# Choices

CAROLE MCKEE

authorHOUSE®

*AuthorHouse™*
*1663 Liberty Drive, Suite 200*
*Bloomington, IN 47403*
*www.authorhouse.com*
*Phone: 1-800-839-8640*

*First published by AuthorHouse 5/19/2008*

*ISBN: 978-1-4343-6964-2 (sc)*

*Library of Congress Control Number: 2008903954*

*Printed in the United States of America*
*Bloomington, Indiana*

*This book is printed on acid-free paper.*

# Chapter 1

**Dr.** Nicholas Bazario held the phone to his ear and leaned against the wall. As he expelled air from his lungs, he stared up at the ceiling, wondering why he had even answered the phone.

"No, Angie. I can't do that," He said through his teeth.

"Nick, please. You're my only *hope*." The caller whined to him.

"It's not my problem, Angie."

"No, not directly.....but if something isn't done, it will end up being everybody's problem. Nick, I can't handle him any more. He won't listen....he won't do anything I tell him to do. He's smoking, drinking, probably doing drugs, too. He stays out all night; doesn't go to school. He's only *sixteen*, Nick. He'll be in prison before he's eighteen at the rate he's going. He's your *nephew*, Nick.... your *only nephew*."

Nick Bazario sighed. "Angie, I don't know anything about kids. I certainly don't know anything about raising them."

"You don't have to *raise* him. He's sixteen. He needs a male figure to look up to. He needs to learn respect. He needs discipline."

"Damn it, Angie! *What…*you want to send him *here?* And *then* what?"

"Nick, ever since his father died….well, he changed. He's…..sullen, secretive. I try to talk to him and he sneers at me. You gotta help me, Nick. *Please.*"

Nick sighed. Still holding the phone to his ear, he walked to his bar in the corner of his living room and poured himself a half a glass of Scotch. He sat down on one of the bar stools and leaned his elbow against the edge of the bar. Sipping from the glass, he checked his watch and sighed again.

"Nick, are you still there?"

"Uh, yeah, Angie……I'm still here. You know if you weren't my only sister, I would have hung up on you and your absurd idea about a half hour ago. Why haven't you asked Louis to help you? He lives right there."

"Because his wife is sick. He's taking care of her, and besides, in her fragile state, she doesn't need the problems. Their two daughters are enough."

"What makes you think I can do any good? I wasn't exactly the perfect child growing up."

"Nick, I don't want him starting school here. The influences…..well, they're bad. He's hanging around with the wrong people. Look, it's not permanent. I want to sell the house and get out of Chicago, too. I just want him to get a fresh start in a better area, better schools, and better environment. Then, I'll move near there when I sell the house. If Ricky can just be there to start a new school year……in a better school……"

Nick sighed again. "Angie, I have an engagement that I'm going to be late for. I'll call you tomorrow morning. I need to think about this. Okay?"

"You'll think about it, Nick? *Really?*"

"Yeah, Angie.....really. I promise I'll call you in the morning. Tomorrow is Saturday. I'm home all day. Give me some time to think....then I'll call you back."

"Promise?"

"Yeah....promise." Nick hung up and headed up the stairs toward his bedroom, undressing as he went.

He sat on the edge of the bed and removed his shoes. 'What is she thinking? What would I do with a sixteen year old punk?' He thought to himself as he stripped off the rest of his clothing and turned on the shower.

Nick let the hot water run over his neck and shoulders to release the muscle tension that had begun to build while he was on the phone with his sister. Maybe if the tightness left his muscles he would be able to enjoy himself tonight and not dwell on his sister's stupid request.

Nick Bazario had come a long way since his youth on the Chicago streets. He was a young punk destined for jail at one time, he recalled. All it took to straighten him out was a near fatal shooting—his fatality in question. He could still see his assailant's scarred face as he pulled the trigger. He remembered the eyes—hard and cold— and the distorted smile—distorted from the scar on his cheek—and then—BANG! Nick didn't remember anything after that until he woke up in a hospital room eight days later. Eight days of his life he spent fighting for it, and he didn't even remember. The first thing he saw was his mother holding her rosary beads between her white-knuckled fingers. She was on his left side, where she had been for eight days. He looked to his right side and saw his father crying—crying openly and unashamedly in front of his brother and sister. Angie and Louis were

3

crying, too. When the family realized he was awake they began crying harder and openly thanking God for giving him another chance.

Nick had been fifteen when he was shot for the first—and the last—time. His parents sold their house and moved to a quieter neighborhood and scraped the money together to put him into a private boarding school, where he discovered that the battle on that turf was a competition for good grades. He didn't have to be tough; he didn't have to have a lot of guts; he just had to get A's to be looked up to. For Nick, that was easy, so he excelled and was looked up to by fellow students. Piece of cake. From high school he went on to college, on a partial scholarship. To cover what the scholarship didn't, he worked nights as a bartender in a local bar. His parents sent him what they could afford so he managed to have a little extra once in awhile. From the time he finished high school he knew he wanted to be a doctor. Not a doctor that saw patients, but a doctor who discovered new diseases and cures for old diseases. He aced all his chemistry courses and thoroughly enjoyed doing scientific research for any of his science courses. As he graduated from college, he got accepted to study medicine at a major university in Western Pennsylvania. After his residency, he eventually worked his way into the research field that he originally strived for. At the age of forty, he was now head of research at a large university hospital, running his own show, and making top dollar doing it. Some of his research had eventually brought him recognition in his field, and the open and outward respect of his colleagues.

Nick Bazario was good in a lab; it was personal relationships he had a problem with. At the age of thirty-two, he married a pretty OB-GYN, and she divorced him when he was thirty-five. Liz said he was an opinionated, hard-nosed jerk whose only tenderness was between his ears. It hurt when she said it, and if he had shown her that it hurt, things may have turned out differently. His early street days had conditioned him to show no real emotion except anger, and that was all Liz ever saw. His anger. When they first starting going out he had made an effort to be "warm and fuzzy" like women wanted. She was charmed, and soon fell head over heels for him. They married quickly—too quickly, perhaps—and divorced just as quickly when Liz realized that the tender moments between them were long gone. She took a position in another hospital several states away. Her parting words suggested to him that he gain sexual gratification by doing an anatomically impossible act, and that she only hoped there would be enough states between them that they never crossed paths again.

He hadn't heard anything concerning Liz or her whereabouts until last week. Another OB-GYN on staff at the hospital informed him that Liz was coming back to head up the OB-GYN Department. He went straight to Tom Siverson, the head of the hospital, and confronted him. Siverson told Nick that the rumor was true. Liz would be arriving the following Wednesday morning to take over the entire Women's Health Department. Hearing this news was all it took for Nick to realize that he had never gotten over Liz; now she was back. She had been on staff two days already, and he hadn't run into her.

It was a big hospital, so if he was lucky he could avoid her from now until he retired in twenty years.

Engrossed in his thoughts, Nick mindlessly dressed and left for the banquet he had promised Tom Siverson he would attend. Generally, he avoided these things, but this one was for a good cause—Research. Still reminiscing, he swung into the country club parking area, slowing to avoid hitting pedestrians crossing the driveway. By the time he had the keys out of the ignition, he knew he would be telling Angie that her wayward son could come stay with him. Maybe the kid needed the same break he got, or maybe he just needed a good, swift kick in the ass. Nick could accommodate him in both areas, whichever was the case. He was thinking that he would call Angie the first thing in the morning to tell her to bring the kid here. He wouldn't take any bullshit from him; that was for sure. Lost in thought, he looked up just in time to avoid a face to face collision with his ex-wife.

"Nick."

"Liz." He shouldered around her and kept walking.

"Still the bullheaded jerk, I see." She didn't exactly shout it, but she said it loudly enough for him and a few others to hear it.

He turned around, and made a small production of offering his hand to her. "How are you, Liz? You're looking well. And it's an *opinionated, hard-nosed jerk* as I recall. Not a bullheaded jerk" His lips were formed into a plastic smile, which looked more like a grimace.

She briefly touched his hand, and then let hers drop. "Nick. You're looking well, too. Now that the formalities are out of the way, let's try to be adults from here on." She gave him a mock smile and turned and walked away.

\* \* \*

Just three miles away from the country club, sixteen-year-old Belinda Riley sat in her room, in the middle of her bed, going over a checklist of the things she needed for school. Her father had put three-hundred dollars on the kitchen table that morning. It was what he had allotted her to spend for school clothes and other items like pens and pencils, notebooks, notebook paper, et cetera. If she hadn't have reminded him, he wouldn't have left anything, so she was grateful for the money he had left. Fortunately, she hadn't grown any since last year, so everything in her closet still fit. She also conserved her school supplies, so she wouldn't need to replace everything from the year before. Three-hundred dollars was good, and she did have her own money that she rarely touched.

Belinda was a pretty teenager. Long blonde hair with just a slight wave to it, and large blue eyes fringed with thick dark, curly lashes gave her an angelic look. She was a small girl, at just five feet, two and one hundred, two pounds, with a lovely figure. And she was quiet—not exactly shy—but quiet. Teachers considered her studious and bright since she maintained a 4.0 grade point average. Since she was a modest girl, very few people knew that besides getting all A's, she could sing like an angel. Her voice was inherited from her mother.

She missed her mom. Stacey Riley died from ovarian cancer when Belinda was fourteen. Things were different when her mother was alive. The house was alive back then. There was music and laughter then. And holidays. Good smells coming from the oven. How Belinda missed that. Everything changed when Stacey died. Her father changed. Now there was nothing but darkness and an unnerving quiet all the time. Belinda felt like she had to walk on eggs most the time. Her father never smiled, never laughed any more. He brooded. He sat and drank, and brooded. He never talked to Belinda; never even looked at her. She used to be daddy's girl—his princess. He used to ask her about her day, her studies, and her friends. Now all he ever did was grunt when she spoke to him. Belinda remembered how handsome her father used to be. He still had his looks but he was unkempt. He didn't shave every day nor did he get a hair cut as often as he once did. Belinda's older brother, Chris escaped to the service shortly after their mother passed away. This left her to grieve alone. How she wanted her father's comfort! He was never abusive or legally neglectful. She had what she needed to sustain her life, but emotionally, she was starving. She found herself grieving for both parents, not for just the one who passed away.

"Lindy!"

She jumped when she heard her name. Her father was outside her room in the hallway.

"I made some stew if you want some. It's in the pot on the stove. Clean up the kitchen when you're done eating. I'm going out for awhile."

"Okay." She responded. Silently, she said, "Wow.... four whole sentences. Maybe he's snapping out of it."

She put her checklist aside and wondered out to the kitchen after she heard his truck pull out of the driveway. She braced herself for the mess she knew he had left in the kitchen. He was usually half-crocked whenever he cooked anything, leaving spills everywhere. Tonight was no exception. She sighed and got a bowl out of the cupboard. After she ate, she cleaned the kitchen and returned to her room well after ten PM. As was her habit, she locked the door to her room. Sometimes her father brought his drunken buddies home, and she always felt uneasy with them in the house. She fell asleep on top of the coverlet and didn't even hear her father when he came home after two in the morning.

# Chapter 2

"Angie? Bring the kid here." Nick sat at his glass-topped kitchen table with a cup of strong, hot black coffee in front of him.

"Oh, Nick! Thank you! I'll get him packed and we'll be there tonight sometime."

"Tonight? Holy shit, Angie! You're not wasting any time. I need to get prepared for this."

"Nick, I checked with the school in your area. School starts Wednesday. I want him there on the first day. And Nick? I want him in school every day after that."

"He will be, Angie. He will be….even if I have to break his butt….okay?"

He heard Angie let out a sigh of relief. "You have full authority, Nick. Do what you have to do to get him straightened out. I'll see you tonight some time." Angie hung up quickly, either because she had so much to do to get Ricky ready, or because she was afraid Nick would change his mind.

Nick sat and stared at the cup of coffee in front of him. "What did I just get myself into?" He asked the cup.

He picked up a medical journal and began reading about a new technique being used in the OR, but his thoughts kept drifting away. He wondered what Ricky looked like. He hadn't seen him in six years. Ricky was ten then; now he was sixteen—a year older than Nick had been when he was shot. Nick ran his hand over his face, feeling the stubble of his facial hair. He rarely shaved on Saturdays, but he knew today would be an exception. Later, though. He just wanted to relax this morning. The banquet the night before had been boring as they usually were, but what made matters worse was knowing that Liz was in the same room. He caught glimpses of her from time to time during the evening, but there had been no contact outside of the initial encounter. He knew he had to stop thinking about her. Maybe having Ricky there would help keep his mind off of her, if Ricky was the problem Angie said he was.

After his third cup of coffee, Nick drifted through his large three-bedroom two-story condo. It was much too big for one person, but all that was available were units with three-bedrooms, and a den. The first floor held a spacious living room and dining area, a fully equipped kitchen large enough for a table and chairs, a good-sized den, and a powder room. Behind the left wall in the kitchen was a laundry room. The second story contained three large bedrooms with a full sized bath, and another full-sized bath with hot tub in the master bedroom. A large walk-in storage closet separated the master bedroom from one of the other two bedrooms on one side of the hallway while a large bathroom across from it separated the other bedroom. The condo was bright and airy with the help of the floor to ceiling glass wall and sliding glass door that opened onto a stone patio. Nick had hired a decorator to do the furnishings, which were all light neutral shades.

He felt that the word 'nondescript' was a perfect way to describe the rooms, but he had to admit, he never grew tired of it.

One thing he loved about the condo was that it was maintenance-free for him. He was never good with repairs, and all tools, especially power-tools, were off-limits to him. He knew nothing about them, didn't want to know anything about them, and he would probably be dangerous with one in his hands. He paid people to do what needed done. If something broke, he could call someone from his maintenance contract to come fix it. He liked that. Once a week, a cleaning lady came in to clean, but he did his own laundry. He also cooked for himself occasionally, but that was as far as his domestic side could go. He hoped his nephew knew how to cook, because if he didn't, he may end up going hungry a lot.

Nick wondered upstairs to check out the bedrooms. He opened up the windows to let them air out a bit. Ricky could have the bigger of the two extra bedrooms. There was a queen-sized bed, a dresser, a chest of drawers and two night stands in the room, and there was a good-sized walk-in closet—more than adequate for a sixteen-year-old boy. The bed comforter and matching curtains had narrow stripes in many shades of brown, from beige to a deep dark chocolate—definitely masculine enough for a boy. Nick made a note to get a computer and a small desk for it. The desk would fit nicely in front of the smaller of the two windows in the room. The bedroom furniture, like all of the furniture in the condo, was a light oak— sunny oak—the decorator called it.

Since the condo was air conditioned, Nick closed the windows before leaving the room. Once again, he looked inside to make sure the room was fine for a teenaged boy. He opened the door to the smaller bedroom. Angie would spend the night in this room. There was a full bedroom suite in this room as well as the other one, but the bed was a double instead of a queen. The closet wasn't as big in this room, but she wouldn't be staying very long, so it didn't matter. The matching comforter and drapes in this room were more colorful than any other room in the house. The decorator called the colors 'brick' and 'ecru'. So be it. Nick called them burnt orange and cream.

Satisfied that the rooms were fine, he wondered down the hall to the bathroom. He rarely used the main bathroom. He peeked inside the door and found it clean and orderly. He wondered if the kid shaved yet.

Nick realized he was hungry. It was after noon and he hadn't eaten anything yet. He showered, shaved, and dressed in casual clothes and headed for his favorite diner for lunch. He thought he might go grocery shopping after he ate. He was sure he had nothing in his refrigerator or cupboards that would appeal to a sixteen-year-old boy. But then again, he had no idea what a sixteen-year-old boy liked. He settled into a small booth and picked up the menu, scanned it quickly and decided that he wanted breakfast food. He placed his order while the waitress filled his cup for him. Too late, he remembered that this was also Liz's favorite lunch place. He immediately spied her sitting at a table on the other side of the suddenly too small diner. He turned toward the window and stared out at nothing, not daring to look across the room again. He jumped suddenly when he heard her voice.

"Do you mind if I join you?" She was standing where the waitress had stood, but it seemed like she was standing too close. "Look….we have to work in the same hospital. Can't we call a truce? Maybe we can't be friends, but can we at least be civil? Can I sit?" She nodded toward the empty side of the booth.

Nick shrugged. "You sit at your own risk. Remember, *you* find *me* unpleasant to be around."

"Okay….touché." She eased herself onto the seat across from him, and attempted a smile. "So….how has life been treating you?"

"Not bad….until today. Why did you come back?" He looked directly into her eyes.

"Wow….that's certainly not an effort to be civil. Is my sitting here wrecking your life? I'll move. I'm sorry."

"No, Liz….stay. I wasn't talking about you being here. I'm sorry. It's just that….well, I get the privilege of having my nephew come live with me today. But why did you come back?"

"Ricky? He'd be about……"

"Sixteen." Nick finished the sentence for her.

Liz stared at Nick and sighed. "I came back because I was made an offer I couldn't refuse. The hospital has offered me a phenomenal salary and a grant to build the best women's health center in the country. I couldn't say no. Now, why is Ricky coming to live with you? Angie is okay, isn't she?"

Nick nodded. "Yeah, she's fine. She just can't handle him any more. Since Enrico died, Ricky became out of control. She's looking toward me to straighten him out. Yeah, go ahead….laugh."

"Well, I wasn't going to laugh, but I just can't see you as a role model for a teenaged boy. When did Enrico die?"

"About three years ago. Massive coronary. I was out of the country at the time. I didn't make it to the funeral."

"I'm sorry to hear that. How is Angie making out without him? Everything okay, financially?"

"I guess. I'll know tonight. They're driving here as we speak. She wants Ricky away from the bad influences of the big city, in a better school, and with a strong male figure. You will concede that I am a strong male figure?" Nick stared directly into her eyes, causing her stomach to do a small flip—something she didn't expect to feel.

"Well, if you need any help, don't hesitate. You know how fond I was of Ricky." As she spoke, she remembered what it was like to be kissed by Nick. "And yes, you are a strong male figure." She had forgotten those brown eyes, and his thick hair. Although it had a few gray strands in it, it was still as black as she remembered it.

"Thanks." He countered. He wondered why he had forgotten her opal colored eyes. It was the most unusual thing about her. Her hair was still blonde, but not as blonde as it once was, but those eyes….they were still like opals, with green, brown and yellow flecks in them. He was becoming annoyed with himself. He needed to stop thinking like this. What they had between them once was over, and they had both gone their separate ways. He regretted letting her sit down.

He ate his breakfast lunch as quickly as he could without appearing rude and ill-mannered. He explained to her that he had to grocery shop for things that a teenager might like to eat. He lied by telling her he had to get the room ready. It was as ready as it was ever going to be. With what he hoped was a reasonable amount of time spent after finishing his meal, he escaped to his car in the parking lot. She stayed there a little longer, enjoying her coffee and the first of her three daily cigarettes—a habit she just couldn't quite give up.

# Chapter 3

$\mathcal{N}$ick braced himself when he heard the car doors slam. He knew his sister and nephew had arrived, and they weren't having a pleasant conversation. He went to hold the door open for them, thinking there would be luggage coming in.

"Ricky….*listen*….listen to me! You have a chance at a better life! You're bright, Ricky! Do you want to spend your life in the gutter?" Angie's tone was pleading.

"Hey….I have neighbors. Get inside if you're going to argue."

Ricky stormed past Nick into the living room, nostrils flaring and eyes glaring. Nick stared after him, seeing a tall, skinny kid, with hair too long, dark peach fuzz on his upper lip, and an extreme attitude. Certainly not the same sweet kid he remembered. He had the Bazario eyes—dark brown that turned black when angry. They were black right now. Ricky's raven black hair was poorly kept and looked uncombed, but what caught Nick's attention were his oversized pants falling off of his waist down around his hips. Nick could see he had a lot of work to do. He hugged Angie.

"Sit down. Anybody hungry? Want a soda or something? Ricky?"

Ricky stared at Nick, but gave no response.

"Kid, rule number one….when I talk to you I get an answer. Is that clear?"

Ricky stared at the off-white carpeting. He didn't see Nick come up on him suddenly, so it startled him when he found himself looking into a pair of dark brown eyes exactly like his own.

"Are you deaf?" Nick's voice was a low growl, as he spoke through his teeth. Ricky thought he looked like a wolf. "Let's get something straight, Punk. You're sixteen; I'm forty. I can, and I will, kick your ass if you give me a reason. Do we understand each other?"

Ricky nodded.

"Good. Now what do you say we order pizza? Angie? Sound good to you?"

"Yes, Nick, that sounds great." Angie spoke quietly. She was in awe of her brother. Already Ricky was more subdued than she had seen him in three years.

Nick picked up the phone and ordered two large pizzas with toppings, and then went to the refrigerator and got sodas for Ricky and Angie and a beer for himself.

"Rule number two…..you never, ever….touch my alcohol. It's here, but it's for me. I bought it. You don't touch the beer, the scotch, the bourbon, or the wine. There are plenty of sodas in the fridge. You can drink as many as you want and I'll replace them. But don't ever let me catch you drinking my booze."

Ricky stared at Nick, wondering just how far he could push him.

"Rule number three…..you pick up after yourself. I don't ever want to come home to a mess. That includes your room. You keep your room neat at all times. A cleaning lady comes in every week, so you have to have everything up off the floor and put away when she comes in. Rule number four…..no smoking. Rule number five…. no drugs…..plain and simple. Rule number six…..you will have a curfew and you will obey it. Rule number seven……no punks, creeps, or thugs in this house. You want to bring somebody home; you do it with my approval. There are plenty of nice kids around that you don't have to bring riff-raff in. Rule number eight….you will go to school….every day. If you say you're sick….remember, I'm a doctor. Rule number nine….you will bring in decent grades and you *will* do your homework. Rule number ten…..you break something in this place and you will find a way to pay for it. And we're just getting started, kid."

Nick stopped to answer the door to the pizza delivery man. He paid him and carried the pizza boxes to the kitchen table. "Come on….get it while it's hot."

Ricky wanted to stay behind just to ruffle his Uncle Nick's feathers, but the smell of the pizza made him realize that he was really hungry. If he stayed back from the kitchen, he fully believed his uncle would not allow him to eat later.

In the kitchen, Nick handed Ricky plates, silverware, and napkins to put on the table. Knowing that Nick wanted him to set the table, he hesitated. He had not set a table for dinner since his father died. He was used to his mother doing it. He did what Nick expected of him, rather than have the wolf in his face again.

When they were all seated with pizza on their plates, Nick took up the conversation again. "Ricky, you will have an allowance of twenty-five dollars a week. Buy one drug with it, and you'll not get another dime. I want you to account for the money at the end of the week. Tomorrow we are going shopping. You will want some decent clothes since those rags you're wearing are going to be thrown out. People wear pants that fit. Do you have any questions so far?"

"Music….what about music? Can I have that?" It was the first time Ricky had spoken since he walked into the house. Nick was surprised by his deep voice.

"These places are sound-proof. Yeah, you can have music as long as it's in your room and the door is shut. I don't want to hear that crap you kids listen to, so keep your door closed. Oh, and rule number eleven….no foul language. I don't want to hear it coming from you or the music you listen to. Are we clear on that?"

Reluctantly, Ricky nodded.

"After we eat, I'll show you your room. You *do* have luggage or belongings to bring in, right? We'll get that after we eat. So tell me, Angie….how are you doing?" He turned toward his sister and smiled for the first time since they entered the house.

\* \* \*

As promised, Nick showed Ricky his room after they ate. Ricky was impressed, but tried not to show it. He was equally impressed when Nick told him they would be buying a computer and desk for him to have in his room. Maybe it wouldn't be so bad after all. Those rules were going to take some work, especially the smoking and drinking ones. Drugs…..he could take them or leave them, but he did like the cigarettes and booze. Nick and Angie left Ricky alone to unpack, while they went downstairs to catch up on everything.

"Nick, you didn't say anything to him about girls, and….sex."

"Should I have?"

Angie nodded.

"That skinny little kid has girlfriends?"

"Yes and not just girlfriends. Sex partners. I've come home and caught him several times….with girls, naked…. doing things."

"Jesus, Angie….please. I just ate." Nick shook his head. "Girls sure have changed, huh? Didn't get that lucky when I was sixteen."

"I know. We didn't give in so easily back then. It took a ring on your finger to make you go that far. Now….. girls have no pride."

"Oh, Angie, guess who I had lunch with today. Liz."

"Liz? She's back? You know I always liked her, Nick. She was good for you."

"Yeah, well….things happen. So what about you? Seeing anybody? It's been three years, now."

Angie laughed. "No, Ricky's all I can handle right now. He's been a real handful, Nick."

Nick nodded. He could see that.

# Chapter 4

"Ricky! Let's go! Time to get up!" Nick knocked on Ricky's door for the third time. It was the first day of school and he was determined that Ricky would be there, on time. He had taken the morning off to get him registered and he was going to make sure the kid got to school on time.

He was about to knock again when the door opened. Ricky was standing there fully dressed and ready. Nick looked him over with approval. The new clothes looked good on him. He actually didn't look as skinny with clothes that fit well. The caterpillar on his lip was gone, and his hair was trimmed. Nick conceded to letting him have it a little longer than he would have liked, as long as Ricky kept it clean and combed.

Ricky felt apprehensive as Nick pulled into the high school parking lot. He was willing to bet that in the entire school there wasn't one other kid named Enrico. He never saw so many blondes in one place. In Chicago, his school was full of Italians, Hispanics, and African-Americans. He was not going to fit in; he knew it. He looked over at his Uncle Nick and got what he thought may have been a reassuring smile.

"It'll be okay, Ricky. I'll see if I can register you as Ricky DeCelli. That way you won't have to go around correcting people. Is that okay?"

"Yeah, that'll work." Ricky expelled air in a sigh of relief.

The registration went without a hitch. Ricky was given his schedule and a list of rules and regulations. He was handed a calendar of events, which he knew he would be throwing away. He didn't do school activities. A girl in a modest skirt and sweater approached them.

"Hi! I'm Carrie. I'm your 'buddy guide'. That's what they call us, anyway. I'm here to get you to your homeroom, and, oh.....here's a map of the school."

Ricky took the map, but didn't as much as glance at the girl. Already, he didn't like her....the perky little cheerleader type. Phony. He could imagine her doing cartwheels as she led him to his homeroom. 'Rah, rah, rah...here you are!' He said his goodbyes to Nick and started to follow this silly girl, hoping there would be no cartwheels.

"Oh, hey, Ricky!" Nick caught up to him. "You'll need this." He handed Ricky a key. "I'll see you when I get home."

Throughout the day, Ricky was handed things. Nick had paid for a lock for his locker, and he found the locker at lunchtime. He slipped his brand new books into the locker, and went to the cafeteria for lunch. He was surprised by the quiet order of the lunchroom. There was no screaming or shouting, nobody was throwing anything, and, most importantly, there were actually chairs to sit in. He looked at his schedule and the map while he ate.

He was interrupted by Miss perky. "Ricky! Hi! How's it going? Need any help?"

"No….I'm good. Thanks."

"Well, if you need anything….just let me know. That's what I'm here for."

As he watched her bounce away he wondered what she would have done if he had told her he needed a blow job.

Getting through this first day would be the hardest part. Once he studied the map, he realized that the school was actually easy to get around in, and everything was either color coded, in numeric order, or alphabetically in order. He didn't think he would need Miss Perky's help.

With his first day behind him, he strolled home, looking left and right, until he was sure he was in no danger. That would take some getting used to. Feeling safe was not a luxury he knew. He unlocked the door of the condo and bolted up the stairs to his room. Once inside, he stared at everything, still not believing that this was his room. He tossed his books on the bed, but stopped and retrieved them. He stacked them on his new desk beside the new computer. No sense in antagonizing the big bad wolf. He changed into sweatpants and a tee-shirt, remembering to hang up the clothes he just took off. He figured he had about two hours before his Uncle Nick got home, so he decided to get his homework out of the way. If it was done, maybe Uncle Nick would let him go out for awhile. He really wanted to explore the area, but he also wanted a cigarette. He looked through the box he usually kept cigarettes in and found two. Grabbing a lighter, he ran down the stairs and out the back door to the patio, and lit one of them. He sucked the smoke into his lungs and enjoyed the buzz he got off of it. He continued to smoke the cigarette, watching for the front door to open just in case his Uncle Nick decided to come home early. He managed to smoke the entire cigarette with no interruption. He butted it out in the grass, ran his hand through it, and carried the butt out the front door to the street and dropped it down in the sewer. He returned to his room and started his homework.

When Nick came through the door, Ricky was watching television.

"Homework done?" Nick asked him, pointedly.

"Yes." Ricky responded.

"Good. Let's go eat somewhere."

"Really?" Ricky couldn't hide his surprise.

"Yeah, really….unless you want to cook."

"Uh, no….not really."

"So….let's go. Change your clothes first."

Ricky ran up to put his new jeans and shirt back on. Nick looked him over and decided he looked okay to go to the diner.

\* \* \*

Belinda used her key to unlock the front door, reached into the mailbox and retrieved the mail, then kicked the door closed behind her. She was met with the dead silence, to which she had become accustomed. She set her books down and rifled through the mail. Nothing from Chris. She put the mail in its usual spot, and carried her books to her room.

After completing her homework, Belinda went out to the kitchen. Her father had left dirty dishes in the sink again. She quickly washed them and opened the refrigerator to see what was in there. She grabbed a diet soda and closed the door. In the freezer she found one freezer bag full of stuffed shells and another bag full of pre-made spaghetti sauce. There was more than enough for two, so there would be enough in case her father came home. She popped the bags into the microwave and put the settings on thaw. While the microwave was thawing the bagsful of food, she quickly threw together a green salad and added Italian dressing. Maybe tonight would be the night her father would look at her and speak to her. She had been hoping that it would happen for almost two years now.

Her father didn't come home—at least not while she was awake. She ate in silence, and then washed up her dishes. She put the remainder of the food in plastic containers and left them in the refrigerator. If her father didn't eat it, she would have it for tomorrow night. It was still early, so she got out the vacuum cleaner. After dusting the furniture and vacuuming the carpet, she watched a little television, and then went to bed. She did not hear her father come home again, but in the morning she knew that he had. She saw that he had eaten the leftovers she put into the refrigerator and left the dishes in the sink again. Walking to school, she had to wipe her eyes several times. Although she tried not to cry, she just couldn't keep the tears from flowing. She was so lonely!

# Chapter 5

Ricky had sixth period free, but had a class seventh period. He believed the school did that on purpose to keep him there all day. If the free period could have been the last period he would be out of there and home. They took role in every class in this school, so there was no ducking out of them, especially since his uncle had put down his cell phone number, as well as the number at the hospital, and instructed them to call him if Ricky was not in any class for which he was scheduled. He spent the free period wondering around outside, smoked a cigarette, and then decided to explore the halls. He stopped outside large double doors that stood partially open. He assumed this was the auditorium. He started to pull the door open but stopped. Coming from somewhere on the other side of the doors was the sound of an angel. He gingerly peeked into the auditorium and spotted a tiny blonde standing in front of the stage beside a piano. She was singing. Her clear voice floated through the auditorium and wafted in mid-air like a bell. Quietly, Ricky slipped inside through the doors, and took a seat in back of the auditorium. He was mesmerized by the clear quality of her beautiful voice. He wondered what she looked like up close, since he really couldn't make out all of her features from where he sat. The person who played the piano, probably the music teacher, praised her and encouraged her to sing another song.

Close to the end of the sixth period, the pianist stopped playing. Ricky watched the girl gather her books, say a few words to the pianist, and start up the aisle toward him. His first instinct was to get up and walk out, but he felt as though his body was rooted to the seat.

Belinda was unaware that anyone was sitting in back of the auditorium until she was almost on top of him. Startled, she gasped.

"Oh! You scared me! I didn't expect to see anybody there." She spoke breathlessly.

"Sorry, I didn't mean to. You sing like an angel. I couldn't help but sit and listen."

"Thank you."

She was standing directly in front of the auditorium seat that held him. He looked up into the most beautiful eyes he had ever seen and he felt something inside him stir. Their eyes connected and Ricky felt something like an electrical shock go through him. He knew he must look stupid, but he couldn't look away. Their eyes locked, and he felt a feeling that he had never felt before. Warmth—a warmth that left him breathless. She was staring at him. Had she spoken? Was she waiting for him to answer her?

Belinda felt it, too. That feeling of electricity momentarily stopped her breathing. She opened her mouth to speak but no words would come out. She settled for a smile. She was relieved when he smiled back.

"My name is Lindy—Belinda, really, but everybody calls me Lindy. Hi."

Carole McKee

"I'm Ricky—actually Enrico, but I'd rather be called Ricky. And hi back at you."

"You're new here, aren't you?" She asked him.

Her voice sounded so sweet to him, and she wasn't anything like that perky broad, Carrie. She was genuine, real, and.....well, sort of low-key were the words that came to his mind.

"Yeah, I'm new. From Chicago. Ever been there?"

She shook her head. "No."

"Well, you're not missing much. It's nicer here. I guess I better get to class. English Lit."

"Me, too. Room two-oh-one?"

Ricky looked at his schedule, and nodded. "I guess we're in the same class. Can I walk you there?" What was wrong with him? He never asked a girl that before. In Chicago, if he wanted to walk with a girl, he would just grab her and pinch her nipple. That always got more than just a walk—he usually got laid after school, too.

"Okay." She answered.

They entered the classroom together. Neither of them saw Carrie until they heard her. "Ricky! Hi! Sit here!" Her bouncy voice cut through the murmur of the other students in the half-full classroom.

"No, I'm going to sit over here." He moved past Carrie to the far side of the room, barely touching Lindy's elbow, but just enough to get her to go in the same direction.

He grabbed two desks for them and arranged them so they would be sitting next to each other. When they both were seated, he smiled at her.

"Thanks."

"For what?" She asked.

29

"For sticking by me and getting me past that bubbling idiot."

"Oh. Most boys probably want to be with that bubbling idiot." She shrugged as she finished the sentence.

"Well, I'm not most boys. Personally, I can't stand her, or girls like her. Fake. Phony. And besides, if I had my choice between you and her, I'd choose you."

"Really?" She looked up into his face to see if he were joking. Their eyes met, and there it was again—that electric jolt. Lindy was the first to look away. Class began.

When class let out Ricky made a right into the corridor and Lindy made a left. Ricky was disappointed, but realized that she had to get to her locker and maybe she had to be right home after school. Maybe she had a job to go to. He locked his locker and walked out the front entrance thinking about her, and there she was—walking down the front steps. For the first time he noticed what she was wearing. He thought she looked so cute in her three tiered light blue denim shirt and her stylish white top.

"Hey! Lindy!" He quickened his pace to catch up with her. "Do you walk home?"

"Yeah, every day. It's good exercise."

"I could think of better ways to exercise." He countered. "Can I walk with you?"

"Of course. Where do you live?"

"In those condos off of Carlisle. Is that anywhere near where you live?"

"Well, I live past them, but I walk past that road that goes down to them."

"Good. How about I walk you home?" Ricky smiled at her. "I mean you can't be too careful…..right?"

Lindy laughed. Ricky thought her laugh was beautiful and was about to tell her that when the sound of a horn interrupted their conversation.

"Ricky! Do you want a ride?" It was Carrie.

"No. Thanks. I'd rather walk."

"Oh, come on! Hop in!" She persisted.

"No. Can't you see I'm busy?"

Carrie finally noticed Lindy standing there next to Ricky. "Oh. Well…..whatever." She glared at Lindy, and then drove away.

Ricky looked at Lindy, playfully. "Well…..I guess you won't be invited to her birthday parties."

Lindy laughed.

"You have a beautiful laugh; did you know that?"

Lindy laughed again. "No, I didn't know that." She turned her face toward Ricky, their eyes connected, and again, they both felt the electricity between them.

Ricky was fighting the urge to touch her. He asked questions about the area, and Lindy answered them, offering extra information and insight regarding many of his questions. 'She's so sweet and pleasant to be around,' he thought to himself. He had never spent any time with a girl like this. Mostly, whenever he was with girls in Chicago, they either got drunk together and had sex, or shoplifted together. Just walking and talking was something he never even imagined himself doing; but he soon realized that he liked it. Maybe it was a pleasant experience because it was Lindy, or maybe it was because everything in the area seemed so bright and pretty. She stopped when they got to the small bridge on Carlisle Street.

"I love looking over this bridge. It's so pretty down there."

"Did you ever go down there?"

"No."

"Why don't we, then? Maybe not today, but over the weekend? What do ya say? We can figure out a way to get down there; I'm sure. Want to explore?"

She grinned at him, and replied, "Sure."

Ricky was busily looking down around the sides of the bridge trying to find a way to get down there. He thought he could see the way, but didn't say anything, lest he look foolish if it didn't pan out.

"I guess we part here. The condos are down that way." She smiled and gestured with her left arm.

"I was thinking I'd walk you all the way home. Just so you're safe." He returned her smile. "Then I would know where you live, too." He stopped abruptly and stared down into her eyes. "And I really want to know where you live."

Lindy stared up at him for a moment, and then nodded. "And I think I want you to know where I live."

Ricky stopped at Lindy's front door and grinned at her. Although he wanted to, he refrained from kissing her. Instead, he told her he'd see her tomorrow, and turned and walked away. As he walked home, his thoughts were in turmoil. He never even spoke to a girl that sweet, let alone walk a girl—any girl—home. He knew instinctively that she didn't smoke or drink, and that she had never had sex. He knew he had to make a decision—either find girls that were more into his normal lifestyle, or change his style and make Lindy his girlfriend. He glanced back toward her house as he stopped to light a cigarette.

# Chapter 6

Nick opened his front door and listened for sounds coming from inside. There were no sounds at all—no radio, no television, no footsteps. He glanced around the room and saw nothing out of place, and no evidence that anyone had even touched anything. Was Ricky at home like he was supposed to be? As he walked toward the kitchen his nose picked up a familiar smell—spaghetti sauce. He leaned on the door frame and stared at Ricky's back as he stood in front of the stove.

He cleared his throat. "What are you doing?"

"Making spaghetti. Ever have my dad's sauce? He taught me how to make it when I was twelve. It was always way better than my mother's....even she admits that."

Nick was trying to hide his smile. "Who said you could cook and mess up the stove?"

"I'm not messing up the stove. Look....I'm wiping up as I go."

Nick rubbed his hand over his mouth and chin to hide the smile. What he was seeing pleased him, but he didn't want the kid to think he was that easy to please.

"So do you do this very often?"

"No….only when I need to think." Ricky glanced at his uncle and quickly looked away, regretting having said that. Hopefully his uncle wouldn't ask him what he had to think about. Thankfully, he didn't ask.

"It will be ready in about fifteen minutes, so if you want to change or shower, or anything, you have fifteen minutes." Ricky instructed him as he added the pasta to the boiling water. "Oh, and I used one of your beers…. for the sauce…..like my dad taught me."

Nick stopped and turned around. Ricky thought he was in for it, and he braced himself in defense.

"Was that his secret ingredient? Is that what he used to make it so different?"

Ricky nodded.

"Well, I'll be damn!" Nick headed toward the stairs and Ricky breathed a sigh of relief.

He didn't know why, but he was a little bit afraid of his uncle. That wolf face on the day he arrived may have had something to do with it, but it was more than that. He detected anger—an anger way deep inside of Uncle Nick—an anger that he had only seen one other time….when he witnessed his friend Paulie gutted by a hunting knife. He remembered the murderous look in the eyes of the assailant, who fortunately, could not see him. Many times, he was awakened in the middle of the night because those eyes haunted his dreams. During those times he would relive the events that took place up to the minute Paulie was killed. They had been running from the cops, he and Paulie. They had just stolen three cartons of cigarettes each and some cash, when the police car pulled up. They ran. They ran into an alley that was too narrow for a car to go. Running hard and watching their backs, they rounded a corner and headed south down another alley. Before the next corner, Ricky stopped to catch his breath, and Paulie continued around the corner to the left. When Ricky's breathing slowed down he heard voices coming from the direction Paulie had run. He looked behind him and saw no police coming, so he quietly made his way to the corner, staying in the shadows. Underneath a single lit bulb in the alley stood his friend Paulie, held up against the wall by the throat. The holder was an extremely big, mean lunatic everyone called "Punch".

Rumor had it that 'Punch' punched his father to death when he was twelve. Ricky never knew if the story was true but he believed the guy was capable of it. Nobody messed with Punch. He was mean and angry all the time. His own mother and sister were terrified of him, with good reason. On-lookers had watched him slap his mother around and grab his sister and pull her home by her hair on numerous occasions. Nobody ever stepped in, lest they suffer the consequences of his wrath at another time. On this particular night, for a reason unknown to everybody, Punch was in the alley. Paulie must have charged right into him without seeing him. Ricky remembered crouching down behind a dumpster and listening to what Punch was saying to Paulie. All he could make out were the words, "You touched me, you slimy little maggot. Nobody touches me." Ricky saw Punch lift Paulie off the ground with one hand and plunge the knife into Paulie's stomach and pull down on it. He remembered the blood curdling scream coming from Paulie, as he sat behind the dumpster biting into the back of his hand to keep from screaming himself. Suddenly there were cops running around the corner. Ricky saw Punch turn toward them, and that was when he saw his eyes….full of murder, hate, and rage. He charged at the uniforms with the bloody knife still in his hand. Ricky heard the gunshots—all three of them—and watched Punch fall to the ground. He stayed where he was for what seemed like hours. He watched as they hauled Paulie away on a stretcher, sheet covering his entire body. He watched as they hauled Punch away, in the same fashion. He watched the police, wearing plastic gloves, pick up the murder weapon and put it into a bag. There would be no reason to work the crime scene since both the victim and the attacker were dead. Before too long, everyone was gone and the alley returned to its quiet, dark state. Ricky didn't know how long he sat crouched there but he remembers his joints were stiff when he finally stood up.

He never told anybody what he saw. Maybe if he had, he wouldn't keep having the nightmare of Punch's eyes watching him.

"Hey, kid! Are you in there somewhere?" Nick's voice was raised.

Ricky jumped.

"What the hell were you thinking about? You're not in any kind of trouble already….are you?"

"No. It's ready. Hope you're hungry." Ricky tried to smile and shake off the dark cobwebs of that memory.

Nick sat down and reached for the bowl of steaming pasta while Ricky ladled enough sauce for the two of them into another bowl and brought it to the table. When he was seated, Nick spoke.

"So you must have been in pretty deep thought. I asked you twice how school was going."

"Oh….sorry.…..it-it's going okay. I mean, it's only the second day. Can't fail in two days' time, you know."

"That's not what I was talking about. How are you getting along there?"

"Okay. I don't really have much time to make friends, if that's what you mean. And the teachers haven't singled me out as a trouble-maker yet. So it's going okay."

Nick studied his nephew hard, trying to read him. "So do you like it?"

"Like what? School? No. Does anybody? How's the sauce?"

Nick looked down at his plate and realized he had eaten more than half of the food he had dished onto it. "Great. I mean that, Ricky. It's great…and…it is every bit as good as when your father made it. So I guess you can be taught something after all." Nick ended his sentence with a laugh, hoping that Ricky would also see the humor in his little joke.

Ricky just smiled a little. He felt now was the time to bring it up that he wanted to explore the woods with Lindy. He realized after they made the plans that he might have to get permission—something he never thought about in the past.

"Do you mind if I do some exploring on Saturday?"

"Exploring what?"

"Well, I have never been in the woods before. There are some woods over the bridge off of Carlisle. I would like to just go there and see what it's like to be in them."

"That can be dangerous if you've never been in them. It's easy to get lost."

"I thought of that. Can we go to a store and get some….I don't know.…..maybe colorful tape? I could put tape on some of the branches to make it easy to find my way back. It's better than bread crumbs." He hoped Uncle Nick caught the humor and that it would lighten him up a bit. He was relieved when he saw Nick's smile.

"Anyway, I sort of made a friend, and we thought we would just go into the woods and explore them."

"Your friend....has he ever been in them?"

"Yeah, a couple of times, but not very far into them."

"Is he a pretty good kid? No drugs?"

"Doesn't do any of that. Besides, that would be stupid to do in the woods, wouldn't it? I don't want to get lost and never find my way out, and end up as bear food. So can I go?"

Nick stared at Ricky for a moment, making eye contact. Ricky looked sincere. "Okay, yeah....I guess you can. Do you have a cell phone?"

"No....you know I don't."

"Well, we're going to get you one. However, it probably won't work in the woods. You're going to get one anyway. That way I can call you when I can't find you no matter where you are. Okay? We can go to the mall after we clean up here."

Ricky cleaned up the kitchen while Nick caught the last part of the television news broadcast. He didn't know why he did it, but he let his uncle believe that his friend was a guy. Silently, he apologized to Lindy for it, but he instinctively knew it was better that his Uncle Nick not know about Lindy just yet. Besides, he had to think about the whole situation and sort it out himself, first. Lindy was so pleasant to be around—so sweet. But on the other hand, that could get boring. But then again, he knew there would be no vices, either, which would keep him out of trouble. Also, there would be no sex. No sex for a long time, anyway. He felt the chemistry and the electricity between them, but he knew she was not promiscuous. If they did go that far, it would be her first time. He heard girls cried when that happened for the first time. He wouldn't know. Those 'Ho-Bags' he hung out with in Chicago had been doing it since sixth grade. Did he want those kinds of girls, or did he want a decent girlfriend? He could have Lindy and cheat on her, but....if she found out she would be hurt. Somehow hurting her seemed very offensive to him. Kind of like deliberately stepping on a defenseless baby bird—stupid and cruel. What should he do? He had to decide before anything went too far with her. He didn't want her to think she was his girl and then suddenly dump her. That wouldn't be fair. He had to think—decide—by morning.

At the mall, Nick purchased a cell phone and a contract for unlimited minutes for Ricky. While Nick went into a clothing store to look for ties, Ricky ran down to a hardware store to look for colorful tape. He found exactly what he was looking for—red electricians' tape. It would be perfect to attach to tree branches in the woods. If he went to the woods, that is. After all, if there was going to be no Lindy in his life; then the woods would be out of the question, too. He bought the tape since he hadn't made a final decision yet. He passed an arcade where there were lots of young people hanging out, playing games, and talking. Two girls in provocative clothing stood leaning against the wall, fishing cigarettes out of their purses. One of them was wearing a black lace top that left no room for the imagination. He felt he was on familiar ground again, and just as comfortable. "Toto, we're back in Kansas," he murmured to himself. Ricky watched them for a few minutes before he approached them.

# Chapter 7

Lindy grabbed her book bag and her house key and walked outside. She was surprised when she saw him leaning against the lamppost, ankles crossed. He had a Styrofoam cup in each hand—one hand was extended, offering a cup to her.

"Hi," she said, tentatively, with a slight smile. "I can't believe you walked down here. Now you have to go all the way back up the hill."

"Well, good morning to you, too." He retorted. "It's no big deal. I'm in pretty good shape."

Lindy's smile broadened. "Good morning. Is that coffee?"

"Sorta. I thought you might like one. It's a Starbuck's special sold at the store-slash-gas-station up at the corner. So it's not really Starbuck's. It's a Starbuck's knock-off."

Lindy's broad smile turned into a small laugh. "That's great! Thank you." She accepted the cup from his extended hand and they started up the hill towards school. They talked. They compared their schedules and discovered that they had three other classes and a study hall together, in addition to the English Literature class. During the first three days of school, the classes were disrupted and out of the normal sequence because of registration and late book deliveries. The homeroom periods were sometimes two hours long, eliminating classes during the day, so students could get caught up with registration. The following Monday, classes would be on a normal schedule. Lindy and Ricky would then have four classes and a study hall together.

"Trig. I *hate* math." Lindy spoke harshly for the first time since Ricky met her. To him, she still sounded sweet, though.

"Well, I'm pretty damn good in math…..so I'll make you a deal. I'll help you in trig if you'll help me with English, and writing any papers I have to write. Deal?"

"Yeah. Deal. That's a good deal." Their eyes connected and the electricity shot through them once again.

They stopped to look over the bridge again.

"Tomorrow? We're going to get down there tomorrow, remember?" Ricky stared at Lindy to see if she remembered.

"Yeah. I remember. What time do you want to start?"

"Ten good?"

Lindy nodded in agreement. "We meet here? At ten o'clock? If you don't show by quarter after, I go in without you." Lindy grinned at him.

"And if you don't show by quarter after, I'll wait. I'd be scared to go in there by myself." He shot back at her.

"Really?"

"No. Compared to where I came from, these woods are a piece of cake. You have no idea what a jungle that place is. Danger at every corner. I spent much of my time looking over my shoulder, but I had to go out. Had to be tough; act tough. If not, I'd be the one the other jungle

43

animals would get. I did things I'm not proud of, but it was the only way to survive."

Lindy shuddered, involuntarily. She couldn't imagine a place like that. She couldn't imagine Ricky doing anything to hurt anybody, either.

They parted at the front steps of the school, since they didn't have the same homeroom. It was uncertain if they would see each other before lunch, since the classes were still not on a normal schedule. They agreed to meet in the lunchroom, since they both had the same lunch schedule.

Ricky sat in homeroom staring out the window. He guessed he had made his choice. He thought about those girls at the mall the night before. He had walked outside and smoked a cigarette with them, but that was all. The three of them were cracking dirty jokes and laughing, but all he could think about was Lindy. Halfway through his second cigarette with them, it dawned on him that he really was not enjoying himself. He enjoyed walking home with Lindy. He butted the cigarette out and told them he had to go. The girl wearing the revealing black lace jotted down her phone number and handed it to him. He accepted it, but had no intention of ever dialing the number. He stopped inside the mall and bought a roll of breath mints to hide the tobacco smell from his uncle, and went back to the clothing store where he left Nick, who was now trying on a suit. Ricky went out to the mall corridor and sat on a bench to wait. He noticed a small store that sold nothing but trinkets, as was advertised on the window front. He walked over to it and spied cute tiny stuffed animal key chains. He wondered what animal was Lindy's favorite. He went into the store and purchased one with a brown teddy bear. He just remembered that he had forgotten to give it to her. It was still in his book bag. Lunch time......he'd give it to her then. He also forgot to tell her about the cell phone. He had to give her the number, too. She would be the first to have it. As he sat there staring out the window and thinking, he realized how much he was looking forward to lunch.

* * *

The key chain was a big hit at the lunch table. The smile on Lindy's face was well worth the two dollars he spent. Not that the money was a big deal; but Ricky thought the little piece of junk was way over-priced. Lindy loved it, and that was what counted.

He didn't know how she could be so sweet all the time, especially after she had to practically fight to sit next to him. He got to the cafeteria first and sat down with his tray. He looked around for Lindy and saw her coming in through the double glass doors. He waved at her and waited for her to get her lunch. Before she got to the table, Carrie plopped down next to him.

"Hi, Ricky. Everything okay?"

"Yeah....you don't have to baby-sit me any more. I'm fine."

"Well, can I sit with you and have lunch?"

"No. You're sitting in Lindy's seat."

"Well, Lindy can sit somewhere else. There are a lot of chairs."

"No, she can't. She's going to sit here. I *want* her to sit here. I *invited* her to sit here. I can't recall inviting *you*, however."

Lindy was standing beside the table, holding her tray, trying to keep from laughing. Nobody ever talked to Carrie that way.

Carrie stared at Ricky like she didn't understand what he had just said.

"Carrie, like you just said…there are a lot of chairs. So get your ass out of this one and go sit it in another one. No, never mind…..we'll get another place to sit. I don't want Lindy sitting in the same chair you sat in. Annoying pains in the ass might be contagious."

Ricky slid out of the chair and he and Lindy went to another table and sat down. "Damn it, she's annoying. She just rubs me the wrong way; you know?"

Lindy smiled and nodded, but didn't say anything for a moment. Suddenly, she burst out laughing.

"What's so *funny*?"

"Her face….did you see her face when you said that to her? It was priceless. Too bad the yearbook photographer wasn't around. What a shot he missed." Lindy chuckled and smiled at Ricky.

Ricky relaxed and laughed, too. Then he opened his book bag and pulled out the key chain. "Hope you like bears."

Lindy gasped in surprise. Her smile told him she did like bears. "Thank you." She told him, and then quickly and unexpectedly, she raised herself up and kissed him on the jaw. He was pleasantly surprised by her action. He knew he wanted to kiss her back, but he also knew that he couldn't kiss her in the lunch room. He opted for taking her hand as they left the lunch room together. So engrossed with each other were they, that they both missed the hard, nasty stare from Carrie, as her narrowed eyes bored into their backs.

# Chapter 8

$\mathcal{L}$indy reached the bridge at exactly ten o'clock. Ricky was already standing there, waiting. He noted the worn jeans and tee shirt she was wearing, which were not too different from the clothes he had on.

"Ready?" He asked. He brought coffee for them, and he also had a couple of sandwiches and a bag of chips in the small knapsack he carried. "Didn't want us to get lost and starve to death in the woods, so I brought us each a sandwich and some potato chips."

"Great. We want to be well-fed when we become the dinner of bears or wild cats. I brought a couple bottles of water and a couple granola bars. I have an ice pack in my case. Do you want to rearrange things so that the sandwiches stay cold?"

They took a couple of minutes to separate the perishables from the non-perishables before they started off through the trees, Ricky leading. Every few yards Ricky pulled off a piece of tape and tagged a branch with it by draping it over the branch and pressing the ends together so it would not fall off.

"How did you know to do that? You've never been in the woods before."

"Survival instinct. I'm a survivor. So stick with me and you'll always survive." He smiled broadly at her as he said it, hoping that she believed it more than he actually did. "Actually, I remember the Hansel and Gretel story."

He smiled at her and she reciprocated.

They followed what looked like a natural path, downward. The terrain was steep, but not too dangerous. Except for the complaining of an occasional bird they had disturbed, it was completely quiet. They made their way down near the bottom of the steep hill, where they could hear the running water of the wide creek. The last leg of the hill was a drop-off of almost six feet. Ricky jumped down easily, but Lindy hesitated.

"Come on. Try running down real fast if you can't jump it. I'll catch you."

Lindy took a deep breath and ran down the drop-off, falling into Ricky's arms. He was pushed back by her momentum, but he dug his heels in, stopped and held onto her.

Laughing, he looked down at her. "See? Piece of cake."

She looked up at him and their eyes locked. Slowly, Ricky dropped his face down and placed his lips on hers. The first kiss was soft and quick. He pulled his lips away and stared into her eyes, and then brought his hand up and touched her cheek, drawing her in close to him. They kissed again—this time a long passionate kiss with just a hint of Ricky's tongue. He knew she wasn't a girl who he could choke with his tongue. He had to move slowly with her.

The kiss ended with Ricky lightly kissing the tip of Lindy's nose. He smiled down at her. "That was nice. Let's do it again sometime." He winked at her.

She laughed and winked back. "Okay." She turned and looked around them. "So now what? We have to walk back up the way we came? That's going to be….."

"A bitch….I know." Ricky finished her sentence. He looked around and then focused on something Lindy couldn't see, and started grinning. "Well, now….I don't think so. Come on; let's go check this out over here." Taking her hand, he started walking away from the bridge that was now high above them. About twenty-five yards in the opposite direction of the bridge, they stopped at a set of wooden steps.

"Do you think that goes back up to the top?" Lindy asked him.

"Well, I know it goes *up*. Where it comes out, I wouldn't have a clue. Let's eat the sandwiches and then we can go up the steps. Okay?"

They walked toward a large flat rock, and Ricky helped Lindy up onto it.

"See, I figure it this way. We eat the sandwiches. If we have to bribe a wild animal to let us pass, all the animal will get is the granola bars. Make sense?"

Lindy laughed and nodded in agreement.

Ricky stared at the surroundings. It was beautiful in this place. The trees and the rocks alongside of a babbling creek were something he had only seen in pictures. The sunlight was bright, but not harsh. He never imagined that places like this actually existed. He looked over at Lindy. It was the same with her….he never knew girls like her existed.

"What are you thinking right now?" He asked her. 'Damn, that was a chick question.' He thought to himself.

"It's so peaceful and beautiful here. That's what I was thinking. You know…you can be alone down here and not be lonely, yet sometimes.…..up there.….." she nodded her head toward the top of the hill. "You can be lonely with people all around. Do you know what I mean? Does that make any sense?"

Ricky nodded. "It makes perfect sense to me."

He reached for her, pulled her close, and kissed her again. They kissed over and over again, each kiss getting more passionate and more intense.

Ricky pulled away first and expelled air from his lungs. "We better quit this. It's driving me crazy." He smiled at her. "I really want you, but not on this rock. Ready to make the climb up?"

They gathered up the trash and put it into the knapsack, jumped down off the rock, and headed toward the wooden steps. They began the ascent up to what they hoped would be civilization.

Feet dragging the last few yards, they came to the top of the steps and looked around. Ricky was lost, but Lindy was smiling.

"We are a few streets down from where my house is. If we walk up that street for about three blocks, we'll come to my street."

"Are you sure?"

"Positive."

"Okay. So let's make a pact right now. That's our place down there at the bottom of the steps. If either one of us is ever in trouble or danger, we go there and wait. If you ever need me, go there and wait. I'll be there. I'll know."

Lindy stared at him, appreciating the gesture, but not quite understanding the thought behind it.

"Hey, how about some real lunch now? The sandwiches were sort of breakfast. Let me buy you lunch at that little restaurant over there. Sound good?"

They walked hand-in-hand to the small corner restaurant. It was nearly deserted when they went in, since it was past the lunch hour. They chose a small booth toward the back and sat down. The waitress took their order after they made their selection from the menu.

"So do both of your parents work?" Ricky asked her.

"My dad does. My mom is dead."

"Oh. I'm sorry; I didn't know."

"That's okay. It was two years ago. Cancer. I miss her."

"Yeah, I miss my dad, too. He died when I was thirteen. Heart attack."

"Wow....that's sad. So you live with your uncle? I heard you say it yesterday."

"Yeah.....my mom made me come here. She said the place where we lived had too many bad influences. I was getting out of control. Probably all true, but the fact is.... she annoys me. I find it hard to listen to her."

"Why?"

Ricky sighed and took a sip of the water the waitress had placed in front of him. "Because....she never says anything nice when she talks to me. And....she never mentions my dad to me. I mean....sometimes I feel like she's trying to forget he ever existed. I want to talk about him. He was a great guy. She won't."

"Yeah, I have the same problem….except my dad won't talk to me at all. It's like I don't even exist any more. We used to be close. When my mom died, I lost him, too."

Lindy looked at Ricky and he could see the sadness in her expressive eyes. Suddenly, he had an urge to hold her and take the sadness away. Instead, he changed the subject.

"So why don't you have a boyfriend?"

"I thought I did." She looked at him pointedly.

"Well, you do now, but why didn't you have one before?"

It was Lindy's turn to sigh. "Well, I think it's because everybody knows about my mother dying. People treat me differently. Kids at school do, anyway. It's like….they're afraid that if they get close to me, they'll catch it."

"Catch what?"

"Catch the death disease. It's like….okay…..my mother died….so if they get close to me…..their mother will die. Maybe that's not the way it is, but that's how it feels. Maybe boys just don't like me. I don't know."

"That's a stupid reason to stay away from you. And….. I like you."

"Good." She smiled at him.

After they ate, Ricky paid the check and left a tip. They walked out into the bright sunlight and headed up the hill. Just as Lindy promised, her street was three blocks from where they came out from the trees at the steps. Ricky walked with her to her door, after Lindy noted that her father's truck wasn't in the driveway.

"Hey, you know what?" He asked. "I don't have your phone number. Can I have it?"

"Oh, yeah....of course." She stepped inside, grabbed a piece of paper and a pen, and wrote down her phone number. Ricky handed her a piece of paper with his cell phone number and the number at the condo written on it.

"Can I call you later? I know I won't be allowed out, but can I call? I mean, you'll be home, right?"

Lindy smiled and nodded. "Yeah, I'll be home."

"Hey.....tomorrow.....what are you doing tomorrow?"

Lindy grinned at him. "I usually go to the zoo on Sundays. I have a pass."

"The *zoo*? I've never been to a zoo, which is funny because Chicago has a nice zoo, I hear. How do you get there?"

"Bus. Want to come along?"

Ricky looked at her and laughed. "Yeah....I do. I'll call you later and make the plans. Okay?"

They looked at each other briefly, and then came together in a kiss that was sweet, but at the same time, warm and passionate. Lindy watched him walk away long after she closed the door. For once, the hollow spot in her chest didn't feel so hollow.

Ricky fairly sprinted home. He got to the front door and remembered to take his shoes off. They were covered with a reddish dust from the edge of the creek and the rocks around it. He had totally enjoyed the day. He thought of Lindy as he walked up the stairs to his room. He noted that Uncle Nick wasn't at home, so he decided to jump into the shower and get the dirt from the woods off of him. He would take his clothes downstairs and put them into the washing machine, along with some other things that needed washed. He knew how to wash clothes. His dad taught him one day when his mother was in the hospital having gall bladder surgery. His dad told him he had to know how to wash his own clothes, since there might not be someone around to do it all the time. So he learned how to separate clothes, and how much detergent to use. He found it to be a valuable lesson in the past three years, just like many of the other lessons he learned from his father.

\* \* \*

Nick heard Ricky leave to go to the woods. He briefly wondered if he would be okay and if he was telling the truth. Quickly, he decided that the answer was an affirmative to both questions. He was pleasantly surprised when he went downstairs and discovered that Ricky had made coffee. 'That kid is not so bad,' he thought to himself, as he poured himself a cup. As he was sitting down, the phone rang. He instinctively knew it would be his sister.

"Hell, Angie, let me get a cup of coffee in me first." He growled into the phone.

"Nick, good morning….how's it going? Any problems yet?"

"Actually, no…the kid's been great. Actually made a pot of spaghetti the other night. He's in school and hasn't caused any problems there. He's not as bad as you said he was."

"Well, that's a relief….I guess. I don't know….maybe he has no respect for me…"

"Angie….what happened to him in Chicago?"

"Wh-what do you mean, Nick?"

"Something happened to him....something bad. You must have a clue as to what it was."

"No, Nick....I don't have any idea. How would I know?"

"Because you're his mother. You are supposed to know that kind of stuff. Didn't you ever hear him cry out in his sleep at night?"

"Well....yes....but...."

"But, what? Didn't you ever ask him about it?"

"No...he wouldn't have told me."

"How do you know that? Angie, something terrible happened to him...or he saw something terrible....real terrible. I hear him at night. I used to do the same thing, Angie.....cry out and wake up in a cold sweat, trembling. The kid has been through something....and as a parent, you should have found out what it was."

He knew he had hurt her feelings, but he couldn't help himself. He saw the signs that Ricky had been through something. What Angie was calling 'out of control' was actually post traumatic stress and a cry for help. He knew he would have to take some extra-special care, but he intended to find out what Ricky had been through. It just angered him that Angie wasn't on top of it.

"Can I talk to him, Nick?"

"Uh, he's not here."

"Where is he?"

"He went off to explore the woods with a new-found friend from school. I tell you, Angie, you're going to see a difference in him."

"Well, I hope so...as long as it's a change for the better."

"I think he….I don't know…..feels safe here. He still has that wariness in his eyes, but he seems more relaxed. But he hasn't given me any problems, I can tell you that."

"Well, I'm glad of that. I put the house up for sale yesterday. Hopefully it will sell quickly. Listen, I have to run. Give Ricky my love. Does he need anything?"

"No, I got it all covered. Just take care and get down here and be a parent. Love you, Ange."

He disconnected the call and leisurely drank his cup of coffee, plus two more. He planned on going to the lab for a couple of hours, even though it was Saturday. Since Ricky would be gone for a few hours, it would give him a chance to get caught up on some paperwork. Maybe they could go out for dinner together later. He wanted to spend as much time with Ricky as he could, because he intended to find out what caused the nighttime screams; but beside that, he liked the kid. He found that he enjoyed his company.

On his way to the hospital, he stopped at his favorite diner for a late breakfast. He ordered his breakfast and thought about Ricky while he waited. He recognized that, although he was on the thin side, Ricky was a good-looking boy. He imagined he had female admirers. How was he—Nick—going to handle that one? He remembered what Angie had told him about Ricky having sex partners. He tried to think back and remember if he had them at sixteen. No, he didn't think so. What if Ricky wanted to bring a nice girl home with him? Or a not-so-nice one? How would he react to that? A nice one? Yes, Nick could handle that. The other kind….hmmm, Nick didn't think so. How do you tell the difference, though?

Totally engrossed in his thoughts, he didn't see his ex come into the diner from the side door. He was taken by surprise when he heard her ask if she could sit down.

"Liz, of course…have a seat."

"You were lost in thought; I could tell. Everything okay?"

"Yeah, everything's fine. How's the women's center coming along?"

Liz sighed. "Slow but sure. How are things going with Ricky?"

"Good, actually. I'll tell him you asked about him."

"Good, thanks…..I'd love to see him. I'll bet he's pretty grown up now, huh?"

"Yeah, I guess. He's got a lot of growing to do….in every way except height. He's about six feet tall."

"Oh, my *stars*! You're *kidding*!" Liz laughed.

"No, I'm not. He's a little taller than I am. Well, Enrico was tall, so I guess that's where he gets the height from. He has the unmistakable Bazario eyes, though."

"Well, that certainly isn't bad. I'll bet girls just swoon over those eyes. I did."

Nick looked across the table from her and smiled. "Yeah?"

"Yeah, but then things change." Liz quickly changed the subject. "So listen…I'm planning on having a fund raiser at the hospital. Can I count on you to lend a hand for it? Maybe even get Ricky involved?"

"Depends on what it is."

"Well, I was thinking of holding a talent show. You know; local talent….sell tickets. What do you think?"

"Sounds like a lot of work, but not a bad idea. What is it you would want me to do? I don't have much talent….

that I could perform on stage, that is." Nick offered her a suggestive smile.

"Funny, funny man! No, I just meant that maybe you'd buy a couple of tickets."

"Oh, well, if that's all….sure." He was interrupted by the arrival of his breakfast. Liz ordered coffee and toast. "Very light and soft with the butter melting on top." Nick finished the order for her.

She favored him with a smile. "You remembered."

Nick nodded, as she automatically, without hesitation, passed him the salt and pepper for his eggs. "Speaking of remembering…." He smiled at her.

They were both distracted from their conversation by a young couple standing outside, obviously exchanging harsh words. Nick tensed when he saw the guy grab the girl by the arm, and then grab her face, holding it so she couldn't look away. Whatever he had said to her, it subdued her as she walked to their car, her head down. The guy still had a grip on her arm and quite a sneer on his face. The girl looked familiar to him and he wondered why he thought he knew her. Maybe she was a candy-striper at the hospital, or something.

"Does that remind you of us?" He asked Liz.

"No….we never fought in public. That's why our divorce was such a surprise to everybody."

Nick nodded in agreement. He noted that the couple who had been fighting just five minutes ago were making up in the front seat of the car they sat in. The guy put the car into gear and quickly sped away. "A happy ending." He nodded toward the car pulling out of the parking lot, and smiled hollowly at Liz.

Nick finished his breakfast at the same time Liz finished her toast. He got up to go and was reminded of her usual habit. He reached for her check and smiled down at her. "I have this. Now have your cigarette. I have to run."

She nodded, and silently marveled how much they remembered about each other.

\* \* \*

It was close to five when Nick returned home from the hospital. Ricky was in his room, maybe listening to music or sleeping. Nick was disappointed, since he wanted to hear all about the trip to the woods.

Nick wasn't disappointed for long. Ricky heard him come in through the front door and came out of his room and down the stairs. He had showered earlier and was dressed in clean clothes.

"Hi, Rick. How was your day? Have fun in the woods?" Nick glanced at him.

Ricky's eyes took on that wary look. "It was okay. Why do you ask?"

Nick felt his suspicion begin to rise, and his voice took on a tight note. "Why shouldn't I ask? You said you had never been in the woods….I just wanted to know if you liked it. It's a normal question." He stared hard at Ricky.

"Oh," was Ricky's response. "It was fun, I guess. It was more fun going downhill than it was coming back up. Hey, trees can be pretty big; can't they? Kind of makes you know how insignificant you are."

Nick chuckled, and expelled air in a sigh of relief. The wariness in Ricky's eyes must have been a normal reaction—a conditioned response from his life in the streets.

"Where would you like to eat tonight? I'm buying dinner."

Ricky thought for a moment. "You pick. I don't know anything around here. You must know some good places to eat."

"Steak? How does that sound?"

Ricky nodded. "That sounds great. I'm starving, too. Being a woodsman takes a lot out of you."

They both laughed as they headed out the door to go to dinner.

# Chapter 9

Ricky met Lindy at the bridge again. They would have to walk for a few blocks to get to a bus stop, get on a bus, and then change busses once to get to the zoo. This was a new adventure for him. Not only had he never been to a zoo, but he had never ridden on a port authority bus. In Chicago, he walked everywhere. Busses were for old people and the weak. It wasn't like he ever went anywhere very far, so there was no need to get on a bus.

He smiled when he saw Lindy coming up the hill. She was like a breath of fresh air all the time—so sweet and innocent, but yet fun to be with. She had a wonderful sense of humor that was similar to his, and he realized that he really looked forward to seeing her every day. He was thinking about his uncle's reaction when he told him he was going to the zoo. At first Ricky didn't think he believed him, but then he offered Ricky money so he could pay his way in. Of course, Ricky took it. Now at least he would have a little something to spend on Lindy—definitely buy her lunch and maybe a zoo souvenir. He was surprised when it dawned on him that he no longer thought about buying booze with money he got. He bought a pack of cigarettes, but he didn't smoke as frequently as he once did. He was smoking a cigarette now as he watched Lindy. He quickly butted it out and popped a couple of breath mints into his mouth as she got closer. He knew it wouldn't mask the smell completely, but she wouldn't find the smell as offensive.

"Hey, Babe." His arm went around her as he greeted her, and his lips brushed hers.

Lindy wrinkled her nose. "You've been smoking again."

"Busted. Sorry......just one, though." He smiled down at her.

She smiled back up at him. "I just worry about your health; you know? I don't want you to get lung cancer."

"I know. I promise I'll quit eventually. Hell, I gave everything else up......just let me give this one vice up gradually. Okay?"

He took her hand as they started walking in the direction of the bus stop. He knew cancer was a big worry with her because of her mother. He guessed that it was that way with most people who lost someone to cancer. But the funny thing was....Lindy never asked him to give up anything. He gave up booze and sex for her, but not because she asked him to; he just did. She never really asked him to quit smoking, but he could tell she really found the smell offensive, and...she did worry about his lungs. He looked toward her and smiled, knowing that the sacrifices were all worth it.

They had a wonderful time at the zoo. Ricky was fascinated by the wild animals as he stopped to read the history and characteristics of many of them. Aside from the animals, he was fascinated by the tranquility of the zoo, even with all of the patrons roaming around and occasional squawks from birds, especially the peacocks.

He decided it was a great way to spend a Sunday afternoon. He bought Lindy and himself a soft drink and a box of popcorn, and they sat on a bench and fed the small birds with it. Since there was no restaurant inside the zoo, they made a lunch of hotdogs and cotton candy as they sat at a small table overlooking the lions. One lion roared at them, causing them to laugh. They agreed it was because he wanted their hotdogs. On the way out of the zoo, they stopped in the gift shop. Ricky bought Lindy a small stuffed lion to commemorate the roaring. It had been a wonderful day and they both hated to see it end. Ricky walked Lindy all the way to her house and kissed her at the front door. He fairly sailed back up the hill, only stopping to light a cigarette.

* * *

September turned into October, forcing the leaves into their yearly spectacular show of colors. Lindy and Ricky walked along the creek, arms around each other. The air was crisp and clean smelling; the sun, high in the sky, brilliantly showed off its blaze.

They had returned to this place—their place—several times since their first discovery of it. On one occasion, they erected a small shelter out of branches and some wood they had found halfway up the stairs. This would provide protection from the rain if they should get caught in it. They made sure that the shelter was hidden so that it couldn't be seen from the bridge above or from any other angle. Neither of them told anyone about their special place—it belonged to the two of them, and nobody else. More than once Ricky reminded Lindy that if she ever had to hide, she should go there, and he would find her.

She still didn't understand why he thought that way, but she assumed that it had to do with where he came from.

On this clear, crisp day in October, Ricky and Lindy were lying on their backs on 'their' rock, enjoying the heat from the sun. They weren't speaking; they didn't have to; and except for their fingers being laced together, they weren't touching. Whenever they were together, a feeling of serenity engulfed them, making them feel safe and at peace with the world. Ricky was toying with breaking that serenity and telling Lindy about Paulie. He decided that if he could tell anyone, it would be her. He looked over at her, noting that her eyes were closed and there was a half-smile on her lips. That meant she wasn't sleeping.

"Lindy?" His voice was barely above a whisper.

She opened her eyes and turned her face toward him. She instinctively knew that he was going to tell her something, so she waited.

He told her the terrible story of Paulie's demise and how he had watched because he couldn't do anything else. He showed her the scars from his teeth where he bit his hand to keep from screaming. She had noticed them before but she never asked why they were there. When he stopped talking, he saw the tears glistening in her eyes.

"I think that's why I sometimes wake up screaming. It's because I couldn't scream then. Anyway, that's why I always have to have a safe place to hide. And that's why I want you to have a safe place. We have to hide from the Punches in this world, because we're just not capable of fending them off. And we need a place to scream. Do you understand any of that? I mean, does it make sense to you?"

Lindy stared at him for a moment, and then nodded. "It does."

She rolled onto her side and placed her arm on his chest. He rolled and met her halfway and they joined in a kiss. Ricky ran his hand through her silky hair and then brought it up under her chin. He kissed her again as he held her chin. He wrapped an arm around her and held her, his cheek pressed against hers. Lindy felt a sensation as his breath lightly grazed her ear. She labeled it as desire. Ricky was feeling his own sensations, but lower. He knew he had to pull away from her if he wanted to be able to get up off of the rock and walk. But it felt so good holding her that he didn't want to let go just yet. He looked down into her big blue eyes and traced her jaw with his index finger.

"You look like an angel," He whispered as he smiled down at her.

She responded by smiling up at him, and then grinning. "And you look like….the devil." Then she broke up laughing.

Ricky grabbed her up and pulled her on top of him, laughing. Lindy quickly met his lips in a long passionate kiss, causing his heart to pound erratically.

"We better stop this….'cause if we don't……you're going to see my horns….or at least one in particular." Ricky's breathing was as uneven as his speech.

"Right on this rock? That would hurt!" Lindy laughed as she spoke.

Ricky conceded that it would, and then sat up with her still on top of him, causing her to fall into his lap. He sighed and stared at her.

"So what are we going to do about this? I know I want you really bad…..and it hurts. So what do you think we should do about it?"

"I….I don't know. I've never…..you know…."

"I know you haven't. But…..I…….I'm used to girls who have….and I didn't even have to ask them. It's just so hard….to keep stopping all the time….especially when you are so desirable." He nuzzled her ear, and she felt the sensation again.

"I…..I'm afraid….."

"I would be extra-careful with you….be gentle…not hurt you. What do ya think?"

Lindy stared at him for a few moments. "Ricky, I don't know. What if….I get pregnant?"

"I would take care of that. I'll make sure you don't. Come on, Baby….please? At least think about it?"

Lindy nodded. "Okay….I'll think about it. It's just that…..if we do….and you find someone else…."

"Don't even say that. It won't happen. Besides, I just want you to think about it. I didn't say we would. I mean, I can't afford a motel and I'm not going to jump your bones on the rock or in the woods."

He jumped down and pulled her down off of the rock, and then put his arms around her waist. "Relax…..I'm not about to force you." He kissed the tip of her nose and released her. Together they made their way up the steps toward the world above, brushing the dust off of each other at the top of the steps.

# Chapter 10

Ricky sat in the back of the auditorium watching Lindy and the rest of the student actors rehearse for the musical. This year's selection was *Grease*, with Lindy playing the lead role. Ricky chuckled as he watched. Lindy was good. Her singing was wonderful, but so were her moves, up on stage. Her voice carried well, which surprised Ricky, since she was usually soft-spoken. She played the part well. Ricky would be attending both performances since he knew Lindy wouldn't have anybody else there for her. He was a little worried about Nick letting him attend the Thursday night performance since it was a school night, but he promised Lindy he would be there. He was going to approach Nick about it tonight. Actually, he was going to tell his uncle about Lindy, too. He had begun to recognize Nick as a straight-up guy, and felt he could trust him.

He waited for Lindy after the rehearsal, and after a quick kiss, they headed to their English Lit class together. Ricky reached for Lindy's hand as they walked.

"I'm going to tell Uncle Nick about you tonight. It should be okay, unless he has plans for me to be a priest." Ricky smiled at her. "But wish me luck anyway. Okay?"

"Of course. So how did I do in rehearsal?"

"You were wonderful…..as usual." He raised her hand to his lips and kissed it.

Luke, one of the other students in their class came up behind them, making kissing sounds. "Hello, young lovers." He sang to them. "Lindy, do you have tickets to the musical to sell?"

"Yeah, Luke….I do. Want one or two, or three or four?" Lindy was reaching into her purse for her tickets.

"Two will do. Ricky, you're going, right? I mean you wouldn't miss your girl at her finest, would you?"

Ricky laughed. "Absolutely not. I'll be there….both nights, as a matter of fact."

"Ooh…..a sign of real love." Both Ricky and Lindy laughed. They both liked Luke and he seemed to like them.

"So how many do you have to sell now?" Ricky asked her when they took their seats.

"Two more."

"I'll buy them."

"I don't think they're worth scalping." Lindy looked at Ricky laughing.

"I think I'm going to ask Uncle Nick if he would like to go."

"Really?" Lindy's face lit up into a beautiful smile.

"Really." Ricky responded.

\* \* \*

Nick walked through the front door and immediately smelled the food from the kitchen. In spite of his rough day, it brought a smile to his face.

"Hey, kid, I could get used to this," he said as he stood in the doorway.

"Yeah? Well, don't. I only do it when there's something on my mind."

"So what's on your mind? Want to share it?"

"When dinner is ready….which is in about ten minutes. Meatloaf, garlic mashed potatoes, and cold asparagus in Italian dressing."

"Sounds great. I'm going to change, and I'll be right down." Nick was pleased as he ran up the stairs. He realized that he was famished when he smelled the food.

He hurried back downstairs and poured himself a glass of wine, and as an after-thought, poured a small portion into a smaller glass for Ricky. 'Hell, we drank wine when we were kids,' he thought to himself. He set the glasses on the table where Ricky had already had plates and silverware, and sat down. Ricky joined him after he had set the food on the table.

Nick sampled the meatloaf and found it to be surprisingly good. It was better than good; it was excellent. He complimented Ricky for his effort, and Ricky beamed.

"So what's on you mind?" Nick's curiosity got the best of him.

Ricky put his fork down, sat back and sighed. He looked down at his plate, and then looked his uncle square in the eye. "Uncle Nick, I have a girlfriend. She's a nice girl. I really like her and I want you to meet her. It's important to me that you like her."

Nick was not quite prepared for this, even though he had thought about it before. He stared at Ricky for a few moments before he answered. "Is she someone you think I would like? I mean, I've seen what girls look like and act like today….and I don't like much of what I see."

"Lindy's different. She's….sweet…..and decent."

"Pretty?"

"I think she is. She looks like an angel. She doesn't wear makeup and she doesn't need it. I think you'll like her."

"And when do I get to meet her?"

"Well, here's the thing. She's in a musical at school Thursday and Friday night. I have tickets to go both nights, because she won't have anybody there for her. I bought an extra ticket thinking maybe you would like to go….Thursday night. Actually, I bought two extra tickets. So what do you say?"

Nick was studying Ricky as he talked about Lindy. He saw the light in his eyes and he knew that Ricky was crazy about this girl. 'How far had it gone with them?' he wondered. Did she feel the same about Ricky?

Nick heard himself say, "All right, I'll go with you."

Ricky smiled at him. "Thanks, Uncle Nick. Hey, I know you'll like her. I can't wait for you to meet her."

"Why won't she have anybody besides you…and me…there for her?"

"Well, her mother is dead, and her father is still grieving. He barely speaks to her, let alone get active in her life. It hurts her really bad, but she still loves her father…a lot."

"You know…..I never had the chance to raise any kids….but if I had, I know I would have done right by them. How do you ignore your child? Yeah, Ricky…I'm looking forward to meeting her."

\* \* \*

Nick and Ricky entered the school through the front doors. The auditorium doors were open and the overhead lights were on. Ricky could see that the seats were filling up already.

"Let's hurry up and get good seats. I want to be able to see Lindy when she's on stage."

Nick let Ricky lead him down the aisle toward the empty seats closest to the stage. After they claimed their seats, Nick went to out to buy them drinks and snacks, while Ricky stayed to save their spot. He watched the activity in front of the stage, but his mind was on Lindy. He had walked her home from school earlier that day, and told her he would see her after the performance tonight. Luke had agreed to pick her up and drive her to the school, and Ricky would provide the ride home if Nick actually decided to go to the musical with him. He hadn't told Lindy that his uncle was definitely going, because he didn't want her to be nervous on stage. He told her that he would walk her home if there was no ride, and she was fine with that. He was quite anxious for Nick to meet her. He was tired of hiding her from everybody. She was the first decent girl he had ever been with and he wanted to show her off; make her a part of the family. She was his girl, and he was damn proud of that. He also realized something very important. Although he wanted her so much it drove him crazy, he wanted Lindy, the whole person, more than just her body. He knew eventually they would end up in bed together, but for now he just enjoyed having her near him.

Nick brought their drinks and a bag of chips to the seats and settled into the one next to Ricky. The lights dimmed and the play was ready to begin.

Halfway through the first act, Nick leaned over and asked which one was Lindy. Ricky nodded toward Lindy and said, "Her. She has the lead role."

Nick's smile turned into a large lopsided grin. "Yeah? That's her? That pretty blonde? Man, can she sing."

Ricky nodded and shushed Nick. "Shh."

Nick studied Ricky's face and saw the admiration in his eyes as he watched his girlfriend perform. He turned back to the stage and focused on the girl and decided that he liked her already.

After the last curtain call, Nick and Ricky hung around in the hallway waiting for Lindy to come out. Nick knew when Ricky spotted her by the way his face lit up.

"Lindy, this is Uncle Nick." Ricky took her hand and led her to Nick. "Uncle Nick, this is Lindy Riley."

"Hello, Lindy. Nice to meet you.....you can really sing. How about we go for a pizza? I'm starving since all I had were those stale chips."

"Sounds great....it isn't that late." Ricky said as he looked at his watch.

"Okay, but I want to buy one of my CD's. They're selling them over there." She pointed toward a table that had been set up in the hall before the musical began. "The proceeds go to a local charity of my choice—the Humane Society."

"Well, then I guess I'd better buy one, too." Nick smiled down at her.

\* \* \*

After each of them purchased a CD, they went in Nick's car to a local pizza den that had a reputation for making terrific pizza. Ricky and Lindy sat together in the bucket seat on the passenger side, even though Nick suggested that they might be more comfortable if one sat in the back. He knew they would decline that idea, and he chuckled to himself. They found a booth toward the back of the pizza den and made a decision on the toppings. Ricky and Lindy liked the same toppings—onion, green pepper, and black olives—while Nick liked pepperoni. They compromised by getting all four toppings on the pizza. Nick found Lindy's company to be delightful, and he could see why Ricky was smitten with her. Not only was she pretty and sweet, as Ricky had said, but she was also intelligent with a wonderful sense of humor. She was definitely a keeper, Nick decided. What he couldn't understand was how a father could have such a wonderful daughter and choose to ignore her.

It was almost eleven when they got to Lindy's house. The truck was in the driveway so Ricky quickly walked her to the door and quickly kissed her before she slipped inside. Ray Riley was staring at the television when she walked past him.

"Kind of late, isn't it?" He asked, his voice sounding far away.

"I guess. But the play didn't let out until almost nine-thirty and we went for pizza."

"What play?'

"The musical I was in tonight. I had the lead role. I left you a ticket on the kitchen table."

"Oh…..I couldn't make it."

"Yeah….well….go figure," she answered, and went straight into her room and shut the door, blinking back the tears.

\* \* \*

Nick backed out of the driveway and headed toward the condos.

"Well?" Ricky asked him.

Nick smiled into the windshield. "She's terrific, Rick. Honest. You couldn't do better."

"Yeah, well....that's what I figured." Ricky looked at Nick's profile in the darkened car, and caught the smile on his face. "She can really sing, can't she?"

"Yeah, she can. You should mention to her that the hospital is going to have a talent show to raise money for the women's center. She should enter it."

"Yeah, I'll do that. Isn't she sweet, though, Uncle Nick? She's nothing like the girls I knew in Chicago."

Nick laughed lightly. "I'm glad of that. Your mother told me about those. By the way, she's coming in for the weekend, you know. You said you had an extra ticket.... so why don't you take your mother tomorrow night."

Ricky got quiet. He didn't want his mother to meet Lindy. She would just find something wrong with her. She found something wrong with everybody. He guessed he loved his mother, but he really didn't like her very much. She whined; she complained; she nagged; and she found fault with everything and everybody.

"So why so quiet all of a sudden?" Nick asked.

Ricky shrugged. "I don't know."

The conversation had ended as Nick pulled into his driveway. He watched Ricky get out of the car and walk up the short walk. Nick shook his head and followed him, determined to continue the conversation.

Nick went directly to the refrigerator and got out a beer and a can of soda and set them on the kitchen table. "Hey, kid....let's talk."

"I'm pretty tired. I'm just going to go to bed."

"You weren't tired five minutes ago. Come on…we need to talk. Your mother will be here tomorrow afternoon. She'll be here for the entire weekend, and I need to know what it is that makes you clam up when I mention her. Be honest with me. Sit down, and let's talk."

Reluctantly, Ricky went to the kitchen table and sat down. He opened the can of soda and looked over at Nick.

"So what gives? What's the problem with your mother?"

Ricky stared hard at Nick for a moment, searching for that anger he had seen there before. It wasn't there. There was no wolf-like face; just the face of his concerned uncle. He sighed resignedly.

"Uncle Nick, my mom is constantly complaining…. whining….about how hard it is to be without a husband. When she's not complaining or whining; she's nagging. Always picking at things. She's always so negative about everything. You know, when dad died I made all A's and B's in school. She complained that I spent too much time on schoolwork and not enough time helping around the house. 'After all, she had to work all day,' she would say. So I started spending less and less time on my schoolwork and my grades dropped to C's. Then she criticized me for getting grades that were just average. She would say, 'So that's all you are? Just average?' Then she found fault with everything I did or said. She complained about what I wore, who my friends were, my hair, you name it. I started staying away from the house as much as possible because I just couldn't stand it. I swear she nagged dad to death. Do you know how many times I walked out of the front door with my heart racing because all I wanted to do was smash her face in? I know…..I shouldn't say that…..but it's true. Everybody has a point to where they just can't take any more. My dad had a heart attack…was I going to be next?"

Ricky stopped talking. Had he said too much? He was seeing the anger coming to the surface on his uncle's face. He involuntarily cringed.

Nick had been staring at the table and realized Ricky had stopped talking. He looked over at him, and prodded. "Go on. I want to hear this."

Ricky hesitated briefly, but then continued. The can of worms had been opened. "Well, when you stay out past the good kids' curfew, all that's out there are the bad kids. I met a few of them, we hooked up, and we started getting into trouble. Little trouble, at first. You know….. petty stuff. Puncturing tires….that kind of stuff. Then we did more and more. I got arrested with another kid for breaking a windshield. My mother came to the police station to pick me up and she slapped me in the face, in front of everybody. I hated her at that moment. Well, of course she bitched and moaned all the way home. I tried to tune it out and I couldn't. When we got to the house, I got out of the car and swore at her. Then I took off up the street. I stayed gone for two days."

Ricky stopped to take a drink from his soda can. "Well, anyway, I found that I could cope with it if I just stayed buzzed a little bit. I never really cared for pot or anything like that, but a couple of beers would mellow me out just enough that I could handle her constant yammering. Uncle Nick, I don't want to disrespect my mother, but…hell, could you put up with that?"

Nick had listened up to this point and had not offered any comment. So far, he totally sympathized with Ricky. He was very angry with Angie right now.

"No, I couldn't. Tell me the rest of the story."

Ricky took another swig of the soda before he started again. He looked down at the can like he was discovering that brand for the first time, and then looked over at Nick.

"Well, then I spent as much time out in the streets as I could. Drinking, stealing…whatever it took to fit in. I started smoking cigarettes, and found that they could make me relax a little bit when I didn't have alcohol. But then I discovered a way to stay away from home all night. Girls. Some girls hung out with us and all you had to do was come on to them and you had a place for the night." Ricky smiled sheepishly. "They taught me everything I know….about sex, that is."

"Uh, Ricky, did they teach you about disease?"

"Well, no….but I know about S-T-D's."

"How do you know that they were clean?"

"I don't. But so far I haven't had any changes down there."

"Okay, now I don't want you to get mad….but there are a lot of diseases that you don't see changes at first. Sometimes not for years. I want you to get a physical exam. Please. Uh, have you done anything with….?'

"Lindy? Oh hell, no! You can't tell that she never….?"

"Well, yeah…..I just know that sometimes women can be deceiving."

"Not her. What you see is what you get." Ricky smiled for the first time since they walked into the condo.

"Will you get the exam? I mean, you don't know how far it will go with Lindy. You wouldn't want to inadvertently cause her misery at some point, years down the road; would you?"

"All right."

"Good. I'll set it up for you. Do you want a man or a woman doctor?"

Surprised, Ricky looked wide-eyed at his uncle, and saw the smirk on his face. They both laughed together.

"Well, anyway," Ricky continued. "I had a friend named Paulie. He had a good kids' curfew, but when he found out that I was keeping my own hours, he decided to join me. I was glad, because I always felt so much more comfortable around Paulie than I did around the other guys. They scared me a little, actually. Actually, they scared me a lot….but it was still better than hearing all that miserable yakking at home. For Paulie to fit in, he had to rob somebody. That was kind of an initiation. Well, he did and he got away with it, so he was in. Paulie found that he actually liked robbing people and getting away with it. I never did. I always felt so guilty afterward."

"That's the difference between being a sociopath and not being one." Nick interjected.

Ricky sighed. "Well, that's how we lived our life—stealing, robbing, drinking, smoking, and screwing. It was easy to tune out anything my mother had to say after that. Then the girls found out where I lived, and they started showing up there when I got home from school. Apparently, I was their favorite….fuck-buddy…. they called it."

Nick winced. He remembered the term.

"My mother caught me a few times….girls naked and doing….*things*." He emphasized the word 'things'. "She went off like a maniac. Can't say I really blame her for those times, I guess. I was disrespecting her house. She called the girls whores and she called me a….whore-monger….whatever that is."

Nick couldn't help himself. He burst out laughing. He walked to the refrigerator and took out another beer, stalling to regain his composure. When he had himself under control again, he sat back down.

Ricky sat in silence for a few moments. He was mentally wrestling with himself about whether to tell Nick what happened to Paulie. So far, Nick had been really cool about everything. Ricky decided to proceed.

"Anyway, Uncle Nick…..one night Paulie and I robbed a convenience store. We each grabbed three cartons of cigarettes and a handful of cash. We were running from the cops and we ran down this dark alley. The police car couldn't fit down there so we figured with a few zigzags, we'd be home free. We ran and ran. I stopped at a corner to catch my breath and Paulie kept running around the corner. Suddenly, I could hear voices around the corner. I looked behind me and didn't see any cops, so I slowly peaked around the corner. I saw my friend Paulie held up against the wall by a guy we all knew as Punch. Apparently, Paulie had run into him when he went around the corner. I saw him lift Paulie up by the throat and stick a knife into his stomach and gut him while he held him in the air."

Ricky had to stop. Annoyed, he wiped the tears from his cheeks. "I slid behind a dumpster and watched the whole thing. There was nothing I could do. Paulie screamed. It was the….worst….scream I have ever heard." Ricky remembered his bite mark on his hand. He held his hand up for Nick to see it.

"There. I bit myself so hard to keep from screaming, too, that I broke the skin. Anyway, the alleyway was suddenly full of police and flash lights. They forgot about our petty little robbery when they saw the bloody massacre in the alley. Punch charged them with the knife and was shot to death. It took three shots to bring him down. I hid behind the dumpster the whole time, and nobody saw me. When everybody was gone, I went home. Paulie was dead, of course. I guess I sorta blamed mom for it. Neither one of us would have been out there if she hadn't have forced me out there with all her nagging and complaining all the time. It coulda' been me instead of Paulie. If I had gone around that corner first, it woulda' been." Ricky wiped his eyes again. "Besides Lindy, you're the only person I ever told about this. Anyway, I couldn't even look at my mother for the longest time. Then she told me she was sending me to live with you. She made it sound like she wanted to be rid of me."

"How?" Nick perked up.

"Well, saying things like 'it's too hard to raise a boy by myself' or 'at least I'll be able to sleep at night when you're out of here'….things like that. I was glad to be getting away from her, but it still hurt…'cause it sounded like she didn't want me for a son any more. I mean….after dad died, she never talked about him. I wanted to. I loved dad. But she wouldn't talk about him and wouldn't let me talk about him. So now, she gets me out of her life, and I guess that's forever, too."

Nick looked at Ricky like he saw him for the first time. He realized why Ricky was so hostile around Angie. She made him that way. He focused back to Ricky when he realized that Ricky was still talking.

"Anyway, I don't want her to meet Lindy. My mother will find something about Lindy to criticize and I will hate her for it. Finding Lindy was like finding my way out of a sewer; you know what I mean? I don't want my mother to ever say anything bad about her. Lindy is the sweetest girl I have ever known. I couldn't stand having mom say anything bad about her. Lindy is the best thing that has ever happened to me."

Nick nodded in agreement. He clearly understood what Ricky was talking about, and he was certainly going to have a talk with Angie. She couldn't take her frustrations out on her son. If she did, she would lose him forever.

"All right…..but you should think about taking her. I mean, I didn't know what to expect before I met Lindy. It was a delightful surprise to meet such a sweet teenaged girl. And, by the way, she is very pretty. What could your mother find wrong with her?"

"She's not Italian?"

Nick once again, burst out laughing, and Ricky joined him.

"We had better get to bed. Neither of us is going to be able to get up tomorrow."

Ricky nodded and trotted up the steps. Nick followed, turning out the lights as he went. Neither of them could sleep. Ricky stayed awake reliving Paulie's demise and Nick lay awake staring at the ceiling, wondering how to tell his sister that she was Ricky's problem.

# Chapter 11

Nick dropped Ricky and Lindy off at the school and headed toward the hospital. He was going in for an hour or so, but then would go back home to wait for Angie to arrive. He was going to have a real heart-to-heart with her; he knew that. She had called at seven this morning, and Ricky answered the phone. Nick got wind of the conversation as he was coming down the stairs. He heard Ricky's end of the conversation.

"….Because I don't start school until eight. It's only seven now." There was a pause, and then, "I go to school every day, and yes, my grades are back up. Here's Uncle Nick."

Nick saw the agitation on Ricky's face as he handed him the phone. Nick put his hand over the receiver and asked Ricky, "Do you walk to school with Lindy?"

Ricky nodded.

"Call her on your cell and tell her we'll pick her up. We'll leave here about seven-thirty and pick her up at her house about seven-forty, okay?"

Ricky nodded again, and flipped open his cell phone.

"Yeah, Angie, where are you?" He asked his sister.

"You sound agitated. Is he giving you a hard time?"

"No, he's not. You know, you might have asked him what time he had to be in school before you started accusing him of not going….."

"I just know him, Nick; that's all."

"Unfortunately, Angie, you don't know him. You don't know him at all."

"What's that supposed to mean?"

"Look, I have to go. We'll talk when you get here." Nick had abruptly hung up.

Nick sat at the red light thinking about the conversation. He hated to admit it, but Angie was a lousy mother. He looked down at his console and discovered the CD he bought at the school. The light was still red, so he tore open the cellophane around it and took the CD out and dropped it in the CD player. The CD began playing as the light changed. Instead of moving forward he sat there staring in the direction of the CD player. The sound coming out of the player was extraordinary. First, there was a piano intro, and then Lindy's voice wafted through the speakers sounding like all the angels in heaven. The horn behind him reminded him to drive forward. He listened to the CD all the way to the hospital and continued listening to it, until it ended, as he sat in the parking lot. 'That girl has a real gift,' he thought to himself. He took the CD out and put it back into its cover, got out of the car, locked it, and walked into the hospital.

He pushed the button on the elevator and when it opened; he got in and pushed two instead of seven, the floor where his lab was situated. Two was the floor for the original women's center. He walked down the corridor until he came to the office of the Director of Women's

Health. He tapped on the door, and he heard Liz's voice tell him to come in. He entered.

"Nick….hi. Considering the nature of my specialty I have to assume this is a social call."

"Sort of. Are you still putting together a talent show?"

"Yeah, did you reconsider and come up with a hidden talent? What is it? Flute? Bagpipes?"

Nick laughed. "No, but I think I found the winner of the talent show. Do you have a CD player in here?"

"Yes, why?"

Nick pulled the CD out of his pocket and handed it to Liz. "Listen….just listen."

Staring at Nick, Liz reached for the CD. She turned around and dropped it into her small CD player that sat behind her desk. Then she sat down to listen. When Liz heard Lindy's clear voice, her mouth dropped open and she turned to look at Nick.

"Who is this? She is…..wonderful!"

"Ricky's girlfriend." Nick told her about the performance at the school last night, and how he bought the CD because the profits went to charity.

"That was nice of you. So what's she like? Pretty?"

"She's a little doll, and just as sweet as can be. Ricky's quite taken with her. I'm glad, because he could do a lot worse. I've seen some of these girls nowadays…."

"Yeah, I have, too. I've been meaning to stop by the lab. How are things going with you and Ricky?"

"They're great, Liz. He's a great kid. You know, he wanted me to meet the girlfriend, and he said it was important that I liked her. That made me feel pretty good; you know? I gave them both a ride to school this morning.

You should have seen Ricky's face when she came out of her door. She was a knock-out this morning, I tell you. Long pink and black flowered skirt, down to her calves, black boots, pink sweater.….really cute."

"So what does she look like? Hair and eye color?"

"Long blonde hair, big blue eyes….her face reminds me of Heather Locklear."

"Oh, well.….that's certainly all good." Liz laughed.

"Well, I guess I'd better get upstairs and get some work done. I'm only going to be here a couple of hours. Angie is coming for the weekend and I want to be home when she arrives. Nice talking to you."

"Yeah, same here. Nick, can I keep this?" Liz was referring to the CD. "For awhile?"

"Yeah, you can have it. I'll just get another one. It's for charity." He grinned at her and left quickly.

Liz sat down and quietly listened to the entire CD as she completed some paperwork for the new site. She let the CD play again, and this time she sat there thinking about Nick. If only he could have let go of the anger. They may have still been married. She felt sure that the anger was a wall that held his emotions in check. He couldn't show love or affection because the anger was there, right out in front. Nick was a good man; always had been. She knew he had really loved her, but sometimes love isn't enough. If only he could have opened up to her; talked to her; explained his anger to her; she might have been able to help him get past all that. But Nick remained close-mouthed and tight-lipped, and it had cost them their marriage. Since the divorce, she hadn't met a man who even came close to Nick and certainly nobody who kissed like he did. Liz felt a little stir way down in the pit of her stomach as she remembered the way he made her feel when he kissed her. 'Stop it, Liz,' she scolded herself. 'That was a long time ago.'

\* \* \*

Nick got some paperwork done and hurried home to greet Angie when she got there. He was sitting at his bar drinking a scotch and water when he heard her pull into the driveway, and he immediately went out to retrieve her bags out of her car. He gave her a quick hug and a kiss on the cheek.

"It's a little early to be drinking, don't you think?" She gave him a cold stare.

"Are you going to start monitoring me? I've never abused alcohol in my life. Sometimes it's just nice to sit in your home alone and have a drink. Do you have a problem with that?"

Angie narrowed her eyes at Nick. "What has Ricky been telling you?"

"Angie...we will get to that. Come on in and relax a little."

"That is such a long drive. My eyes are tired from peering out of the windshield all that way."

"Something to drink, Ange? Are you hungry maybe? We can go to lunch."

"I'm tired from driving. I really don't want to get into a car."

"Angie, you sound like an old woman. You're thirty-eight years old, and you talk like you're seventy-eight. So let's just say we sit down at the kitchen table and talk...okay? Do you want to know about your son? How he's been getting along?"

"I just want to know one thing. What is his problem? I call here and ask him why he's not in school and he bites my head off. Just what is his problem?"

"You."

"What? What are you talking about?"

"You're his problem."

"That's absurd. I'm his *mother*. How can I be his problem? I've done my best to keep a roof over his head, feed him, clothe him. *What more can I do?*"

Nick stared at his sister, not believing what he had just heard.

"Have words like encouragement, nurturing, listening, understanding, and paying attention ever crossed your mind? I can't believe you think you have done enough."

"What? You're going to lecture me on raising children? What do you know about it?"

"I know enough to realize it was a wise choice that I didn't have them. But you did. You had Ricky....and you owe him more than just the basics. He's been here almost three months, and I'll bet I know more about him than *you* do. Now I think it's time we had a serious talk."

Angie noisily sat down in a kitchen chair and glared at her brother's back as he poured her a cup of coffee. Nick set the cup in front of her, remembering that she drank it black with no sugar. He walked over to the bar and poured himself another drink and then sat down across from his sister.

"Angie, do you remember his friend, Paulie?"

Angie's head snapped up. "Yeah......he was murdered. Thank God Ricky wasn't with him that night."

"Ricky *was* with him, Angie. They were together. In a split second's difference, that could have been Ricky that was killed. He watched the whole thing….hiding behind a dumpster. He's still not over it, and maybe he never will be. He screams out in the middle of the night."

"My God, Nick…..I had no idea…"

"I know. Remember I asked you what happened to him? That's what it was. That's what's wrong. And he has a problem with you because if you hadn't have driven him out of the house with your constant bitching, complaining and nagging, it might not have happened."

"What are you talking about? Bitching? Nagging?"

"Yeah, Angie……bitching and nagging……and complaining…..finding fault…."

"He said all this?"

"…and more. I know it's true, because I hear you. Everything is so negative with you. You jump down his throat rather than find out what's going on with him. Angie, you drove that boy out into the streets…to do…. God knows what all he did out there. You show no trust… you don't give him any credit. He's basically a good kid, Angie. Quit beating him up, verbally and emotionally. And another thing……why don't you talk about Enrico with him? Do you know how much he needs to talk about his father? He misses Enrico very much."

Angie stared at Nick for a moment before she answered. "Nick, I…..I thought it would be too painful for him to talk about his dad. They were close; you know that. It hurts me to talk about him; I miss him so much. I didn't want to cause Ricky any more pain over Enrico's death."

"Well, he needs to talk about him, Angie. By the way, he mastered Enrico's spaghetti sauce recipe; did you know that?"

"No…..I didn't. Ricky can cook?"

"Hell, yeah, and he's a good cook, too! You know, he looks for approval. He doesn't get it from you, so he finds it elsewhere….like on the streets of Chicago. Those wild girls you told me about? They approved of him. They liked him….a lot."

"Yeah….I could tell." Angie rolled her eyes and stared down into her coffee cup.

"He's got a girlfriend…."

"Oh, God…."

"Now see? There you go! You haven't met her, but already, you've judged her. I met her. Ricky said to me, 'Uncle Nick, I want you to meet her. And it's important to me that you like her.' Well, I *do* like her. She's very sweet." Nick stared pointedly into Angie's eyes. "He doesn't want *you* to meet her."

"Why?"

"Because she means a lot to him. And he feels you'll just find something wrong with her, and he'll end up hating you for it."

Angie had no words as she stared into her coffee cup. Her eyes began to well up with tears. Finally, she looked up at her brother.

"Am I that bad?" Her voice was almost a whisper.

Nick nodded.

"Maybe I can take him out to dinner tonight. Just the two of us….so we can talk."

Nick started to nod an approval, but remembered the musical.

"Probably isn't a good idea….tonight that is. Lindy is in a musical at school. She has the lead role, and you won't be able to drag him away from the auditorium tonight. He dragged me there last night. I enjoyed it, though. Lindy is one talented little girl."

"Is she pretty?"

"Very."

"Nick, I..…I think I'd like to go. Do you think he would let me go with him?"

"Well, he has an extra ticket. Tell him. Tell him that you would love to see his girlfriend in the show. Maybe he'll offer you the extra ticket."

\* \* \*

Angie pulled into a parking space in the parking area designated for those who were there to see the show. Ricky was quiet all the way up to the school, except to tell Angie where to turn. Angie didn't get a very good reception when Ricky walked in the door from school. He was cordial and polite, but very distant and cold toward her. She tried to engage him in conversation, but didn't have much luck; and now that they were alone in the car, he was even more distant. Ricky did seem a little surprised when she said that she wanted to go with him tonight. She even told him that Nick had said good things about Lindy, and she was looking forward to meeting her. Angie knew she had to be careful. Ricky was all she had, and she didn't want to lose him. Above all, she had to remember to say nothing negative, especially about the girlfriend.

Ricky was surprised when his mother said she wanted to go tonight. Since when did she take any interest in what was going on in school? He was glad he had asked Luke to give Lindy a ride again, giving him gas money as reinforcement. Luke was glad to take the money, even though he had plans on attending the show with his girlfriend anyway. At least Ricky knew Lindy would have a ride to the school, so giving Luke money for gas was worth it. His mother had already agreed to give Lindy a ride home. Before they left, Uncle Nick gave Ricky a twenty dollar bill and asked him to get another CD. He explained that Aunt Liz fell in love with the CD and he told her she could have it; but he still wanted a copy for himself. As he was getting out of the car, it dawned on him that his mother hadn't said much on the way there. Not that he minded, but it was certainly a change. He only hoped she would have the good sense not to say anything bad about Lindy.

Luke trotted up the Ricky when he and Angie entered the school by the front door.

"I got your girl here safe and sound…." Luke stopped when he saw the woman standing next to Ricky.

"My mom…." Ricky nodded toward Angie, and then quickly introduced Angie to Luke.

"Hi, Mrs. DeCelli. Nice to meet you."

"Same here, Luke."

"See ya inside…." Luke said over his shoulder.

"What a nice boy, Ricky. Is he a friend?"

"Yeah, sorta. We're cool with each other."

Angie was impressed with the difference in the teenagers here compared to where she and Ricky lived. She hoped that the house would sell soon, so she could move here and be a part of her son's new life. She followed Ricky into the auditorium, stopping to buy them drinks first. As they found seats, the lights dimmed a little, alerting the crowd that the show would start in five minutes.

She smiled tentatively at Ricky. "You know I saw this show when it first came out. Your girlfriend has the lead role?"

Ricky nodded, the corners of his mouth going up ever so slightly. "Yeah. She's really good, too. You'll see."

The lights went out and the curtain opened. The show began.

Angie was indeed impressed with Lindy's talent. "She *is* good!" She whispered to Ricky.

Ricky only nodded, as his eyes devoured Lindy on the stage.

When the last curtain call ended, Ricky and Angie made their way to the corridor to wait for Lindy. Ricky bought another CD for Nick and was especially surprised to see his mother purchase one for herself.

"It's a long ride home. I want something good to listen to." She put the CD into her purse.

When Lindy arrived at Ricky's side, he made the introductions. Angie couldn't help but be impressed. 'Such manners! What a sweet smile. And, of course, Nick was right. She is very sweet,' Angie thought to herself.

Luke ran up to congratulate Lindy.

"Awesome!! You were awesome, Lindy."

"Yes, she was." Angie blurted it out, surprising Lindy, and Ricky.

"Hey, I guess you're going home with your mom? I thought maybe you and Lindy would want to go out for awhile….maybe get something to eat."

"Yeah…well…" Ricky started to answer.

"Ricky, just tell me how to get home. You go ahead with your friends. But Lindy, I want to take my son out for dinner tomorrow night. Would you like to join us?"

"Well…..yeah….if it's okay with Ricky…..I'd love to."

Angie looked at Ricky and raised her eyebrows, and Lindy was staring up at him. She knew it was a difficult decision for him to make since she knew all about his problems with his mother.

"Yeah….sure…..that'd be great. Are you sure you don't mind about tonight?"

"No….go ahead. Your uncle and I have some catching up to do, and then I'd like to make an early night of it."

Luke led out of the parking lot, with Angie following him. He had given her directions, and told her to follow him just to reinforce the directions. When she was out of sight and Luke's car was headed toward the fast food side of town, Lindy leaned her head on Ricky's shoulder and smiled up at him. He gently placed a kiss on her lips.

"Hey, Luke and Sarah, wasn't she really awesome tonight?"

"Who? Your mom? Yeah." Luke teased.

Lindy and Ricky laughed. Sarah was quiet, which made Ricky remember that Carrie was her best friend. That made Lindy the enemy. Luke swung into a fast food parking lot and pulled to the rear where the drive-thru was situated.

"Let's get this stuff to go and then we can go out to "The Circle" and eat it. Okay?"

"What's the circle?" Both Lindy and Ricky asked.

"Oh, yeah, I forgot….you're not from here. And Lindy….well, Lindy wouldn't have a clue…." Luke finished his sentence with a laugh. "It's where we all go to make out."

"Oh." They answered in unison.

Once they had the bags of fast food, they drove off toward "the Circle". The smell of fried food permeated the inside of the car. Ricky grabbed a bag and hurriedly opened it, unwrapping a burger. He fed Lindy French fries by putting the tip of one into his mouth, and offering the tip of the other end to Lindy. They met in the middle, and kissed. Soon the fries were forgotten and they just kissed—long and passionate kisses. So engrossed in each other they were, that they didn't notice that the car had stopped, nor did they notice that Luke and Sarah disappeared from view onto the length of the front seat.

Ricky felt like his head was about to explode. He kissed her and she kissed him back, but he wanted more. Tentatively he ran his fingers down her neck to her throat and then onto the swell of her breasts. Gently, he ran his fingertips over her breast, instantly feeling the hardness of her nipple. His fingers returned to where he felt her nipple and he gently and lightly ran his thumb over it. He felt her respond as he gently stimulated her nipple even more. He moved his lips down to her neck and kissed it, and then he trailed the length of her neck up to her ear with the tip of his tongue. He lightly kissed her earlobe, and then took the lobe between his teeth. His breath in her ear caused her to swoon a little. Ricky slipped his hand inside her blouse and touched the nipple again, this time in the flesh. Lindy didn't protest. With his other hand, Ricky reached behind her and unhooked her bra. He felt her stiffen a little, so he eased back a little. He found her lips and began kissing her again until he felt her relax, and then he slipped his hand under her blouse and quickly found her nipple again. It hardened even more when he touched it. Still kissing her, he eased her blouse up, exposing her breast. Swooping down, he engulfed her breast in his mouth, and gently began sucking on the nipple, running his tongue over it. He felt her excitement, but he knew he had to stop. He couldn't go any further with her in Luke's car—not for her first time. That had to be special—he knew that. He withdrew his hand and wrapped his arms around her, leaning his cheek against hers. His heart was pounding and he felt his blood racing through his vessels. Oh, how he wanted her! But not this way. Not with Luke and Sarah in the front seat. He would wait, but he only hoped he didn't have to wait too much longer.

* * *

Ricky walked Lindy to the door while Luke and Sarah waited in the car. He embraced her and kissed her nose.

"So why did you stop?" Lindy was looking into his dark eyes, her big blue ones full of curiosity.

"What do you mean?"

In the car…..at The Circle. Why did you stop?"

"You didn't want me to?"

"Well yeah….but I didn't say anything. So why did you?"

Ricky sighed and smiled at her. He tightened his arms around her. "Because I'm not going to do you in Luke's car. You're better than that. When it happens…..it will be in the right place. I'll call you tomorrow and let you know what time we're going to dinner. Okay?" He kissed her quickly, and then kissed her again before he ran back to get into the car with Luke and Sarah.

# Chapter 12

Nick was sitting on the sofa in front of the television when Angie came through the door. He diverted his eyes from the television screen and immediately noticed that she was alone.

"Where is Ricky? I thought he and Lindy would be here with you." He quickly searched Angie's face to see if something was wrong.

"Oh, his friends wanted him to go out with them. I told him it was okay. He needs to be around nice kids like that."

Nick was relieved. "And you didn't mind?"

"No, not really. I thought you and I could chat a little before I went to bed."

"Okay....that's fine. So what did you think of Lindy?" Nick involuntarily flinched, expecting a tirade.

"Oh...she's adorable. Very sweet, just like you said she was. Pretty and talented. I bought one of her CD's. Oh.... here's the one that Ricky bought for you, along with your change." Angie dug in her purse for the items.

"Thanks. I didn't expect the change. But you know.... he always gives it back to me. Any time I give him money to get something, he brings the change back. I think that's a pretty good trait."

Angie nodded. "Yes, it is. Listen, I wanted to talk to you about...well, when I sell the house. I want to move into this area, so Ricky can finish school here. What are the prospects of getting a job at the hospital? I've worked in Medical Records for years. And also, not that I'm trying to pry....but what would it run to buy a condo like this?"

Nick stared at her for a moment. "These are pretty expensive. You might be better off to buy a two-bedroom house."

"I just worry about repairs....I can't really do them, and Ricky doesn't know much about it."

"Yeah, I understand that. Think about it, though. These condos are now up around the million mark."

"Oh.....my God! I just want to stay in the same area. It's nice here. Now what about the job?"

"Well, there would have to be an opening, but the hospital is expanding. They are opening a special women's health center. Liz is in charge of it."

"Liz....how is she? Do you see her much?"

"No, not really. We don't work anywhere near each other. I saw her today. I gave her my copy of Lindy's CD, and she fell in love with it. That's why I had Ricky get me another one."

"So....are you two on civil terms? I know you didn't end that way."

"Yeah...we're okay. As long as we don't see each other. The sparks are still there. Unfortunately, both sets of sparks are still there. The anger and the attraction. It's a dangerous combination." Nick laughed.

"So what did you think of the show tonight?" Nick quickly changed the subject as he often did when the subject was his ex-wife.

"It was good. Lindy was....excellent. She can really sing."

"It's good to hear you saying nice things about her. It'll mean a lot to Ricky. He's crazy about her. Hey, how about some tea? I bought it because Ricky told me Lindy drinks it. I thought she would be here tonight. We can plan Thanksgiving. In case you have forgotten, it's next week."

Ricky came home while they were discussing Thanksgiving. He pulled up a chair and helped himself to tea from the teapot Nick had set on the table.

"I thought you were going to bed, Mom."

"Well, I planned on it, but we got into this discussion about Thanksgiving. I guess I could come Wednesday after work, but I wouldn't get here until really late. I could put the turkey in the oven before I go to bed...."

"That's a lot to do for one day, Mom. How about you go to bed early....get up early on Thursday, and drive here in the morning? I'll get the turkey ready and have it in the oven."

"You can do that? Prepare the turkey and stuffing, I mean?"

"Mom, you worked every Thanksgiving. Me and Dad did it every year....*remember?*"

"Wow....I didn't realize......so you can do that, then?"

Ricky nodded. "Now....can I invite Lindy to Thanksgiving dinner?"

"Of course." Nick and Angie answered him in unison.

\* \* \*

Ricky awoke early. It was Saturday, yet he didn't feel like curling up and falling back to sleep. He padded down the stairs and put the coffee on, and headed back upstairs to shower.

Wrapped in a terrycloth robe, he sat at the kitchen table drinking a cup of his delicious coffee. He knew it was good, and he smiled when he thought about Nick raving about it. He wanted to know what Ricky did to make such good coffee. That was Ricky's secret—his and Enrico's. His father had taught him so many things, and he remembered every one of them. He smiled to himself as he remembered his father's philosophy about a man knowing how to cook. 'It doesn't hurt to know your way around the kitchen,' his father had told him. 'Women love a man who can cook….trust me on this.' Ricky thought about Lindy. 'Would she love him for that?' he wondered.

His thoughts turned to the night before. Lindy. Touching her. She felt so good to him. He felt himself becoming aroused as he remembered what her breast looked like—how it felt under his fingertips. He quickly turned off the thought and concentrated on pouring another cup of coffee.

He had gone to bed happy last night. Happy because he had been in the presence of his mother and she hadn't bitched once. Normal…for once everything was like a normal mother-son relationship between them. He wondered why. Maybe Uncle Nick talked to her, or maybe she just missed him and decided to be nice when she saw him. He would wait and see what she said about Lindy before he assumed anything was actually changed. He didn't ask her what she thought about Lindy the night before, because; one, he didn't care what she thought, and two; he didn't want to bring out the negativity in her. Ricky jumped when he heard Angie's voice right next to him. He hadn't heard her come down the stairs.

"You're up early."

"Yeah, I got up and made the coffee. Have a cup." He came close to a smile with his offer.

Angie got a cup out of the cupboard, helped herself to a cup of Ricky's delicious-smelling coffee, and sat down across the table from him.

"So….how's school?" Angie was trying her best to communicate on a pleasant level.

"It's okay. My grades are good. Well….Lindy and I study together, and she's really smart in most subjects. I'm better in math, so we have a trade-off. I help her in math and she helps me in everything else."

"That's nice. Besides math, what other subjects do you have?"

"English, Spanish, History, and Art. Then there's P-E."

"Do you and Lindy have all your classes together?"

"Most of them. Not P-E, of course, and she has music when I have art."

"She takes a music class? She certainly didn't sound like she needed any training. What a beautiful voice she has!"

"Yeah." Ricky smiled. "Her voice is how I met her. The first week of school I had a free period and I was exploring the halls. When I opened up the door to the auditorium, I heard an angel singing. I just had to go in and sit down. I was hooked from that moment." Ricky gave out a short laugh.

"She's a doll, Ricky. I couldn't find anything wrong with her...not that I looked for anything. She's a perfect doll."

Ricky smiled again. "Thanks. She means a lot to me. I never had an actual girlfriend before. One that I can take places, hang out with; bring around the family; you know...stuff like that. Lindy is the first decent girl I ever even spoke to for more than five minutes. She's just so...pleasant to be with. You know, she has the prettiest laugh. I love to hear it."

Angie marveled at the communication that just took place. 'What was different? Living here? Nick's influence? Had she changed? Or could it be Lindy?' Angie didn't care what caused it; she liked it.

"So where do you want to eat tonight? You pick."

"I thought maybe we could try the Japanese Steak House. How does that sound to you?"

"It sounds fine." Angie smiled at her son, thanking God or whoever else may be responsible for his turn-around.

* * *

Lindy was ready when Angie pulled into the driveway. She opened the door at Ricky's first knock. He ducked inside to help her with her coat, and to kiss her. She smiled up at him after the kiss.

"Do I look okay? I miss my mom at times like this. She would know what I should wear."

"You look great. That blue dress is perfect for you. It's probably perfect to wear to dinner with my mother."

"Are you going to be okay with this?" She asked him.

"Yeah….I think so. If you're there, I think I can get through anything." He smiled at her and quickly kissed her forehead. Taking her hand, he led her out the front door, stopping to ask if she had her key before he pulled it shut.

The dinner went better than Ricky had expected. His mother was kind and pleasant to Lindy, asking her questions that didn't sound like she was prying. Ricky tensed a little when Angie asked Lindy about her mother, but it went well.

"I'm so sorry, Lindy. Ovarian cancer…..that's so sad." Angie had said. "For you and for your dad. How is he doing? It must be hard for him. I mean….I know how hard it is for me."

Ricky watched the sadness creep into Lindy's eyes for a moment, and then fade. "It's like he's….angry with her. Like he blames her for dying. He….won't even look at me. I guess it's because….I look exactly like her."

"He'll come around, Honey. He *is* angry. I'm still angry at Ricky's dad for dying on me. It's a breach of contract when somebody promises to love you forever and then dies before forever is up. I felt betrayed for a long time. I'm sure that's how your dad is feeling. And if you look just like your mother, that's like she's taunting him after having the audacity to break the contract by dying. Me…I punish Enrico by never mentioning his name. That'll show him." Angie ended with a short laugh.

Lindy had smiled, and then she requested something from Angie that made Ricky believe that he would love her forever and ever. "Tell me about him." Lindy urged.

The rest of the dinner was spent telling anecdotes about Enrico and stories about him and Ricky when Ricky was little. It was an enjoyable dinner...one that Ricky would remember for a long time. After dinner the three of them returned to Nick's condo for tea and the cookies Angie had spent the day baking. It was close to midnight when Nick offered to give Lindy a ride home. Ricky kissed her at the door, and smiled down at her.

"I think I will remember tonight for the rest of my life. Call you tomorrow."

He waited until she was safely inside before he ran back to the car. It was cold outside, but he didn't feel it. The warmth of the evening clung to him.

# Chapter 13

Ricky had his alarm set for seven in the morning. When it went off he immediately got up and started downstairs to make coffee and begin the preparations for the turkey. If everything went well, dinner would be at three o'clock. Angie should be there by one, in time to make the rest of the meal. Nick would be picking Lindy up at one. She was bringing pies for dessert. Ricky smiled as he remembered her reaction to being invited to Thanksgiving dinner. She was ecstatic. Ricky knew there were no holidays celebrated in her house, and hadn't been since her mother died. This holiday dinner meant a lot to her, and consequently, a lot to Ricky as well. He was busily mixing the stuffing when Nick came down the stairs.

"Wow, you really did get up early enough to start that bird, huh? I can already smell your stuffing.....and great....the coffee is done. You're a good wife, Ricky." Nick teased, and pinched his cheek.

Nick took his coffee over to the kitchen table and sat down. "Oh, and speaking of wives....your mother invited my ex-wife to dinner today. So I guess you'll be seeing your Aunt Liz."

"Wow....that's cool. Aren't you a little surprised she accepted though? I mean...you used to fight all the time...and..."

"Yeah, well....that's in the past. We're trying to keep it civil since she is back at the hospital. Anyway...she doesn't know many people in town any more, so she accepted your mother's invitation to come here for dinner."

"I can't wait to see her. I always liked Aunt Liz." Ricky glanced at Nick to get his reaction, but there didn't seem to be one. He slid the prepared turkey into the oven and set the timer for basting, and then he helped himself to a cup of coffee and joined Nick at the kitchen table.

"Lindy is so excited about being invited here for Thanksgiving. If she weren't coming here she would be home alone with no holiday dinner."

Nick smiled sadly into his cup. "That poor kid. Why can't the father see how badly he's hurting her?"

"I don't know. Selfish, I guess. Lindy looks just like her mom, so he punishes her for it by ignoring her. Other than her brother, Lindy has no other family. Her brother Chris is in the army."

"Well, tell Lindy she has an Uncle Nick now"

Ricky jerked his head up in surprise. "You mean it?"

"Yeah, I mean it. She's such a sweet girl.....I don't know how anybody could help but love her. By the way, your mom does. She raved about her."

"Really? All she told me was that she couldn't find anything wrong with her, and I was happy with that. What time will Aunt Liz be here? I think we should pick Lindy up a little earlier so she can help me with the hors d'oeuvres. I want to have them out right before everybody gets here."

"Hors d'oeuvres? We're serving hors d'oeuvres?"

"Of course. Dad always had them when company came for a holiday dinner."

"Well, call Lindy and tell her we'll pick her up earlier….whatever time you want, okay?"

Ricky nodded, looked at the clock and figured that Lindy would be awake. It was almost nine o'clock. He dialed her number from the wall phone and she answered on the first ring. Nick watched Ricky frown.

"What's wrong? Why are you crying?" Ricky asked into the receiver. After listening he covered the mouth piece and told Nick her dilemma. "She made two pies and her dad came home with a friend last night and they ate them. She's crying."

"Give me the phone." Nick ordered as he reached for it.

"Lindy, Honey, this is Uncle Nick. We'll fix it; don't worry. Get dressed and I'll pick you up at eleven o'clock…. okay?" He handed the phone back to Ricky.

"Feel better?" Ricky asked softly.

"Yeah. He called himself Uncle Nick; did you hear that?"

"Yeah, I did. So go ahead and get ready. I need you here to help me with the hors d'oeuvres, okay? Where is your dad now?"

"He's in the shower. I heard him on the phone earlier. He told whoever he was talking to that he would be leaving here at ten, so I guess he'll be gone all day. He must know it's Thanksgiving…."

"Hey, you have family now, so smile that pretty smile and get ready. Okay?" Ricky smiled into the phone. "See ya in a little while."

* * *

Lindy ran out to the car when Nick pulled in. He reached over and opened her door for her as she reached the car.

"Happy Thanksgiving......Uncle Nick." She smiled at him. "So how are we going to fix the pie problem? Where's Ricky?"

"Ricky had to stay home to watch the turkey, and you and I are going to the pie shop. They are open until twelve today." He smiled over at her. "Don't worry; everything will be fine."

Lindy stared at Nick for a moment, and then a broad smile lit up her face. "It will be fine if you let me pay for them. After all, they were supposed to be my contribution, and I do have money."

"Fair enough. You pay for them, then." He swung his BMW into the parking lot of the store in question. "See? They're open. Now let's go pick out pies."

They selected two large pies, one pumpkin and the other coconut cream, and then headed for the condo. Ricky heard them get out of the car, Lindy laughing. He looked out of the window and saw his uncle smiling, and wondered what was so amusing. It didn't take him long to find out.

"Ricky! The lady at the pie shop thought I was Uncle Nick's daughter. She said I must take after the mother, and Uncle Nick said that I did. When we got in the car, Uncle Nick said he should have said I was his wife, just to shake her up."

Lindy was laughing her beautiful laugh, and Ricky just couldn't help but smile at her. She set the pies down as he reached for her and wrapped his arms around her.

He kissed her lightly. "Happy Thanksgiving," He said softly. "You look really nice." He looked her up and down, approvingly. She was glad she decided to wear a long skirt today. It was both dressy and casual, and very comfortable. The aqua colors in the lightweight tiered skirt matched the light-weight aqua sweater perfectly, and the entire outfit complimented her coloring and her figure.

"Happy Thanksgiving, Ricky." Her smile and her shining eyes said it all.

\* \* \*

Angie entered the condo in a flourish of chatter and activity. It was snowing in Chicago when she left—she said, and it was headed this way—she said.

"Ricky, I can take over now. You have done enough. So, shoo! Both you and Lindy."

Ricky took Lindy by the hand and pulled her out of the kitchen. "Come on; let's not argue with her. Mom, we'll get the hors d'oeuvres out in about an hour, okay?"

"That's fine, Ricky. Now go sit and relax for awhile."

Ricky and Lindy grinned at each other. It was obvious that Lindy was happy. Spending the holiday in a family setting was what she had yearned for ever since her mother passed away. She briefly wondered what her father was doing today, but dismissed the thought of him. He had plenty of opportunity to be part of a family—her family—but he turned his back on her.

"I want to show you a Web site I found. Uncle Nick, can I use your computer in the den? I want to show Lindy something."

"Yeah, go ahead." Nick responded without turning his head away from the football game on the television.

\* \* \*

109

Nick stood in the doorway of the den, just watching Ricky and Lindy in front of the computer. They looked so cute together. Ricky had his arm around Lindy's shoulders and Lindy was laughing. They both were watching the computer screen. Nick heard Ricky tell Lindy that he knew she would like that site, just before he made his presence known.

He cleared his throat to get their attention, causing them both to look toward the door. "Sorry to interrupt, but your mother said it's time to start the hors d'oeuvres. Your Aunt Liz is on her way."

"Who's Aunt Liz?" Lindy asked Ricky.

"She's Uncle Nick's ex-wife. She was always pretty cool with me, but I haven't seen her in years. Let's go get the hors d'oeuvres ready." He took her hand and led her back into the kitchen.

As they were setting out two plates of Enrico's special holiday hors d'oeuvres, the doorbell rang. Ricky opened the door to Liz, who immediately gasped when she saw him. She set her package down and reached to embrace him.

"Ricky? My God, how you've grown! And you are just as handsome as the rest of the Bazario men….even if you are a DeCelli….who were all handsome, too, I might add. She laughed and held him at arms length. "Look at you! You're not a little kid any more! I'm shocked!"

"I told you he'd grown up." Nick came up from behind Ricky to help Liz with her coat. "Glad you could make it, Liz. Come on in, sit down…..can I get you a glass of wine? Ricky has hors d'oeuvres out on the coffee table. You have to try one. I already did." With that he turned to Ricky. "Excellent stuff, Rick."

"So where is Angie?" Liz asked.

"She and Lindy are in the kitchen. You can go join them or be safe out here with me."

Liz laughed. "Oh, I'm not so sure I would say that." She laughed again to let Nick know she was joking, and then headed toward the kitchen, Ricky following, intent on introducing her to his girl.

"Liz!" Angie broke into a big smile that lit up her whole face. "I'm so happy to see you!" She and Liz hugged each other for a moment.

Ricky interrupted them. "Aunt Liz, I want you to meet Lindy."

Liz let go of Angie. "Oh, yes, of course." She turned toward the sound of Ricky's voice, and stopped in surprise. She had no idea what she thought Ricky's girlfriend would look like, but she wasn't quite expecting to see this little angel-doll. Those were the words that came to her mind when she saw Lindy—Little Angel-doll. Liz caught herself openly staring at Lindy, and recovered.

"Hi, Lindy….it's nice to finally meet you. I listen to your CD every day. I must say I didn't expect that such a big voice came out of such a little girl." She smiled and took Lindy's hand. "I love the CD, by the way."

Lindy smiled back at her. "Thank you….and it's nice to meet you, too."

Angie interjected the conversation. "You two…..leave the kitchen. Go check the table to make sure everything is set properly. Dinner will be in twenty minutes! Now, shoo!"

Ricky grabbed Lindy's hand as they scooted out of Angie's way for a second time. Liz looked over at Angie and mouthed to her 'she's a doll!' Angie nodded.

Thanksgiving dinner was delicious, and everybody over-indulged, giving Ricky the full credit for the turkey stuffing.

Angie smiled over at Lindy and Ricky. "Ricky is a good cook. Do you cook, Lindy?"

"Not like *he* does. So I figure it this way…..if we grow up and get through college, and end up getting married some day…..he can do the cooking, and me? Well, I guess I'll just have to sing for my supper." She ended with a shrug.

The humor was not lost on anyone, as they all burst out laughing. Ricky reached under the table and squeezed Lindy's hand, and then held onto it. After dinner, Lindy and Ricky cleared off the table and stacked the dishwasher while the others sat in the living room catching up on each other's lives.

Lindy and Ricky worked well together, having the cleanup under control in short order. When the dishwasher was started, Ricky draped his arm around Lindy's shoulders.

"Do we have to wait that long?"

Lindy looked up at him, puzzled. "For what?"

"To get married. That's a long time to wait. At least six years."

Lindy smiled and her eyes twinkled. "No, I guess not, but….I couldn't say it any other way…to the grown-ups, I mean. I mean, do you really want them thinking we're seeing too much of each other?"

"No, I guess I don't. You're very, very smart, Babe." He kissed the tip of her nose, and then moved to her lips. After a brief kiss, he whispered into her ear. "Do I have to wait that long for sex?"

Lindy pulled away. "Stop," She responded flatly.

Ricky let out a short laugh, and then smiled. "Okay."

# Chapter 14

$\mathcal{L}$indy awoke to the ringing of the telephone on Friday morning, the day after Thanksgiving.

"Look outside." The caller ordered. The caller, of course, was Ricky.

Still holding the telephone, Lindy padded to the front door and peered out through the window. Snow. Lots of it. Angie predicted that it was headed their way, and she apparently was right. Lindy also observed that her father's truck was not in the driveway, nor were there any tracks. He had not come home last night. She was shaken out of her thoughts by Ricky's raised voice.

"Hey! You still there?"

"Uh, yeah, Ricky……sorry. I just noticed that my dad didn't come home last night."

"Oh…..sorry. Do you want to play in the snow today? Build a snowman maybe?"

"Yeah, sure….that sounds like fun. I'll get dressed and come up, okay?"

"Yeah, and my mom said she will make us lunch. You're going to stay for dinner, too…..right? 'Cause the only thing better than Ricky's Thanksgiving cooking is Ricky's leftovers the next day. Come on up and we can make a day of it." When she agreed, Ricky lowered his

voice a little. "Got something to tell you. See you.....
soon?"

"In about an hour....okay?" Lindy hung up the phone,
looked at the clock and realized that it was almost ten
o'clock. She normally didn't sleep that long, but with all
the holiday activity yesterday; she guessed she probably
was extra-tired. She headed toward the bathroom and got
into the shower.

She enjoyed the hot water running over her, but her
mind kept drifting back to her father. Where was he?
Where was he all night? She dressed in her warmest
sweatshirt and heaviest sweat pants, got out her fur-lined
boots, heavy mittens, and fur-lined hat, found her heavy
scarf, and heaviest parka, and began dressing for the snow.
Grabbing her key, she opened the door to a blast of cold
air. She braced herself and headed outside, locking the
door behind her. Halfway up the hill, she spied Ricky
coming down toward her. She stopped and grinned as he
approached her.

"Couldn't let you go it alone....so I decided I'd meet
you halfway. Then I could tell you what I wanted to tell
you on the way to my place. It's no big deal, but I don't
want anybody to think I was spying on them."

"Well? So what is it? You're driving me crazy with
suspense."

"Okay....well, it's really no big deal....but Uncle Nick
walked Aunt Liz out to her car last night....and I saw him
kiss her. Not just a kind of 'thanks for coming, see ya
again some time' kiss, but a kind of 'I want you' kiss."

"And?"

"Well....they used to be married, but now they're
divorced. I thought they hated each other. I mean, at least

I thought they didn't love each other since the marriage ended."

Lindy looked at Ricky and sighed. "Ricky, sometimes people don't stay married for other reasons. Sometimes love isn't enough. Oh, they still love each other....I could see that by the way they looked at each other at dinner. But love only keeps you loving each other; it doesn't keep you together. There has to be other things—the kind of things that do keep you together. Kind of like the mortar that holds two bricks together."

Ricky stared at Lindy for a moment, and then reached around her waist and pulled her close to him. "You're so smart; you know that?"

"Yep." She answered, and then smiled up at him.

\* \* \*

The four-day weekend was drawing to a close. Lindy and Ricky spent as much time as possible together all weekend. Angie had lunch ready when Lindy and Ricky walked through the door on Friday. After lunch, the two of them built a large snowman in the front yard, and then went out to the patio and built a smaller one. 'They're guards,' Ricky told Lindy. 'They protect the house from the cold.' Lindy laughed and told him she thought it was very poetic. When Nick came home, Angie served the leftovers from the Thanksgiving dinner, and as Ricky had said, they were better than the day before. Because the roads were icy, Ricky walked Lindy home after dark, so Nick wouldn't have to drive. On the way home they made plans to go to 'their place' the next day, since neither of them had seen their place covered in snow. Lindy noted that her father's truck was still not in the driveway, and that it hadn't been there, since no tracks were visible.

She bit her lip, and wondered about that, but didn't say anything.

Saturday morning brought sunshine that made the snow sparkle. Ricky met Lindy at her front door and they headed down to the steps that led to 'their place'. The icy steps were very slippery, making them tread very carefully all the way to the bottom. The descent was worth it. Both Ricky and Lindy gasped as they saw the sparkling white snow covering the partially frozen creek. The water shone brilliantly as it trickled over rocks. 'Their rock' was covered in snow with icicles hanging over the sides. The air was still and crisp and the quiet was overwhelming.

"It's beautiful, isn't it?" Lindy thought her voice sounded exceptionally loud in this snow covered haven below the bridge.

"Yeah.....I think we should see about buying this place, and then building a little house right here. Then we can live in it happily ever after."

".......Except that this place floods every year in the spring. Our house would end up full of water." Lindy informed him.

"Oh....well then.....never mind. Hey, look our shelter is still standing." Ricky took Lindy's hand as they made their way to the shelter they had built. Upon inspection, they discovered that the ground under the shelter had remained dry.

"Maybe we should be architects. We sure built this well. It's dry and still standing." Ricky pulled out the plywood and small blanket they had placed inside, and discovered that they were both dry. He arranged the blanket over the plywood, and reached for Lindy's hand. "Come sit on our sofa," he teased as he grinned at her.

Smiling broadly, she sat down beside him, snuggling close to him to keep warm.

"Cold?" He asked and he wrapped his arms around her.

"No, not yet anyway." She looked up into his eyes.

Their eyes locked and they felt that familiar charge of electricity that they had felt the day they met. Neither spoke. Slowly, their lips came together. The kiss was sweet, but soon turned to passionate. Lindy parted her lips and accepted Ricky's tongue. When he pulled it back, Lindy's tongue chased it into Ricky's mouth. Ricky moaned and then took Lindy's shoulders and held her at arms' length. He expelled the air from his lungs.

"Don't *do* that to me. God....you drive me *crazy*, Lindy. I'm only human. I want you so bad. I want to make love to you, Lindy.....I...."

"Ricky, I want you, too. I'm just scared....that's all. I mean.....I want to do it...but...."

"Shhh! It's okay." Ricky expelled air again, and then pulled Lindy close, resting his head on top of hers. He felt her trembling.

\* \* \*

The climb up the steps was slow. They moved slowly, holding onto the railings and testing each step before putting their feet down. Lindy slipped once and Ricky caught her, almost causing himself to slide downward. They eventually made it to the top, where they rested for a few minutes. Ricky noticed that the little restaurant was open.

"Want some hot coffee?"

"Yes!" Lindy responded quickly.

They made their way over to the restaurant and welcomed the warmth as they entered. Lindy's cheeks were flushed, which made her eyes look even bluer than they were. Ricky smiled at her when the waitress walked away to get their coffees. She smiled back.

"Ricky, it won't be like this forever. I promise." She spoke in a hushed voice. "I mean….eventually, we will… you know."

"Yeah, I know. But when you're a guy….eventually is an eternity. But hey, I respect you for putting me through this torture all the time. It will be worth waiting for. All good things are….right?" He stopped as the waitress set their coffees down in front of them. "It's just….well, if you only knew what you do to me…..wow!"

They finished their coffee, paid the tab, and started up the hill toward Lindy's house. When the house was in site, Lindy saw that her father's truck had still not been there. She looked up at Ricky.

"Are you tired of turkey yet?" She asked.

"What did you have in mind?"

"Well, a movie and a pizza. You can call Uncle Nick and tell him to pick you up later. Want to? I mean, I see I'm still alone in my house."

"Well, okay…but what happens if he comes home? Will he get pissed if I'm there?"

"I haven't the slightest idea. But I'll hide you in the bedroom if he comes home."

Ricky looked down at Lindy and saw that she was joking, and then laughed.

"Okay, I'm game. We have to cross paths eventually, I guess."

"Maybe not. He and I barely cross paths."

Once inside the house, Lindy checked for notes and voice mail messages. There were none. "I'll call for pizza if you select the movie." She spoke over her shoulder as she reached for the magnet that held the name and phone number of a pizza delivery place on the refrigerator door. Ricky was already searching through the stacks of DVD's that sat on the bottom shelf of the entertainment center.

"Let's wait for the pizza to get here before we put the movie in. Show me your room."

"What?"

"I just want to see where you sleep....then I can picture you there when I think about you at night when I'm in bed."

"And do you think about me at night?"

"All the time." He rested his arms on her shoulders, and stared into her eyes. "Come on....show me."

She took his hand and led him to her room and switched on the light. Ricky smiled.

"Perfect. It's so you. I knew there would be teddy bears." Ricky's eyes swept around the room; taking in the lavender walls, the comforter and matching curtains in a pink, lavender, and blue floral print. There were, indeed, bears everywhere. Bears, and cats and dogs, and a menagerie of other stuffed animals. On top of the comforter on the bed sat the lion he had bought her at the zoo. The furniture was white. In the corner of the room a computer was set up on a white computer desk, her school books stacked beside it. The room was neat—nothing out of place. An oval white faux fur rug lay on the floor beside her double bed. Her kitty-face slippers were there on the rug. Ricky noticed a picture on the dresser. It had to be of her and her mother. There was another picture on the night stand. This one was of the two of them—taken by Cindy, a girl in their English Literature class. Lindy had bought a little frame for it. The other night stand held a picture of a young blonde guy in uniform—probably her brother Chris. Ricky felt that the room was lovely—a perfect blend between teenager and woman.

"So is this your haven?" He asked her.

"I guess. Sorta." She smiled as she answered.

"I'll have to show you my room sometime. It doesn't have all these animals in it, but it's nice."

"No stuffed animals? Are you under-privileged?"

"Yeah, I guess."

"Then you have to take one of mine." She looked around the room until she found the one she thought would be perfect for Ricky. "Here….Sherlock…he's perfect for you." She picked up a brown dog wearing a plaid hat like Sherlock Holmes, thus the name. "Now when you think of me at night, you'll have something of mine to hold."

Ricky hesitated for a moment. "Do they all have names? You don't really think I'm going to walk out of the house with that in my hands, do you? My Uncle will laugh at me for years to come."

"I'll put it in a bag. He won't know what it is…. okay?"

"Okay…but on one condition." He looked into her eyes for a moment. "That some day I get to hold the real thing in my bed—and not just a symbol of you."

She nodded. Ricky moved toward her bed and sat down on it. He picked up the picture of the two of them and smiled. "This is a good picture, isn't it? We look good together."

Lindy sat down beside him and took the picture from his hand. "We do. And yes, they all have names."

She returned the picture to its proper place, and looked up at Ricky. He already had his arms around her, his lips reaching for hers. She returned his kiss as she clung to him. He eased her down onto the bed, and partially covered her body with his. He put his arm around her and cupped her chin in his hand, kissing her passionately. His other hand trailed down to her waist and up under her sweater. She didn't resist. He felt what he was looking for—her hardened nipple. In one motion he unhooked her bra and exposed her breast, lightly running his hand over her nipple. She responded. His lips trailed down her neck to her breast. He teased her nipple with his tongue and he heard her moan a little. His other hand moved toward the waist band of her sweatpants, and slid down inside them. He found her mound of pubic hair and gently petted it. Again, she did not resist. His finger found her sensuous spot and she parted her legs slightly. Ricky went back to her mouth and kissed her, while his finger made its way inside of her. She gasped. He slowly moved his finger in and out, breathing raggedly, as he planted kisses on her neck and ear. His hot breath in her ear gave Lindy a wild sensation. Ricky moaned, "Oh, Baby."

A sharp knock on the front door ended the moment. They looked at each other and simultaneously said, "Pizza guy." Lindy was up off the bed first, adjusting her clothing. She went to the door, accepted the pizza, and paid the delivery boy. He stood there for a few minutes staring at her.

"Is there something wrong? There is plenty there for a tip."

"No....I....you're so....." Ricky came out from the bedroom, and the delivery boy ended his sentence with, "Forget it. Have a nice night."

"What was that about?" Ricky asked her.

"I have no idea. Smells good, doesn't it? I have sodas in the fridge."

Lindy disappeared into the kitchen, and returned with cans of soda, napkins and paper plates. Ricky called home while Lindy was putting the pizza onto the plates, and inserting the DVD into the player. Ricky came in and sat down.

"Eleven-thirty. He'll be here at eleven-thirty."

"Why don't you get your license?" Lindy wanted to know.

"Nothing to drive." Ricky told her. The truth of the matter was that Ricky was on probation and was not permitted to get a license until the probation was up next year. He finally admitted that to Lindy after the second piece of pizza.

"Oh. Well, we're doing fine without it, I guess. I was just thinking how much of an inconvenience it is on Uncle Nick to have to come out that late to pick you up."

"Oh, he doesn't mind. He told me the other night that he didn't mind at all, as long as it's for you and me. Let's watch this movie. It gets good after this part."

They turned back to the television and became engrossed in the movie Ricky had selected. They snuggled up together, Ricky's arm around her for the rest of the movie.

* * *

Angie was getting her things together for the trip back home. The roads were once again clear, thus making the drive back to Chicago safe. Lindy walked up to the condo to say goodbye to Angie.

"I'll see you soon, Lindy," Angie hugged her while Ricky was putting her luggage into the car.

Lindy and Ricky, arms around each other, watched Angie's car pull out of the driveway and go on up the street. They watched until she was out of sight. When they could no longer see the car, they went inside and spent the afternoon playing gin at the kitchen table, while Nick watched football on television. Around dinner time, Ricky heated up leftovers for everybody, proving that leftovers were even better the third time around. Shortly after dinner Nick drove Lindy home so she could get her things ready for school in the morning.

Her father wasn't there when she got home. She threw in a load of laundry, did the few dishes that were in the sink, took out the trash, and then tidied up the living room. She was sitting on her bed reading, waiting for the dryer to stop, when her father's truck pulled into the driveway. She quickly got up off of the bed and shut her bedroom door. Her weekend had been wonderful— she didn't need him to spoil it for her. She needn't have worried. He went straight down the hall to his room and shut the door. Lindy heard the dryer buzzer and went out to collect the clothes out of the dryer. She hurriedly took the clothes back to her room and was about to shut the door again, when he came out of his room. He stood there staring at her like he didn't recognize her, and then he spoke.

"Hi," was all he said. He stood there staring for a few moments, and then turned back into his room and shut the door.

It was all Lindy could do to keep from screaming at him, 'did you have a nice weekend, you son of a bitch?' But she said nothing as she choked back a sob and wiped away the involuntary tears. She shut the door to her room, folded the clothes and went to bed.

# Chapter 15

Ricky was waiting for Lindy when she came out of her house to return to school on Monday morning. On the way to school she told Ricky of the incident with her father the night before. He was sympathetic as he put his arm around her. Ricky had become the light in her life.

As they walked through the front doors together, they spotted Carrie. Ricky groaned as she approached them.

"Ricky….hi, how was your Thanksgiving?" She asked him, totally ignoring Lindy.

"It was great. Lindy and I cooked a great meal for my family. My mother helped, but we did most of it." He turned to Lindy. "Right, Honey?"

Lindy nodded. Carrie abruptly turned and walked away, but not before Lindy caught the venomous look in Carrie's eyes.

"She's evil. She scares me." Lindy whispered to Ricky.

"I'll protect you." He hugged her and smiled.

* * *

Lindy entered the gym dressed for Physical Education class. She normally didn't mind P-E, but they were going to play basketball. Being small was always a disadvantage when playing basketball, and to make matters worse, she shared the class with Carrie. Today they wouldn't play a game against each other; it was just going to be practicing throwing shots into the basket. The class lined up on each side of the two baskets, while one girl took her turn. Each girl got five shots. The balls were to be retrieved by the girls on the sides and returned to the girl making the shots. Carrie stood closest to Lindy when it was her turn. Lindy missed her first two shots, but made the basket with her third and fourth. The fifth shot bounced off the rim right into Carrie's arms. Carrie grabbed the ball and immediately swung around, deliberately smashing into Lindy, hitting her in the eye with her elbow. Lindy flew across the floor and landed in a heap several feet from the basket. The instructor blew her whistle and grabbed Carrie by the arm.

"You go sit in my office....NOW!" And then she ran to Lindy who was having a hard time getting up.

As Carrie was walking toward the locker room, she heard Cindy holler, *"You did that on purpose, Bitch!"*

"Hey, are you okay, Lindy?" The teacher was leaning over her, eyes full of concern. Already Lindy's eye was purple and swelling shut. "Can you get up?"

Lindy nodded, and started to sit up, but slid back down again.

"Cindy, go get the nurse." The teacher instructed.

Cindy nodded, and ran down to the nurse's office. On the way, she spied Ricky in the hall. It was his free period. *"Ricky, Lindy's hurt.....in the gym!"*

Ricky turned ashen, and then ran towards the gym. In a flash he was at Lindy's side. "What happened?"

Surprised by the intrusion, the teacher answered matter-of-factly, "She got hurt playing basketball."

Cindy retuned with the nurse, who immediately took charge. Ricky stood back to let the school nurse examine Lindy. "There doesn't seem to be a concussion, but you're going to have a real shiner for awhile, Honey." She helped Lindy to her feet as Ricky materialized on the other side. "Uh, young man, I'm helping her into the girls' locker room. You can't go in there. You can wait for her outside the gym. Go down to my office and tell my assistant that you need some ice packs. She's going to need ice on that eye. She'll be ready when you get back....okay?"

Ricky nodded and took off running to the nurse's office.

The nurse yelled after him, "No running!"

Armed with two ice packs, he waited for Lindy to come out of the locker room. Carrie came out first, head held high, with a smug look on her face. Ricky ignored her, and for once she ignored him. Lindy came out with the nurse at her side. The nurse smiled at Ricky. "Here she is. Do you have the ice packs?" Ricky held them up. "Good....just keep ice on the eye; it will help with the swelling. Any problems....come to my office."

Ricky led Lindy down the hall toward their English Literature class. They were a few minutes early, so Ricky sat down and put his arm around Lindy and applied the ice pack to her eye.

"Wow! That's a hell of a shiner. Does it hurt?"

Lindy nodded. Carrie walked in and took her seat, not looking back toward Lindy and Ricky. The classroom began filling up with students, all curious about what happened. Cindy took her seat in front of Lindy and Ricky, and turned around to look at Ricky.

Cindy narrowed her eyes, and whispered, "It was on purpose. Carrie did it on purpose."

Ricky stared at Cindy and then looked over at Carrie. "It was on purpose? It better not have been…."

"It was." Cindy assured him.

Carrie looked back at Ricky, saw the anger in his eyes, and quickly looked away.

Shawna, who sat in back of the row between Ricky and Carrie, piped up. Shawna was a female bully, with more male characteristics than female, who believed in justice and fairness. She believed Lindy to be a 'good egg' and Carrie to be a 'bad penny' as she expressed it. "Ricky….give me a buck and I'll kick her ass."

Ricky laughed, and Carrie visibly flinched.

"That's all you want is a buck?"

"That's all she's worth." Shawna countered. Both Ricky and Shawna laughed.

"Okay, so if I decide to get you to kick her ass, all I have to do is give you a buck…any time….and you'll do it?"

"Yep…any time. It will be my pleasure. In fact, maybe I should pay *you* for the enjoyment." Shawna grinned at Ricky, showing two gold capped eye teeth. She ran her hand through her short cropped spiky hair, brought the hand down, and pointed her finger at the back of Carrie's head, pretending to have a gun. "Pow! Right to the back of the head. It would be my pleasure."

The teacher brought the class to order, staring over at Ricky with his arm around Lindy. After a moment, she realized that he was holding an ice pack over her eye for her. She walked back toward them, asking, "What happened, Lindy? Oh, my! How did that happen?"

Lindy smiled a little. "In P-E class."

"Well, are you able to sit up and hold that yourself? I appreciate Ricky's caring concern, but….well, for the sense of decorum, I would rather you held the ice on your eye yourself. You understand; don't you, Ricky?"

Ricky shrugged. 'No, I don't understand,' he thought to himself. He looked over at Carrie as she turned to look back at them. He glared angrily at her, and she quickly turned away.

They got through the class. When the bell rang, Ricky jumped up and bound toward Carrie, grabbing her arm. "Touch her again, Bitch, and you'll get your ass kicked. That's a promise."

Carrie jerked her arm away and darted out of the classroom. Ricky returned to Lindy, helped her up, and walked her out of the classroom toward her locker, and then to his. In his locker he found a pair of sunglasses. "Here, you'll need these for the light outside. I'm sure it'll hurt." He was right, so Lindy was grateful for the glasses.

*   *   *

Nick was staring into a microscope when he felt someone present. He looked up into the opal eyes of his ex-wife.

"Well, hi. You surprised me." Nick's smile was genuine.

"Yeah, well, I just wanted to come up here to your ivory tower and thank you again for the wonderful dinner."

"Ricky deserves most of the credit, I'm afraid. He did most of it. Learned everything from his old man."

"Ricky…..my, he has grown! And so handsome! He's really a great kid. And Lindy…..well, she's an absolute doll."

"Yeah, they're both great kids. I just worry about them….you know, getting too close. I know Lindy is still pretty innocent, but Ricky isn't."

"And you're afraid he will show little Lindy the ways of the world."

"Something like that."

"Well, you can only hope things don't progress, but you can't stop them from progressing. I wouldn't worry. They both seem responsible."

"Yeah, they are….but they're crazy about each other….and it's that old saying….where there's smoke, there's fire."

Liz stared at Nick for a moment. "You're beginning to sound like a parent."

Nick mocked a high-pitched voice, *"Oh, no….not that!"* Then he laughed.

An awkward moment passed between them as their eyes connected. They both remembered the kiss on Thanksgiving night. Nick hadn't meant to kiss her; he was just being courteous by walking her out to her car. 'After all, that's what you do when a lady visits, right?' He justified to himself. Liz broke the silence.

"Are you going to the hospital Christmas ball? I know you hate them, but I thought I'd ask anyway."

Nick shrugged. "Maybe."

"What? You're actually considering it?"

"Well, the invitation came to both me and Ricky. I know he would love to take Lindy to something fancy like that. Impress her…..you know how it is. I thought it might be good for him….them….to mingle with professionals for a night. I haven't mentioned it to him yet…."

"But that's a noble idea. Can I help?"

"How?"

"I'll volunteer to take Lindy shopping for a gown and shoes if you get Ricky to a tux rental….I mean….I'm sure he probably doesn't have his own."

"Oh…I forgot about that. It *is* black tie. I'm not sure he will go for that."

"Oh, he might. He and Lindy can get to play dress-up for the night. Come on….I already know the dress for her. It will be perfect."

"You don't even know if she can afford it. She's very proud, so don't think you can just offer to buy it for her…."

"No….but I can work it so that she's paying less than the dress is worth. Give the kids a special night out…. what do ya say?"

Nick studied Liz for a moment before he answered. "Only if you'll agree to go with us. What do *you* say?"

Liz bit her lip as she ran her hand through her hair. "Sure….why not? Tell the kids tonight and I can take Lindy shopping this week. The ball is less than two weeks away, you know. Hey, I gotta run. Some of us actually work around here. I'll get back to you…." She fled out of the laboratory door. 'What have I just done? I agreed to a date with the man who made me so unhappy for almost five years. I must be insane."

Nick stood there smiling at Liz's back as she darted out of the lab. "I just asked my ex-wife out. I'm a jerk." He shook his head and grabbed up a sponge to clean the sink.

\* \* \*

Nick smelled food the minute he opened the door. Ricky was standing in front of the stove stirring a pot of something, and Nick could see the tension in his shoulders.

"Need to think about something again? It always smells so good when you think."

Nick was hoping for a favorable response to his little joke, but got nothing more than a nod. Ricky barely acknowledged him. Although Nick was curious as to what was wrong, he decided to let it be for the time being; opting to run upstairs and change clothes instead.

Ricky's newest cooking venture of beef tips and noodles was sitting on two plates when Nick returned to the kitchen. A glass of red wine had been placed in front of the plate.

"Wow, you even know which wine to serve. You're not bad, kid."

Ricky thanked him without a smile, and then brooded all through the meal. Nick was seeing the kid he saw back in August when Ricky first arrived, and he wondered what brought it on. He had to ask.

"Hey, what's wrong? Something happen today?"

Ricky nodded, but didn't offer any explanation. Nick prodded until Ricky finally opened up. He told Nick about the incident in the gym and how bad Lindy's eye looked. Nick listened to Ricky's story with great concern.

"Should I take a look at Lindy's eye? Do you think she needs more medical attention?"

"I don't know. I just hurts me to see her injured like this because of me."

"Why because of you?"

"The girl did it on purpose….because she's been hitting on me since the first day of school. I wasn't interested in her to begin with…but after I met Lindy, Carrie didn't even exist as far as I was concerned…..so she's been pretty mean to Lindy because of it. What I'm afraid of is that Carrie is much bigger than Lindy. I'm worried about Lindy really getting hurt."

"Who is this girl? What's her name?"

"Carrie Siverson. You met her…..my 'buddy guide' the first day of school, remember?"

Nick's brain grabbed onto the last name. "Siverson? As in Tom Siverson?"

"Oh……I don't know any Tom Siverson."

"I do. He's the head of the hospital. I wonder if that's his daughter……" Nick's voice trailed off.

"You're not going to go telling on her or anything; are you? I mean…..that would make me a rat."

"Well……..here's the way it is, Ricky. As head of the hospital, he has an image he has to maintain…..a reputation, so to speak. If he or any of his family does something wrong to somebody……well, his integrity suffers. If I mention it to him, I am doing him a favor. Something like this could damage his image….especially because he is on the school board as well. And besides, this is how it's done here. There are no rats…just concerned citizens."

Ricky was not entirely comfortable with this, but let it go. Whatever it took to keep Lindy safe from Carrie was fine with him.

"Oh, Rick….there is something I wanted to talk to you about. First, how bad is Lindy's eye? Does she need more medical attention?"

"Naw, just a steak on it, I think." Ricky chuckled, showing humor for the first time since Nick walked through the door.

"Well, call her and tell her I'll give you kids a ride to school tomorrow; and then I can look at her eye. But that's not what I wanted to talk to you about." Nick paused, wondering how to approach the subject correctly. "Okay, here goes…..the hospital has a formal Christmas ball every year. This year, I got the invitation with your name on it, too. Would you like to take Lindy?"

Nick studied Ricky, waiting for a reaction, and then continued. "I mean….you would be going with me……. and your Aunt Liz."

This got a reaction. Ricky's eyes opened wide with surprise, a grin spreading across his mouth. "What? I'm not agreeing to anything until you give me some details on how this is happening." Ricky's grin became a laugh.

Nick filled him in on the conversation with Liz earlier in the day. "I don't know…she just took a real interest in Lindy, Rick. I think she's the daughter Liz never had, or something."

"You know, Uncle Nick….Lindy won't take anything from her. I mean, I hope she isn't looking at Lindy as a charity case. That would hurt Lindy….might actually piss her off."

"Well, Liz says that's not it….I hope not, too. I don't look at Lindy that way. I just think she's cute as hell, and a nice girlfriend for you. So what do you say? I know girls like that sort of thing, and with you not having a license, you can't take her many places…..it would be an opportunity to give her a fancy night out…."

"......And give you an opportunity to date your ex-wife." Ricky sniggered at his own remark, and then became quiet for a few moments. Nick knew he was thinking. Suddenly Ricky's face lit up. "Yeah.....I think she would like that. I just hope her eye heals by then. And if it's for her, I can stand a monkey suit for a night. I'll ask her."

"Most facial wounds heal more quickly than others. But I'm sure Aunt Liz will know how to fix it if it isn't completely healed. Now Liz says she wants to go shopping with Lindy. They both need dresses so that should work out okay. You and I will go to rent black tie monkey suits together. Hey, how cool is this? We're going to the prom together!" They both burst out laughing.

# Chapter 16

It was the day of the ball, just two weeks before Christmas. Liz picked Lindy up around two in the afternoon, since they both had hair appointments at Liz's favorite salon. Lindy was showered and ready when Liz pulled into her driveway, but she opened the door and held up one finger, indicating to Liz that she needed a minute. She opened the door again and ran out with something in her arms.

"I just wanted to ask you if this would be okay." Lindy held up a short black faux fur jacket with silver braiding around the cuffs, collar, and around the bottom edge of it. She tried it on and Liz saw that the length was halfway between Lindy's shoulders and ribcage—a perfect evening wrap.

"Yes! It's perfect…..really. Are you ready to go?"

Lindy handed Liz the wrap and ran back to get her purse, jacket, and house key. She pulled the door shut behind her and jumped into the car, smiling at Liz as she pulled the car door shut.

"Excited?" Liz asked her.

"A little. I've never been to anything like this before. I can't wait to put my dress on."

Lindy remembered the dress she and Liz had shopped for. She fell in love with it from the moment she saw it. The saleslady helped her try it on and from that moment she knew that it was the one. The dress was white with white three-inch ruffles with silver edging. The ruffles were sewn at an angle, wrapping around the dress like garland on a tree, and ending around the hemline. Thin silver straps, attached to the dress just above the breasts, brought out the silver in the ruffles. The soft material clung to Lindy's torso, accenting the lovely curves on her size two figure, and then dropped straight to the floor. The saleslady brought out silver high heeled sandals to go with it, and Lindy was sold. While her purchases were being rung up, Liz tried on a green gown with a plunging neckline. It was simple but elegant and sophisticated, and looked great on her. Liz opted for gold high heeled sandals. She looked fabulous, Lindy told her. Liz purchased a crystal pendant on a silver chain and matching teardrop earrings and gave it to Lindy. "It's a little gift. I think it will go well with the dress," she told her. Lindy accepted it graciously. They went to dinner after the shopping, and exchanged secrets and phone numbers to make arrangements for the hair appointments on Saturday. By Saturday, Lindy and Liz were good friends.

"I can't wait for Ricky to see you in it." Liz laughed.

"Yeah, me neither." She looked over at Liz and grinned.

* * *

The stylist piled Lindy's hair on top of her head, letting wisps fall to the sides and on her forehead. The wisps were curled with a curling iron.

"Oh, Lindy.....you're breath-taking." Liz told her.

Lindy's smile was gigantic as she looked into the mirror. "Wow! I hardly recognize myself." She giggled.

"Who is hitting you, Sweetie?" The stylist piped up. "Your right eye is going to need a little shadow to match the left one."

Liz had forgotten the injury that had been prominent the night they shopped for dresses. She walked over to the chair and inspected Lindy's eye, observing that there were still traces of injury showing. "I can fix that. Nobody will even notice it. It happened in gym class," She assured the stylist.

* * *

Lindy was dressing in one of Liz's spare rooms while Liz got ready in her own room. Before she went to dress, Liz dabbed a little cover-up onto Lindy's eye and added a little shadow to each eye. Upon careful inspection, Lindy was satisfied that what was left of the bruises on her eye could not be seen. She stood in front of the mirror in a strapless bra and matching panties, moving her arms up and down until she was sure that she would be able to keep the bra up. She had never had one before Liz talked her into buying this. It was almost time for Uncle Nick and Ricky to show up, so she took her dress out of the closet and unzipped the plastic garment bag the saleslady had placed it in. She zipped the back of the dress as the doorbell rang. Liz ran in and told her to stay in the room until she called her.

"I want to see his reaction to you. Oh, Lindy.....you look like....the most exquisite angel I have ever seen. That boy is going to fall in love tonight." Liz grinned at her and then went to answer the door.

"Well, don't you two just look….handsome! Ready, Lindy? Come on out!"

Liz watched Ricky's face as Lindy emerged from the bedroom.

"Wow…..aw, wow! You look…..you look……wow!" Beyond those words, Ricky was speechless.

"I think he's trying to say you look gorgeous, Lindy. And he's certainly right." Nick added.

Lindy smiled at Nick and thanked him, then turned back to Ricky, who still could not speak. He just devoured her with his eyes.

Nick turned to Liz. "Uh, Liz, you look beautiful. That green does something very special to your eyes."

Surprised by the detailed compliment, Liz couldn't say anything more than a thank you. Ricky still was not speaking; he just stared at Lindy.

\* \* \*

"Are you okay?" Lindy asked Ricky as he took her wrap from her shoulders once inside the country club.

He let out a short laugh. "Yeah…….I'm sorry….I just can't stop staring at ya. You look so….gorgeous….really gorgeous. Everybody is looking at you. You're the most gorgeous one here tonight."

Lindy laughed her beautiful laugh. "Oh, come on… stop. I know I look nice, but not really gorgeous. There are a lot of pretty women here tonight. Look at Aunt Liz. She looks beautiful."

Ricky smiled down at Lindy. "Yes, she does….but not as gorgeous as you."

They made their way to their designated table and found that they shared it with another doctor and his fiancée, who both proved to be delightful company, even if the young doctor kept staring at Lindy, causing Ricky to be a little annoyed. The young couple got up to dance, which prompted Ricky to ask Lindy to dance.

"Bet you thought I didn't know how; didn't you?" Ricky teased.

"It's a surprise." Lindy admitted.

"My dad taught me." Ricky winked at her as he passed that information along to her.

Ricky led Lindy to the dance floor while Nick and Liz sat and watched. Liz leaned her chin on the heel of her hand and watched Ricky and Lindy.

"Oh, to be young and in love like those two." She said half to Nick and half to herself. She looked at Nick, and then looked back at the dance floor. "Look at them. It's magical. Don't you agree?" She turned toward Nick with her question.

"Agree to what? They're just two kids with the hots for each other. Young love doesn't last."

"Perhaps…..perhaps not. I just think they look so beautiful together."

"With Ricky tripping all over her feet? Beautiful."

"Oh, come on. Where's your sense of romance?" She began to get annoyed with his cynicism.

Nick laughed. "Hey, I'm just teasing you. The truth is…..I believe in young love. I believe it's more real than the love you feel when you're older. I believe that when young people like those two fall in love, it's the purest and sweetest love there is. The problem is with the maturity. They aren't mature enough to handle all the problems that come with an adult world. That's why it doesn't last. Now….when you're older and fall in love, the obstacles of the world have already been set in front of you at least once. You can't really…..openly…..love with all your heart, because your heart has seen so much…pain….sorrow…. hurt. You can't give your whole heart because part of it is already being used to carry all that stuff from the past. But the love lasts longer…..because you expect less."

Nick stopped talking when he realized that Liz was openly staring at him like she was seeing him for the first time. "Sorry….didn't mean to go off on a tangent."

"You know, I think you said more this one time than I got out of you in a month when we were married. If you could have been that honest and open with me when we were together, we may have been able to work it out. I think you've matured. Maybe Ricky being there is good for you."

The corners of Nick's mouth turned slightly upward. "Maybe. I just know that I care a lot about those two out there on the dance floor. I don't ever want to see anything bad happen to either one of them. And Liz….for the record….I see the magic, too. Now…….would you like to dance?"

"I thought you'd never ask." Liz smiled at Nick and got up from her chair.

\* \* \*

The dance music changed to dinner music as the waiters began serving the pre-ordered meal selections. Lindy got up to use the restroom but quickly returned to the table and whispered in Ricky's ear.

*"Carrie is here."*

Ricky saw the fright on Lindy's face. "Aw, damn it!"

He turned to Liz and asked if she would mind going to the restroom with Lindy. He quickly gave Liz a short version of the animosity between Carrie and them. Liz could see that Lindy was visibly shaken by the fact that Carrie was nearby. She agreed to go but planned on talking to Tom Siverson about his daughter's behavior. She got her opportunity on the return from the restrooms.

"Liz…..are you enjoying yourself?"

Tom Siverson fell into step with her as she headed back toward her table. Liz quickly introduced him to Lindy and watched as Lindy walked back to their table after the introduction.

"Lovely girl." Siverson commented.

"Yes…..she is." Liz began. "Tom, we have a problem. It seems that….your daughter Carrie has been bullying Lindy at school. I had to accompany her to the restroom when she realized that Carrie was here. She's scared to death of her."

"My Carrie? Are you sure?"

"Yes, unfortunately….I'm sure." Liz quickly told him the story about the eye injury in P-E class, and how Lindy was visibly shaken when she realized that Carrie was on the premises.

"Is there any foundation for it?" Siverson wanted to know.

"Well, according to them it's over Ricky, Nick's nephew. Ricky and Lindy have been together since the beginning of the school year and apparently Carrie had designs on him."

Liz watched Siverson's jaw tighten. "So it's jealousy over a boy?"

She nodded.

"Well, I will deal with it. Thanks for letting me know. Oh, and….you can let Lindy know that she can enjoy the rest of her evening without incident. I'll see to it."

Liz thanked him, hoping that she had done the right thing. The rest of the evening did pass without incident. Lindy and Ricky danced several dances, as did Liz and Nick. The four together created a night to remember, just as Liz had hoped.

Nick swung the car into Lindy's driveway way past midnight. He noted that there was no other vehicle in the driveway, probably meaning that Lindy would be spending the night alone in an empty house. This disturbed him. He knew it wasn't a good idea even if the neighborhood was a relatively safe place. Most criminals came from outside the neighborhood.

Lindy and Ricky got out of the car, and Ricky stopped by Nick's car window.

"I'll be a few minutes. I just like to check to make sure there's nobody hiding in there when she goes into the house alone."

"Good idea." Nick answered, a little relieved that Ricky was that concerned for Lindy's safety.

"How sweet." Liz added.

Ricky did a quick check of the house, turning on a couple of lights along the way. When he was sure that all doors and windows were locked and everything was the same as Lindy had left it, he came back to Lindy and encircled her in his arms.

"Did you have a good time tonight?" He whispered against her temple.

"Hmmm, yes. Did you?"

"Of course.....I was with you." He tightened his arms around her. "You looked so beautiful tonight. I know I keep saying it, but it's true. You were the most beautiful girl there."

"And did you see yourself in the mirror? You look so sexy and handsome in a tux...do you know that?"

She and Ricky locked eyes, feeling that familiar bolt of electricity pass through them. Their night ended in a kiss—sweet and tender, sealing their devotion to each other.

# Chapter 17

$\mathscr{L}$indy was walking from store to store inside the mall. Ricky would be meeting her around noon, so she wanted to get his gifts bought before that. She had already purchased a gold ring that held a diamond of one-third carat. She knew Ricky would love it. Before leaving the house she checked her bank balance and was greatly surprised by what it held. Since her grandfather had passed away four years ago—two years before her mother had died—an amount of money had been going into the account every month, for her expenses. She had been issued a VISA debit card so that she could use the money as she needed it. She rarely touched the money in there since she had no real expenses. The amount had grown to a sizable proportion, and it wasn't any part of her education fund. It was just money for her to spend, so if she wanted to, she could spend lavishly on gifts for those she cared about.

After a few more purchases for Ricky, she looked for something nice for Uncle Nick and then for Liz. It was almost noon when she remembered she hadn't gotten her father anything, but then wondered if she should. She remembered looking into his closet one day during the summer and in there she had discovered that every gift she had bought for him over the past two years was in the closet, still wrapped. He had never opened anything she bought him. That memory brought the sting of tears as she walked passed the brightly lit holiday stores.

"Happy times, happy times." She murmured to herself. 'This is Christmas and it will be different this year. You have Ricky and Ricky's family.' She reminded herself. She stopped outside of a women's clothing shop, remembering that she had to get something for Ricky's mother. She saw the perfect sweater in the window and darted in to purchase it. Ricky's mother had dark hair and eyes like Ricky's and Nick's. The sweater was a soft knit in either pink or green. Lindy chose the pink one, knowing that it would bring out her dark eyes. She checked her list to see if she had forgotten anyone and was satisfied that all had been covered. She headed toward the restaurant to meet Ricky, and spied him heading in the same direction.

"Ricky!" She shouted to him.

He turned around, smiling when he recognized her voice. "Hi. How's the shopping coming?" He asked as he kissed her cheek.

"I think I'm done. I didn't get my dad anything, but….why bother?"

"That's something you have to decide all by yourself, Sweetie. I'm starving. Are you?"

They were lucky to get a booth inside the restaurant, since the shoppers were filing in to eat before shopping some more.

"I think I'm done shopping. How about you?" She asked him. She had noted the two shopping bags he carried.

"Well, almost. I got my mother a couple of things, Uncle Nick, and Aunt Liz and then…you. I have to get one more thing for you, and then I'm done. Want to catch a bus and go to my place for awhile? I'll cook us dinner later."

\* \* \*

When they arrived at the condo, Nick was in his den. Ricky ran his shopping bags up to his room while Lindy set hers inside the guest closet in the living room. Nick came out of the den obviously in a good mood.

"Hey, you two! Christmas is next week! We don't even have a tree. Want to go get one?" Nick noted that Lindy's face brightened. "We have to get ornaments, because I have none, and we have to get window and door decorations. You guys up for it?"

It was unnecessary to ask Lindy that question. He could see that she was already into it. He loved to see her smile like that. Ricky bounded down the stairs after putting his purchases into his closet and was taken in by the smile on Lindy's face.

"Yeah, let's go do it."

"And the two of you can do the decorations tonight, because I have a date."

Ricky and Lindy stopped, looked at each other, and the two of them burst out laughing.

"Now what the hell is so funny?" Nick tried to keep a straight face, but the corners of his mouth kept moving upward. "You think dating and romance is just for young people?" This caused them to laugh harder. Nick shook his head as he opened the door to the outside.

\* \* \*

Nick and Ricky set the tree in the stand and Lindy assured them that it was straight. Ricky cooked a quick dinner while Nick got ready for his date. Ricky and Lindy laughed every time he said the word.

When he came down the stairs, Lindy told him he looked handsome. Ricky asked him if Aunt Liz had a date, too, and got no answer.

"Okay, you two. You can decorate the tree and the windows and door. No hanky-panky, okay?" This brought waves of laughter from them. "I'm serious. I'm trusting you both. The tree should be finished when I get home. I won't be too late, so I can give Lindy a ride home….okay? I'll call if…well, no never mind….I'll be home before midnight."

With that, he left. Lindy and Ricky once again burst out laughing.

Ricky grabbed Lindy around the waist and whispered into her ear. "Let's hurry up and get the tree done so we can get to the hanky-panky, whatever that is." They burst out laughing one more time, before they set about decorating the tree.

\* \* \*

Lindy was mesmerized by the tree. She and Ricky sat together on the sofa, admiring their work. All the lights were out except for the ones on the tree, as they sat together, Lindy's head on Ricky's shoulder, his arm around her.

"We do good work." He joked as he hugged her closer to him.

Neither of them spoke as they stared into the lights of the tree. Lindy closed her eyes for a moment and sighed. It had been a long time since she had felt this happy and this content. She was remembering the last Christmas before her mother died. Her father had cooked the Christmas dinner that day, while her mother sat on the sofa with her and Chris. They were watching a Christmas movie on television and laughing at the funny parts together. Lindy remembered laying her head on her mother's bony shoulder very much the same way as she had her head on Ricky's shoulder. Her father joined them for a few minutes right before dinner was ready. She remembered his arm over the back of their sofa, his hand just touching the nape of her mother's neck. He was crying. Lindy remembered the tears rolling down his cheeks. He wiped his tears away and told her he was crying because he didn't get the BB gun he wanted. Of course, she knew that wasn't true, and she remembered laughing at his words. Then she remembered the sadness in her mother's eyes—sad because she didn't want to leave any of them.

Ricky heard Lindy's sob. "Hey….Baby…..what's wrong?"

She buried her face in his shoulder, trying to get control of her sobs.

"Nothing….everything…..I….was just remembering my last Christmas with my mom….that's all. I…..oh, Ricky…..I *miss* her….*so much.*"

Lindy no longer tried to control the sobs or the tears. She couldn't any more. Ricky held her tightly and rocked her gently, stroking her hair.

"I'm sorry, Ricky….."

"No…..don't be. It's okay….I understand."

Ricky's voice was soft as he spoke to her. He did understand. If he weren't a guy he would cry for his own loss. He missed Enrico all the time, but especially around the holidays, because they had done everything for the holidays together.

Lindy wasn't crying any more, save for a few tell-tale sniffles. Ricky continued to hold her and stroke her hair. They continued to stare into the lights on the tree.

"Lindy?" Ricky said her name softly as he stared into the tree. "Lindy?" He turned to look into her face. "I think I love you."

"Oh, Ricky." She responded softly, as she reached up to touch his cheek.

They fell asleep on the sofa in front of the tree, and awoke when Nick came home. It was still early—way before Lindy's curfew, if she had one. She really didn't know if she did or not, because her father never spoke to her. Ricky made tea for everyone, and they sat around the table making plans for Christmas. Of course, Lindy would be there for Christmas Eve and Christmas day. Dinner would be comprised of a ham and sweet potatoes, vegetables, mashed potatoes and the ever-present pasta. Ricky agreed to do the majority of the cooking. It would be the three of them, Liz, and Angie for dinner. Ricky promised to go to midnight mass with his mother, and asked Lindy to go with them. Lindy was looking forward to it.

Nick looked from Ricky to Lindy and realized the deep affection he had for both of them. If only he and Liz had had a child.....maybe they would have made it. His own child would be about two years older than these two kids. His child. He tried not to think about her. That was a part of his life not even Liz knew about. It was the source of his anger.

# Chapter 18

Christmas Eve. Lindy had spent the last three days wrapping the gifts she had purchased. They were stacked in the shopping bags, ready to be carried to Ricky's. She was dressing with extra care tonight, choosing a festive long red dress with a high turtleneck and long sleeves that held twelve gold buttons on each side. The material was soft—the kind that moved and stretched with the body. It clung to Lindy's torso. The skirt of the dress flared out from the waist, making her waist seem miniscule. She tied her hair at the nape of her neck with a matching red chiffon bow. The red color brought out her big blue eyes even more and gave her cheeks a rosy look. She thought she looked pretty and hoped Ricky would think so, too.

She checked the clock on the dresser. Uncle Nick would be there soon, and she wondered if her father was still at home. She peeked out and looked down the hallway in time to see him walking out the door. No, he wouldn't be there when Uncle Nick showed up, she guessed.

She squared her jaw and said out loud, "Go to hell, Daddy dearest." She immediately felt guilty.

Gathering up her shopping bags full of wrapped presents, she turned off the lights in her room and headed toward the living room to wait for Nick. There was a note waiting for her on the counter. Under the note was a hundred dollar bill and an envelope addressed to her from her brother Chris. She quickly read the note which simply stated that her father would be away until the day after Christmas and the money was for her to use to eat on for the next couple of days. "And a jolly merry Christmas to you, Father. Where would I go to eat on Christmas day? Everything is closed." She shook her head, determined not to let her father's physical and emotional absence ruin her holiday this year. She turned her attention to her brother's envelope and quickly tore it open. It was a short note written on a homemade Christmas card.

*Lindy—I hope you're fine. I'm okay. Can't tell you where I am but I'm over-seas. Have a nice Christmas—love, Chris*

"I love you, too, Chris. I wish you were here." She said this to the air around her, and then thought to herself, 'I better be careful. I'm doing a lot of talking to myself lately.' She laughed to herself as she heard Nick's car pull into the driveway.

The evening was warm for December, and all the snow from Thanksgiving was gone. Lindy slipped into a pair of black dress shoes that held a heel of an inch and a half high. The shoes were plain except for a small gold buckle on the top of the shoe. Nick got out of the car to help her with her bags.

"Did you buy something for everybody on my entire block?" He laughed as he picked up the bags by the handle and felt their weight tug on his arm. Lindy laughed at his remark, too.

"Actually, Lindy, I wanted to see if we could invite your father for dinner. I see he's not here...."

"No...he won't be here for the entire Christmas holiday..." She showed Nick the note her father left for her.

Nick just shook his head and set the note back down on the counter. "Well...are you ready to celebrate Christmas Italian-style?" He offered her his elbow as he carried her bags out to the car.

The condo was ablaze with holiday lights. Ricky had added more to the windows during the week, and to Lindy it looked beautiful. She found him in the kitchen stirring a pot of cheese dip. He kissed her lightly on the lips and held her around the waist, while he continued stirring.

"Wait 'til you taste this. My dad made this one up, himself." They smiled at each other. Ricky kissed the top of her head. "Merry Christmas." He whispered to her. "I can't wait for you to see what I got you."

"Same here." She laughed. "And Merry Christmas to you. All this food...who is going to eat it?"

Ricky laughed. "Hey....it's the Italian way. Seriously, though....Uncle Nick invited some people from the hospital to come over tonight. It's like a real Christmas Eve party. Are you cool with that?"

"Yeah, I am." Lindy grinned.

"Well, then....help me get this food out on the dining room table. By the way...you look beautiful." He stepped back and looked at her. "Yep....really beautiful."

She smiled at him appreciatively, and grabbed a tray to take to the dining room table, just as the doorbell rang and people—strangers to Lindy—began filing into

Nick's condo. People came and people left, and then more people came. Ricky and Lindy were busily serving and replenishing trays all evening, Lindy loving every minute of it. Angie made an appearance shortly after Lindy got there, and Liz was not far behind. It was almost midnight when the last guest left the condo, and Angie, Ricky, and Lindy got ready to leave for the church.

"See….I'm not totally stupid." Ricky grinned at Nick. "If I go to church, I get out of cleaning up this mess."

"Oh….it will be here when you get back." Nick laughed.

"No, it won't, Ricky." Liz jumped in. "I'll take care of it. No….*we* will take care of it…..right, Nick?"

Ricky, Lindy, and Angie laughed when they heard Nick say "Yes, Ma'am."

Ricky added, "I'm not sure we can leave you two alone. Remember….no hanky-panky." Both he and Lindy burst out laughing.

\* \* \*

Angie swung the car into the driveway in front of Lindy's house. Lindy got out of the car, followed by Ricky, who reminded his mother that he would be a few minutes.

"I always check out the place, Mom….to make sure nobody has been in there."

Angie watched Lindy unlock the front door. Suddenly, not being able to stand it any longer, Angie rolled down her window and called to Ricky.

"Ricky, why don't you have her get her things together and come spend the night with us? I don't want to see her here alone on Christmas morning. Lindy! Honey, come spend the night with us." She appealed to Lindy as she joined Ricky at the car window.

Ricky turned to Lindy. "What do ya say? Pack whatever it is you sleep in and whatever you're planning to wear tomorrow. Spend the night at our place. We can stay up late and sit in front of the tree, or we can get up early and open presents, just like we did when we were little kids. Okay?"

"Well, will it be okay with Uncle Nick? I mean….it *is* his house."

"Of course it will be. He loves you, Lindy." Angie assured her.

"Well…..okay then. Why don't you come in and wait while I pack something?"

Angie nodded and got out of the car, grateful for the opportunity to get out of the cold. The temperature had dropped rapidly since Nick had picked Lindy up earlier in the evening.

Angie sat down on the sofa while Lindy and Ricky went to gather her things. Angie glanced around the room approvingly. It was a lovely home and kept very clean. She imagined Lindy did most of the cleaning. She heard Ricky calling her.

"Mom! Come see Lindy's room."

Angie smiled as she made her way down the hall toward the lit room. "Oh, this is darling." Angie spied the picture of Chris. "Is that your….brother?"

"Yes, it is. I just got a card from him. He's overseas somewhere, but he says he can't say where. This is my mom." Lindy handed Angie the picture of her and her mother, just before she snapped her small suitcase shut, indicating that she was ready to go.

"Before we go, I want to show you my favorite part of this house besides my room." Lindy led the way through the kitchen and snapped on the lights that lit up the family room on the other side of the kitchen. The room was large enough to hold a dining room table and chairs and a sofa and loveseat. Windows stretched across the entire length of the room, while a big screen TV sat in an entertainment center against the far wall. "This has become my dad's hangout when he's here. We all used to gather in here, though. Hardly ever used the living room. The room beyond this has a pool table in it."

"Wow….it's really cool in here. Good place to have parties." Ricky spoke quietly so as not to disturb the peacefulness of the room.

\* \* \*

"Psst! Psst!" Lindy opened one eye and cocked her head toward the door of Ricky's bedroom. She saw Ricky's eye staring in at her. "Hey, it's daylight. Get up. Come on, I want to give you one of your presents before anybody else gets up. Come on."

Lindy reluctantly got out of bed, and quickly made it up. She grabbed her robe and padded down the stairs a couple of minutes after Ricky. He was in the kitchen making coffee when she got to the bottom of the stairs. He smiled when she came into the kitchen.

"Ever have my morning coffee?"

"No, I don't think so."

"Well, it's good. I make really good coffee….another of my father's secrets."

Ricky grinned at her, and then reached for her. He hugged her tightly and kissed her hair.

"I'm glad you stayed here last night."

Lindy nodded. "Me, too. Where are the cups?"

Ricky pointed to the cupboard that held the cups as he opened the refrigerator to retrieve the cream. The coffee was not quite done yet, so he ran into the living room and plugged in the lights for the tree. Then he returned to the kitchen, smiling.

"You have to open one present before my mom and uncle get up, okay?"

"Only if you will open one from me."

"Deal."

Armed with fresh cups of coffee, they went into the living room and sat down on the sofa. Ricky dropped off the sofa onto his knees and reached under the tree, pulling out a small box wrapped in gold paper and tied with a red ribbon. He brought it up and set it in front of Lindy.

"Here….open this."

Lindy held up her finger, got down on her knees and crawled to the tree. She, too, pulled out a small box, wrapped in blue foil paper with a silver bow on it.

"And you open this one….okay?"

Ricky hesitated. "You first."

Lindy shrugged, tore off the paper, and opened the small box. She gasped. The box held a gold pearl ring, diamonds flanking the pearl.

"Oh, Ricky…..it's beautiful." She reached for the ring but her hand was intercepted by Ricky's hand.

"Allow me." Ricky took the ring out of the box and slipped it onto her third finger, left hand. "That's where I want you to wear it…..okay?"

Lindy nodded, and then pointed to the box she had for Ricky to open. Ricky unwrapped the package and opened the box.

"Oh, Baby…..this is beautiful. I love it."

"Will you wear it on the same hand? The left, I mean?"

"Of course." Ricky took the ring out of the box and slid it onto his left ring finger. "So….it's official. You're mine and I'm yours….right?"

He looked up into Lindy's face, and saw the tears trickling down her cheeks. She was biting her lip and smiling at the same time. He reached for her face and held it between his palms.

"I love you, Lindy. I really do."

She nodded, and then answered. "I love you, too, Ricky."

Ricky moved to the sofa and sat down next to her. His arms surrounded her and he whispered into her ear. "Merry Christmas." They dozed off in front of the tree, Lindy wrapped in Ricky's arms.

* * *

Angie and Nick came out of their bedrooms at the same time. Angie held her index finger up and told Nick to wait a minute.

"Nick, Lindy's here. She stayed all night. I….just couldn't let her go into that empty house and spend the night alone on Christmas. I know I should have asked you…but…when I saw her going into her dark house….. I had to ask her to come and stay here. I'm sorry…"

"That's fine, Angie. Your heart was in the right place. I should have thought about it and asked her to stay when I picked her up. So….where did everybody sleep?"

"She slept in Ricky's room and he slept on the sofa. I hope that was okay…."

"Yeah, yeah…..fine. So where are they now? Nobody's in Ricky's room."

"I heard them go downstairs about an hour ago. Ricky came up and got Lindy and they went down to sit in front of the tree. Lindy loves that tree." Angie whispered.

Both she and Nick had been whispering through the entire exchange. They quietly made their way down the stairs and spied Lindy and Ricky, heads together, sleeping in front of the tree. Nick tiptoed up to them and leaned down very close to their ears.

"Boo….." He whispered into their ears.

Lindy and Ricky jumped, and then laughed. "Merry Christmas, Uncle Nick!" They responded in unison.

Angie and Nick poured themselves coffee and the gift exchange began. Nick surprised Lindy with a watch. He had noticed that she never wore one, and thought it would be an appropriate gift. She was delighted with it, as he was with the shirt, tie and sweater she bought for him. Angie gave Lindy a pink running suit and Ricky a black one very similar to it. They laughed when they discovered that Ricky had gotten a black one for Lindy just like the one Angie bought for him. Angie loved the sweater from Lindy and the slacks and blouse from Ricky. Nick gave Ricky a gold chain and a television for his bedroom. Angie and Nick exchanged gift certificates for their favorite stores. Ricky had something very special for Nick. Along with a pair of gold cufflinks, Ricky had copies of Nick's achievement awards bronzed for him. Nick was truly touched by his thoughtfulness. All that was left under the tree were gifts to Liz from everybody, including Nick. Liz would be there later.

Angie started a breakfast of eggs and bacon, sausage, home fries and toast. Ricky and Lindy set the table; Lindy poured the juice while Ricky made a fresh pot of coffee. Still in her robe, Lindy sat down at the kitchen table with everybody when breakfast was ready. She looked radiant. For the first time in three years she was celebrating Christmas, family style, and she couldn't have been happier.

*   *   *

Lindy awoke in her own bed the morning after Christmas. She sighed and snuggled further down into the blankets. It had been a wonderful holiday, and she was still basking in the warmth of the Bazario-DeCelli displays of affection. Yesterday had been wonderful, especially after Liz arrived. She had gifts for everybody and good tidings along with it. Uncle Nick had surprised her with a pair of diamond earrings, and Ricky had given her a gold bracelet. Angie bought her a nightgown and she, in exchange, had given Angie a new robe. Liz loved the silk blouse from Lindy. It was a bronze color that really made her unusual eyes stand out. For Lindy, Liz had a pair of designer jeans and a turquoise designer top to go with them. Proving that Liz had a sense of humor, she gave Nick a small oblong box to unwrap. In it, he found a pair of argyle socks, which brought peals of laughter from Lindy and Ricky. Inside one of the socks was a gold and onyx pinky ring, similar to the ring Liz had thrown at him once. That ring had bounced off his car and was never found. This was the replacement for it. Nick quietly smiled and chuckled to himself as he slid the ring onto his little finger.

Lindy smiled to herself remembering everything about the day. She wondered if Ricky was awake yet. She looked over at her clock and saw that it was only seven o'clock. Probably not a good idea to call him yet. She rolled back over and dozed off again, briefly wondering if her dad was home, but not really caring.

She awoke again to the ringing of the telephone. It was Ricky calling her.

"Hey…..are you awake?" He asked.

"Barely," she yawned as she spoke.

"My mom wanted to say something to you before she left. She's packed and ready to go. Here she is."

"Lindy? Honey, it was wonderful having you here for Christmas. I hope you enjoyed it."

"Oh yes….I did. Thank you so much. Hope to see you soon." Lindy smiled into the receiver as she hung it back up.

Angie was smiling, too. "You take care of that girl, Ricky. She's very special."

"Yeah, Mom…I know. And I will take care of her."

"Good. And take care of yourself. You're doing good. I'm proud of you. Your dad would be, too. I can just hear him saying…'I taught that boy to be good to his woman….and he is. I taught him well'. Your dad gave you all the gifts he possessed, Ricky. He was a wonderful man. You remember to treat Lindy like he treated me. She deserves it."

"I do and I will….always."

"Good. I love you, Ricky. Take care." Angie hugged him.

"Love you, too, Mom. Be careful driving back."

# Chapter 19

Nick was peering through a microscope, making adjustments with his right hand as he intensely stared at the microbe on the slide. He had been working on this project since before Thanksgiving and was becoming frustrated that he hadn't seen much progress. His lab assistants were out with either the flu or holiday vacation time, making him short-handed on the project. He didn't hear Liz come in.

"Dr. Bazario, I presume." She spoke, adding a small laugh at the end of her sentence.

Nick looked up from his microscope lens and smiled at her. "Liz….did you enjoy yourself yesterday?"

"Immensely. It was like old times….except Ricky's bigger. Truly, Nick….I had a wonderful holiday, thanks to you and your family. Thank you….again, and again, and again."

"Well, I'm just glad everybody had a nice time. How about that Lindy, huh? She was so enthralled with everything. It was nice to see her so happy."

"Yeah, I agree. Ricky's got a keeper there, huh? She is so adorable, and so sweet."

Nick scowled for a moment. "Yeah, she is. I can't imagine what her old man is thinking. That girl practically lives alone. You know she stayed with us on Christmas Eve night. Angie couldn't bear to see her go into that empty house alone, so she invited her back to the house to stay over."

"Well, that was nice of her. Where did everyone sleep?"

"Lindy in Ricky's bed, Ricky on the sofa. It worked out. Those kids are at my place a lot. I don't mind it, though….they're good kids…..and…I know where they are when they're at my place."

"Oh, I almost forgot why I came up here. What are you doing New Year's eve?"

"Haven't even thought about it," Nick admitted. "What'd you have in mind?"

"Siverson is having a party. He asked me to invite you since he never sees you. He says he doesn't come into your domain and you don't bother him for anything, but he would like to have you come to his party."

"Oh. Well, I don't know. I guess I could go."

"Lindy and Ricky are invited, too, but I think we can count them out."

"Yeah, Lindy won't go anywhere near Siverson's daughter, and Ricky can't stand her. How is it they got invited?"

"Apparently his daughter is having a party in their game room that night. Tom invited them to his daughter's party; she didn't invite them. But you can go. How about it? Be my date for it?"

Nick cocked his head and stared at her. "Liz….are you hitting on me?"

* * *

Ricky watched the headlights on Nick's car as they backed out of the driveway. When Nick's car swung toward the top of the hill, Ricky called Lindy.

"Hey, what do you want to do tonight?"

"Be with you."

"Well, yeah…of course….but what do you want to do? Go eat somewhere? See a movie? Whatever you want." Ricky hesitated for a moment. "Hey…are you okay?"

"Yeah, I guess. Listen to this."

Ricky could hear paper rattling through the phone.

"Going to New York for New Year's. Be back late New Year's Day. No happy new year, no name, nothing. I…I'm about as important to him as the garbage man."

"Aw, Honey….You're damned important to me. You're my everything." Ricky could tell she was on the verge of tears. "Do you want me to come down there?"

She didn't respond.

"Honey?"

"Yeah." She finally answered. "Listen, how about we splurge for a couple of movies? The Blockbuster is not far from me. We can order a pizza….and I have a surprise for you. Okay? Everything my treat. He left me fifty dollars. Can you come down soon and then we can walk to the video store?"

"Yeah, sure. I'll leave in fifteen minutes." After he hung up he thought about what she said. What kind of surprise did she have for him? He ran upstairs to change his clothes.

\* \* \*

"Oh God, it's so cold out!" Lindy exclaimed as they slipped into the warmth of her house. "My eyes are watering from the cold."

Ricky looked at her face and saw that her cheeks and nose were red. "I guess I should have gone down there and left you here. I'm used to cold like that. Chicago always has bitter cold winds in the winter."

"And let you get your selections of movies? Not on your life. That was a joint decision." She laughed through her chattering teeth.

"Well.....since you put it that way....suffer." He responded, laughing.

She was already on the phone ordering the pizza. She hung up the phone and complained, "We have to wait a whole hour for it."

"So what's the surprise you have for me?"

"You'll see. Do you want to start watching one of these or do you want to wait for the pizza? Oh.....tell me where Uncle Nick went tonight."

"Okay, yeah....he went to Siverson's for a party....but he took Aunt Liz out to dinner first. They're going to the party together. She asked him."

"Wow! Do you think they might get back together?"

"I'm hoping. Oh, yeah, Mister Siverson invited us tonight. Carrie is having a party in their game room and he invited us to it."

"No way..."

"That's what I said. Uncle Nick just laughed because he knows how we feel about that bitch."

"Anyway, Ricky, wouldn't it be cool if Uncle Nick got back with Liz? I'm hoping, too. She'd be my Aunt Liz, too, then."

Lindy disappeared into the kitchen and returned with plates and napkins for the pizza when it arrived. She removed the centerpiece from the coffee table, replacing it with three trivets covered with a couple of placemats. It was just short of an hour when they saw the headlights from the pizza delivery car swing into the driveway. They waited for the knock before going to the door.

"I'll get it....in case it's that same guy mooning over you." Ricky chuckled, and Lindy laughed. It was the same guy. Ricky paid for the pizza and tipped him well, hopefully getting the message across that Lindy was his and he was in charge there. He set the pizza down and opened the box to let the steam out. It looked good. Lindy disappeared once again into the kitchen. She came back holding two beers.

"Ta-da!" She exclaimed, holding them up. "Here is the surprise."

"Where did you get them?"

"The refrigerator in the back. There are a couple of cases there. He won't miss a couple. Besides, there are some in the kitchen refrigerator, too. We'll just have to get rid of the bottles. So.....Happy New Year!"

Ricky reached for the bottles and smiled at Lindy. "You're going to drink one, too?"

"Yeah....I've never even tasted it before, but....what the hell..."

"Whoa! Drinking and using profanity...my kitten's gone wild." Ricky teased as he grabbed her by the waist and pulled her down beside him. He popped the caps off of the beers and drank from one. He looked over at Lindy and then suggested she get a glass for hers. "I don't want you to drink it fast....you'll get sick, okay? Eat a piece of pizza first."

"Why aren't you following those orders?"

"Because I have had many beers before tonight. I know what I'm doing…..seriously. Just take it easy."

It didn't take long for Lindy to feel the effects of the alcohol. She wasn't quite halfway through that first beer when she felt a little dizzy. She snuggled close to Ricky and put her head on his shoulder. He looked down into her face and kissed the tip of her nose, laughing a little.

"Are you okay?" He asked. She grinned back at him. He could tell she was feeling the alcohol. He rubbed his cheek across her forehead and tightened his arm around her.

"I think you're already a little drunk," he whispered.

"A litter." Lindy answered him.

"A litter drunk, huh?" Ricky laughed and so did Lindy.

They stared into each other's eyes and felt the bolt of electricity shoot through them again. Ricky took her face between his palms and gently kissed her.

"I love you, Lindy…I really love you."

"And I really love you, Ricky…a lot."

Ricky kissed her again and she responded. The kisses turned passionate and their breathing became heavy and ragged. The pizza, the beer and the movie were forgotten as their kissing and touching intensified. Ricky, after removing his shirt, slowly removed Lindy's sweater and bra. He peered into her face and pulled her closer.

"Some day we are going to get married, Babe….I can feel it."

Lindy grinned crookedly at him. "I hope so," she smiled and wrinkled her nose up at him.

"Let's go lie on your bed."

Maybe it was the alcohol, or maybe she was just ready, but it surprised him when she said okay. He took her hand and led her to her bedroom. They took their relationship to a whole new level that New Year's Eve night.

Exhausted, Ricky lay beside her, trying to get control of his breathing. His body was spent. Lindy lay there quietly with her eyes closed. When his breathing was a little better, he draped his arm over her nude body.

"Hey….it gets easier every time after the first."

She stared at him for a moment. "I should hope so. I can't imagine talking somebody into doing that twice." She turned her head away from him but not before he saw the tears.

"Hey, hey….shh…shh, Baby, don't cry." Ricky reached for her and surrounded her with his arms. "Did I hurt you?"

Lindy nodded. Ricky could feel her trembling, and he sighed. This isn't what he wanted.

"I promise you it won't hurt like that again." He rested his cheek against her temple. "I guess girls kind of get the bad end of the deal when they first do it. It doesn't hurt for guys. I'm so sorry I hurt you." He raised his head above hers, brushed her hair back and smiled at her. "Smile and tell me you love me….please?"

She tried to smile, but only managed to raise the corners of her mouth a little.

"Ricky, I *do* love you."

"I know you do, Babe……I know. And I love you…. so much."

They dozed off and awoke in time to celebrate the entry of the New Year. Lindy heated up the pizza and disposed of the warm beers. Ricky turned the television channel to the New York festivities so they could watch the ball drop. He watched Lindy bring the warm pizza into the living room. She looked so fragile to him.

"I think I'll have a soda. Do you want another beer?"

Ricky shook his head. "No, soda is fine."

"Hey, maybe I'll see my dad."

"You think?"

"No…..I was being funny." She smiled at him.

They watched the ball drop, kissed each other for New Year's, and then returned to Lindy's bed. They made love, and as Ricky promised, it wasn't as bad for Lindy; just not wonderful. He held her in his arms in the darkened room.

"It will get better and better. There will come a time when you will be chasing after me for it."

"Really? Do you *think* so?"

Ricky laughed quietly. "I *know* so. When we get married, you'll want it as much, if not more, than I do."

They fell asleep and woke just past dawn. After helping her clean up, he dressed quickly. He stared down at the reddish-brown stain on her sheets and felt something in his chest tug at him. Lindy came up beside him and saw what he was staring at.

"I guess I better wash those today."

"I'll call you when I get home. Hopefully, Uncle Nick doesn't know I didn't come home all night."

He kissed her quickly and opened the door to leave. "You know I don't want to leave, don't you? I have to. If he discovers that I didn't come home all night…."

"I know."

She watched him walk away from the house and head up the street. She watched until she couldn't see him any more, and then went into the bathroom and turned on the light. She stared into the mirror, wondering if anybody would notice that she was different. She took the sheets off of the bed and poured peroxide onto the stain. It came right out. As she was putting the sheets into the washer, the phone rang, startling her a little. It was Ricky.

"Hey.....I needn't have worried about Uncle Nick. He didn't come home all night."

Lindy let out a short gasp. "Are you sure?"

"Yeah, because I left a light on in the living room and it's still on." Ricky paused.

In a softer voice he spoke to her almost intimately. "I miss you already. I wish I hadn't have left. How about some of Ricky's famous cooking for dinner tonight? Traditional New Year's Day food. Up for it?"

She imagined he was smiling into the phone when she realized that she was doing the same. "Yeah....I'm up for it. What's traditional food?"

"Well, let's see.....I can have ham and cabbage or pork and sauer- kraut. What do you like the best?"

"Doesn't matter. I dislike them equally." She laughed.

"Well, I'll have something special for you. Want to walk up around two?"

"Sounds fine. See ya then."

"I love you, Babe." Ricky waited for her response.

"I love you, too. See ya then."

Lindy hung up and Ricky rested the telephone receiver against his cheek. He wished he had stayed there a little longer. He could have helped her take out the trash or wash the sheets….anything. He would make it up to her, he promised himself.

# Chapter 20

Ricky knocked on Lindy's front door bright and early on their first day back to school after the holiday break. She opened the door and smiled, and then laughed.

"You look cold!" She laughed again. "It is friggin' cold out there! Even colder than I remember in Chicago. Are you ready?"

"Yeah, let me get my book bag."

Ricky was right. The temperature must have been around zero. The two of them trudged up the hill, feeling the cold through their clothing. As they were nearing the convenience store where Ricky usually bought their coffee, a yellow cab pulled in. Ricky picked up the pace a little.

"Come on…let's see if we can get a ride."

They approached the side of the cab and Ricky asked the cab-driver if he would give them a ride to school.

"Not for free, kid," the cabdriver stressed.

"I didn't mean for free. I can pay you."

"Well, okay, then…..let me get a cup of coffee first."

Ricky followed him into the store while Lindy climbed into the back of the cab, grateful for the heat that was already warming her face. Ricky and the cabby came out of the store together, holding three cups of coffee between them. The ride was expensive and short, but worth it to both of them. Ricky handed the driver a twenty dollar bill and told him to keep the change. The driver grunted his approval, and added that they could have a ride any time. They hurried up the steps to the front door of the school, and were met by Lukas.

"I didn't just see you two get out of a cab." Luke challenged.

"Yeah, you did. It's friggin' cold out there. We froze our asses off just coming up her hill."

"Well, don't bother to take your coats off. No heat in the school. No lights either. A transformer or something blew. Hasn't been any heat in here in days. May even have broken pipes from the cold; I don't know. We're standing here to see whether they are going to cancel school for the day."

"Oh, great! We can't even get warm before we start the walk home." Ricky turned to Lindy and added. "We may be calling a cab again, Babe."

"Hey, no problem….I'll give you guys a ride home. And the car has a good heater."

"Really? Thanks, Luke."

The school principal, carrying a bull horn, came halfway down the hall announcing that classes were canceled for the day, and advised them to listen to the local news to see if school would be open tomorrow. There were some cheers, but mostly the students were just glad to get out of the icy cold school. Lindy and Ricky followed Luke to his car, and waited for him to unlock the doors. The car started, but it grinded a little before the engine kicked over. Ricky and Lindy huddled in the front passenger seat together while Luke revved the engine a little, trying to warm it up.

"It will be awhile before it's warm. So how was your Christmas? What did you get each other?"

Both Lindy and Ricky took off a glove to show Luke their rings.

"Nice. So is it official? You two are formally a twosome?"

"Yep. It's not like we weren't before, though."

"I agree with that. So what else did you two get?"

Lindy gave Luke the run-down on what all she got, and Ricky did the same.

"So what did you get, Luke?" Lindy asked.

"Oh, clothes….TV for my room…..gift certificates."

"What did Sara get you?" Lindy asked him.

"A couple of sweaters, a pair of jeans, a couple of CD's. I got her a gold chain and a sweater. I guess she liked it; she never really said. Are you both going to the same place or home alone?"

Ricky looked at Lindy. "Want to go to my place and help me dismantle the tree for Uncle Nick? I'm sure he would appreciate that."

"Okay….that's a good idea. Ricky's place, Luke."

As Luke pulled up in front of the condo, Ricky asked him if he'd like to come in for a cup of coffee. Luke accepted and pulled into the driveway. Ricky set about making coffee while Lindy retrieved cups from the cupboard, and the cream and sugar. Luke watched them from a chair at the kitchen table.

"I envy you two; you know that?" He sounded almost wistful.

"Why?" Ricky responded.

"Oh…I don't know. You work so well together…it's like you're the perfect couple. You get along so well."

Ricky laughed and grabbed Lindy around the waist. "She's my baby." He kissed Lindy quickly. "But seriously…. there are no head games here. I love her and she loves me. We don't try to get over on each other, or compete with each other. We're devoted to each other. We know where we want to be, and that's together. Do we always get along? Yes. Do we always agree? No. But we both want what is best for the other, so it works out. We don't get mad at each other; that would be a waste of precious time. We're always there for one another; you know? And we tell each other everything. We have no secrets and we are honest with each other. We can be honest, because we are both secure in knowing that no matter what we say to each other, we will still love each other. That's why we are so perfect together."

He grabbed Lindy's hand and kissed her fingers. Their eyes locked and they felt familiar electricity course through them. They realized the coffee was done and Ricky went to the counter to pour it into cups.

Luke drank a cup of coffee with them and got up to leave. Ricky and Lindy, arm in arm, walked him to the door. They watched him drive away, and then turned toward each other and embraced.

"Want to see my room?" Ricky whispered.

Lindy nodded. It was almost noon when Ricky and Lindy emerged from his bedroom. At the top of the stairs Ricky stopped and wrapped his arms around Lindy and pulled her close to him.

"I'm so in love with you; do you know that?" He whispered into her ear.

Lindy nodded. "I'm in love with you, too. Let's get the tree down and maybe….just maybe we can go back to your room." She smiled and wrinkled her nose, causing him to laugh from his throat.

He took her hand and started leading her in the opposite direction from the stairs.

"No, not now! Let's get the tree down first." She snapped.

"I'm leading you to the storage room to get the empty boxes for the lights and the ornaments. Gees! Is your mind always on sex?" He shot her a comical look which made her laugh.

They laughed together as they entered the storage room. When they had the empty boxes downstairs, Ricky called Nick to let him know that school had been canceled for the day and that he and Lindy would be taking down the tree.

"Is that okay with you, Uncle Nick?" Ricky spoke into the phone as he watched Lindy line up the boxes across the cushions of the sofa.

"Yeah, that's fine. So what happened that they had to cancel classes today?"

Ricky gave him the rundown about the power being out and having no heat, and about the pipes bursting.

"We have to watch the local news to see if there will be school tomorrow. With all the work that needs to be done, I doubt it."

"Yeah, me, too. So does this mean you'll be home an extra couple of days?"

"I guess…..why?"

"Oh…..I was just thinking of all the good meals I may be getting….that's all." Nick laughed at his own joke.

After Ricky hung up he relayed to Lindy what Nick had said.

"You know….he's been in a pretty good mood lately. I think he and Aunt Liz are back in love. She's been here a lot and he's been at her place a lot. Remember…..he spent the night there on New Year's Eve. He fell asleep…he said….right."

Lindy and Ricky laughed, and then set about dismantling the tree. By three o'clock the tree was ready to be carried outside. Lindy was glad she had suggested the tree bag that sat under the tree, ready to envelop the tree to be carried out. Ricky held the tree while Lindy removed the stand and then they wrapped the tree in its bag. Ricky carried it outside while Lindy began closing and stacking the boxes, now full of holiday decorations. After depositing the tree at the curb for pick-up, Ricky ran back inside and helped Lindy get the boxes up to the storage room. When the last box was put into its place, Ricky grabbed Lindy around the waist and led her to his room.

"Come here….I want to show you my desk top on my computer." When the screen came up, Lindy let out a short gasp. Ricky was using a picture of her as his desk top wall paper. "Cool, huh?"

Lindy stood behind him and surrounded his shoulders with her arms. "How did you do that?"

Ricky pointed to a flat oblong computer accessory sitting next to his computer. "That thing. It's a scanner. It came with my computer and I just recently learned how to use it. Really cool, isn't it? Here, let me send this to your computer." Ricky went online and typed in Lindy's email address on his Internet Explorer, and then went into his files and added her picture as an attachment to the email. He clicked on the 'send' icon. "When you open your email, you will have the picture from me. That's really cool, isn't it?"

"Yeah, it is. Maybe I should get one, too. Can you add it to a computer you already have?"

"I think you can, unless your computer is too old to be compatible for it. But what the hell are we talking about computers for?"

Ricky twisted around, pulled Lindy down onto his lap, and covered her mouth with his. Her lips parted and she accepted the tip of his tongue, as she met it with hers. They made their way to the bed, Ricky undressing her as they slowly moved across the room.

\* \* \*

It was almost five-thirty. Nick would be home at six. They quickly made the bed and dressed, and then ran downstairs. Ricky immediately began pulling out pots and utensils, while Lindy opened the refrigerator and went to the vegetable bin. The kitchen was full of cooking smells when Nick walked through the door at six o'clock. He smiled at them as they stood in the kitchen together.

"The place looks good. How did you get it all done so fast? I thought there would be stuff still lying around to be carried upstairs. You two must have worked non-stop all day. I'll have to come up with some sort of reward, I guess."

Lindy and Ricky laughed.

"Sure....we'll take it." Ricky grinned at Nick.

Lindy's attention became focused on the television news broadcast. The newscaster mentioned their high school, and ended with saying there would be more when they came back. The station then went to a commercial. Lindy waited until the news came back on and listened for the details of the school's problems. It was declared that there would be no school again tomorrow, and possibly not until the following week, since there had been extensive damage due to the cold.

"That's okay by me. Maybe it will be warmer by next week." Lindy said as she sighed.

"Yeah, we froze our rear-ends off, Uncle Nick. I finally hailed a cab to take us the last few blocks. We couldn't take it any more."

"Wimps. When I was your age I walked 2 miles to school and two miles back....all uphill." Nick burst out laughing. "Seriously...maybe I should change my schedule a little bit and give you kids a ride to school just until this cold snap ends. Think you'd like that?"

"Oh, yeah! That would be great." They both answered.

\* \* \*

Lindy ran out when she heard the BMW pull into the driveway. After an extra week off from school she was ready to return to the academic environment. She and Ricky spent a lot of time together during that week, even braving the cold to go to the mall one day. Of course, they also spent quite a few hours in bed together, just learning and exploring each other. Lindy was experiencing less and less discomfort, but still wasn't enjoying it like Ricky said she would. Ricky seemed to be having all the pleasure and she was beginning to resent him for it. She knew it was time to express her feelings, or it would drive a wedge between them.

Ricky held the door open for her as she hopped into the front seat.

"Are you ready to go back?" Nick smiled at her.

"Yeah, I guess. The longer we stay out the longer we have to go in June, so it's better to go back now."

"Good thinking." Nick smiled at her again.

Nick dropped them off at the school and continued on his way to the hospital. He was meeting Liz for breakfast in the hospital cafeteria. He wondered to himself how this had happened. They parted as enemies, and now here they were, seeing each other—going out together—again. Neither one of them tried to hide their feelings this time, so maybe they stood a better chance than they had last time. Nick parked the car in a 'Reserved for Doctors' space and headed toward the cafeteria. She was waiting for him.

"So did you get the kids to school?"

"Yeah….they said they could get a ride home, so I won't have to go pick them up. It's damn cold out. I'm glad I'm able to give them a ride, because it's definitely too cold to walk. So what are we having for breakfast? Do you want to eat here or play hooky for awhile and go to the diner?"

Liz's face lit up. "That's a marvelous idea. I'm ready."

They left the cafeteria and drove to their favorite diner. Although it was crowded, there were still tables and booths available. They chose a small booth and slipped into it, turning over the coffee cups in preparation for the coffee that they knew the waitress would come by and pour out of the pot.

"So are you going to that conference next weekend?" Liz asked.

"Yeah, I booked a couple of months ago. Why? Are you going?"

"Actually, yes. I booked my flight before Christmas, but I haven't gotten a hotel room yet. I'm having a hard time finding one close to the conference center."

Nick smiled at her. "I have a room….a double room. Interested in bunking with me?"

Liz stared at him and chewed on her lip. Nick knew she was considering the offer when she did that.

"Take in a show and a couple of dinners?"

"Sure."

"It's a deal, then." She smiled her widest smile.

Nick's face took on a serious look. "I hope Angie will come down here next weekend. I don't feel comfortable about leaving Ricky alone."

"My God, Nick….he's almost seventeen."

"Yes, and so is Lindy. Hormones. I don't know…it's an open invitation to put the hormones in gear."

"Oh. Do you think they've gone that far yet?"

"I don't know. Listen….could you maybe talk to Lindy about….you know, birth control? The way those two look at each other sometimes…."

"Okay. Next time I see her I'll suggest we go for lunch or something. This is a mother's job, you know."

"I know….but Lindy doesn't have that luxury."

"True. I'll do it. We have a good rapport."

\* \* \*

Angie answered the phone on the second ring.

"Nick…..what's wrong? Is Ricky okay?"

"Yeah, yeah, Angie….he's fine. Listen….I have a conference I have to go to next weekend. I was wondering if you would be able to come here that weekend. You know.....to keep an eye on things."

"Oh.....you scared me. I thought something was wrong. Yeah, I can come then. I'll be glad to. Hey, Nick, listen.....I think I may have a buyer for the house. The couple is coming back to look again tomorrow. They really like it; especially the room that Enrico refinished. I only hope they can get the financing."

"Well, that's good news, Angie....if the deal goes through. Say a prayer."

"Oh, and even better news is that the realtor says he can help me find a place in your area, since they have a branch there."

"That's great, Angie."

"So how is Ricky? Still not giving you any problems?"

"No....not at all. I enjoy having him here....and Lindy, too. They're like a breath of fresh air all the time."

"So that relationship is still going strong, huh?"

"It appears that way. That's one reason why I would like you to be here while I'm in New York. To, you know....keep the hormones in check."

Angie laughed. "I know all too well, Nick. I'll be glad to come. Listen, there's the doorbell. It's another couple coming to look. Can't put all my eggs in one basket, right?"

"Right, Angie. Talk to you soon."

Nick hung up satisfied that the worry of leaving Ricky, and Lindy, alone was taken care of. He picked up his itinerary for the conference and began reading through it, already picking and choosing what he wanted to sit through. He was looking forward to this conference, mainly because he would be there with Liz. Liz….how did this start again? He remembered how it had been on New Year's Eve. The passion….the hunger. It had been a night to remember. No matter what they didn't have, they still had that wild abandon in bed going for them. But who was he kidding? They had all the rest of what it took to make a relationship as well. She said he had changed. Maybe. Matured? Definitely. The anger was still there, but he controlled it better. Liz had changed, too. She wasn't that up-tight, proper bitch she used to be. She was more relaxed; easier to get along with. Everything doesn't have to be 'just so' like it had in the past. She is more down to earth now. His thoughts were interrupted by the ringing telephone. He picked up the receiver, thinking it might have been Angie calling back. It was Liz.

"Hi." She spoke tentatively.

"Hi. What's up? I was just going to call you. Ricky must be at Lindy's so I thought maybe you and I could go for a quick impromptu dinner somewhere. Up for it?"

"Yeah, I am. Do you want to pick me up or meet me somewhere?"

"I'll pick you up. Leaving right now." He hung up.

# Chapter 21

$\mathcal{L}$indy and Ricky were walking up the hill on their way to school. The temperatures had gone up within the past week. It wasn't exactly sweater weather, but it was bearable. Nick had left early that morning and would not be back until late Sunday night. While Ricky watched him pack his suitcase the night before, Nick told him his mother would be there after school sometime on Friday. He relayed all of this to Lindy as they walked. Lindy was exceptionally quiet.

"Something wrong?" He asked her.

She started to shake her head in denial, but changed her mind. "It's…..nothing…..really. Maybe I'm being overly sensitive…or maybe I'm expecting too much too soon."

Ricky stopped walking. "What is it? Talk to me."

"Well….it's just….well, you seem to be the only one of us who is enjoying the sex. I mean…..it doesn't hurt much any more…..but…."

"It's not feeling great yet…..right? No orgasm, no climax…."

Lindy shook her head.

Ricky stared at her for a moment. "Well, guess what? We're going to change all that…next time. I promise. Next time will be different. Trust me. I'm glad you told me how you feel." He took her face in his hand and kissed her lightly. "That's all you ever have to do. Just tell me." He put his arm around her shoulders and squeezed them lightly. "I love you." He said.

They parted just inside the main entrance, knowing that they had a class together in a little more than an hour. The school smelled clean and appeared to be brighter than before Christmas. Lindy imagined that they must have done some major cleaning over the long holiday and the extended break after the New Year. She hurried to her homeroom, already missing Ricky.

Ricky entered his homeroom feeling as though a part of him was missing. He knew it was Lindy that was missing. They had grown so close, especially over the holiday and the extended week, that it was hard not to have her next to him.

They got through their morning classes and met for lunch. Lindy was wearing a striking two-piece black and white striped dress with a short fitted black knit bolero over it, and Ricky couldn't help but comment on it.

"You look great in that. Wow! Those boots go with it perfectly." Ricky noted as he looked down at her soft kid black boots that ended at the bottom of her knee.

"Thanks. You always say the right things; you know that?" She leaned over and kissed his cheek; taking note that Carrie was watching them from two tables over. "We're being watched," she whispered.

"I can guess by whom. She's in my first period class. All she talked about was her stupid party before the class started. She told me I should have come, so I told her I was going to, until I found out she was going to be there.

Lindy laughed. "Why doesn't she take a hint that you're not interested?"

"She's not used to being turned down, I guess. That's one of the first things I don't like about her. Spoiled. Oh, and Luke told me she got into trouble with her dad for what she did to you in the gym. Sara told Luke that Carrie's dad told her he was really disappointed in her and that she could destroy his image by such behavior. She got grounded for two weeks."

"Not long enough." Lindy quipped.

"I agree. Let's take a walk out in the hall. She's staring at us again."

They walked out of the lunchroom, hands linked together, unaware that Carrie's eyes were once again boring a hole in their backs. On their way out, Lindy was complimented on her outfit by a couple of the other students, which annoyed Carrie even more.

Ricky went to a study hall and Lindy went to her music class. They would meet at the auditorium and walk to their last class together. After the music class, Lindy waited for Ricky. She grinned when she saw him, and he slipped his arm around her waist. They walked to their English Literature class quickly and found their usual seats. The class began promptly; the teacher surveying the room.

"Class, today we begin to read the love story of Romeo and Juliet. Now….Romeo and Juliet were very much in love….so much in love that they were willing to die for each other. Can you imagine anyone being that much in love?"

"Yeah…..those two." Luke piped up and pointed to Ricky and Lindy. "We have our own Romeo and Juliet right in this classroom."

The class roared with laughter, Lindy and Ricky included.

"Hey…I'm not ashamed of it." Ricky grinned at Luke.

"So….Ricky…..would you commit suicide for Lindy?" The teacher thought she was being cute.

"No….I'm not suicidal…..but I'd kill to protect her." He replied pointedly.

"And, Lindy….would you commit suicide for Ricky?" The teacher pressed on.

"No, I'm not suicidal either. But I'd die defending him." Lindy spoke with conviction.

"Well…..close enough, then. All right……let's begin reading." The teacher quickly turned to page one of Romeo and Juliet.

\* \* \*

Classes ended for the week. Lindy and Ricky moved quickly out of the school and down the steps to the sidewalk.

"Wow….those clouds are creeping in." Ricky stared up at the sky. "I think it's too warm to snow just now…but I think we're going to get some rain. Let's get moving so we don't get caught in it. My mom should be at Uncle Nick's soon, so I'll just have her come down and pick you up a little later…okay? We can play cards or watch TV….maybe rent a movie. Sound okay to you?"

"Yeah….sounds fine. You sure she won't mind picking me up?"

"Of course not. She really likes you."

They were halfway down the hill to Lindy's house when she spotted her father's truck in the driveway.

"What's *he* doing home?" She wondered aloud. "Go ahead back to your place. I never know what mood he's going to be in. It goes from sullen to angry then back to sullen, and then miserable. Call me when your mom gets there....okay?"

She kissed him quickly, and then made a bee-line for her front door. Ricky hesitated, wondering if she were going to be all right. He felt uneasy about something, but he didn't know what. He turned and walked toward home, lighting a cigarette on the way.

Lindy could hear voices when she entered the house. She heard her father's voice, and then a woman's voice. Slowly, she made her way down the hall, being careful not to make any noise.

"Let's hurry up.....she'll be home soon." She heard her father say to the unknown woman. They were in her father's bedroom, but the door was standing open.

Lindy heard the unknown woman say, "When are you going to tell her about us? It's been six months."

"I will. She was close to her mother. I think it will be hard for her to accept another woman into the house; you know? Besides, we don't talk much. I want to leave before she gets home....I guess I should write her a note."

Lindy went to the doorway of her father's room. They hadn't seen her yet. She stared at her father's and this strange woman's back. The woman was blonde—dyed blonde—not natural like her mother's hair. Lindy spoke, forcing the words around the lump that suddenly appeared in her throat.

"Would the *she* in question be *me*?" Her voice was just above a whisper.

Ray Riley jumped and turned around. "Lindy....I've been meaning to talk to you..."

"For almost three years now." Lindy finished the sentence. "Sure you have." She stared at her father, unwavering. "So who's your friend?"

The woman made an effort to be friendly. "Hi, Lindy.... my name is Diane. I've been dying to meet you....."

"Why?" Lindy wouldn't budge toward friendship with this woman.

"Well, because.....I like your father....and....I would like for you and me to be friends."

"Why do you think that's necessary? My father hasn't spoken to me in almost three years. He has forgotten every holiday, every birthday, and every event of my life. Did he tell you I was in a musical? I had the lead role. Did he tell you that? Probably not, because he didn't care enough to attend."

"Lindy...." Ray spoke.

"No........let her know the truth. You have ignored me for almost three years. *THREE YEARS*! What do you think about that, Diane? I thought it was because he missed my mother. I thought it was because he was hurting. I thought it was because every time he looked at me he saw her. I made excuses for him." Lindy swallowed, and wiped the involuntary tears from her cheeks, and then began again. "I created reasons for why you ignored me, Dad. But you're not sad; you're not lonely; and you don't miss mom. The real reason is that you ***JUST DON'T FREAKING CARE!!***"

Diane touched Ray's elbow. "Ray, maybe we better postpone this weekend. Maybe you should stay here."

"Oh, no….by all means….go! Go have a good time with her! Maybe it will make you talk to me eventually!" Lindy was sobbing now.

Ray spoke for the first time. "Lindy…I'm going away for the weekend. I'll be back Sunday night. We'll talk then. Yes, I miss your mother, but I….I have needs, Lindy."

*"Well, what about my needs?"*

*"Your needs?* You're sixteen. What needs to *you* have?"

**"I need a father!"**

"We need to talk, Lindy."

"It's too late for that. ***You can go to hell, for all I care!***"

Lindy ran into her room and slammed the door and locked it. Leaning against the door, she sobbed and sobbed. She had never spoken to anybody like that. She heard her father and the woman—Diane—go out through the front door, and then she heard the truck pull out of the driveway. Still sobbing, she grabbed some things and threw them into a small suitcase. She tried Ricky's number and got a busy signal. She then tried the cell phone and it went to voice mail. "Probably on the charger." She said aloud. Pulling on sweatpants and a sweatshirt, she grabbed a jacket and the small bag she had packed and ran out the door. Before pulling the door shut, she stepped back in and grabbed her purse and key, and then re-exited the door, closing it behind her. It was pouring—pouring hard. She ran. She ran and ran until she got to Ricky's front door. She pounded on the door and rang the doorbell at the same time, still crying.

Ricky yanked the door open, angered by the rude urgency of the intrusion. He stopped when he saw Lindy standing there out of breath and sobbing, and drenched to the skin.

"Baby, what's wrong? What happened?"

He extended his hands toward her, and that was all it took for her to fall against him, crying. She was soaked to the skin, and soon had the front of his clothes wet, too. He held her in his arms for a few minutes, and then held her at arm's length.

"Wait right here. Let me get you some towels….and something dry to put on. Take your shoes off."

He ran up the stairs and disappeared. He reappeared with two towels and a heavy terrycloth robe.

"Come on in here." He led her through the kitchen to the laundry room. "Here….take your clothes off and throw them in the dryer. You can put this robe on. Dry your hair the best you can. Damn, Lindy….I don't want you getting *sick*. I'm going to put on some water for tea. Then you can tell me what the hell happened….*okay*?"

Lindy nodded, still shivering from the cold rain. Ricky went out to the kitchen and she could hear him filling the tea kettle with water. She stripped down, dried off, wrapped a towel around her hair, and slipped into the terrycloth robe. It felt so warm and soft against her skin. She pulled the robe's sash tightly around her waist and tied it. Ricky was pouring water into two cups with teabags in them. He looked up when she emerged from the laundry room, and noticed that she had quit crying for the moment. He carried the cups to the kitchen table, and got out the sugar and lemon juice, and then he reached for her.

"Now come here." He pulled her down on his lap and kissed her. "Tell me what happened."

Lindy related the story about her dad and the woman. She was crying again. "I told him to go have fun with her, and then I told him to go to hell…."

"My baby's got some fight in her….how about that?" He gently tweaked her shoulders.

Lindy started talking again. "All this time….I thought he was lonely….I thought he was hurting…sad because my mother was gone. I made excuses for him. Ricky….he had *Thanksgiving* with her….he had *Christmas* with her…. all the while…ignoring *me*."

This brought on fresh tears. Ricky surrounded her with his arms and held on to her tightly. It was breaking his heart to see her like this. He held her, gently rubbing his hand up and down her back, until she stopped crying. He sighed.

"I hate seeing you hurt. I love you so much. Hey…. are you hungry?"

"Probably. I haven't eaten. I'm just so upset right now." Lindy remembered that Ricky's mother was supposed to be there. "Where's your mom?"

"She's not coming. She called a little while ago. Somebody hit her car and demolished it. She wasn't in it….it was parked."

"Oh….I'm glad she wasn't in it. She's insured, I hope."

"Oh, yeah….but anyway, this means it's just….you and me….all weekend. What do you think about *that*?" He smiled at her and stared into her eyes. The electricity between them emerged immediately.

"I think it's as it should be." She smiled for the first time since he opened the door to her.

Ricky made a light dinner of grilled cheese and tomato soup—Lindy's favorite. They sat together at the kitchen table eating and talking.

"You know....I don't care that he has a girlfriend..... that's not it. But to give her all the attention while he ignored me for all these years....that's what hurts."

"I know. I know exactly how you feel, Babe. He could have included you in on the holiday with her. Brought her around once in awhile, maybe."

"Or how about just speaking to me for the past three years? Remembering my birthday? Coming to see me in musicals? Bought me a Christmas present? Oh, I'm done...I am so *done*!"

"So what's the woman like?"

Lindy sighed. "She's probably not that bad. She tried reaching out to me, I guess. It's shame she got caught up in the middle of it all."

"So would you make an effort to get to know her if you had the chance? Just asking."

Lindy shrugged her shoulders. "I don't know. Maybe. But I think my dad would have to make a very big effort toward me first. She's not the issue....he is."

"Hey, let's watch some TV or a movie. Want to?"

They got up from the kitchen table, stacked their dishes in the sink, and then curled up on the sofa together; putting Ricky in charge of the remote. A good comedy on 'pay-per-view' not only held their interest, but kept them laughing until almost midnight. Ricky got up and retrieved Lindy's clothes from the dryer, and folded them for her. He returned to the sofa with the pile of dried clothing, and wrapped his arms around her.

"You don't have a thing on under that robe, do you?"

"Uh….no…no, I don't." She gave him a sly grin.

"Remember my promise?" He whispered.

"Um-hmm." Her voice was barely audible.

"I'm going to keep my promise, Sweetie. Let's go upstairs to bed."

Ricky turned off the television, locked the door, and turned out the lights. He took Lindy's hand and led her upstairs to his room, where he shed his shirt and pants. He turned to Lindy and very slowly undid the sash to the robe, and then peeled the robe from her shoulders, letting it drop to the floor. Slowly and deliberately, he kissed her, caressing her cheeks with his thumbs. Still kissing her, he picked her up and deposited her gently on the bed. He quickly shed the rest of his clothing and lay down beside her. Ever so lightly, he caressed her body, just barely touching it. His mouth trailed down her neck to her throat, and then lower to her breasts. He teased her breasts with his tongue, causing the nipples to harden. Lindy moaned a little.

"Like that?" Ricky whispered.

"Um…hmmm." She swooned.

His mouth went lower to her navel, his tongue making circles around it. His mouth traveled lower and then lower. He gently parted her legs and his tongue reached out for her clitoris. He teased it until he felt it harden a little, and then plunged into her with his tongue. Lindy gasped.

"Oh my God!" She was breathless. "Oh, Ricky….oh my God!"

Ricky continued to work his tongue in and out of her until her felt her stiffen.

"Oh God, Ricky."

He felt her spasms begin, and he quickly positioned himself on top of her, sliding into her and holding it deeply inside of her while the spasms continued. He was aroused to the fullest, her spasms heightening his erection. He felt his own spasms begin as he pressed deeply inside of her. He exploded inside of her, causing more spasms from her. She clung to him, her breathing ragged. Ricky could feel her heart pounding. His own heart was booming in his ears. He slipped his hands under her and held her tightly, feeling a little dizzy. They lay that way for several minutes, until they both were breathing normally. Ricky was the first to move. He pulled himself up on his elbows and stared down into her face. She smiled up at him and he kissed her lightly.

"Wow…that felt incredible." She gasped. "You kept your promise." She smiled at him again.

Ricky rolled off of her and cradled her in his arms. They slept fitfully in that position until morning.

\* \* \*

Ricky awoke first. He quietly slipped out of bed so as not to wake her, and padded down the stairs. First he started the coffee and then he got out the frying pan. Quickly and efficiently, he made a breakfast fit for a queen and king and carried it upstairs on a large tray. Lindy opened her eyes when Ricky approached the bed. He smiled down at her.

"Breakfast, my love."

"Oh, wow….Ricky. You spoil me."

"And I love every minute of it."

"Yeah, well…me too." She smiled at him.

"And….I have a surprise after we have breakfast."

Lindy cocked her head. "What is it?"

"It's a surprise….that's what it is. You'll find out. Now….are you ready for breakfast?"

They grinned at each other just before they demolished the food. Ricky set the tray aside when they had finished, and took Lindy's hand and pulled her up out of bed.

"Now for the surprise. Grab the robe."

She put the robe on and followed him out of the room. He stopped and put his arm around her and covered her eyes with his free hand.

"Keep your eyes closed."

She obeyed his command, as he led her down the hall. She heard a door open and they walked a little further. He stopped her and told her to open her eyes. To her delight, they were standing in front of Uncle Nick's Jacuzzi.

"The water's already hot. I turned it on before I made breakfast. Want to sit in it awhile?"

He didn't have to ask her twice; she already started down the steps into it, shedding the robe. Ricky followed her, dropping his robe, as well. After spending an hour in the Jacuzzi, they wondered downstairs together in their robes. Ricky stopped in the bedroom and picked up the breakfast tray first. Lindy poured fresh coffee into their cups and they sat down at the kitchen table, content and happy to be together.

"You know, Babe….I could get used to this. You and me together, alone. It's like we're married….and it's nice."

"Do you think Uncle Nick will let us get married and live with him?"

Lindy's question took Ricky by surprise. He jerked his head up in time to see her hiding her mischievous grin behind her hand. They burst out laughing together. After cleaning up the kitchen, they showered and dressed. It had gotten very cold outside during the night. There was ice on the windows, and by the looks of the streets, they were icy. It was a good day to spend playing cards, which is what they did. Ricky's mother called to check up on him, and he told her he was studying for a test, and 'no, Lindy was at home because it was too icy to come out.' Angie seemed satisfied by that, because she didn't call again until the next day. Ricky was satisfied by that. Toward evening, they ordered pizza and found a good movie on the television. Curled up together on the sofa, they ate their pizza and watched the movie, then turned to the news, just to make sure they weren't missing anything big happening in the world. At eleven-thirty, they went to bed. Their love-making was slow and tender, bringing Lindy to another orgasm. Afterward, they lay spent in each other's arms, falling asleep happy and contented. Sunday morning. They lazed in bed all morning, making love more than once. They couldn't get enough of each other. When they finally got up for the day, they stripped the bed and washed the sheets. Ricky cooked brunch for them while the sheets were being washed. Lindy put the sheets into the dryer and they went back upstairs to take a shower—this time together. They touched and teased each other until they ended up on the unmade sheetless bed, making love again. Their weekend was coming to an end. Nick would be home by nine that evening and Lindy's father would be returning, too. Lindy got her things together and Ricky walked her home. They embraced inside the door, and then kissed.

"I don't want to leave you. It's like every time we separate, I feel like my arm is cut off or something....you know? Something is just missing when you're not with me."

"I know. I feel it, too. I love you....so much, Ricky."

"Me, too, Baby....me, too."

Ricky kissed her again and then headed up the hill toward home. Lindy took her things into her room, got out her clothes for the next day, and then turned off the lights, locked her bedroom door, and went to sleep. She heard her father come in around ten o'clock. She lay there in the dark listening to his movements. She heard him walk down the hallway and stop in front of her door. She waited silently. He stood outside her room for a minute or two, and then walked down the hall to his room. She heard him go in and shut the door. 'Nice talk we just had, dad,' she thought to herself. She knew she was being unfair, because he probably thought she was sleeping and wouldn't want to wake her; but she didn't care. He had been unfair to her all this time. She fell back asleep, thinking of Ricky.

\* \* \*

Nick unlocked the door and dropped his suitcase to the floor. 'Home, Sweet, Home', he thought to himself. The conference had been tedious, long, and boring for the most part. He looked around and saw that nothing seemed amiss. He wondered when Angie left. Ricky came out of his room to greet him.

"Hi....welcome home. How was everything?"

"Boring. When did your mother leave?"

"She never came."

"*What*? Why the hell *not*?"

"Her car got demolished."

Nick turned his head toward Ricky quickly. "She all right?"

"Yeah, she wasn't in the car when it happened. The car was parked. Anyway, now she needs a new car. Good thing she has insurance."

"Yeah…I'll say. So what did you do all weekend? Hanky-panky with Lindy?"

Ricky laughed, and then told Nick about Lindy catching her father with a woman.

"Lindy was really upset. It took quite awhile to calm her down. It's not the woman Lindy is upset about…that she could handle. It's that he spent all the holidays with this woman. He had a Thanksgiving and a Christmas with this woman, and ignored Lindy. Poor Lindy….she really snapped on him. Told him to go to hell. You know Lindy doesn't talk like that; so you can imagine how upset she was."

"Man….her old man is so insensitive. What an asshole. Lindy okay?"

Ricky nodded. "Yeah, she's okay. Just very sad. It broke my heart to see her crying like that. So…Uncle Nick…. are you hungry? Want some coffee or something?"

"Ricky, your coffee would hit the spot right now. Would you mind making a pot?"

Ricky grinned and moved toward the kitchen to start a pot of coffee.

# Chapter 22

Ricky and Lindy stopped on the bridge and looked down at 'their place'. It was the last day of February and the weather was showing promise of a few spring-like days ahead. It was that time of year when Mother Nature teased her audience with a couple of nice days here and there, only to turn cold and blustery again. Today was one of those nice days. The temperature was close to fifty degrees, the sun was shining, and the air was still. Lindy had been silent most of the way up the hill from her place, leaving Ricky to do most of the talking. She felt the weight of her book bag pressing into her shoulder, but it was not as heavy as the weight pressing on her mind.

"You're quiet, Baby....Something wrong?" Ricky's face showed real concern.

Lindy didn't answer him. She just stared over the railing at the place below the bridge.

"Hey...Lindy? Okay....what's up? I know something is wrong." He pressed.

Lindy sighed. "I'm late."

"No, we have a lot of...."

"No. *Me....I'm* late."

The realization finally hit him. "Oh.....no. How late?"

"Twelve days…." Lindy began to cry.

Ricky dropped his book bag and reached for her, wrapping her in his arms.

"Okay….don't cry. Let's not panic. No, too late…. we're panicking. Okay….uh, look…..I know we're young…..but we do love each other, right? We can handle this. There's nothing we can't handle as long as we're together…right?"

"Oh, Ricky….I'm scared. I don't know what to do… I…"

"Shh….okay….don't cry, Honey. We have to think. Twelve days….that's not all that late…..fuck…who am I kidding? It was that weekend….that weekend when Uncle Nick was in New York. I just know it. That's the only time I wasn't really careful." He sighed. "I was just caught up in us being together…like we were married. It was so great….."

"Oh, God….and now I'm *pregnant.*" Lindy started sobbing.

"Honey….don't. We'll figure something out. Don't worry." He took her face between his palms. "Look at me, Sweetheart; look at me."

She looked into his eyes, her vision blurred by tears. She was shivering all of a sudden.

"Lindy, for the record……*You're* not pregnant….*we* are. Okay? *You and me.* Us. We're in this together. I'm right beside you, just like I'll always be."

Lindy fell into his arms, clinging tightly to him. "Oh, Ricky….I love you so much."

"And I love you, Babe….forever."

They walked the rest of the way to school with their arms around each other. As they entered the school through the main entrance, Lindy handed Ricky her book bag.

"Hold this…..I'm going to be sick."

She made a bee-line for the girls' bathroom and barely made it to a stall before heaving up her breakfast. Ricky stood outside in the hall waiting for her. He saw Carrie and Sara come out of the bathroom. He knew that their visual communication with each other and the smirk on their faces had to do with Lindy, and he wanted to smash them both in their faces. Looking drained, Lindy finally emerged from the bathroom. Ricky hugged her and kissed the top of her head.

"We'll be okay….I promise." He whispered.

\* \* \*

It was a balmy day in mid-March. Lindy and Ricky walked home together as usual. When they got to Lindy's Ricky followed her into the house and shut the door behind him. Lindy was about to take her third pregnancy test, using the test kit they bought at the drugstore on the way home. The other two tests came out positive, but they still hoped there was a chance that they could be wrong.

"Go ahead. I'll wait." Ricky gave her shoulders a quick squeeze for encouragement, and then he sat down on a stool in front of the kitchen counter to wait. He spied a note for Lindy from her father, and picked it up to read it. In very neat handwriting, the note simply stated that he had to go out of town to work and would not be home until late the following Friday. Under the note were three one-hundred dollar bills that were for whatever she needed, according to the note.

Lindy sighed when she came from the bathroom. "It couldn't get any more positive. What's that?" She asked Ricky, referring to the note and the money in his hand.

"Well, apparently you will be alone all week." He handed her the note.

"And this is different *how*?" She dropped the note on the counter and sighed again.

"I don't have to go right home…..can I stay for awhile?"

"Of course. Let's see what we can eat here. Maybe it'll be my turn to cook. I'm not as good at it as you are, but…. I try." She smiled at him.

Ricky opened the refrigerator door and Lindy opened a cupboard door.

"Hmmm…..don't know. See anything appealing?" She asked him.

"Pancakes. You have bacon in here and I see pancake mix in that cupboard. How about pancakes? I love those for dinner. My dad and I used to eat them when my mother worked late. It was one of our special times we had together….mom working and me and dad eating pancakes."

"Pancakes it is, then." Lindy turned and reached for the box of pancake mix, but not before Ricky saw the tears in the corners of her eyes.

He reached for her and pulled her to him. "I'm sorry. That was insensitive of me. I….I'm really sorry."

"It's okay. I like it when you talk about your dad. Your whole face lights up. It still hurts, but I guess I'm sort of getting used to not having parents. Funny, now I'm going to be one."

"Wow.....yeah...we are; aren't we? Kind of scary, but kind of cool, too. When do you think it will be born?"

"Well....let's see." Lindy silently counted on her fingers. "I think mid-October. I guess I have to see a doctor before too long."

"I think we should see about getting married."

"Ricky, no state is going to allow it. We have to be eighteen or have our parents' consent."

"Well....maybe we'll get the consent."

"Fat chance of that. Your mother plans on you going to college. My dad...well, I have no idea what he plans for me....but I sincerely doubt that he'll allow me to get married."

"Other people have done it...."

"Yeah, I'm sure....but....."

"Lindy, you're not thinking about an abortion.....are you?"

"It would be the easy way out.....but....I'm not sure I could go through with it. No....I'm not thinking of abortion. Are you....thinking....?"

"*Oh...hell, no*! That's my kid in there....*our* kid..... no...not a *chance*."

"So what do we do? God, I miss my mother....." Tears sprung into her eyes as she looked away. Ricky saw the tears and pulled her to him, resting his cheek on her hair.

"Hoping for a laugh, Ricky quipped, "You're crying.... that means I have to cook."

Lindy did laugh. Her laugh sounded like a melody to him.

\* \* \*

205

Nick disconnected the call on his cell phone by snapping it shut. The phone rang immediately.

"Hi, Uncle Nick……"

"I just tried to call you. Where are you?"

"Uh, I'm at Lindy's. I called to say that I'm having dinner here….."

"Oh, well….I called to tell you I wouldn't be home for dinner….so that works out. Be home by midnight…. got it?"

"Yeah, got it." Ricky hung up and turned to Lindy. "I think he's having dinner out…with a certain ex-aunt I have….who happens to be his ex-wife….." Ricky raised and lowered his eyebrows several times, making Lindy laugh.

"So, Sherlock…..I'm going to cook these now. I'm hungry."

\* \* \*

Nick helped Liz into his car, and then went around the front of the car to the driver's side. Liz had already unlocked his door, as he knew she would. It was one of those little things that he always appreciated about her. He still thought he must be nuts, going out with her. Considering where it led last time they started going out, he had to wonder why he was setting himself up again. Why did he ask her to dinner tonight? It's not like he was lonely and dying for company. There was Ricky, and most of the time, Lindy, to talk to.

"Well, you're a million miles away." Her voice broke into his thoughts.

"Oh…..sorry…..I'm right here now. Any place in particular you would like to have dinner? I didn't get a reservation anywhere since.....well, I hadn't planned on going out for dinner. It was completely spontaneous."

"Oh, well, there's a new side to you. Spontaneity."

"What? You don't think I was spontaneous?"

"Nope...not at all. Volatile, yes...but spontaneous? No."

Nick laughed. "Okay....touché. So where do you want to have dinner?"

"Anywhere, as long as it's seafood. Is that okay with you?"

"It's better than okay....now I know where we're going."

They rode in silence until Liz broke it. "Do you think we....I don't know...that we could have stayed together if we had gone for counseling?"

"I don't know. The big question is....would I have gone for counseling?"

"That's a good point."

"I think I would now....but back then, probably not. I was a real hard ass....I know that. I know I've softened some....well, maybe a little."

"I think a lot. You've softened a lot. You never would have even admitted to being a hard ass. I don't know, Nick.....I see you with Ricky, and even Lindy, and I see a side I never saw before. Maybe we should have had kids.... I don't know. Maybe we should have given the marriage more of a chance....."

"We could try again...." Nick inwardly winced. 'I don't believe I just said that!'

"Let's give it some time; shall we? Go slow....slower than we did last time." Liz paused for a moment. "Nick, can I say something?" She dove in without waiting for his consent. "You've changed….you've change a lot. So far…. I like what I see."

Liz studied his profile after the words were out, waiting for a reaction. She saw his lips go up in a smile—exactly the reaction she had hoped for. He reached over and grabbed her hand and squeezed it gently.

He found a parking space in the restaurant parking lot. The place was not crowded for a Friday night, he noted gleefully. He never did get used to large crowds. He always preferred an empty restaurant to a crowded one, no matter how terrible the food might be.

Once they were seated, Liz asked him about Angie.

"She thinks she may have the house sold. Now she wants a job in the hospital. She's a medical records-patient information specialist. I told her there would have to an opening…"

"But with the expansion, there just may be. As soon as either of us hears about an opening, we need to get a hold of her right away. I'm sure Tom would consider her, since she's your sister, and my ex-sister-in-law."

"Well, it's not up to him. She would have to go through Human Resources."

"But he could endorse her…."

"Yeah, that's true."

They stopped talking as the waiter brought their water and silverware. They ordered drinks from him, and watched him head toward the bar to get them. Nick was staring at Liz's eyes. 'They're incredible,' he thought to himself.

"So…how are the young lovers doing?"

Nick's reaction was a combination of a sigh and a laugh. It came out more like a snort. He shook his head.

"They are cute. Ricky waits on her hand and foot. I have no idea if they are actually lovers yet. It scares me to think about it. They're so young, yet they have every element to make a good union. They're considerate of each other, they never fight, they work well together, and they always seem to be on the same page. And I see the chemistry between them. It's scary."

Liz smiled. "They look great together....have you noticed?"

"Yeah, I have. They're what people call a beautiful couple....like us. Remember when people said that about us?"

"Do I ever! It used to drive me crazy because all we ever did behind the scenes was fight."

"I wonder why that was. We aren't fighting now."

"Maybe we both had something to prove...or maybe we both expected more than we were getting."

The waiter brought their food to the table. Liz had gone with the seafood platter, where there were three different types of seafood on the plate, and Nick had opted for the lobster. Liz immediately placed a sample of each on Nick's plate.

"Old habits...." Nick chuckled.

They enjoyed the meal as well as each other's company, lingering over coffee much longer than they had planned. It was well past ten o'clock when Nick paid the check and they walked out of the restaurant, arm in arm. The ride to Liz's apartment was spent in pleasant and comfortable silence. Nick pulled up in front of her building, cut off the headlights, and turned off the engine. He turned to look at Liz, who simultaneously turned to look at him.

"Want to come in for a nightcap?" Liz's voice was almost a whisper.

Nick nodded.

\* \* \*

Ricky and Lindy finished the dishes and sat down at the kitchen table.

"Cards? Do you have any board games? Or do you want to watch television?"

Lindy smiled at him, got up and reached for his hand. She led him to the bedroom, and then closed and locked the bedroom door. Smiling up at him, she whispered, "I can't get pregnant *now*."

Surprised, Ricky just stared into her eyes. He took her face between his palms and kissed her, running one hand through her hair. He was already aroused. He took her hand and led her to her bed.

They made love slowly. Lindy responded to Ricky's touch, her body quivering with desire. Afterward, they lay facing each other, just studying each other's faces; communicating without speaking.

# Chapter 23

$\mathcal{L}$indy awoke to find Ricky gone. She knew he had to get home or Uncle Nick would be furious. Lindy didn't want Ricky to be grounded; she needed him, so she wasn't upset to find that he had left. She got out of bed and felt the queasiness in her stomach. She knew it was morning sickness, and she briefly wondered how long it would last. Grabbing her robe, she went to the kitchen and put coffee on. It was still very early; not quite six-thirty. She sifted through the envelopes on the counter and found a letter from Chris. 'How did I miss that?' she wondered. The coffee was just about finished, so she got a cup out of the cupboard and poured coffee into it and added the cream. She sat down at the kitchen table to read Chris' letter. She smiled as she read the contents of the letter, and she couldn't help the tears that sprung into her eyes. She hoped he would come home soon, but more than that, she hoped he would continue to be safe. In part of his letter, he told her that he was in no danger, which was something for her to hang onto. Most of the letter consisted of funny stories about military life and things he and his friends did together. He thanked her for writing to him and asked her to keep it up. He also asked about her life. How was school? Was she still singing? Did she have a boyfriend yet? She refolded the letter and made a mental note to answer his letter; maybe even tell him about Ricky.

After her second cup of coffee, Lindy set about doing the weekly cleaning. Since the house was vacant most of the time, the cleaning was easily and quickly accomplished. Lindy took a shower and decided to start a letter to Chris. She got out her stationary and a pen and began writing, but was interrupted by someone knocking on the door. She opened the door to Diane, the woman who had been with her father. Lindy just stared at her for a moment.

"Hi." Diane smiled at her. "May I come in?"

"What do you want?" Lindy asked out of curiosity.

"I think we should talk."

"Why?"

"Because I think we should. May I come in?"

Lindy stood aside and let the woman enter. "You know…you don't need my blessing, or my permission to be with my father. I don't really care. You are not an issue with me."

"May I sit down? I see you have coffee made….may I?"

Lindy shrugged. "Yeah, sure." Lindy reached into the cupboard and brought out a cup. She poured coffee into it and set it on the table. "Cream and sugar?"

"No….black. Thanks. Sit down with me, Lindy."

Lindy shrugged and got herself another cup of coffee. She sat down across the table from this woman who insisted on trying to develop a friendship with her.

"Lindy…..I know your dad hasn't been fair with you….in fact, he's been downright mean. I know that, and I feel bad about it. I just wonder why. Do you have any idea?"

"There is no why, Diane. I'm his daughter; he's supposed to love me, be there for me. He doesn't and he isn't." Lindy sighed deeply. "At the funeral….he stood there and let everybody else offer me comfort. I was devastated, Diane. I loved my mother so much! I cried and I cried. And I wanted my father….to hold me, to say something to ease my pain, to assure me that I still had him….but that didn't happen."

Lindy stopped to swallow the lump in her throat, hoping that she wouldn't have to throw up. "Anyway…. after everything was over…my mother was laid to rest…. we came home and….he went straight to their room and shut the door. From that moment, he not only shut the door to the room, but he shut me out of his life. Do you know how it hurt to find out that he spent all the holidays with you while I was here? When he lost his wife…he discarded me. Do you know how that feels?" Lindy wiped her eyes. She was fighting to keep from crying, but she was losing the battle.

"No, Lindy….I don't. I can't even begin to know how it feels. But I know that he is aware that he's hurt you. He doesn't know how to make up for it…."

"He can't. He can never make up for turning his back on me. For almost three years…..three years, Diane…. I have lived alone, taken care of myself alone. Do you know I have no curfew? He doesn't even know if I go out or not. I have no rules to follow, except one….stay out of his sight."

"Lindy….we're talking about getting married…."

"Fine….I don't care."

"Things would be different…."

"It's too late to change things. So…..*what*? You get married and move in here, and then what? All of a sudden I have rules and curfews, and somebody asking me what I'm doing and where I'm going? I don't think that would work….not now…after all this time. My father had his chance to be a parent….and he blew it. And I don't need a step-mother to suddenly take an interest in me. So you see, Diane….whatever you and my father do….I really don't care….but just don't think I'm going to let it affect me. And for the record…..I created my own rules and my own curfews. I'm always home by midnight on weekends, I don't drink, do drugs, or smoke. I get all A's in school. These are the rules I set for myself and I live by them. I think I've done a pretty good job so far."

"Yes, you have. I was thinking more along the lines of family dinners, holidays again, family outings….that sort of thing. I'd love to hear you sing."

"That sounds great, Diane. You and my father can enjoy all that together….I don't care. But don't expect me to be involved in any of it. I won't….I can't forgive my father for what he has done. He should have been there because he wanted to be—not because you entered the picture. It's nothing against you. You are not an issue with me at all. Being the intelligent person I am; I understand that he would eventually need someone like you in his life. But I will never understand why he turned his back on his daughter."

"He realizes he was wrong…"

"Maybe he does, but the damage is done. There is no going back and fixing it."

The telephone rang just then, giving both of them a chance to stop talking. It was Ricky.

"Hey, Uncle Nick and I are going grocery shopping….. want to come along? I know you need some things. The cupboards are looking kind of bare. Uncle Nick said to ask you…."

"That sounds good. Yeah, when are you going?"

"We're leaving here in about a half hour….okay?"

"Great. See ya then." Lindy hung up and turned back to Diane.

"I'm getting a ride to the grocery store. See….my father leaves me money for food, but has not figured it out that I have no way to go shopping on my own. No license, no car, and the supermarket is kind of far to walk to it. So I have to get ready to go. I think we've said all that is needed to be said. Go ahead….marry my father….but the two of you can just leave me alone."

Lindy stood there waiting for Diane to get up from the chair. She took the hint and stood up.

"Thank you for talking with me, Lindy. I….I only hope that we…can be civil with each other."

"That won't be a problem, Diane. My mother taught me how to be polite."

Lindy made no effort to walk her to the door, but stood and watched as Diane let herself out. As soon as Diane shut the front door, Lindy made a beeline for the bathroom and threw up the three cups of coffee in her stomach. She brushed her teeth and dressed. When the BMW pulled into the driveway, she was ready to go.

Ricky got out of the car so she could get into the front seat when she pulled the door shut. Since the temperature outside was still a pleasant fifty degrees, Lindy was wearing her lavender light-weight nylon jacket, but she kept the lining in it.

"That color looks good on you." Ricky said it as soon as she reached the car.

Nick turned to see her and he had to agree that the color made her eyes look the bluest of blues. Ricky shut the car door and put his arm around Lindy's shoulders.

"Uncle Nick didn't come home last night." Ricky loudly whispered into her ear, meaning for Nick to hear.

Lindy let out a loud gasp. "Uncle Nick....."

"You two are about to get on my S-list." He tried to say it with conviction but his mouth was betraying him as his lips turned up at the corners into a wicked looking smile. "Okay...here is the way it is. We're going to get something nice to make for dinner tomorrow. Lindy, you'll come for dinner, won't you? Ricky's cooking."

"What? Who made that decision?" Ricky tried to look angry.

"I did." Nick laughed. "Anyway, I invited Aunt Liz to Sunday dinner. Do you mind, Rick?"

"No....that's okay. I'll cook. My baby here will help me....Right Lindy?"

Lindy turned to Ricky. "Right. Guess who came to see me this morning."

"I don't know...but if it was the pizza delivery guy, he and I are going to have a talk."

Lindy laughed. "No, it wasn't the pizza guy. Diane, the woman with my dad...."

"Oh....are you okay? What did she want?"

"I don't know. Somehow she believes that she has to get along with me. She said they're talking about getting married."

Nick's ears perked up. "How do you feel about that, Lindy?" He asked her.

Lindy shrugged. "I don't care."

"Things might be better for you….."

"Things will still be the same. Do you think that after all this time I can just forgive and forget? Do you think that if they get married I'll just be part of their happy little family? I may be friendly to Diane; I may even like her…. but my father? No way….I can't forgive him. The scars go too deep. Almost three years of wanting my father; needing him….no….I'm over it."

Nick chewed his lip. He knew that someday a certain Mister Riley was going to be sorry for pushing his daughter that far away. He swung into the parking lot of the local supermarket, found a parking space, and got out of the car. Lindy and Ricky took their time, sharing a kiss first. Nick shook his head, hoping he had nothing to worry about with those two.

Lindy was glad to have the chance to get some groceries into the house. She made sure she had a box of saltine crackers to help with the morning nausea she had been experiencing almost every morning. So it wouldn't look suspicious, she grabbed a couple of cans of soup. When she was ready to check out, Ricky disappeared and then reappeared with a bouquet of fresh flowers for her, purchased through the express line. She rewarded him with a smile that lit up her entire face. Nick just shook his head. After loading the groceries into the car, Nick suggested they go for lunch at a nearby restaurant. He drove the short distance to the restaurant and parked again. As soon as they entered the restaurant Lindy knew it was a mistake. The smell of the food brought on the queasiness she had experienced earlier in the day. She looked for the restroom and quickly excused herself. Ricky knew why she went and he glanced at his uncle to see if he noticed her urgency. He didn't seem to notice. Ricky searched Lindy's face, looking for signs of distress, when she came back to the table. She looked fine, but she ordered light, settling for a cucumber salad and bread sticks. The conversation over lunch was mainly about the Sunday dinner the next day. Ricky teased Nick by saying he and Lindy would be happy to chaperone him and Aunt Liz any time.

"Seriously, Uncle Nick….are you and Aunt Liz going to get back together?"

"I don't know……maybe. We never fell out of love…. just fell out of like. We stopped liking each other. I'm trying…..harder than I did before. So is she. We'll see what happens. Now….no more questions about my personal life." He tried to sound stern, but couldn't pull it off. Lindy and Ricky laughed.

Ricky reached under the table and grabbed Lindy's hand. "Aren't you glad we don't have to *try* to be nice to each other, Babe?"

"Yeah….being nice comes naturally with us." She grinned at Ricky.

"Okay…..funny…..very funny. You're really working toward my S-list; aren't you?" Nick tried to sound annoyed, but failed that one, too.

Lindy and Ricky just laughed.

Ricky helped Lindy carry in her groceries when they got to her house.

"Hey, I'll be down later, after I get ours put away." He hugged her tightly. "Someday when I say 'our groceries',

I'm going to mean yours and mine. So….want to do anything special tonight? Uncle Nick is taking Aunt Liz to see a play at the theatre in the city. Maybe we could go down to that place behind Blockbusters. Looks like a fun place…..want to?"

Lindy nodded, "Okay…..sounds like fun."

They kissed each other and Lindy stood and watched the BMW pull out of the driveway and go up the street. She set about putting her groceries away and then got a vase out for the flowers Ricky had bought her. She carried the vase into her room, looked longingly at the bed, and decided to take a nap.

# Chapter 24

$\mathcal{L}$indy awoke to a beautiful April morning. The sun was streaming through her bedroom window and from where she lay; the sky looked to be a perfect shade of blue. April fourth—Ricky's seventeenth birthday. Her birthday was ten days away. She smiled when she thought about the cards she had for Ricky. She planned on giving him one in every class they had together today, and then giving him his gift tonight after they went out to dinner with Uncle Nick and Aunt Liz. Lindy didn't have any idea what to get for Ricky until she saw the full-length black trench coat. It would look so great on him—she knew it. It was an expensive one—one with a zip-in lining—but she knew it was perfect for him.

She got out of bed gingerly, as she did every morning. The nausea was there again. "I hope this stops soon," she mumbled to herself. She made it to the kitchen, not needing to run into the bathroom for once, and saw that there was coffee in the pot. She felt the pot….still hot. Her father must have made it before he left for work. Strange. She shrugged her shoulders and got out a cup, and carried a cup of coffee into the bathroom with her. Quickly showering brushing her teeth, and drying her hair, she picked up her coffee cup and carried it into the bedroom. Since she always had her clothes ready the night before, there was no time wasted on deciding what to wear. She wanted to look extra nice for Ricky today on his birthday. Shedding her robe, she stood in front of her full-length mirror, turning sideways in both directions. She felt fat, but her stomach still looked the same—flat. 'How long will *this* last?' she wondered. She dressed carefully in a two-piece light purple dress that was stylishly cut, with the hem of the skirt being slash-cut to give a hap-hazard uneven effect. She knew she looked good in it. The color was flattering and the style gave her the willowy look of a much taller girl. Make-up was unnecessary. Her long dark lashes and dark eyebrows gave her eyes a dramatic effect, and her skin took on a healthy glow.

Carrying her empty cup, she wondered out to the kitchen. Since she still had plenty of time, she decided to have another cup of coffee and go through the mail that had piled up on the kitchen counter. She guessed her father didn't look at it any more, but hoped that he was paying the bills. There was nothing exciting in any of the envelopes, most of it being junk mail, until the last one. The bottom envelope was addressed to her from a company she had never heard of. She tore open the envelope and began reading, but not fully understanding. It had something to do with the stock market, and a portfolio, whatever that was. If she had one, she didn't know anything about it. Apparently she did have one, and it was considerable in size. She read over the names listed on the stock deeds and realized that her grandfather must have put everything into her name before he died. She knew about the money in the safe deposit box at the bank. She knew that he put it there for her in case of emergency. She had a key to the box and her name was on the signature card for whenever she needed to get into it. This new information overwhelmed her. She was considerably wealthy—or would be at the age of eighteen. She quickly filed everything back into the envelope and took it to her room. Inside of her closet she kept a large suitcase with a secret pocket. She added this envelope with its contents to her stash. She had no idea why she did it, but she always stored any extra money she had in that pocket. It was as if she expected to make a quick getaway at some point in her life—silly as it sounded to her. As she closed the closet door, she heard Ricky's familiar knock on the front door. She ran to let him in, and then wrapped herself around him.

"Happy birthday!" She smiled up at him.

"Thanks.....and whoa! Very pretty! I couldn't ask for a better birthday gift." He held her at arm's length and looked her up and down. "You look gorgeous."

She grinned at him, feeling a rush of love coming from deep inside. They both heard the honking of the horn, and laughed. Uncle Nick was getting impatient. Grabbing up her book bag and her light-weight coat, they quickly moved to get out of the house.

Nick dropped them off in front of the school and reminded them to be ready to go by six that evening. They waved at him as he drove away, and then they turned and walked up the steps together.

"When I'm big and fat, are you still going to tell me I look gorgeous?"

"Well, yeah....you probably will still be gorgeous. How are you feeling, anyway? Sick this morning?"

"Nauseous, but I didn't bow to the porcelain God if that's what you mean."

"Well, that's an improvement; isn't it?"

Lindy nodded, spying Carrie staring over at them as she did. "Oh, hell! She is watching us again. Doesn't she have anything better to do?"

Ricky shrugged. "Guess not." He put his hand on Lindy's elbow and led her away from the main entrance down the hall toward the lockers.

As planned, Lindy gave Ricky a card in every class. He enjoyed reading them, but he also enjoyed her thoughtfulness. He was going to have to do something equally special for her on her birthday ten days from now. Lindy saved the best card for last—their seventh period class—English Literature. Ricky read the card with emotion showing on his face.

"Thanks, Babe…..I love you."

They stared into each other's eyes and felt the familiar bolt of electricity shoot through them from head to toe. Their connection was broken by loud, raucous Lukas.

"Hey, Rick….is it your birthday?"

"Yeah, it is."

"Cool! Happy birthday. Lindy, yours is coming up soon, isn't it?"

Lindy nodded. "In ten days."

Many other students wished Ricky a happy birthday before the class began. Ricky thanked them, but ignored Carrie when she offered her wishes. Crazy Shawna told Ricky that for his birthday she would kick Carrie's ass for free, causing Ricky to laugh. He realized he was happy here. He had a wonderful girlfriend, good friends and classmates, and a clean life. Other than the occasional cigarette, he put no substances into his body any more. He felt great and he was beginning to look great. The weights in the gym were adding bulk to his arms, shoulders, chest, and legs, giving his muscles definition. He looked over at Lindy, smiled, and grabbed her hand, planting a light kiss onto her fingers. Life was good.

* * *

Lindy let Ricky in as soon as she heard his knock, and immediately wrapped her arms around him. "Happy birthday again, Birthday Boy!" When can you open your gift?"

"After dinner, I guess. You didn't have to get me anything..."

"Yeah, I know....but it's always nicer when it comes from the heart rather than a required gesture. Don't you agree?"

"Yeah....sure do. You look great, by the way."

"Thanks...you, too. Did I ever tell you I'm a sucker for a man in a suit?"

"No...but I'll start wearing one to bed...."

Lindy burst out laughing, causing Ricky to laugh, too, as he helped her with her coat.

Ricky chose the restaurant—a popular steak house—and Nick had made the reservations. Dinner was enjoyable; the food exquisite, and the company pleasant. After dinner they went back to the condo where Ricky got to open his gifts from Nick, Liz, and Lindy, saving Lindy's for last because he knew it would mean the most to him. And he loved it. It was a perfect fit, and it looked just as good on him as Lindy believed it would. Liz surprised Ricky with a birthday cake after the gifts were opened.

Ricky couldn't remember when he had a nicer birthday, he told them.

"Now I have to come up with something just as great for your birthday." He announced.

"When is that?" Nick asked.

"In ten days." Ricky answered for her.

"Well, I'll do the dinner thing again….how about it, Liz? Dinner in ten days? For Lindy's birthday?"

"Yep….I'm up for it. You'll be seventeen as well, Lindy?"

Lindy nodded.

"Oh, I have something for you, Lindy." She reached into her purse and pulled out a folded sheet of paper. "It's an application for the talent show, which is two weeks from this Saturday. The Saturday after your birthday, actually. You will perform in it, won't you?"

Lindy nodded, again. "It's for a good cause….right?"

"Right." The other three answered in unison.

Lindy filled out the application, silently hoping that the morning sickness, which lasted all day sometimes, would be gone by then.

Nick offered Lindy a ride home since it was close to ten o'clock and it was a school night. Ricky walked her to the door, stepping inside as usual, making sure that nothing was out of place or unusual inside the house. After checking, he kissed Lindy goodnight and thanked her for the wonderful birthday.

"You'll get the rest of your present Saturday, maybe." She offered him a sly grin.

"Would that one be given horizontally?" He answered as he ran his hand up and down her back.

"It might....I don't see any chandeliers in this place."

They both burst out laughing. Lindy watched as the car pulled out of the driveway, sighed and locked the door.

# Chapter 25

Lindy woke before the alarm, turned toward the window and saw that the sun was just coming up. She stretched and swung her feet over onto the floor and sat up. No nausea—good. She was seventeen today, and that was the best birthday present she could have—a morning without that terrible queasiness. Listening for sounds in the outer rooms, she quietly unlocked the door and turned the doorknob. Satisfied that she was the only one awake, or more than likely the only one in the house, she walked out to the kitchen to start a pot of coffee. On her way to the kitchen she peeked out the window and noted that her father's truck was not in the driveway. She didn't hear him come in last night so she assumed that he probably hadn't. She snapped on the light in the kitchen and stopped dead. Sitting on the table was a large package wrapped in birthday paper. A balloon was attached to the ribbon.

Walking past it, she mumbled, "Nice try, Diane." She made the coffee and didn't as much as glance at the package again. She took her shower and went back to get a cup of coffee. The package was still there, looming up from the table like an ominous icon. She sat down at the kitchen counter with her back to the package and leafed through the mail. There was a card from Chris. She tore it open and was delighted that it was another homemade card. He apologized for it, saying they couldn't get cards in the area in which he was located. He had no idea how much she loved the homemade cards. She would have to write to him and let him know that. She also found a letter, which brought tears to her eyes. In her last letter she told Chris about Ricky. His answer was encouraging, saying that he hoped he was a nice boy and that he was good to her. He wrote that he wanted to meet Ricky when he came home. Lindy hoped that would be soon, reminding herself that Chris was going to be an uncle. It was time to get dressed, so she picked up the letter and the card and took them into her room and slipped them into her nightstand drawer.

As usual, she studied herself in the full length mirror, and frowned this time. Her abdomen was protruding a little. Not much, but a little. She chose to wear the pink running suit that Ricky's mother had given her for Christmas. With a loose-fitting white tee-shirt under it, the pouch was not noticeable—she hoped. She heard Ricky's knock on the front door. He was a little early. She ran to the door and opened it to a large bouquet of red roses, in a large clear bevel cut vase.

"How did you get them at this time of the morning?" She hugged him and laughed.

"Florist opens at seven. They were ready for me when I got there."

"Oh, wow! They're beautiful! Thank you!" She set them on the coffee table and wrapped her arms around Ricky again, kissing his chest.

He reciprocated by tilting her chin up and kissing her lips. "Happy birthday, Sweetheart. Wait 'til you see what I got you. Uncle Nick got you something, too. Speaking of which….he's in the car waiting for us…what's that?" Ricky's eyes were on the package on the kitchen table.

"Oh….I'm sure it's something Diane picked up for me. Don't care. Ready to go?" She grabbed her book bag, purse, and keys and led Ricky out the door by his hand.

Ricky could hardly contain his excitement. He had cards to give her in all their classes, except the last one. He had something special planned for that class. He couldn't wait until then.

Finally it was seventh period. Just as the teacher shut the door and called the class to order, there was a knock on the door. The teacher opened the door to a gorilla—a gorilla holding balloons. She was visibly shaken by it for a moment, but regained her composure. The gorilla handed her a slip of paper and she began to laugh.

"Lindy….I believe this is for you."

The gorilla barged into the room, and started dancing to music only he could hear. The class was in an uproar over it. Lindy put her hand over her eyes, put her head down, and laughed. Her face was red from embarrassment. She looked at Ricky, saw the love in his eyes, and wiped the tears that were running down her cheeks. The gorilla was gesturing for her to come to the front of the class.

"Go ahead, Babe….it's not over yet."

"Oh, God…." She laughed. She went up to the front of the room and the gorilla gestured for quiet throughout the room. When the room was quiet, he pushed the button on the tape recorder he was carrying.

Ricky's voice came through the small speaker: "Happy birthday to you, my Juliet, my love, my life. I will always be there for you and I will love only you forever. With love, from your Romeo."

Lindy was sobbing now. The gorilla hugged her and nuzzled her cheek. Much of the class was crying now, including the teacher.

"Man, Dude, you are a class act." Lukas broke in. "I got tears in *my* eyes. Will you marry me, Rick?"

The crying turned to laughter. Ricky went to the front of the class to hand the man in the gorilla suit a ten dollar bill, and to retrieve Lindy, who still had not regained composure.

The teacher shook her head. "Not even Romeo did anything that romantic. I agree with Luke. You *are* a class act. Happy birthday, Lindy."

"Thank you." Lindy responded to the teacher. She looked up at Ricky and shook her head. "And thank you."

Her smile was all that mattered to him at that moment, until he glanced over at Carrie and saw the look of hatred on her face. Her lips were pursed, making them look like a slash across her face where her mouth should have been, and her eyes were narrowed into an evil glare. The class returned to order, taking up where they left off reading Othello.

When the class ended, well-wishers came over to wish Lindy a happy birthday. Luke shook Ricky's hand. When Shawna appeared Ricky whispered into her ear that he was afraid that Carrie was going to do something to Lindy.

"Why do you say that?" She asked.

Ricky glanced at Lindy and saw that she was talking to Cindy, so he told Shawna about the evil look on Carrie's face. "It was damn scary. If she does anything to her…."

"Don't worry; I'll take care of it. She's afraid of me."

"Thanks, Shawna."

"No problem. I know how much Lindy means to you. She's a lucky lady."

\* \* \*

Lindy chose a family-style restaurant, with real mashed potatoes, for her birthday dinner. The food was comfort food, she said. Liz laughed when Lindy told her the story about the gorilla. The meal consisted of good food, good stories, and good company; a birthday dinner for Lindy to remember. She shared with Nick and Liz the part about the mysterious wrapped box on the kitchen table.

"What is it?" Nick asked.

"Don't know."

Well, aren't you going to open it?"

"I will….right after he opens all those gifts from me….the ones in his closet that still have wrapping paper on them from two years ago. You see, those came from the heart. This one comes from guilt—or Diane—I don't know which."

After dinner, they went back to the condo, just as they had done for Ricky. Lindy was excited when she saw the birthday cake, since she hadn't had one in three years. Nick gave her expensive perfume that wasn't too strong for her, and Liz gave her another designer outfit. Lindy gasped when she saw the gift from Ricky. It was the most beautiful gold chain she had ever seen. It was made up of clusters of gold nuggets, soldered together. It was exquisite.

"Damn….where do you get all this money?" Nick asked Ricky.

"I'm robbing you blind….why?" Ricky laughed. "No, really…I have money. Besides the social security I get from the government because my dad died, I get a check every month from something my dad invested in. He put my name as beneficiary on it, and apparently, it pays real well. The Social Security check goes into a college fund, but this is mine. I save some of it, but it's what keeps me independent. I don't have to keep bugging you for money….or my mom, either."

"I had no idea. So you spend it all on Lindy?" Nick made it sound like he was joking, but he actually wanted to know.

"Some of it. She's my baby." Ricky smiled at Lindy and winked.

"I'll be damned. Things we don't know about our kids."

\* \* \*

Lindy thought about that conversation after she got home that night. She had said nothing about her spending money or where it came from. She wondered why she didn't.

Ricky had walked her to the door and slipped inside with her to kiss her good night. He did his little inspection of the house before he left, noting that the box was still on the kitchen table. Lindy thanked him for giving her a wonderful birthday.

"You make me so happy, Ricky."

Ricky smiled down into her face. "Well, I sure try to." He kissed her one more time before he left.

She watched the BMW pull out as she always did, letting out a sigh of happiness. She picked up the flowers Ricky had brought that morning and carried them into her room, and then she went back to the living room to get the balloons she brought home from school. She was gathering them together when Ray Riley walked through the door. He stood with his hand on the doorknob poised like he wasn't sure he should stay. Lindy turned her back and walked to her room and shut the door. She listened for sounds in the outer rooms before she got undressed.

Before too long, she heard Ray walk down the hall toward his room. He stopped at her door and spoke.

"The box on the table is for you." His muffled voice came through the door.

"Thank you." Lindy's response was crisp, as though she just thanked a stranger for picking up something she had dropped. She undressed and got into bed, thinking of Ricky as she wrapped her arms around herself.

\* \* \*

The school days were uneventful for the rest of the week. On Tuesday, Lindy went to see her music teacher to ask him to accompany her on stage Saturday night for the talent show. He agreed to play for her while she sang, and then they set about choosing a song that was sure to be a first place number. 'Something dramatic', the teacher said. 'Something that shows your range and the strength of your voice'. They settled on the song *The Impossible Dream*.

"The song is perfect, Lindy. It has drama, depth, and range. You can do it. Let's start rehearsing now."

They spent the sixth period rehearsing the song, Lindy taking hints and ideas from her teacher, perfecting it as she sang. By the time Ricky got to the auditorium, the song was almost perfect. Lindy sounded wonderful, and Ricky didn't hesitate to tell her.

"It's the song I'm going to do for the talent show. Mr. Wise will be there to play for me when it's my turn."

"Well, I'll tell you this, my love…..if you don't win, it's fixed."

They laughed and walked toward the seventh period class, arm in arm.

* * *

Lindy dressed carefully for the scheduled event. She wanted to look pretty, but she also wanted to look sophisticated. She had done her hair in a French braid and had strategically placed small bows along the length of it. The bows were turquoise, a perfect match for the outfit she had chosen. The straight skirt of her silk outfit just brushed the top of her feet, and the matching straight, sleeveless, v-necked top was fingertip length. Staring into the mirror, she was satisfied that there were no telltale signs of her growing stomach. She chose comfortable small white heels to wear, since she had a fear of walking out on stage, tripping, and falling flat on her face. One last glance into the mirror assured her that she looked fine. Ricky's whistle sealed it. He knocked before he opened the door, but entered before she got to it. One look at her, and he let out a cat-call whistle.

"You look beautiful……and you're going to win. I know it."

Lindy smiled at him and picked up the light shawl she planned on wearing when the sun dropped from the sky for the day. Nick was in the car waiting for them, getting impatient since he promised Liz that he would help behind the scenes until the show started. Ricky handed Lindy his cell phone so she could call Mr. Wise to make sure he was on his way. He was in his car when he answered his cell phone, and he assured her he would be there.

\* \* \*

Lindy did win. The song choice was right, showing the strength and range of her voice. Ricky and Nick sat in the audience, both of them beaming at her performance. When her song ended they both gave her a standing ovation, followed by the rest of the audience. The judges were unanimous in their decision, bestowing Lindy with a bouquet of fresh-cut flowers, a trophy and a gift certificate worth one hundred dollars. Ricky watched with pride as she was called back to the stage to accept her winnings. He watched her as she posed for a picture for the morning newspaper, and smiled into the camera for a local television station. She looked so beautiful to him. When the stage lights dimmed, signaling that the show was over, Ricky and Nick got up and headed toward the rear of the stage to find her. Lindy was thanking her music teacher when Ricky appeared at her side.

"Congratulations, Baby.….I knew you would win…." Ricky said as he embraced her.

"There wasn't a doubt in my mind," George Wise contributed. "I have to run, Lindy. Again…you were great. Any time you need me to help you out, let me know." He tweaked her shoulders quickly and left out the side exit.

"Baby, you were magnificent….awesome….the bomb…." Ricky held her in his arms tightly and kissed her hair.

"Any chance I can say my congratulations to her?" Nick came up behind Ricky, smiling. "Lindy, you were wonderful. You stole the show."

"Thanks, Uncle Nick." Lindy smiled at him. "Hey, I think I'm going to be on TV."

"I'm *sure* you're going to be on TV." Liz's voice came from behind Lindy. "Looks like we were both successful tonight, Sweetie. You won and I took in a lot of money for the Women's Center."

"Well, I think we should all go somewhere and celebrate. What do you say, Lindy? Where would you like to go?" Nick laid his hand lightly on Lindy's shoulder.

"Somewhere where there's a television." Lindy laughed.

\* \* \*

Ray Riley sat at the bar in his local hang-out watching the end of a hockey game. The game buzzer sounded and the station went to a commercial. A couple of his buddies entered and joined him at the bar, ordered drinks, and began talking about a planned fishing trip they all had signed up for. The local news came on while they talked. Joe Finch, Ray's best friend glanced up at the television to catch the headlines.

"Hey, there's *Lindy*, Ray." Joe was pointing to the television screen. Ray looked up in time to see his daughter's smiling face across the screen. The four men got quiet to catch the details, but had missed most of it. They would have to wait for the actual story to find out why Lindy was on television.

It was the third news story, right after the related events of a deadly car crash and a small store robbery. The details of the talent show were then related and that the winner, Belinda Riley was a seventeen-year-old high school student with 'a voice from heaven'. The camera switched to Lindy holding the microphone, and singing part of her song. The news anchorwoman commented on Lindy's extraordinary voice and that she was pretty, too.

All four men at the bar stayed quiet. Ray's three friends knew how he rejected Lindy the last three years. They felt that it wasn't right—in their words. Lindy was always a sweet girl and they couldn't understand why Ray turned his back on her. After seeing her on television and hearing her sing, they wanted to say something, but didn't know what to say, since they didn't know how he would react. Joe Finch couldn't hold it in any longer.

"Ray, she's....so....talented. I had no idea she could sing like that."

Ray said nothing; just stared down into his beer.

A younger patron, in his mid-twenties, sitting at the corner of the bar interjected his thoughts into their conversation. "Hey, Asshole....if she was in a talent show tonight, why is it that you are sitting here and weren't there to support her? What an asshole you are....to have a daughter like that and not give a shit about her."

"Shut up....that ain't none of your concern." Joe Finch ordered. "Let's get outa here, Ray." Joe didn't understand Ray's indifference to Lindy, but he was his friend. He wasn't going to judge what he knew nothing about.

Ray nodded, stood up to leave, and threw a few dollars on the bar. 'If people only understood the pain in my heart', he thought to himself.

* * *

"I was so proud of you tonight, Baby." Ricky hugged her as they stood just inside her front door. "You were....

awesome. You know….you could probably get a singing career going. You're that good."

Lindy smiled gratefully at Ricky. "Who knows? Maybe I'll get discovered tonight, and then we can go to Hollywood and live there together." She rested her cheek against Ricky's chest, closed her eyes for a moment and sighed.

"I'll go home and start packing." Ricky laughed and pulled her closer to him. "I'll call you tomorrow. If it's nice out, want to go to the zoo?"

His question was rewarded with one of Lindy's best smiles. "Okay!"

\* \* \*

Diane opened the door when she heard Ray's knock. "I figured you'd be here tonight."

"You saw the news?" He asked her.

Diane nodded. "She's good, isn't she?'

"Yeah….she is." Ray moved to the sofa and sat down. "You know….nothing is her fault. She's not to blame for anything….I don't know what happened….I love my daughter….I just can't…show it….since…."

"…Stacey died?" Diane ended his sentence with a question.

"No….since….the day before Stacey died. I can't talk about it. How about a beer?"

Diane got up to get Ray a beer, his statement ringing in her head. She wondered what had happened the day before Stacey died to make him turn his back on that beautiful child. Diane could see that Lindy was a very sweet child who had been hurt very badly by her father. Why? She wondered.

# Chapter 26

Lindy was a mini-celebrity in school on Monday. Many of the students and teachers saw the Saturday night news broadcast, and those who didn't, heard about it. Those who saw the news clip told her she was awesome and congratulated her on her winning. Those who missed it congratulated her all the same. The news was buzzing all over the school. Lindy took it in stride, but Ricky was so proud of her and proud that she was his girlfriend.

Carrie had other things to think about when Lindy's name came up. She had been scrutinizing her for two weeks now, and she was fairly sure that Lindy was pregnant. 'Miss Innocent isn't so innocent,' Carrie thought to herself. Lindy had walked past her on her way to her locker that morning and Carrie took a good look at her. Lindy was wearing a loose-fitting tee-shirt that dropped down almost to her thigh, over a pair of running pants. Carrie could see the tell-tale rise under the tee-shirt. She smiled to herself. She had a little gift for Lindy, and she could hardly wait for seventh period to give it to her. She saw the two of them sitting together across the lunchroom. Ricky had his arm lightly around her shoulders and hanging on to every word Lindy said. They smiled at each other. Carrie watched Ricky pick up Lindy's milk carton and put the straw to her lips, making her drink from it. 'Oh my God! He's feeding her!' Carrie's mind screamed. She could feel anger and jealousy bubbling inside of her.

Carrie didn't realize that she was being watched—by Shawna. 'Ricky was right. She does look evil,' Shawna thought to herself. Nonchalantly, Shawna got up and walked toward Carrie's table. She glared at Carrie for a moment.

"You know.....you are really ugly." Shawna sneered at her and then followed Carrie's line of vision. Shawna let out a low chuckle. "They're so cute together....aren't they, Carrie?"

Carrie just glared back at Shawna without saying a word. Shawna laughed and walked away.

Ricky walked Lindy to music class before he went to art class. The music teacher was waiting there and gushing over the triumph of the previous Saturday. Ricky smiled, quickly kissed Lindy's cheek, and headed to his class. Lindy and Mr. Wise began choosing sheets of music to work on for the next hour. The hour flew by, and Lindy was surprised when Ricky appeared at her side by the piano. She told Mr. Wise she would see him tomorrow and she gathered her things and went with Ricky to English Literature class. They sat in their usual seats, waving at Luke when he came in.

"Hey, Hollywood! Caught ya on the television the other night. Awesome!"

Lindy grinned at Luke. "Thanks, Luke. I won't forget ya when I'm famous."

Lindy, Ricky, and Luke were laughing when Carrie made her entrance into the room. She walked determinedly

toward Lindy and dropped a baby rattle on Lindy's desk
and then continued walking to her desk. Lindy just stared
at it. Ricky blew. He grabbed the rattle and flung it as
hard as he could, hitting Carrie between the shoulders.
She jumped out of her seat, and so did Ricky. He knocked
his desk out of the way and started toward Carrie. She
screamed. Luke jumped up and intervened. He grabbed
Ricky in a bear hug and put all his weight and strength
into stopping him.

"Rick, easy…..she's not worth it. Easy….come on…
stop." Luke managed to hold Ricky back.

Ricky glared at Carrie with a murderous look. "Leave
her alone! Leave *us* alone! You're jealous, Bitch! You're
jealous because I've never been interested in you! I can't
*stand* you! I couldn't stand you from the moment I met
you. Even if I hadn't have met Lindy, I would not have ever
looked at you! Now…leave…Lindy…and me…alone!"

Carrie gathered her books and hurried out of the
classroom. She had tried to humiliate Lindy in front of the
entire class, but it had been she who had been humiliated
instead. Her anger brought the sting of tears to her eyes.
'You'll pay for that, Lindy. You'll see!' she whispered to
herself. Already, she was formulating a plan.

\* \* \*

Nick pulled into the driveway as Ricky came flying
out the front door in a full run, causing Nick to slam on
the brakes to avoid running him down.

*"Hey, Rick! Where the hell are you going?"* Nick yelled,
getting out of the car.

Ricky kept running. Nick jumped back in his car
and began to chase Ricky up the hill. He rolled down the
window and shouted again.

"Ricky! What the *hell* is going *on*? Where are you *going*?"

Ricky stopped to catch his breath. "To Lindy's. She's hurt."

"Get in."

Ricky ran around the front of the car and jumped into the front seat, and slammed the door.

"What happened?" Nick's voice was full of concern.

"Her dad beat her….with a belt."

"*What? My God! Why? Why would he do something like that?*"

Ricky hesitated a moment, but decided it was time to get it out in the open.

"Because she's pregnant."

"Aw, Jesus Christ, Ricky! How could you let that happen?"

"Look, it just happened. We….just weren't careful enough. Anyway, we'll talk about that later. I'm more concerned about how badly she's hurt."

Nick nodded in agreement, and pulled into Lindy's driveway, thanking his lucky stars that her father's truck wasn't there. Ricky jumped out of the car before it came to a complete stop and was up at the front door before Nick put the car into park. He followed suit and got out, too. Lindy may need medical attention, he rationalized. Ricky knocked on the door, shouting Lindy's name. He turned the door knob and the door opened. He ran inside with Nick close behind him.

"Lindy!" Ricky called to her again, as he moved down toward her bedroom. He entered her room and snapped on the light. Lindy was on the floor leaning up against the bed, sobbing. Ricky ran to her, knelt down and cradled her head in his arms.

"My back......don't touch my b-back." Lindy cried.

Nick knelt down and lifted Lindy's tee-shirt. "Oh my God. Let's get her out of here. Get some of her clothes together; she can't stay here. Let me help you up, Lindy."

Nick took her arm and helped her stand up.

"I'm going to be sick." Lindy started down toward the bathroom, Ricky following.

"Where the hell are *you* going?" Nick asked him.

"She's going to be sick. *She needs me.* Do you think it's all about *sex*?"

Ricky stayed by Lindy's side as she threw up and then he wet a washcloth and wiped her face. He was wiping her face for her when Nick came to the bathroom door.

"Come on. Lindy, you're going to stay with us for a couple of days. Let's get some clothes together. And let's get out of here before your father comes home."

Ricky got Lindy's large suitcase out of her closet and began opening drawers. Lindy grabbed the three frames with her favorite pictures from the nightstand and set them in the suitcase and then started pulling clothes down off of the bar rack in her closet. She gathered her underwear and shoved it into a smaller piece of luggage. When the suitcases were full, Ricky closed them and zipped them shut.

"This should hold you for awhile." Anything else you want to take?"

Lindy grabbed up the lion Ricky had bought her at the zoo. "This."

Ricky nodded. "Okay. Where did Uncle Nick go?"

Nick was standing in the living room waiting for Liz to answer his call. She finally answered on the fifth ring.

"Hey….Can you meet me at my place? Bring your bag. Lindy….well, Lindy is hurt. We're taking her to my place."

"Oh my God, Nick. Of course I'll be there. Is it serious?"

"You'll have to tell me. Liz? She's pregnant."

"Oh….I see. I'll be right there." Liz hung up and grabbed her bag and left the same way she came in not more than two minutes prior.

Ricky and Lindy emerged from her room, Ricky carrying both pieces of luggage. Nick walked ahead of them and opened the trunk, leaving Lindy and Ricky to turn off some of the lights and lock the door. Nick stood waiting beside the car, his shoulders slumped and his head down.

"Lindy, get in the back. That way you don't have to press against the seat." Nick spoke to her very softly.

No one spoke during the short ride to Nick's condo. Lindy was still sobbing very lightly as she sat halfway turned toward the back of the seat, her arms outstretched, pushing her palms into the back of the seat. When the car stopped, Nick got out and helped Lindy get out while Ricky got the luggage.

"Get her up to the spare room, Rick. Aunt Liz is on her way over to examine her."

Nick turned and walked inside, and went straight to his den. He refrained from turning a light on, but immediately sat down at his desk. He sat in the dark, holding his head up with his hand. The doorbell brought him to his feet.

"Hi." Liz came in sounding out of breath. "Where is she?"

"Up in the spare room."

"What happened?"

"Her father found out she's pregnant and....beat her....with a belt."

"Oh, no....how bad?"

"Bad."

Liz headed up the stairs, and Nick returned to his den. Inside the small spare room, she could see a light, and the door was partially open so she pushed it open the rest of the way. She could see Lindy lying on her stomach on the bed with her head resting on Ricky's arm. Ricky sat on a chair beside the bed, stroking Lindy's cheek with his thumb on the hand of his free arm. He looked up toward Liz when he detected her presence. Liz snapped on the ceiling light and approached the bed. She lifted Lindy's tee-shirt and it was all she could do to keep from gasping.

"Lindy? Honey, I want to look at your back, okay?"

Lindy nodded. Ricky kissed her forehead. Liz lifted the shirt and felt the bile begin to rise in her throat. It sickened her to see the huge purple and blue welts from where the strap had connected with Lindy's delicate skin. Liz noticed that there were some slash marks where the strap had cut into the skin. Liz hoped they weren't deep enough to leave scars. She wanted to see the rest of Lindy's battered body. She looked at Ricky, pulled out her prescription pad and began writing.

"Ricky, take these down and give them to Uncle Nick. Ask him to go right now to the pharmacy and fill them.

One of them is a local anesthetic. I can't touch her until I can ease the pain a little. Okay?"

Ricky grabbed the slips of paper with the prescriptions written on them and nodded. Liz smiled at him.

"And Ricky? How about making Lindy a cup of tea?"

"Sure…you bet, Aunt Liz. You, too?"

"Yeah, me, too."

Ricky left the room and they could hear him going down the stairs. Liz looked over some of the other welts that went down below Lindy's waistband and then looked to see how far they went toward the front of her. She reached for Lindy's hand.

"So….you're going to be a mother. How far along?"

"I think four months."

"Have you and Ricky done any thinking about this? You're both responsible."

"I know." Lindy responded sincerely.

"It's too late for an abortion, probably."

"Aunt Liz….that was never an option. For me…or for Ricky."

"Okay. So now what?" Liz cocked her head stared into Lindy's face, offering her a tight smile.

Lindy started to cry. "I-I….don't know."

"Don't cry. What does Ricky want?"

"Ricky wants to marry her." Ricky answered for Lindy as he stood in the doorway holding a tray of steaming cups of hot tea, creamer and sugar. "Because I can't imagine life without her."

He set the tray down on the nightstand and added sugar and cream to Lindy's tea. Liz observed as he stirred in both the cream and the sugar, knowing just how much to add. She sighed as she rolled her thumbs over her temples.

"You're both so *young*….just…so…*young*. Do you know what you're up against? Marriage is tough….on most people, but when the two people are…"

"…..When the two people are me and Lindy…it's not so tough. All we want is to be together. As long as we're together, we can handle anything. We love each other, Aunt Liz."

"I know you do, Sweetie. I can see that. But what about…well, what about all the obstacles that come with marriage and responsibility? Things like money….or should I say lack of money? What about school? College? Career? Ricky, Honey….you don't even have a driver's license yet…and you want a marriage license? Where would you live? How would you live? Kids, I'm not trying to paint a dismal picture here…but this is reality."

"So Aunt Liz….what do *you* think is best? Lindy goes through the pregnancy, then childbirth, and then we just give our baby away? Like it's a puppy? It's our kid….with our genes….our DNA. Is that what people call responsibility? It's inconvenient….so give it away? I think we should be responsible for taking care of it."

"Ricky…I couldn't agree with you more….but it's not practical. It's unrealistic."

"No….no, it isn't. It can be done. We can do it. It won't be easy….I know that. But to me, Lindy is worth it….our *baby* is worth it."

Lindy looked up at Ricky and smiled. He made her feel so special.

"Ricky, I heard Uncle Nick's car. Can you run down and get the prescription from him?"

Ricky nodded, and ran down the stairs and retrieved the bag from the drugstore from Nick. He returned with it and handed it to Liz.

"Okay….now…how about food? Lindy, when did you eat last?"

"Noon, I guess."

"Not acceptable. It's past eight now. What do you have that won't be too heavy on her stomach?" Liz asked Ricky.

"Her favorite. Grilled cheese and tomato soup."

"Perfect. How about it, Lindy? Let Ricky make that for you?"

Lindy nodded. Liz began to apply the local anesthetic to Lindy's back, and immediately Lindy felt some relief of the pain. Liz examined the welts more closely, using her medical flashlight. The cuts wouldn't leave a scar; she was sure.

"Have you seen a doctor?"

"No, I haven't." Lindy spoke quietly.

"Want to see me? This *is* my specialty."

Lindy twisted her head around enough to see Liz. "Yes….I'd like that."

"Good. I want you to rest tomorrow and then the weekend. Monday, come to the hospital with Nick. He can bring you to my office. Okay?"

"What about school?"

"Oh, you're getting a couple of days off. I have a light sedative for you to take. It will help you sleep. It's safe for the baby, but I don't want you walking around while you're taking it. And I want some of these welts to go down before you try to maneuver a crowded hallway.

Okay? Ricky can bring you your work so you don't miss any."

"What about Uncle Nick?"

"What about him?"

"Well, I'm sure he's….disappointed in me. He might not even want me around any more. He might even hate me for ruining Ricky's life."

"I doubt that. He brought you here, so I guess he wants you to stay here. Temporarily, at least. I don't know if he can legally let you stay here indefinitely. We'll see. I have some friends. I'll try to pull some strings. Now after Ricky brings you something to eat, I want you to rest. Okay? Oh…and Lindy? You didn't ruin Ricky's life. He didn't ruin yours either. This is something you both did….to yourselves."

Lindy nodded. "Thank you."

"You're welcome, Sweetie." Liz leaned over and kissed Lindy on the cheek. I hear Ricky coming so I'm going down to talk to Nick for awhile. I'll leave you in his care. Goodnight. I'll stop in the morning, by the way. Just to see how you are."

Liz passed Ricky on the stairs, only hesitating to tell him to take care of her. The door to Nick's den was standing open and a small light was burning, so she knocked lightly and entered.

"How is she?" Nick asked her.

"Well…the belt marks will vanish eventually…. she's….distressed. Nick….you're crying."

"Am I?" Nick hurriedly wiped away his tears with the backs of his hands and sighed. "Liz….sit down. I have something to tell you. Something I guess I should have told you years ago….before we got married."

Liz eased herself into a wing chair that sat in front of Nick's desk. "What is it?"

Nick cleared his throat and sighed again. "Years ago…. I was a junior in college. I met a girl and fell in love with her. She was beautiful, sweet, and Greek. Well, things progressed….and she got pregnant. I wanted to marry her….she wanted to marry me, so she wrote to her parents telling them just that….we wanted to get married. Within two weeks, her father appeared at our door, telling her to get packed…she was going home. She put up a fuss….he would hear nothing of it….told her to get her stuff…she was leaving." Nick sighed again. "Then he turned to me. He told me I must never contact her, that if I did I would be killed, and so would she. He took her back to Greece. She had the baby over there. I heard from her sister after the baby was born."

Nick made eye contact with Liz before he continued. "It was a girl. She named the baby Nikoletta. After Ahna had the baby, her father stripped her naked and beat her until he drew blood. Ahna's sister told me she would try to write again, but it probably wouldn't happen; lest her father beat her, too. Her parents adopted the child as their own." Nick's eyes dropped to his desk again.

"Oh, Nick…..why didn't you ever tell me?"

"It hurt to talk about it. It was baggage…..I didn't want to put that on you." Again, he sighed. "If I had told you…..well, I don't know….maybe getting it out into the open would have helped. I don't know." He looked up at Liz again. "You had a right to know…..I'm sorry."

Liz nodded.

"Anyway….You might think I'm nuts, and maybe I am, but…..I'm going to help those two. It might not be sensible, or ethical, or moral, or even legal….but whatever they want to do…I'll help them any way I can. I'm furious with them right now…but, Liz….if they want to have that baby and raise it, I will do anything it takes to make their lives easier while they do…."

As Nick spoke those last words, Liz rose from the chair and moved around to the other side of the desk. She bent down and planted a passionate kiss on his lips.

"What was that for?" He asked, with a half smile on his face.

"For being the human being I always knew you could be. Now….mix me a drink. After seeing her back I could use one."

\*   \*   \*

Diane heard the truck pull into the driveway. She peeked out the kitchen window and watched Ray get out of the truck and slam the door. By the way he was walking, she knew something had happened. His shoulders were slumped, his head was down, and his gait was slow and heavy. She went to the back door and opened it. He looked terrible when he entered the kitchen and sat down on a chair at the table. Diane got a beer out of the refrigerator, set it in front of him, and waited. She knew he would talk eventually. Ray sat quietly, staring into some unseen place. Still staring ahead, he began to speak quietly, as though no one else was present.

"The day before Stacey died….Lindy and I were sitting in her hospital room. We had been there for hours. Poor Lindy. I felt so sorry for her. I could see how it was killing her to watch her mother suffer like that. I also realized that she was scared….scared because she was losing one of her life lines—her security."

Ray stopped talking, and took a gulp from the beer bottle in front of him. He began again.

"I wanted to reassure her...you know? Let her know that she still had me. I watched her face as she stroked her mother's hand. God...how it hurt to see her do that. I just wanted to grab her up and hold her....tell her everything will be all right." Ray paused. "I pulled her down on my knee and put my arms around her....tight....and....well.... the unthinkable happened. I got an erection. It scared me....it scared me so bad. My God...was I some kind of a pervert? My own daughter? It sickened me. I....hated myself. How could....God, it made me so *sick*...."

Ray felt as though he were being smothered. He stopped to drink some more from the bottle. "My own daughter....." His voice trailed off.

Diane touched his arm. "Ray...you're not a pervert. You know that kind of thing happens sometimes....for no reason...."

"Anyway, I had to stay away from Lindy. I wouldn't let myself get close to her, touch her, or even talk to her very much. I was so scared it would happen again. Diane....I don't have those kinds of feelings toward Lindy. She's my daughter. She was always my little princess....the thought that I could...do anything to her.....never, ever crossed my mind....but when that happened....it made me wonder about myself...you know?"

He looked at Diane for the first time since he got there. "I know, Ray...but you would never do anything like that. I know you....."

"Anyway...these past couple of years...she has become so beautiful....just like Stacey. I...I been avoiding her.... staying away....protecting her from....*me*...."

Ray finished the bottle of beer. Diane took the empty away and got another one out of the refrigerator. She was becoming nervous, not sure whether she wanted to hear what he was eventually going to get around to telling her. Ray was staring straight ahead again.

"Anyway.....tonight I get this phone call.....some snotty girl....she says.....why don't you ask Lindy what she has in her belly, grandpa, and hangs up. I stared at the phone for a minute....and then shouted for Lindy to come out of her room. I asked her if she was pregnant.... she says yes." Ray choked on a sob, but continued.

"I beat her, Diane....I beat her. I took my belt off and I beat her. It was like I snapped or something...." Ray was in a full cry now.

"Oh my God, Ray....where is she? She could be really hurt. How did she....? Does she have a boyfriend?"

"I don't know. I have never seen evidence of a boyfriend at the house. I don't know...." He was sobbing as he put his head down on top of his forearms.

"Ray, you didn't ask? How do you know she wasn't raped or something? Let's go....we have to get there....if she's hurt....she may need medical attention."

Diane already had her purse in her hand. Ray got up to leave, too, grateful that he had Diane beside him. He knew she cared and that she loved him. At the moment she was probably the only person who did. As for Ray, he loathed himself.

They didn't speak on the way to his house. Diane was silently praying that Lindy was all right when Ray pulled into the driveway. The house was dark. Ray unlocked the door and waited for Diane to enter. She looked at Ray before heading down the hall toward Lindy's room. She had only been there once, but she remembered which room was Lindy's. She pushed open the door and switched on the light. The room was empty. The silence told her that the entire house was empty. She backed out of the room and returned to the living room, where she had left Ray standing.

"She's gone."

"Gone? Gone where? Are her clothes gone?"

Diane shrugged. "I didn't open her closet. Should I?"

"Yeah….please."

Diane went back to Lindy's room, with Ray close behind her. She pulled open Lindy's closet door and stood there. Ray peered over her shoulder.

"Her suitcase is gone….so are a lot of her clothes. Where would she go?" Ray turned to look at Diane for an answer he knew she didn't have.

He walked back to the living room; shoulders slumped, and dropped onto the sofa. Sitting on the coffee table was the trophy Lindy had won at the talent show. Ray hadn't noticed it before tonight. He picked it up and rolled it around between his thumb and forefinger. Diane stared at him, seeing the pain in his face. He set the trophy back down and looked up at Diane, who was looking at the kitchen table, noting that the wrapped gift for Lindy was still sitting there, untouched.

"I really fucked up. I tried to protect her…instead I may have destroyed her. When I got over my rage…. I went to her. Diane, I wanted to hold her. She put her arms up like she was trying to protect herself from me…. she tried to cover her face. She screamed. My daughter

was terrified of me. What am I going to do, Diane? I'm…
a….monster."

"Well, first of all….we have to find out where she
went. We have to find her, Ray. Who are her friends?"

"I…I don't know. I'm sorry to say that…but I haven't
known for a couple of years. I don't know who she hangs
out with, where she goes….nothing. I failed her, Diane.
As a father, I failed her. If she's pregnant, it's because I
wasn't a good enough father to her. Even if she was raped,
where have I been? I was so busy protecting her from me
that I forgot to protect her from the rest of the world."

Ray covered his face with his palms and sat silently.
Diane listened to the clock on the wall ticking, realizing
time was passing, and time was important. She went back
to Lindy's room and opened a couple of drawers. Nothing.
She moved to the nightstand and opened the small drawer.
In there, she found birthday cards, and a small card like
the one that comes with florist shop flowers. Everything
was signed 'with love, Ricky' or 'all my love, Ricky'. "Who
is Ricky?" Diane wondered aloud. She scooped up the
cards and carried them to the living room.

"I think we may be able to rule out rape." She said, as
she put the cards down in front of Ray.

Ray picked one up and read it. "Who is Ricky?" He
mused, as he looked at another one. "Boyfriend? It must be.
Why didn't I see any signs of that? Never found anybody
here. She always seemed to be alone. But then, how often
was I here anyway? She could have had a battalion in here
for all I know."

Something was tugging at his memory, but he couldn't
figure out what it was. He sat there trying to remember
what he had seen. It finally hit him.

"The ring." He said it like he just saw the light.

"What? What ring?" Diane questioned.

"Right after Christmas....she came past me and got something out of the fridge. I noticed it, but I figured she may have bought it herself."

"A ring? What kind of a ring?"

"I don't know....I think it had a pearl and a couple of diamonds. It was pretty, I remember that. She had it on her left hand. I didn't think anything of it. I noticed it because Lindy is left-handed—like her mother. When she opened the refrigerator door with her left hand, the ceiling light caught the ring; causing it to sparkle...do you think this guy....Ricky....is responsible for her getting pregnant?"

Diane shrugged. "All indications point to that....I suppose. Ray, we have to find out where she is."

"Yeah....we do....and we have to find out where this Ricky is, too. I want some answers from him."

# Chapter 27

$\mathcal{L}$indy awoke feeling very stiff. As she looked around her, it took her a minute to realize where she was. Her mind went back to the night before and she involuntarily shuddered. As she struggled to get up, she remembered that she wasn't going to school today—doctor's orders— so she gladly gave up the fight and lay back down. There was no clock in the room. She listened for sounds, trying to figure out what time it was. Was Ricky still home; or had he left? She didn't have to wonder for very long. Ricky knocked lightly on the door, before he opened it.

"Hi…how do you feel? I brought you a phone to plug in. Uncle Nick says there's a jack behind this nightstand." Ricky pulled out the nightstand as he spoke. "Yeah…here it is. Now you can be connected." He winked and smiled at her.

She smiled back. "Thank you. A clock would be nice, too. What time is it?"

"Right around seven. Are you hungry? I have time to make you breakfast."

"No, but a cup of coffee would be wonderful."

"Be right back."

Ricky disappeared out through the door, and Lindy could hear him going down the stairs, two at a time.

Once again, she attempted to sit up, this time being more successful. Using her arm as a brace, she swung her legs over the side of the bed, and pushed herself into a sitting position. Now she remembered—the watch that Uncle Nick had given her was in the suitcase. She would ask Ricky to get it out for her. Ricky returned with her cup of coffee, sat down next to her, and kissed her cheek.

"Hurt much?"

"A little. That stuff Aunt Liz put on me works really well. It takes the pain away for a long time. Where's Uncle Nick? How mad is he? He doesn't want to see me; does he?"

"He hasn't said a word…..yet. Do you want some of that stuff on your back?"

"No…Aunt Liz will be by in a little while….but could you get my watch out of the suitcase?"

"Sure…then I'll put that stuff on for you when I get home, then….okay?"

"Okay." Lindy gave Ricky a little smile and rested her temple against his shoulder.

"Lindy….we'll be okay. I promise. I can feel it." Ricky touched her cheek with his fingertips. "Don't worry about anything. We'll be fine."

"Let's go, Ricky!" Nick's voice boomed from the bottom of the stairs.

Ricky kissed Lindy and quickly got her watch out of the suitcase. "I'll call you at lunch. Remember, stay in bed and rest. I'll be home after school and bring all our work home. We can do our homework together then. I love you." He kissed her forehead and left the room before Nick started to shout again.

As they were getting into the car, Liz pulled up. Nick left the car running and went back to unlock the door for her.

"What's that you're carrying?" He asked her.

"Breakfast. Lindy and I are going to have breakfast together. Is that okay?"

"Only if you agree to have lunch with me."

"Deal."

He followed her inside and kissed her lightly. "I think there is still some coffee left. Ricky usually makes a full pot. Gotta run...see you at noon." He kissed his fingers and blew the kiss to her, and ran out the door.

Liz climbed the stairs and peeked inside the room Lindy had slept in. She found her sitting on the edge of the bed, her feet dangling over the side, holding the cup of coffee Ricky had brought her.

"Hi! I brought you breakfast. How do you feel this morning? Any better?"

"Yeah...actually a little better. I'm just....hurt...you know? My dad never, ever laid a hand on me before.... last night. It hurts."

"Emotionally? I'm sure it does. Lindy...do you have any idea how he found out that you're pregnant?"

"No....I don't. I took a pregnancy test....but Ricky and I threw that in the trash and took the trash outside. The trash was picked up the next morning. I don't think he kept track of my tampons...." Lindy laughed, and then added, "I really don't know."

"Okay, give me your cup and let me get us some coffee, and then we'll have breakfast. Bagels with cream cheese, and a blueberry pastry, bought from the best bakery in western Pennsylvania. You're gonna love it!" Liz's voice faded as she took the cup downstairs to refill it and get one for herself.

Lindy thought about the question while she waited for Liz to come back up the stairs. How did her dad find out? She wondered. She also wondered if he knew she was gone, and did he care? Would he look for her or just be glad to be rid of her?

"Okay....fresh coffee, plates, napkins, utensils.....oh, Honey, you're crying again."

Lindy quickly wiped her eyes. "I was just wondering if he will look for me or if he just won't care that I'm gone."

"Oh....I think he'll look for you...and you know what else I think? I think he cares very much. I think he...knows he should have been there more for you...and he feels partially to blame for you getting pregnant....and he took it out on you. Your dad loves you, Lindy....how could he not? You're pretty damn lovable."

Lindy started to laugh, and then winced. "I guess the anesthetic wore off."

"I'll put some more on before I leave, and then I want you to rest. I'll see about having Nick put a television in here for you...."

"Oh, no.....don't do that. I mean....I don't want to be a bother to him."

"Honey, you're not. Uncle Nick is very concerned about you. He hasn't been in to see you because he has his own thing to deal with right now. He'll be in here to see you when he's ready. Don't think he doesn't care. He cried, Lindy. Don't tell him I told you, but...he cried when he saw how hurt you were."

Lindy stared at Liz. She couldn't imagine Uncle Nick crying. She sighed and smiled. "Thanks for telling me that. I was afraid that he might hate me now."

"Couldn't be further from the truth. Honey, you'll be okay? I have to get to the hospital. Let me put some of that on your back first, and then I gotta go."

"Okay." Lindy rolled onto her stomach while Liz applied the cooling foamy ointment to her back.

"Now….stay in bed and sleep. Sleep heals."

Liz patted Lindy's shoulder and left for the hospital. Lindy snuggled under the covers and fell asleep until Ricky called her at noon.

\* \* \*

Ricky felt like only half of him was in school, since he was so used to having Lindy beside him. He felt strange—and lonely. He attended his morning classes, not really speaking to anyone, outside of a nod to those who spoke to him. He called Lindy while he was eating lunch.

"You're not missing the food today. It sucks." He told her.

"It sucks every day." She laughed.

"How are you feeling? Did you have a nice breakfast with Aunt Liz?"

"Yeah, I did. She told me Uncle Nick doesn't hate me. I'm glad."

"How could he hate you? You're lovable."

Lindy laughed. "That's what she said."

"Well, see there? Majority rules." Ricky got serious again. "I really miss you. I can't wait for this day to be over. Oh, a couple of our teachers asked about you; if you were sick or something. I told them you hurt your back. They were all sympathetic and hoped you would be better

soon. That's what I told anybody else who asked, too....
okay?"

"That's fine. Actually, good thinking on your part. I
always knew you were a genius." Lindy teased.

"Yeah? It's about time you finally said it then. Go
back to sleep; I gotta go. See you in a little while. Lindy?
I can't even begin to tell you how much I love you. See
ya later."

Ricky disconnected the call, gathered up his lunch
remains on the tray and started to walk out of the cafeteria.
He passed Carrie and Sara on his way out. They both
stared up at him, but said nothing. He continued on to his
art class where he was working on a special piece of work.
He hadn't told Lindy about it, since it was supposed to
be a surprise. He was doing a charcoal sketch of the two
of them, and the likeness was quite good. Ricky always
knew he had art talent, but until he came to this school,
he had never been able to pursue it. He would have been
called a fag in his other school, which would have gotten
him beaten up as well. Here, in this place he lived now,
he could freely expose his art ability and nobody had
anything to say beside praise for his work. He was almost
done with his sketch, and then he was going to mount and
frame it. He didn't know what occasion he would use to
give it to her, but he would think of one. He worked until
the bell rang, and then he quickly cleaned up and headed
toward his last period class.

He walked into the classroom and sat down in his
usual seat, missing Lindy even more. This was the first
class they shared together and it was special. In this room,
they were known as Romeo and Juliet—a couple—a

team. Lukas came in and looked straight over at Ricky. He immediately sat down beside him.

"Is Lindy all right?" Lukas asked him.

Ricky shrugged. "No....not really."

"I know what happened."

"How do you know?" Ricky sat up straighter and stared at Lukas.

"Me and Sara broke up over it. Anyway, I caught her and that Carrie bitch on the phone. I heard what they said to Lindy's dad."

Ricky stiffened. "What? Carrie and Sara called Lindy's dad?"

"Yeah....and they told him she was pregnant. They were laughing their asses off about it when they discovered me standing there. I told Sara it was over between us.... that I didn't want to be with anybody who would do something that underhanded and cruel. Then I walked out. She chased after me, but...well, what they did made me sick. Poor Lindy. What happened to her? Why isn't she here?"

Ricky made eye contact with Lukas and sighed. "Between you and me....right? Her dad beat her with a belt. She's pretty messed up. Big black and blue and purple welts all over her."

Lukas blanched. "My God! Where is she?"

"She's at my place. My uncle told her she couldn't stay at her place. We gathered up some of her things, and took her to our place. She's in the spare room. Uncle Nick called his ex-wife to come over and treat her. She'll be okay, eventually...physically, that is. The emotional part....well...."

Ricky stopped talking when he saw Carrie walk in. Carrie stiffened when she saw Ricky and Lukas talking, and she quickly sat down and glanced furtively over her shoulder at the two of them. Throughout the class period, Carrie felt uncomfortable, since every time she looked over her shoulder, Ricky's eyes were boring into her. She suddenly became very afraid. When the bell rang, Carrie took a chance and approached Ricky.

"Ricky, let me…."

"Let you what?" Ricky cut her off. "I wouldn't even let you blow me. Now get the hell away from me." He edged past her and quickly darted out of the room.

Lukas narrowed his eyes and stared at Carrie for a moment. "Carrie, does your dad know about that twenty-eight-year-old guy you're screwing? Hope he doesn't find out." Lukas sneered at her and walked past her the same way Ricky had. He wanted to catch up with Ricky and give him a ride home.

Lukas pulled up in front of the condo to let Ricky out. "Hey, can I come in to see her for a moment?"

"It's okay with me, but I don't know if she's up for visitors. Come on in and we can ask."

Lukas shut the car off, took the key from the ignition, and followed Ricky into the condo.

"Wait here a minute while I find out if you can come up." Ricky ran up the stairs and into the room. He found Lindy awake and leafing through a dictionary she had found in the drawer of the nightstand. He made a mental note to get her something to read, if not a television.

"Hi, Honey…I'm home." They both laughed at the cliché. "Hey, Luke is downstairs. Wants to know if he can come up and see you."

Lindy nodded. "Luke and I have known each other since grade school. You know that, don't you? Does he know anything....?"

"Yeah....wait until you hear. He knows more than you do." Ricky went to the top of the stairs and called for Lukas to come up.

Lukas entered the room like he was walking on eggs. Lindy looked so tiny in that bed. He couldn't see any telltale signs that she had been beaten, though.

"Hey, kid...how are ya doing?" He smiled at her, relieved that she wasn't a big bloody mess, which is what he had pictured in his mind when Ricky said her dad beat her with a belt. This still surprised Lukas. He knew Lindy's dad and always thought of him as a loving, supportive father. He couldn't imagine him ever hurting Lindy.

"So...where are you hurt?"

Lindy looked at Ricky and then pulled up her pajama top, exposing the horrid welts. Lukas felt as though his insides crumbled and fell to his feet.

"My God, Lindy. How could he do that to you?"

Lindy's eyes welled up with tears, and Ricky moved close to her, taking her head in his arm. He knew he couldn't touch her shoulders or back.

"Tell her, Luke." Ricky turned to Lindy and said, "Listen to what Luke told me."

Lukas quickly related the story about Carrie and Sara calling her dad, and how he and Sara broke up over it. Lindy listened to Lukas's tale, stunned that someone would do something that cruel to another person.

"So is the baby okay?" Lukas asked her.

"Yes…Aunt Liz listened to his heartbeat and she says he's fine. I'm going to go to her office on Monday for a proper exam."

"You said he….how do you know it's a he?"

"I don't, but why wouldn't it be?" She laughed, and then smiled at Ricky.

"I gotta go, but, uh….if you two need anything, just ask. Do you have something to write on? I'll give you my phone numbers. Call….for any reason."

"I might take you up on that, Luke. I want to get Lindy some looser fitting clothes. Not maternity, yet, but something not quite as tight. I might want to go to the mall."

"You got it, Rick….just holler." Lukas let himself out, leaving Lindy and Ricky alone in the house for the first time in more than a month.

Lindy smiled at Ricky. "I took a shower and washed all that stuff off my back. It's starting to hurt. Can you put some on for me?"

"Of course. Want to do homework and then be done with it for the rest of the weekend? Maybe if you're feeling better, with Aunt Liz's permission, we can do something together on Sunday. Anything you want."

"Okay," Lindy said as she lay down and rolled over onto her stomach. Ricky gently applied the prescription ointment, taking care not to apply pressure. He noticed that the welts were going down, but were leaving mottled purple and blue bruises in their place. He knew she would have signs of the beating for a long time.

"Okay….anywhere else?" He asked. She showed him some on the backs of her legs and another across her left breast. He applied the ointment there as well. "Give it a few minutes to work. I'll set up the table for our homework, and get us something to drink. Hungry?"

"No….I'm good. Aunt Liz left the rest of the breakfast here. I ate it after I talked to you at lunch."

"Okay….well…..let me get the portable table and drinks. I'll be right back."

After he set up the table, and brought their drinks, they spent the rest of the afternoon doing their homework. They finished the last bit of it as Nick came in the door, followed by Liz, at six o'clock. Ricky moved the table out of the way so Liz could examine Lindy again. He decided against putting it away, thinking that maybe they could play cards on it later, or at least give her a table to eat dinner. At the moment, he was taking the liberty of hanging Lindy's clothes on hangers in the closet. He would let her do the drawers herself later.

"Oh….I almost forgot. We're ordering Chinese delivery. What do you both want?"

"Lindy likes the sweet and sour chicken, and I like that General Something chicken. Right, Hon?"

Lindy nodded. Again, Liz marveled over how well Ricky knew Lindy. She went down the stairs to add their selections to the order, and then called the local Chinese delivery. Nick was setting the kitchen table for the delivery of the food. He had lit several candles and placed extra plates, silverware, and napkins on the table. He had not ever acquired the ability to use chopsticks, and he knew Liz hadn't either, so the option of silverware was necessary. He planned on having Ricky and Lindy join them for dinner; since he had something to say to them.

\* \* \*

Ray pulled into Diane's driveway, cut the engine, got out and quickly walked to her back door. She opened it before he knocked.

"Did you see her?" He asked.

"No….I got to the school before classes let out and I stayed until the last kid left the school. She didn't come out of the building. I don't think she was in school today. I'll wait there every day next week if I have to."

Ray nodded. "Diane….thank you."

"For what?"

"For being there….for caring…..for loving me even though I'm a piece of shit….and for caring about my daughter."

"Oh, Ray…..You're a good man…you just made a couple of errors in judgment. I know you love Lindy…you thought you were doing the right thing by staying away from her. That must have been so hard….but you thought you were doing it to protect her. And Lindy? Well, she's easy to love."

Ray smiled at her and then frowned. "How can I ever make this up to her? How can I make up the past three years? I'm afraid it's too late. I've lost her forever."

Diane came around behind Ray's chair and encircled his shoulders with her arms. "We'll get through this. We'll be a happy family….you'll see." She rested her head on his. "I'll find her….I'll go to that school every day until I see her."

\* \* \*

Nick accepted the bags from the delivery boy, paid him along with a healthy tip, and took the food to the kitchen and set it on the counter. Liz had gone upstairs to alert Ricky and Lindy that Nick wanted them to eat downstairs. She looked in the closet and found something for Lindy to wear in lieu of pajamas.

"This is perfect, Lindy. It's comfortable, it won't put any pressure on your wounds, and….it's pretty."

She was holding a long caftan Lindy always wore when she was sitting around her house with nothing to do. It was comfortable, so she opted to put it on, and then she pulled her hair back and fastened it with a clip. She and Ricky started downstairs when Nick called to them that the delivery had arrived. They both braced themselves for what they assumed would be a tirade from Nick, telling them how stupid and irresponsible they were. He greeted them at the bottom of the stairs.

"How are you feeling, Lindy? A little better?" Nick asked her.

"Yes….a little better. Thank you."

Nick looked at the bed pillow in Ricky's hand. "What's that for?"

"So she won't have to sit against the hard frame of the chair."

"Oh…good thinking. I didn't think about that."

"When it comes to her comfort, I think of everything." Ricky responded.

"Yeah….everything except condoms….idiot. Sorry…. this is supposed to be a pleasant dinner….but I couldn't resist that one. Come on and sit down."

Ricky had stiffened at Nick's remark, but relaxed again when he apologized. The truth was that he might have had condoms if he had planned to have sex with Lindy. How could he convince his uncle that the sex was just as unplanned as the pregnancy? It just happened. They made their way to the kitchen table, their eyes taking in all the lit candles. Lindy thought it looked romantic. Ricky pulled her chair out for her and placed the pillow behind her. They smiled at each other, and their eyes locked briefly, telling each other that no matter what happened, they were in this together. Nick and Liz sat down at the table, across from Ricky and Lindy, and passed their food to them.

"Okay." Nick began. "Let's get right to it." He looked at Ricky and then at Lindy. "We have a situation here…. one I wish we didn't have to deal with….but we do. From what Liz tells me….you two want to have this baby and keep it…is that correct?"

Ricky and Lindy looked at each other for a moment, and then both of them nodded. "Yes." They answered in unison.

"I'm not going to go over how young you are, and all the problems that arise….how tough it is. I think you both know that. The question is….are you two capable? Are you up to this challenge? Can you both make the necessary sacrifices for a child, and yet still maintain your own hopes and dreams? See, that's what is important. You may be able to take care of a child, but at the expense of losing all hope for your own future. You don't want that. The kid is doomed from the beginning, and so is your relationship. Do you both understand this?"

"Uncle Nick….this is our baby. No, we didn't plan it, but we can't wish it away either. I know I love Lindy and she loves me. Yes, we are young, but we may just know a little more about love than adults do."

Ricky reached for Lindy's hand and held onto it.

"Uncle Nick, we don't fight because we agree on most things. What we don't agree on, we discuss. We're honest

270

with each other....open....and we trust each other. I know that I want Lindy to be happy and she wants the same for me. I think about what she would like....what would make her smile....what would make her happy...all the time...not just when I'm with her. As far as sacrifices.... we're both willing to do that. Now I know you would like to take the credit for the changes in me....and yes... you did give me an opportunity to have a better life..... but I quit the booze because of Lindy...I quit smoking because Lindy didn't like it...and hell, we waited to have sex longer than most couples our age do. When it's for love, it's easy to make sacrifices. And for the record....I have never made Lindy cry."

Nick sat quietly, mentally digesting what Ricky had said. He glanced at Liz and saw that she was touched by what Ricky said. He reached for Liz's hand, and she nodded, encouraging him to go on.

Nick sighed. "Okay....then if this is the way you feel, I'm going to help you. Right now...I'm mad as hell at both of you....but that doesn't mean I don't love both of you. I'm going to do my damnedest to help you two be together, and raise the child. Now, Lindy...your dad could throw a wrench into the mix, and change everything.... I want you to know that. You are still a minor and may be here in my house illegally. But for now...this is what's going to happen."

Nick looked from Ricky to Lindy and then back to Ricky.

"Ricky, you are going to work this summer. I got you a job in the lab. We need an extra person to do the odds and ends we never get to."

Ricky's face lit up. "That's cool! I love laboratory work."

"And Lindy….you're not off the hook either. Can you type?"

Lindy shrugged. "Yeah….I'm not bad at it."

"Good. Here's the deal. We always need our experiments and the results typed up in report form. The hospital has transcriptionists, but patient reports come first. Ours sit. The hospital is willing to pay for our own typist. You will get paid by the line as well as an hourly salary, just as the others do, but you will type our reports and get them done in a timely manner. Also, you can do it from home. Agreed?"

"Yes, of course." Lindy nodded.

"Now….you two are going to pay rent and buy food. Two hundred dollars a month, plus food. That's through the summer. When you go back to school in the fall, it will get reduced to one hundred dollars a month. You can both work part time then, except for when Lindy gives birth. When is that?"

Lindy shrugged again. "I think in October."

Nick forced a smile. "I knew it was that weekend I was at the conference."

Lindy and Ricky looked at each other, and Ricky's hand tightened over Lindy's. They said nothing.

"Well, anyway…you both have a home here, and when the baby comes…that will be three of you. If you are still together when you turn eighteen, you can legally get married….that's up to you. I will continue to help you until you graduate from college. It won't be easy, but I could make it a lot tougher on you, too. I don't want to see your lives ruined, but I want you to know that this should have been avoided. Understood?"

Lindy and Ricky nodded in agreement. "Thank you." Lindy whispered.

"Now, for some happier news." Nick squeezed Liz's hand before he spoke. "Liz and I are going to try again. She'll officially be your Aunt Liz again. And to be honest with you…we are taking a few lessons from the two of you on how to work a relationship."

Lindy and Ricky's faces lit up in smiles. They smiled at each other and then smiled at Nick and Liz.

"I'm so happy for you!" Lindy told Liz. "Both of you." She added, including Nick.

Liz directed her words toward Lindy. "What we are looking into for you, Lindy…is what legal recourses we have to keep you here. From what I have learned through a few friends in social work is that as long as you are pregnant or have a child, you are under your own jurisdiction…which means you can legally stay here. I'm going to check further to make sure…..but hopefully, it'll be fine for you to stay here. Now…for what he did, your dad could be arrested. The problem with that is….Social Services will get involved…"

"NO! Aunt Liz…..I don't want that….."

"Okay…..I didn't think so. So let's just see what your rights are."

Nick had something to add. "Oh, and one more thing…I know if I tell you no sex under my roof, it would be like talking into a vacuum. Just use a little discretion, and always put the baby first. As long as you two are not married, you will not share a bed in my presence. Fair enough?"

Lindy and Ricky nodded in agreement.

"Ricky, have you told your mother yet?" Nick stared into Ricky's eyes.

"No….I haven't. I really don't have a death wish."

"Good….because I want to be the first to call her grandma."

All four of them laughed. Nick got the look of mischief in his eyes. "Are we done here?" He looked at everybody's plates. "Good….let's call her now."

He got up to retrieve the phone from its cradle and sat back down, already in the process of dialing Angie's telephone number. She answered on the second ring.

"Angie? How are ya?"

"Nick? Is something wrong? Is Ricky all right?"

"Yeah, Angie…Ricky is all right. I just called to tell you that Ricky has a surprise for you…..Grandma." He instinctively pulled the phone away from his ear.

"*WHAT*! NO! Ricky and….Lindy? Lindy is pregnant? Oh, NO! Now what? Their lives are ruined!"

"Not if I can help it." Nick retorted. "Would you like to know when it happened? That weekend I went to the conference, and you were supposed to be here. Remember that?"

"Nick…..I couldn't help it. My car was wrecked. I couldn't get there."

"And….I notice you haven't been down here since. You even missed Ricky's birthday."

"Nick, I know. I've had some difficulties. I sent him something. The sale of the house fell through. The people couldn't get a mortgage. I have a couple more people looking at it this weekend. I want to be out of here by

August. I had planned on Ricky moving in with me and finishing his last year of school. Now what?"

"Well, if you get your ass down here we'll talk about it. There's more than just Ricky to consider. Lindy and the baby get a part in this, too."

"All right....I'll be there next weekend. I have somebody looking at the house tomorrow and there is another open house here on Sunday. I'll be there next weekend....for sure."

"Okay, Angie....and one more thing....Liz and I are getting married again. Bye."

Nick pressed the end call button and counted to five before the phone rang again. He handed it to Liz and she answered.

"Liz! Is that true?"

Liz started laughing. "Yes....fortunately or unfortunately....it's true. We haven't decided when, but it will be soon. I'll keep you posted." As she spoke with Angie, she was watching Lindy and Ricky, their heads together, discussing something. When she hung up, Ricky and Lindy looked up at her.

"We found out how Lindy's father found out. Carrie Siverson. She called Lindy's dad and told him."

"That girl is a real bitter pill, isn't she?" Liz commented. "Ricky, does she still chase after you?"

"Yeah....she had the nerve to come up to me today. I put her in her place. I don't like that girl....not at all."

"Well....your dad would have found out eventually.... but there was a better way for him to find out."

"He may not have ever found out, for all the attention he paid to me."

"Good point. How are you doing now? Starting to feel pain again? I think it's time you got back upstairs to bed. Nick and Ricky can clean up here...not that there is much to do. Come on, I'll help you back upstairs and get some of that magic stuff on your wounds. Ricky can join us after he's done here." She turned and appealed to Ricky. "Bring tea?"

He nodded. "Okay."

"Can I come with him? I'll bring the fortune cookies..." Nick asked.

Lindy and Liz laughed. "Of course." They answered.

* * *

Lukas showed up on Sunday to see if Ricky and Lindy wanted to go to the mall. Liz vetoed it for Lindy, but Lindy encouraged Ricky to go with Lukas. Ricky and Lukas drew Lindy into the kitchen.

"We're going to shop for you, so act like you like everything we bought when we come back....okay?"

"Oh wow...nothing slinky or sleazy....okay?" Lindy laughed at the thought.

"Don't worry, Baby....I know what you like and what you look good in. Trust me." Ricky winked at Lindy and smiled. "You'll be okay here, right?"

"Yeah, Uncle Nick wants me to look at some templates and standards for the job. That will keep me busy."

"Don't forget to rest. I'll be back soon. I love you."

"I love you, too. Luke...no women. Got it?"

The three of them laughed. "Got it." Lukas answered.

Lindy watched them drive away with a slight smile on her face. She loved and trusted Ricky and she knew she could trust Lukas, too. He had been her life-long friend since they were five years old. In grade school, they were sweethearts, but as they got older a strong friendship replaced any romantic feelings they may have had toward each other. Lukas was like a brother to her. She sighed, walked away from the window, and went to find Nick. He was in his den. The two of them spent a good part of the afternoon going over the standards she was to use for his reports. He gave her a sample report as a guide, and then told her that he would be bringing home a computer for her to use—one that had all the information she would need already on it. They were so involved in her training that they lost track of the time. Both of them were surprised when they heard Ricky open the front door and call for Lindy.

"In here, Ricky." Lindy answered him.

Ricky entered and stood just inside the doorway, frowning. "You didn't get any rest, did you?"

"I'm okay. I had to learn all this stuff....."

"Uncle Nick, you *know* she was told to rest...."

"Yeah, and I'm sorry. We just lost track of time."

"Ricky....I'm really not tired."

Ricky smiled at her. "Okay....I just don't want you over-doing it...that's all. Are you done for now?" He looked from Lindy to Nick.

"Yeah, she's got it. Smart girl....quick learner." Nick observed.

"With excellent taste in men, I might add." Ricky smirked and reached for Lindy's hand. "Come on and see what I got you."

"What did you get me?" Nick joked.

"You get rent money....which I have for you already." Ricky said over his shoulder as he led Lindy toward the stairs, stopping to grab the packages he had left in the middle of the living room floor.

Nick started to protest the two of them going upstairs together, but remembered Lindy's injuries and realized that they wouldn't be violating his rules. He smiled to himself. He had no intention of keeping their rent money; he planned on investing it for them, giving them something to build upon when they got older and wiser.

Ricky dropped the packages on the bed and reached for Lindy. He held her face between his palms and kissed her. She slid her arms around his waist and kissed him back.

"I can hardly wait to be able to hold you again. Hey, I missed you. Luke and I had fun, but I wanted it to be you I was with. Come on….look at what I bought you. I hope you like all of it."

Ricky took things out of the bags and held them up for her, and she was thrilled with his selections. Everything he chose was straight cut or flared, and nothing would show her belly. The colors were perfect for her. She tried on a few things, and was pleased with how they looked on her.

"It's all great!" She told him.

"See? And you were worried…."

They laughed together, and their eyes locked, causing that jolt of electricity they were becoming familiar with.

"We're going to make it, Baby.….I know we are." Ricky gently kissed her and ran his thumbs across her cheeks.

# Chapter 28

$\mathcal{L}$indy returned to school on Wednesday of the following week. On Monday, she kept her appointment with Liz and made arrangements for a sonogram for the following Thursday after school, so Ricky could be there, too. Lindy awoke on Wednesday morning feeling refreshed and ready to go back. Liz had given her a note for the school and a note to keep her out of gym class. Liz suggested to her that if there were any questions, to just show them a little bit of her back and say she fell down the steps. On that first day back, Nick dropped them off at the front entrance and watched them enter the building. As he drove away he silently hoped that Lindy would be all right.

Just inside the front doors they ran into Lukas.

"Welcome back, Lindy. How are you feeling?"

"Okay, I guess." She answered him.

"Well, I'm glad you're back. This guy was lost without you." Lukas indicated that he was talking about Ricky. "He moped around here for three days."

Lindy laughed at Lukas' remark and reached for Ricky's hand.

The first day back was tiring for Lindy, but she managed to get through all of her classes. Many of

279

the other students showed their concern for her injury, especially when she deterred them from hugging her by saying her back was really hurting. Some of the students gave her sidelong looks, trying to see for themselves if the pregnancy rumor was true. Ricky was by her side most of the day, except for sixth period when she had music and he had art. Mister Wise gushed when he saw her, and even more when she shared her little secret with him. He liked Ricky and believed they were a couple that would stay together. When the class ended, Ricky showed up to walk her to their last class for the day. After they were seated in their regular seats, Ricky took both of Lindy's hands in his, and stared into her eyes.

"Rough day?" He asked softly.

"Yeah, I'm a little tired. Don't look now but she just walked in, and she's staring at us. Here comes Luke, too."

Ricky turned around to greet Lukas, noting that Carrie was intensely staring at Lindy. He couldn't let it go. "Carrie, I wish you wouldn't stare at my wife like that. She's a straight chick." Those who heard it, which was almost everybody, burst out laughing.

Cindy had to ask. "Wife? Did you two get married?"

Ricky looked earnestly at Cindy. "Cindy, we've been married since the day we met."

"That's so romantic!" Cindy squealed.

Carrie's face was red. She dropped down onto her seat and opened a book to look like she was reading, but the opened book was upside down.

The class ended in what seemed an eternity, causing Lindy discomfort as she tried to sit in the hard chair.

When the bell rang, Ricky and Lindy let everybody else go out first since Ricky was worried about someone jostling her and hurting her. He had all the books so she had nothing but her small purse to carry. They went to her locker and then to his, and got what they needed before they left the building. Ricky held her hand as they went down the steps and crossed the street, oblivious to others around them. They had only walked a few yards when Lindy heard someone calling her name. She turned around and was face to face with Diane.

"Go away, Diane. I don't want to talk to you."

"Lindy….your dad is sick over what he did. He wants to say he's sorry."

"Diane….go away. I can't forgive him. I won't."

"Lindy, please…..he's….really sick over what he did. He loves you. He loves you very much."

Lindy began to shake, her voice quivered, and tears sprang to her eyes.

"Yeah? He loves me?" Lindy turned around and pulled up her top, exposing the mottled purple and blue welts all over her back. "Is this what he calls love?"

Diane gasped, and closed her eyes. It was much worse than she expected.

"Oh, Lindy….I'm so sorry…he….didn't mean it. He even told me why he avoided you these past three years. He loves you, Honey….and he wants to see you."

Lindy was crying. Diane reached for her and Lindy backed away.

"No…I don't want to see him. I don't care what his excuse is…he doesn't have one good enough…..not for the beating….and not for the past three years. Go away, Diane." Lindy sobbed.

Diane reached for her again, and Lindy shrank back against Ricky.

"Please, Lindy…" Diane pleaded as she put her hand on Lindy's arm.

Lindy shrieked and moved even closer to Ricky.

***"Stay the fuck away from her! Don't ever try to touch her again."*** Ricky's tone was threatening.

Lukas pulled up and called to them, asking if they needed help. Ricky told Lindy to go get into the car, and then turned around to confront Diane.

"Leave her alone…..that's all I have to say…just leave her alone."

Diane stared at Ricky for a moment. "Are you the father of the baby?"

"Yes, I am. And you know what? I will never turn my back on Lindy or my child. Mister Riley lost something so precious…..he just didn't appreciate what he had. Now leave us alone."

Ricky strode away from Diane and got into the car. Lukas drove away quickly, not giving Diane a chance to get into her car and follow them. Lindy leaned against Ricky and sobbed during the ride home, and was still sobbing when they entered the condo. Ricky insisted that she let him take her upstairs to rest. He got her a glass of water and gave her one of the sedatives Liz had prescribed, and then pulled a chair up to the bed and sat down. He held her hand and stroked her hair until she fell asleep.

\* \* \*

Diane was leaning against the kitchen counter, holding a glass of bourbon over ice, when Ray walked in. He knew by the look on her face that she had seen Lindy.

"Well?" He searched Diane's face for some glimmer of good news.

Diane sighed. "I saw her."

"And?"

Diane shook her head. "She doesn't want to see you. She showed me her back...where you hit her.....it's awful....."

"What did she say?" His voice aired his irritation.

"She said she didn't want to see you....she can't forgive you...and she won't. She was crying....so the boyfriend stepped in and told me to stay away from her....no, stay the *fuck* away from her...were his words."

"Some asshole punk, huh? Garbage mouth and all."

Diane shook her head. "No, not really....he genuinely cares for Lindy. I asked him if he was the father of the baby, and he said he was. He also said that he would never turn his back on Lindy or the baby....that *you* lost something precious...and *you* didn't appreciate what you had."

Ray sighed, and then dropped into a kitchen chair, staring at the pattern on the table. "The kid's right....you know that? He's right." Ray's voice was barely above a whisper, as he felt a renewed sadness creep into his heart. He fell silent as he sat there staring at the table. Once again, he looked up at Diane who was still standing at the counter.

"There are marks...where I hit her?"

Diane closed her eyes for a moment, fighting back tears.

"Yes, Ray. Really bad."

Ray fell silent again; pain and misery surrounding him like a cocoon.

\* \* \*

Nick tapped lightly on the doorframe to Lindy's room. He had been in the house for ten minutes, and upon hearing no sound or movement, decided to investigate. He peeked in and saw Ricky sitting beside the bed, and Lindy lying on it, sleeping. Ricky put his index finger up to his lips, appealing to Nick to stay quiet. He got up and walked out into the hallway with Nick.

"What were you doing in there?"

"Just watching her sleep. Come on, let's go downstairs. She took a sedative, so she may sleep for awhile."

"Did something happen?" Nick felt himself becoming agitated.

Ricky told him about the encounter with Diane and how upset Lindy was. He ran his hand over his face to keep his composure.

"You know….Uncle Nick….I don't want her hurt any more. I can't stand it when she's hurt. She cries and it's all I can do to keep from crying, too. I just want to hold her and shield her from all the hurt…you know what I mean?"

"Yeah, kid….I do." Nick smiled at Ricky. "You've grown up…you know that? The way you care about Lindy….take care of her…..protect her….well, you're more of a man than…a lot of men I know…who are a lot older than you."

"Well, Uncle Nick….I had a choice to make…and I made it. See, when I first met Lindy…it was a decision for me….either make her mine or find someone who was more like what I was used to. I met a couple of girls the night after I met Lindy…they were like the girls I used to hang out with. Well, I decided….even though I knew there would be things I would have to give up…that I wanted to be with Lindy. I remember….smoking a cigarette with these girls…exchanging crude remarks…and all I could think about was Lindy the whole time. That's when I knew…I was hers. I don't regret it, and I know what I have. I would never do anything to cause me to lose it…and as far as taking care of her….well, it's what I love doing, but it's also right. Agree?"

"One hundred percent. I'm starving. What do we have to whip up real fast?"

Ricky and Nick walked toward the kitchen, Nick's hand on Ricky's shoulder. They were more than just uncle and nephew; they shared a bond now, each respecting the other for different reasons.

* * *

Lindy survived school the rest of the week. By Friday afternoon she was exhausted. She had gotten up briefly on Wednesday evening, the day Diane approached her, and said she was not very hungry. Ricky heated up a can of soup for her and sat with her while she ate. They did their homework afterwards, but they really didn't have all that much to do, so they finished it quickly. Lindy was sound asleep before ten o'clock. Ricky was becoming a little worried about all the sleep she seemed to need. After she fell asleep, he asked Nick about it. Nick immediately dialed Liz's number and handed Ricky the phone. Ricky voiced his concerns to Liz.

"Aunt Liz, is it normal for Lindy to sleep so much? She slept over three hours after school and now she's already in bed for the night. Is this normal? She's pale, too."

"Well, Ricky….usually a woman is very tired the first three or four months, but in Lindy's case…..the emotional

stress is taking its toll. That's what is making her sleep….
emotions. She's been through a lot."

"Yeah….she has….and more today." Ricky told Liz
about their confrontation with Diane.

"Well, see? There you go! Do you want me to stop
by?"

"No….that's okay. She's sleeping. We'll be there
tomorrow for the sonogram…right?"

"Right, Ricky. I'll talk to both of you then. Now let
me say goodnight to your uncle."

Ricky handed the phone to Nick, and told him he was
going upstairs to bed for the night. He stopped by Lindy's
room to check on her once more before going to his room.
He stared down at her with a half smile on his face. She
looked so beautiful and so peaceful just lying there. He
bent down and kissed her forehead, and whispered, "I love
you" before turning around and going to his own room.

After school on Thursday they took a bus to the hospital
and went up to the second floor where Liz was waiting
for them. Fascinated, they watched the technician as she
prepared the ultrasound equipment for the sonogram.
Liz joined them when the pictures began. The technician
pointed the baby out to them.

"That's it? Lindy…I think we're having a seahorse."
Lindy was trying to remain still, but was finding it
difficult since she was laughing over Ricky's remark. The
technician laughed as well.

"Darn….the baby won't turn around. I thought
maybe we could see what it is—a boy or a girl—but the
baby won't cooperate. You'll be having another one in a
couple of months, so we should be able to tell by then."

"We don't want to know anyway. We want to be surprised. Right, Ricky?" Lindy appealed to Ricky, hoping he still felt that way. They had talked about it and they both agreed that they would wait until it was born to find out the gender. He nodded his agreement.

They rode home with Nick and Lindy wasn't so tired on Thursday night. They did their homework and watched a movie with Nick.

Friday afternoon dragged for Lindy. She was so tired that all she wanted to do was go home to bed. She knew she couldn't be doing that all the time, so she insisted that she and Ricky walk home after school for the exercise and fresh air. Lukas had offered to give them a ride, but he understood her need to walk. On the way home, they stopped at the convenience store for something to drink. Lindy disappeared down one of the aisles and came back with a jar of green olives. Ricky took the jar from her and set it on the counter. He leaned over and whispered, "Is this a craving?" She nodded. Ricky chuckled, and asked if she wanted two jars. She shook her head.

The walk home helped. She was not nearly as tired when they got home. They opted to do their homework on the patio since the weather was warm and lovely. The color had returned to Lindy's cheeks by the time the sun set. Ricky was relieved.

\* \* \*

Monday brought a new buzz around the school. The prom was the following Friday. Neither Ricky nor Lindy had even thought about going, but a remark from Carrie changed their minds. The talk before the seventh period class began was of the prom and who was going. Carrie opened her mouth and hurled a cheap remark at Lindy again.

When an unknowing student asked Ricky and Lindy is they were going, Carrie interjected an answer for them. "I don't think they make maternity prom gowns."

Ricky glared at Carrie and then turned to Lindy. "Wanna go? I'll bet we can find something….we'll call Aunt Liz for help. I'll get the tickets right now. Sean up there in that first seat, first row, sells them. Want to?"

Lindy nodded, and Ricky got out of his seat and went up to Sean. He couldn't help notice how Carrie flinched when he got up. Sean gladly sold him two prom tickets, and as Ricky passed Carrie's desk on his way back to his seat, he couldn't resist. "We'll take pictures of Lindy in her maternity prom gown, since you won't be there to see her…I mean…. you didn't even get asked to the prom, did you?"

Carrie shrunk with embarrassment as the class snickered. Shawna couldn't help taunting her more. "Hey, Carrie….want to go to the prom with me?" This caused more laughter.

When class was over, Ricky and Lindy went right home and called Liz. She answered her office phone immediately when it rang.

"Hi, Aunt Liz. This is Ricky."

"Hi….everything all right, Ricky?"

"Uh, yeah….we need a favor."

"Sure….what is it?"

"Well….Carrie Siverson was taunting Lindy about not going to the prom because they don't make maternity prom gowns….and well…I bought two prom tickets.

Can you help Lindy find something that she could wear to the prom?"

"Ricky, I'd be delighted. I'm leaving here at five today. Tell Lindy to be ready...oh...and see Uncle Nick about what you will need. Tux, flowers, transportation....I'll take care of Lindy. Ricky? I think it's important that you two go. It's what Nick was talking about...not losing out on your own dreams. I think he'll agree with me. See you at five-fifteen." Liz hung up and smiled to herself. She would see to it that Lindy looked beautiful that night.

\* \* \*

The week flew by rather quickly with so much to do to get ready for the prom. Lindy and Liz found the most beautiful gown for Lindy at one of Liz's favorite exclusive shops.

"Not many girls can afford to shop here, including Carrie Siverson," Liz told Lindy. "But no arguments from you...we will find something in here and you will be beautiful....no matter what it costs. Don't worry about it."

They found the perfect dress. Not only did it hide her belly but it also hid the still prominent bruises on her back. The neckline of the dress was a vee in the front and a vee in the back. From each shoulder, both front and back, soft, pleated lengths of silk material were draped, crossing in the front and in the back. The back panels came around to the front while the front panels went around to the back. The full skirt was lavender and each panel was a pastel shade of blue, pink, yellow and green. Lindy looked soft and delicate in it; like a true princess. The sales lady recommended shoes in the very same soft pastel colors, which the shop just happened to have. Liz would not let Lindy see the price of the dress or the shoes; she was determined that Lindy would have them.

While Liz and Lindy were shopping for her dress, Ricky and Nick were busy trying to find a last minute limo rental and a tux for Ricky to wear. They were not having it as easy as Lindy and Liz had it, but they managed to find what they needed. Nick took Ricky to the flower shop where Ricky had gotten Lindy's birthday roses and they ordered a corsage with white roses and colored carnations, with the promise to call the color in no later than the next day.

On Tuesday evening Ricky called the florist and told him to make each of the five carnations a pastel color—blue, pink, green, yellow, and lavender. His pearl gray tux would have a lavender cummerbund and bowtie.

Lukas told Ricky he was going to the prom with another girl other than Sara, and he would share the expense of the limo, if that was okay. Ricky agreed to it, and Nick was happy to share the cost of the limo.

Friday arrived. The school was buzzing with excitement about the prom. Lindy and Ricky were excited, too; even though they tried not to be. In the lunchroom on Friday, Lukas introduced them to the girl he was taking. She was nice and very friendly. It was obvious that Lindy and Ricky fascinated her. She told Lukas later that they reminded her of Romeo and Juliet; which caused Lukas to laugh. Carrie was noticeably absent from classes that day, which surprised no one.

Liz picked Lindy and Ricky up after school and drove Lindy to the salon to get her hair done, and Ricky to pick up the flowers and tux. She wanted this to be another night they would remember forever, just like the formal

Christmas party. Building memories adds strength to the relationship, she reminded herself. It dawned on her, that while she and Nick remembered everything about each other, they had very few memories of their life together when they were married. This was something she planned on working on. After she dropped Ricky off at the condo she went to pick Lindy up from the salon. They arrived home in plenty of time to eat and then get ready. Ricky already had a plate of sandwiches and potato salad on the table when they walked in. Ricky complimented Lindy on her hair as she was digging in to the food.

When it was time to get ready, Liz went upstairs with Lindy. Ricky was already upstairs dressing. Nick made Ricky go down to the living room and wait for Lindy to come down, insisting that it was prom etiquette. Nick didn't forget pictures; he had the camera loaded with film. Finally Lindy was ready to walk down the stairs. The look on Ricky's face when he saw Lindy made every penny spent on the dress and the shoes worth it. He was spellbound. Nick took a multitude of pictures while they waited for the limo. Lukas arrived and parked his car off to the side in the driveway. They would go in the limo to pick up his date. Liz had tears in her eyes when they left in the limo.

Nick sidled up to her and put his arm around her. "Our kids are growing up." He joked. "What do you say we go out somewhere and dance tonight?"

Surprised, Liz caught her breath. "Really? I'd love to."

"Well, then….let's go." He offered her his arm and swept her out the door.

\* \* \*

The ballroom at the Marriott was decorated with soft party lights and flowers. Picket fences surrounded the dance floor. Lindy, Ricky, Lukas and his date, Shayla arrived by limo at the front entrance of the hotel. Shayla wore a ruffled mint green gown that looked lovely on her with her auburn hair. Lindy and Shayla seemed to get along well, making the guys happy, since they were becoming best friends. As they walked through the lobby toward the ballroom, they heard 'oohs' and 'aahs' from hotel guests. They made a handsome foursome.

As they entered the ballroom they were given ballots to vote for prom king and queen and tokens for free soft drinks. After finding a table for four, Lukas mysteriously disappeared for awhile, leaving Lindy and Ricky to entertain Shayla. Lukas reappeared when the music signifying the first dance began. He led Shayla away, leaving Lindy and Ricky at the table.

Ricky reached for Lindy's hand. "Come on…I want to dance with my wife. Legally, you aren't, but…in my heart….you are." He winked at her as they got up to dance.

Ricky held Lindy like she was fragile. He smiled down at her. "You look so beautiful tonight. I'm glad we decided to do this."

"Me, too. And you are a handsome devil…you know that? Wow, you turn me on."

"You turn me on, too. You know that."

"What? Fat as I'm getting? You're turned on? I think I'll keep you out of barnyards." Lindy joked and laughed.

The night was magical for them. They danced and laughed and danced some more, hanging on to every precious moment of the evening. Soon it was time to announce the king and queen. A drum roll came from the stage, and the vice principal took the microphone.

"Students....good evening. I have the utmost pleasure of announcing this year's prom royalty. The votes have been counted....and....it was almost unanimous....this year's prom king and queen are Ricky DeCelli and Miss Belinda Riley. Will you two come forward, please?"

Lindy was stunned. Ricky was shocked. Never in a million years could he have imagined them calling his name for something like this. He looked over at Lindy and saw that she was covering her face. Lukas stood up to get them moving up to the stage.

"Come on, you two...your subjects await you!" He made an effort to pull out their chairs.

On shaking knees, Lindy held onto Ricky as they made their way to the stage.

"Congratulations, Ricky and Lindy." The students applauded as the crowns were secured on their heads. Lindy was sobbing and laughing at the same time. Ricky was a little embarrassed by it all, but was so happy for Lindy.

"Will you two go down to the dance floor and dance the royal dance together, please?"

Ricky led Lindy down to the floor and encircled her in his arms. He could feel her trembling. She was biting her lip to control her sobs. Looking up at Ricky, she started to laugh. "Who would have thought...that we would...?"

"Win? Yeah, who would have thought? But it's just one more reason I believe we belong together."

The music ended as Ricky gently kissed Lindy's lips. The crowd applauded them again.

Hand in hand they walked back to their table where they had another surprise waiting for them. This time Lukas was involved. He held a poster that said

### "Congratulations, Ricky and Lindy— Our school's very own Romeo and Juliet."

There was a picture of them in the middle of the poster and the signatures of almost everybody at the prom were all over it.

"How did you have the time to do this?" Ricky asked him.

"Well, I had a feeling you two would win. The word around the school was that everyone was voting for you. I mean….if you hadn't won, nobody would have seen this, but…since you did….while you were dancing I had everybody come over and sign it. It's been in Sean's car since yesterday."

"Sly, aren't you?" Lindy grinned at him. "We'll keep it forever."

\* \* \*

Liz and Nick were almost ready to call it a night. They decided to stop in a local tavern to have one more drink before going home. By now it was assumed that they would spend the night together at Liz's place, so the tavern they chose was close to her apartment. It was almost eleven o'clock and they both wanted to catch the news. The bar was nearly empty, so hearing the news would not be an effort. Nick ordered drinks as they sat down at the bar. The news was just starting when the bartender set the drinks in front of them. The newscasters were announcing the headlines when Lindy's face crossed the screen.

"Lindy!" Liz and Nick said it at the same time.

They sat through each news story until the featured story of the evening came on. The newscaster started out by saying that there was new royalty in the neighborhood. They talked about the local high school's prom and announced the names of the prom queen and king— Ricky and Lindy. Their faces appeared on the screen as they danced together, each wearing a crown. The story ended with the newscaster commenting on what a beautiful couple they were, and that they looked to be so much in love.

Nick and Liz stared at the television, thinking the exact same thing. "They really are Romeo and Juliet." Liz mused, mainly to herself, but overheard by Nick.

"What do you mean?" He asked.

"Oh….Lindy told me everybody calls them Romeo and Juliet in their English Lit class….that's all. It seems that everybody in school approves of them being together…except Carrie Siverson, that is. For some reason, she thinks Ricky should be with her."

"Instead of Lindy? The girl must be psycho or something."

"Yeah…..I agree. I couldn't imagine Ricky with Carrie. She's so…bossy…pushy. I saw her in the hospital with Tom one day about a month ago. She was standing there with her hand out, while he pulled his wallet out. She snatched the money he took out of his wallet and left the hospital. I don't think she even thanked him for it."

"Ricky says I met her the first day of school, but I don't remember what she looks like. I could tell Ricky didn't like her, though."

"Well….I'm not real happy with their situation right now…but I'm happy he and Lindy are together." Liz commented.

"And I couldn't agree with you more." Nick conceded.

\* \* \*

Diane and Ray sat in front of the television waiting for the news to come on. Diane saw the brief glimpse of Lindy's face before the news started.

"Ray….that was Lindy."

"What? Where?" He had been dozing off but came fully awake.

"On the news. Let's watch."

As Nick and Liz had done, Ray and Diane sat through the entire headline news stories until the feature story came on. They sat and watched Lindy and 'that Ricky kid" as Ray called him, dance together, both wearing crowns, and they listened to the comments made by the newscaster when the film clip was over. Neither of them spoke until the station broke for a commercial.

"So…Lindy is prom queen." Ray's smile was sad. "And that was Ricky?"

Diane nodded. "That was him."

"That's the kid who knocked up my little girl. I'd like to blow his balls off….sneaking around in my house, probably….taking advantage of her innocence."

"Now, Ray…that's just sick talk. It happens. Remember when you were a teenager. Teens fall in love, hormones rage, they go too far….it happens. Don't talk about hurting either one of them…it's not right."

"I know….I guess it's easier to blame him than to blame myself. Damn it, Diane…I should have been there more. I should have overcame my fear….and been there for her."

"Ray…it might have happened anyway…whether you were there or not. Lots of girls who have doting parents end up getting pregnant. Stop seeing it as something you didn't do. You saw them on the television just now. The love in their eyes when they looked at each other…. nothing could stop the passion they feel for each other. You just have to accept it for what it is….your daughter fell in love and is going to have a baby…making you a grandfather. You don't have to like how that happened, but you should be willing to accept it and deal with it."

Ray turned a deaf ear to what Diane was saying. He was not going to accept that his little girl was pregnant and nobody was to blame. Maybe he wasn't there for her, but that Ricky kid did this to her—took advantage of her. He planned on finding him and making him answer for it, too. Love—they don't know what love is—not at their age.

# Chapter 29

$\mathcal{L}$indy and Ricky awoke side by side in Lindy's bed on Saturday morning. They jumped up and Ricky quickly went to the window to see if Nick's car was there. It wasn't, so Ricky pulled Lindy back into bed and wrapped his arms around her.

"We're safe for awhile…I think." He whispered against her temple.

They had come home from the prom quite late, noting that Nick and Liz weren't there. The first things that came off were Lindy's shoes. As cute as they were, they were just as painful. She carried them up the stairs and into her room, where she began to remove her dress. Ricky already had his tie and cummerbund off, and he dropped them on his bed. Lindy called Ricky to come unhook her dress and things progressed from there. They made love for the first time in almost two months. Because Lindy's wounds on her back were still tender, Ricky was extremely gentle. Lindy gasped with pleasure more than a few times, causing Ricky's arousal to heighten. Afterward, they lay contented, and drifted off to sleep.

It was early morning now. Neither of them wanted to rush out of bed, but they knew they would have to move soon, both remembering Nick's rules.

Ricky groaned. "I just remembered….my mother is coming today."

Angie had postponed her visit from last week to this week, saying she had too many people coming to see the house during the week. She just wanted to rest last weekend, but she would be here for sure this weekend.

"As we lie here she's probably on her broom right now flying towards this house."

Lindy laughed. "You're terrible."

"And you're gorgeous." He pulled her close, his hand dropping down to rub her belly. "You *are* getting big; I have to say. Wait until the wicked witch of the west sees you. Don't worry…I'll protect you from her." He dipped down and kissed Lindy's belly. "I love you…both of you." He said as he patted her belly one more time. "Want to get up for coffee?"

"You go make it and I'll go shower….okay?" She was already up off of the bed, and heading toward the shower. Ricky watched her for a moment, reminding her to take a robe in case Uncle Nick should come home at any minute. He reluctantly got out of bed, went to get his robe, and headed downstairs to make coffee.

Lindy was out of the shower, and wearing sweatpants and a tee-shirt when the coffee was done. They sat at the kitchen table and drank their morning coffee together and talked about the prom. After his second cup, Ricky ran upstairs to shower before Nick or his mother got there. When he came back down, Lindy was looking at the poster Lukas had made for them.

"This was so nice. I think we should frame it."

"I was thinking the same thing." He said over her shoulder. "Hey, I'm hungry….and guess what….I'm also cooking. Interested?"

"Uh…yeah….I'll set the table and make the toast."

* * *

Nick walked in just moments before Angie's car pulled into the driveway. Lindy and Ricky were relieved that Nick got there before Angie, since they knew that he would serve as a buffer between them and Ricky's mother if she started screaming at them.

Nick saw the car first, and made it known to Ricky and Lindy that she was in the driveway.

"Go say something about her new car. I think it may be a Ford."

Ricky went outside and intercepted his mother and her suitcase. "Nice car, Mom…what is that?"

"Focus….it's made by Ford."

Of course Ricky knew that. He was trying to soften her before the inevitable tirade began.

"Is this all? Anything else you want me to carry in for you?" He was hoping she wouldn't start outside. No such luck.

"So….you couldn't keep it in your pants, huh? Ricky, I'm so pissed off at you….and Lindy, too. How could you!"

"Mom….let's get in the house. Uncle Nick has neighbors." He held the door for her but he couldn't shut her up.

"Ricky….why couldn't you have been careful? I can't believe this! I'm going to be a grandmother at thirty-nine. And Lindy….I thought she was a nice girl, too."

"Mom…." Ricky's tone had a warning in it.

She stopped abruptly and glared at him. "Don't you take that tone with me! You had better learn some respect, young man! And just put that suitcase up in the spare room."

"Uh....you're sleeping in my room. The spare room is Lindy's. I'll be sleeping on the couch."

"Lindy's? She's....living here now? Oh great! So now you can have a sex marathon right here under your Uncle Nick's roof! Good God!"

"Mom! It's not like that! We respect Uncle Nick's rules."

"Oh yeah? Well, if you respected his rules, you wouldn't be in the situation you're in...now would you?"

"Uncle Nick never made any rules about that!"

"He has a point there. I didn't....you remember that." Nick interjected. He had been silent through the entire exchange between mother and son.

"Well, you probably didn't think you had to. One look at that angelic face would make you believe that this kind of thing wouldn't happen. How deceiving! She certainly had me fooled...thinking she was such a nice girl. Nice girls don't spread their legs..."

"ANGIE, SHUT UP!" Nick's voice boomed through the living room.

"What? That's the way you talk to your sister?"

"That's the way I talk to anybody who won't shut up when they should! Now just *shut up*!"

"So Nick....you approve of this....situation?"

No...no, I don't....but we're dealing with it. I'm handling it. Shouting hurtful words is no way to handle anything. Besides, it's too late to change anything. We deal with it."

Angie made a noise that sounded like a snort. "So....
*deal with it*? That's the *answer*? What about his *future*?
Diapers at first....and then child support later on? While
he works at McDonald's or some other minimum wage
job? Working just to pay for a mistake he made when he
was thinking with the wrong end?"

Ricky had disappeared into the kitchen when Nick
took over. Lindy was sitting at the table crying. He
immediately went to her and held her.

"Shhh....Shhh...don't cry, Baby. Please don't cry. It
doesn't matter what she thinks, or what she says. You and
I both know that's not the way it is."

He held her gently and stroked her hair for a few
moments. The act was having a calming effect on him as
well as on her.

"You don't know that it will turn out that way. With
family support they can make it....*with family support*.
I'm willing to help them out. You should be, too. He's
your only child....the baby is your first grandchild....
maybe the circumstances aren't exactly perfect, but....
hell, Angie....accept it and get used to it. It wouldn't even
hurt you to get a little involved in it. Maybe even be a
little excited?"

"I want nothing to do with it! That girl will not be
welcome in my house! Not now...not ever!"

Ricky emerged from the kitchen with Lindy in tow.

"Go up to your room...please? And just stay there.
This stops right now. I'll take care of it." He whispered
to her.

Lindy nodded and quickly crossed the living room and
climbed the stairs. Once inside the room, with the door

locked, the sobs came and her tears flowed uncontrollably. She called Liz.

"Honey, what's wrong? Stop crying so I can understand you."

Lindy sucked in her breath in an effort to get control. When she felt she could speak, she told Liz what was going on downstairs, and what Angie had said about her.

"Oh, Honey….she's angry. She doesn't mean it. How could she? You're so easy to love. She's….worried….and scared. She doesn't know what will happen to her only son now….not to mention she thinks she's still too young to be called grandma." Liz chuckled. "Listen to me…Lindy; do you have any sedatives left?"

"Yes." Lindy responded.

"Take one and lie down. Take a nap. It will shut everything else out. When the shouting stops things will look brighter. I'm going to hang up now. In a little while I'm going to call Nick…to see if I can help in any way. And Lindy? Nick and I both love you; remember that. Bye, Honey."

As soon as Ricky heard Lindy's door close, he confronted his mother. "If she's not welcome then neither am I."

"Ricky…that is just ridiculous talk! You are my son and you are underage. You have no choice but to live with your mother….but I *can still* say who comes there and who doesn't."

"For how long? In ten months I won't be underage. Will ten months be enough time for you to make every day of my life miserable? Because after that, you won't get the chance."

Angie's voice took on a noise similar to fingernails being raked down a chalkboard. "*You would take her over your own flesh and blood?*"

"*YES*! Because I love her...and she loves me. She didn't just spread her legs for me! And if you say one more thing about her...you will lose both of us forever, and....any grandchildren we may produce."

"You wouldn't be saying those things if your father were alive..."

"No, I wouldn't. My father was a loving, caring man. He showed his love in every way...and he taught me how to do the same thing. So now...why don't you blame dad? He taught me how to be good to the girl I love.... how to treat her....how to love her...and how to take care of her. YOU taught me to scream and yell....that's all you've ever done. You don't even listen to yourself when you are screaming at somebody. You don't realize the permanent damage your words can cause. When I was living in Chicago and doing things you didn't approve of...you blamed everybody and everything else for them. *You should have blamed yourself*! You drove me out there! Just like you're driving me out of your life right now!"

"YOU WILL STOP TALKING TO ME THAT WAY THIS INSTANT, YOUNG MAN!" Angie's voice had hit a peak. "I...will....not...tolerate...insolence...like that. Now...you might as well say goodbye to Lindy.... because you two are separating."

Ricky's veins popped out on his neck and he could feel his blood pressure rise instantly. Every muscle in his body tightened as his fists clenched. He hated her at that moment. *"Like hell we are! I will never leave Lindy!"*

"You don't get to make that choice....you have to live with me."

"Oh yeah? Is that why dad died? Because it was the only way to get away from you?"

Ricky grabbed a lightweight jacket, walked out the door, and slammed it shut.

Angie sat there a moment staring after him. "See what he's like, Nick?"

"Angie....shut the fuck up." Nick walked into his den and shut the door, leaving Angie alone in the living room.

\* \* \*

Ricky walked briskly up the hill and then down the other side, just trying to get the tension out of his body. 'We're separating....yeah....right. Over my dead body, Mother Bitch.' He silently screamed at her.

He walked until he could feel no more tightness—only fatigue—in his muscles. He felt guilty about walking out and leaving Lindy there. Hopefully she was in her room sleeping. He thought about calling there, but changed his mind. If his mother answered he would be angry all over again. Looking around him, he realized he was in a beautiful park. He made a mental note to bring Lindy here. They had never walked in this direction, which is the reason he had never seen this place before. There were some swings and a slide for kids, and some picnic tables, a couple of shelters, and park benches. He sat down on one of them, just trying to mellow out. He called Lukas, and agreed to wait there for him.

\* \* \*

It was almost dark when Nick emerged from his den. He didn't see Angie in the living room, so he assumed she must have gone upstairs. He went to the kitchen and turned on a light. She was there—sitting at the kitchen table—drinking a cup of coffee. He tried not to speak to her, as he looked through the cupboard and then into the refrigerator.

"You think I'm wrong, Nick…don't you?"

"Yep."

"Why? Why am I wrong?"

"Well, for starters, Angie….You drove Lindy upstairs to a locked bedroom, you drove me behind a closed door in my den, and you drove Ricky out the door. Now…. how can you be right?"

"Nick…this whole…situation….is wrong. And why is Lindy living here?"

"You had no right to say the things you did about Lindy. Lindy is every bit the nice, sweet girl you first thought she was. Can't you see that they love each other? The pregnancy came from love—not lust."

"What do they know about love…?"

"More than we do, Angie…more than we do. I see them together all the time….I've had talks with Ricky…. and with Lindy. They love….I mean….deep down inside of them…they love each other. Talk of them separating is….well; you might as well kiss your son goodbye. Were you talking about taking him back to Chicago?"

"No…I…sold the house. The closing is in mid-July. I came here to see houses this weekend. I'm moving here…. at least I was…." She stopped talking to watch Nick at the stove. "What are you doing?"

"Making Lindy something to eat. Ricky usually does, but….since he's not here…. I will. I just hope he's okay. It's not like him to leave Lindy behind for this long."

"Oh, Nick….you think he might not be okay? I figured he was just trying to cool down."

Nick shrugged. He busied himself by getting the tray ready to take upstairs. He was making what he knew was one of Lindy's favorite meals—grilled cheese and tomato soup. He picked up the tray and carried it upstairs, setting it down in the hallway. He tapped lightly on the door. "Lindy? It's Uncle Nick. Can I come in?"

Lindy was awake. She awoke to a dark room and immediately wondered where Ricky was. She sat up and turned a light on, straining her ears to hear any sounds from anywhere in the condo. She could hear none. She was relieved when she heard a knock at the door, but surprised that it was Uncle Nick. She went to the door and unlocked it. Nick was standing there holding the tray of food.

"Can I come in? I brought a peace offering."

The corners of Lindy's lips turned up into what was almost a smile, she nodded, and stepped aside to let Nick pass. He noted her swollen, red-rimmed eyes as he set the tray down on the portable table that Ricky had left standing.

"Are you doing okay? Looks like you've been sleeping."

"Yeah, I was. I called Aunt Liz and she told me to take another sedative. Where's Ricky?"

"Uh….he stormed out. He'll be back before too long. His mother….well, she really got to him. He left here pretty angry."

"I see….Uncle Nick…..I'm sorry…."

"Sorry for what?"

"For causing all this….getting pregnant….I…." Lindy stopped before she started to cry again.

"Lindy….you didn't do anything….at least not by yourself. I know how you two feel about each other…and you know what? I can see how you have made a difference in Ricky's life. You changed him for the better."

"But look at what I created between Ricky and his mom….."

"You didn't create that. That problem was there long before you came along. That problem is why he lives here with me instead of with her. The real Ricky is the one you and I see….not that fighting vicious monster she turns him into when she pushes his buttons. My sister is not the easiest person to get along with. She's….insensitive, to say the least. Now come on….eat. You know I don't cook very often…so this has to be a special meal…right?"

Lindy smiled and nodded.

"Much better. I like it when you smile….and so does Ricky. When he comes in, I'll send him up here…okay? I know how anxious you are that he's not here. Oh….and for the record? This is my house and you are welcome here any time…no matter what."

"Thanks, Uncle Nick." Lindy rewarded him with another smile.

"Oh….wait….don't shut the door yet…" Nick disappeared down the hall, and then returned pushing a television on a stand. "Thought you might like to watch some television until Ricky comes back." Nick looked quickly toward the door, and then bent down and whispered into Lindy's ear. "The Wicked Witch of the West is downstairs in the living room."

Lindy laughed lightly. Nick put his index finger up
to his lips, and quietly shushed her, and then he winked.
He left after plugging the cord of the television into the
wall socket and quickly hooking up the cable wire. "One
hundred and eight channels to choose from." He said
as he backed out of the room and shut the door behind
him.

Grateful, Lindy took the remote that sat on top of the
television and started flipping through channels, briefly
wondering when Ricky would return.

\* \* \*

Lukas picked Ricky up at the park fifteen minutes
after he called.

"Hey, Buddy….what's going on?" Lukas asked.

"Aw, my fucking mother pissed me off. She came
into town and started right away. Insulted Lindy….made
her cry….I mean, *really* hurt her feelings….then after
Lindy went upstairs to her room…had the nerve to tell
me Lindy and I were separating. Yeah! Right! Like that's
really going to happen. That's just bullshit. Damn it, that
woman pisses me off! Anyway, she said some things….I
said some things…and here I am."

"So where is Lindy?"

"She's home….locked in her room…"

"Home? Where…home?"

"Oh….she's at the condo. Her room. That's home for
her."

"Yeah, but….you left her there with your mother on
the warpath? Will she be all right?"

"Yeah….Uncle Nick's there….he won't let anything
go on between her and Lindy. And my mother better

think twice before she starts anything. You know how protective over Lindy I am."

"Yeah, I do. So what do you want to do? Go to my house and shoot some pool? Hang out there for awhile?"

"Yeah, sure…that sounds good."

\* \* \*

Lukas dropped Ricky off at home at nine-thirty. "Your house looks quiet, so you should be okay."

"Yeah….I hope it stays that way. I'm just going to go straight up to see Lindy and then wait for my mother to go to bed. I'm sleeping on the couch while she's here."

"Well, good luck," Lukas offered, as Ricky got out of the car.

Ricky entered the condo, nodded to Liz, walked right past Angie, and took the steps two at a time up to Lindy's room. He peeked inside, and tapped on the door. Lindy was lying on the bed watching a sitcom rerun. Her face lit up when she saw Ricky.

"Hi." She greeted him.

Ricky strode across the room and scooped her up in his arms. "I'm sorry I left you here…and that I was gone so long."

"It's okay….I knew you had to get away from her…. nothing happened here anyway. Except that Uncle Nick brought me something to eat….and the television."

"I guess I owe him. I think he's on our side…you know?"

"I think he is, too. I called Aunt Liz…because I was crying and hurt over what your mom said….and Aunt Liz told me that she and Uncle Nick love me. Also, Uncle Nick told me that I am welcome in his house any time…no matter what. Oh…and he called your mom the Wicked Witch of the West."

Ricky started to laugh. "See? I told you she was. Want to play cards or watch a movie? I'm staying up here with you until she goes to bed….okay?"

"Oh, God….she'll think we're having a sex marathon up here." Lindy laughed quietly. "I hope she doesn't come up here screaming."

"I doubt it. Aunt Liz is down there talking to her. She may be able to mellow her out. Now…give me the remote…you know it's a guy's job to hold the remote."

They both broke up laughing. Their eyes locked creating the familiar bolt of electricity to course through them, and they stopped laughing. Their lips met in a sweet kiss. They clung to each other long after the kiss ended, Ricky stroking her hair, his lips against her temple. Their quiet bliss was interrupted by another tap on the door. Liz came in and greeted them with a hug.

"Are you okay, Lindy?" Liz asked her.

"I am now." Lindy smiled at her. "I really didn't expect Ricky's mother to go off like that. I mean….it took me by surprise. Wow…now she really hates me."

"So the rest of us have to make up for it. We all love you so much." Liz lightly squeezed her around the waist. "Oh, I'm sorry…how is your back now? Still hurt?"

"A little, but it's getting better….that didn't hurt when you squeezed me."

"Good…I only hope you can heal emotionally…. some day, anyway."

"I'll do everything I can to help in that area, Aunt Liz. I love Lindy…so much."

"I know you do. Hey, Ricky....your mom will come around...eventually. Okay...I'm going to go back down and rescue Nick. Do you need anything? Tea? Something to eat? I brought cookies."

"That'll work. Some tea and cookies." Ricky grinned at her.

"Okay....coming right up. I'll bring it up. I think maybe staying out of your mother's way tonight might be a good idea."

"Me, too, Aunt Liz....me, too."

# Chapter 30

Angie left for Chicago at mid-morning on Sunday. Before she left she made an effort to smooth things over between her and Ricky, but he was not receptive to it.

"Ricky, how about I come back next weekend and you and I go looking at houses?"

"You don't need me to help you pick out your house. Find one you like and buy it….if that's what you want to do."

"Well, you have to like it, too. You're going to live there, too."

Ricky was busy making breakfast for himself and Lindy, and trying to maintain a calm aura. "I told you…. you can only force me to live there another ten months. I'm gone at eighteen."

"Why? Why do you have to be like this? Say these things?"

"You just don't get it; do you, Mom? You really think you can say those things about Lindy and I'm going to forgive you? Forget about it? No….it doesn't work that way. I love Lindy. We are going to be together…and you can't stop that. Now….you can either be a part of it….or be out of my life forever. It's your choice. I made mine…. months ago. I chose to be with Lindy….and that's not going to change. Now if you'll excuse me….I have Lindy's breakfast ready. We'll be eating upstairs since you hurt her so bad that she won't come down here until you're gone."

Ricky picked up the tray and swiftly carried it upstairs, not giving Angie a chance to respond. It was shortly after they finished breakfast that Angie got her suitcase together and started down the stairs with it. Ricky was coming out of Lindy's room with the empty tray as she passed the room. Balancing the tray in one hand, he grabbed the suitcase with the other and carried it the rest of the way downstairs. He set it down and walked to the kitchen with the tray. Angie followed.

"Ricky….Aunt Liz told me why Lindy is living here. I'm…shocked…I…can't imagine anybody….doing that to her. I'm sorry…truly sorry for her."

Ricky didn't answer her. She was going to have to do better than that. He continued rinsing off the breakfast dishes and stacking them in the dishwasher, and then wiped off the counters.

"Want me to put your suitcase in the car? By the way, where is Uncle Nick?"

"He and Aunt Liz met for breakfast early this morning. Yes, please….put my suitcase in the car. Do you need anything before I go?"

"No….I'm good."

"Well….I guess I'll go then." She stood and watched him as he rearranged a cupboard, and then opened the freezer to take something out for dinner. She watched as he tied up the bag of trash, pulled it out of the trash can, and put a new bag in. When he finished that, he picked up her suitcase and carried it to the car, putting it in the back seat for her. Angie stood and watched, realizing that she had better do something to make amends or she would lose her son forever. She had a week to come up with something that would prove that she was truly sorry, and that she didn't really hate Lindy. Grabbing her purse, she followed Ricky outside.

"Ricky, does Lindy need maternity clothes? I think I can help with that…."

"No….I got it covered….thanks. Have a safe trip." He held the door for her to get in. Before he could protest, she put her arms around him and hugged him. She felt him recoil, so she let her arms drop. As she slid behind the wheel, she watched him walk back into the condo, not even looking back. Angie fought back the tears as she pulled out of the driveway and turned her car in the direction of Chicago.

Ricky ran upstairs and peeked out of Lindy's bedroom window until the car was out of sight, and then he grabbed Lindy and started dancing her around the room, singing, "Ding Dong, the Witch is gone." They both broke out laughing and fell onto the bed.

\* \* \*

Lukas pulled up in front of the condo to let Ricky and Lindy out of the car. They had lots of things to carry in since it was the last day of school. Their lockers had to be cleaned out and their work in all of their classes was returned to them. Ricky was grabbing as much as he could, leaving the lighter stuff for Lindy to get. He had his framed sketch, wrapped in newspaper, under his arm, as he grabbed the large pile of items Lindy had stacked up for him. She had the sweater out of her locker and a pair of sneakers from his. They were busy balancing everything as they carried it inside that they missed the truck sitting across the street, two condos down from them. Ricky unlocked the door as the truck pulled away.

Ray had been sitting there for almost an hour waiting to see where Lindy was staying. He would not have thought about this area had that same snotty girl not called him back. He sat there remembering the phone call as he waited. 'That girl is definitely not right in the head,' he thought to himself, as he remembered what she told him.

"I'm not sure which condo it is, but I know which street it's on," she told him. He listened and then he asked. "Tell me why you hate my daughter so much." He was astonished by her answer.

"Because Ricky should be mine…not hers. I saw him first. She took him. I should be pregnant with his baby."

"Did you go out with him?" Ray asked.

"No….because when he met Lindy….all he wanted was her…"

"So why hate Lindy? You both saw him and he wanted her instead of you. That's not her fault."

"You don't understand….he should have been with me. I saw him first! She took him! Little Miss Innocent! HA!"

"So you think if I go get her away from Ricky he'll be with you?"

"I'll see to it that he is with me….after she's away from him."

"You're a very sick girl…do you know that?" He hung up on her.

Ray saw the car stop in front of the condo two doors up and watched that Ricky kid and Lindy get out. They were busy stacking things to carry into the house and didn't notice his truck. He saw how Lindy smiled at that Ricky kid. He had smiled back and said something to her as they walked inside the door. Ray drove away when they shut the door behind them. He was determined to pay them a visit—maybe after work tomorrow. He had decided that he wanted his little girl back home with him. She could have that Ricky kid's baby and then he would persuade her to give it up for adoption. Then things would go back to normal—a father and his daughter living in the same house. He would marry Diane and give Lindy a stepmother. Lindy needed a female figure around, Ray figured. Lindy would need a female shoulder to cry on after Ray forbade her to see Ricky again. He tipped his beer can upside down and drained it before grabbing another one.

\* \* \*

Ray didn't show up the next day. When he went to work that morning, his company gave him instructions for another out of town job, and told him to go home and get ready to leave by noon. If Lindy had known any of this she would have been relieved. She had no idea that her father even knew where she was, much less cared.

Nick told Lindy and Ricky to be ready to go to work the following Monday, giving them five days off. The following morning, Nick left for work, and Ricky immediately got out of bed and climbed in beside Lindy in her bed. Lindy didn't awaken, but turned toward Ricky and curled up beside him in her sleep. They both awoke two hours later and noted the silence in the condo. They lay together, just holding each other, before they made love, and then after.

"You're going to get us in trouble." Lindy whispered to Ricky.

"Well, I can't get you pregnant, so what other trouble were you talking about?"

"Breaking Uncle Nick's rules…."

"He did not say we couldn't have sex….he said we couldn't share a bed in his presence…well, he's not here. He said to use discretion…..well….we are. So….we technically we aren't breaking any rules…..right?"

"Okay….I guess not……..but…..now your mother may call this a sex marathon."

"Oh, gees…..I think my mother needs a sex marathon….or at least a one night stand."

"Ricky!"

"Well, it's true. She is a real bitch. I personally think she needs a little booty." Ricky added, as he nibbled Lindy's ear. "Look at Uncle Nick. Look at how he mellowed when he started getting booty."

"Yeah, I have to agree with you there." Lindy draped her arm over Ricky's chest.

"What do you want to do today? Want to go to that park I was telling you about? Think you're still able to walk it? I mean, you don't really look all that pregnant, but I don't know how you feel……"

Lindy spoke in a deliberate quivering voice as she teased him. "I don't know, Sonny…I'll have to use my walker."

Ricky laughed. "Okay…so you want to go?"

"Um-hmmm," she crooned, as she teased him by running her tongue around one of his nipples. They made love again before they got out of bed for the day.

The next five days were equally as sweet to them as the first. They spent the mornings curled up together, and then making love, and spent the days doing whatever they felt like doing. They took a trip to the zoo, and a trip to their special place down by the creek, and even went to the museum on a day that was overcast and rainy. They never tired of being with each other. They never ran out of things to say, nor did they require conversation. They had their own system of communication—almost as though they could read each other's mind—and maybe they could.

Monday morning, Ricky left with Nick to go to the hospital, and Lindy started her job, in Nick's den on her new computer, typing reports. Ricky called her at lunch to see how she was doing.

"I miss you. You know….I think we're going to have to work together after we get married…..because I can't stand being away from you."

Lindy was smiling into the phone. "Ricky, use the email during the day." She gave him the email address Nick had set up for her.

"So how's it going? Getting any reports done?"

"Oh, yeah. How about you? Do you like it?"

"Yeah…..well, I love chemistry and working in a lab….so this is perfect for me….except I wish you were here."

"I know….me, too. I got something out for dinner. Guess what? I may have to cook…since I'm at home and you're at work. You get to come home to a home-cooked meal….although it won't be anything near as good as stuff you make…."

"Oh, sure it will. What are you making?"

"Don't know yet, except that the meat is pork chops. So something with pork chops. You should be here around six, right?"

"Yeah….unless I stop after work with the boys for a couple of beers."

Lindy laughed at his little play-acting joke. Ricky loved to hear her laugh.

\* \* \*

Two work weeks went by rather quickly for Lindy and Ricky. It was Friday and they were receiving their first paychecks, for one week's worth of work.

"So do you two want to go to the bank and open an account?" Nick asked. "My bank is open until seven. You have forty-five minutes."

"Are we going to open a joint account?" Ricky grabbed Lindy's hand.

"Yes…and no. Ricky, you and I are never going to fight about money. This is what I suggest…..We figure our monthly household expenses and we both contribute half to that. Right now it's rent and food….so say….six hundred dollars…..divided by four….that's a hundred and fifty weekly…half from you and half from me. How does this sound so far?"

"Go on….I'm interested."

"Our second account will be for extras…..dinner out, outings, and later on, vacations. This one we set an amount before we open the account…..say, fifty bucks each. The rest of the money is ours. Yours to do what you want with….and mine to do what I want. This way we never argue or fight because you want something or I want something. If you have the money, you can get what you want. I can use mine for what I want, too. Now….as expenses grow….say, maybe a car….then we have to figure that in with the household bills and each contribute half of the payment. How does that sound to you?"

Nick was impressed. "I don't know how it sounds to him, but it sounds pretty damn intelligent to me."

"Yeah….me, too. So let's see……this check is over three hundred dollars….so only seventy-five is for expenses plus fifty for extras……right?"

"If you want to set the extras account at fifty….then yes. Don't forget…we will have baby expenses soon….."

"Let's make it a hundred from each a week, then…. okay, Babe?"

"Sounds good….now let's get to the bank and open these accounts. Uncle Nick, are we allowed to open accounts if we're under eighteen?"

"Well….I don't know. I'm going in with you….so I guess we'll find out. I think you can have savings accounts. Maybe do that, and have a debit card. If not….maybe they will let me sign for it. Let's go and find out."

Ricky and Lindy opened four accounts that evening. Everything went as planned, including the checking account. They were allowed to have the checking account but no checks, only debit cards. They felt very grown up and very much like they were an established couple. They insisted on taking Nick out to eat after they left the bank. He chose an inexpensive restaurant and let them pay. He could see it made them feel proud to be doing something for him. He smiled to himself, thinking how much he loved these two kids. At dinner they talked about going grocery shopping the next day. Nick knew they were playing house and he knew he was making it easy for them, but he was not going to sit back and let them struggle or suffer. They just might make it—with his help.

# Chapter 31

$\mathcal{L}$indy and Ricky fell into their work routine again the following week. Lindy was busy working hard and earning a tidy sum every week and sometimes earned more than Ricky, since she got paid a small amount for every line she typed. One day while typing one of the lab findings, she stopped and looked at what she just typed. She checked it against what was in the dictation, and was assured that she had typed it correctly. But the calculation was wrong. She quickly got out a pencil and paper and did the equation. She came up with an answer that was different from the one in the dictation. She called Nick's cell phone.

"Hi, Lindy. What's up?" He was a little surprised, since she had never called his cell phone before.

"Uncle Nick, this report I'm typing......the calculations are incorrect."

"Are you sure? How do you know?"

"Because it's a basic equation. The answer should be 'm' equals three....There's a subtraction error. Whoever did this subtracted fifteen from eighteen and came up with a six."

"Release that one and I'll take a look at it. No, wait, since they fall in order that would make the entire series of reports incorrect. It's almost lunch. Take your lunch now, and I'll call you back after lunch. I think I know why I haven't been able to solve a certain something I've been working on. Who did the report?"

"Uh, it says M Connor, report number three forty-eight."

"Okay. I'll call you after lunch. Thanks, Lindy."

"That was Lindy? Why didn't you let me talk to her?" Ricky had come up behind Nick as he pressed the end call button on his cell phone.

"You can call her back if you want. I was just a little too preoccupied to be concerned with the flame of love right then. Your girl genius may have just helped me solve the research project we've been working on in here for the past year. If she's correct.....steak dinners on me tonight."

Ricky smiled at his uncle. "I told you she was smart."

"Yeah, so you did. You go ahead and go to lunch. I'm going to pull this file and listen myself."

Ricky wandered down to the cafeteria, disappointed that Nick was staying behind. He loved the time they spent at lunch. Nick treated him like a colleague rather than a kid, introducing him to doctors he knew, exchanging stories with those other doctors, and always including Ricky in the conversations. Today he would have to sit it out alone, unless he was lucky enough to run into Liz. He carried his tray to an empty table, sat down and dialed home to talk to Lindy.

"Hey, girl genius! How's it going today? I hear you may be responsible for a real breakthrough in Uncle Nick's research."

"Yeah, well….it was a subtraction error…I think. He said he would look at it."

Their conversation was interrupted by an all too familiar spine-grating voice.

"Ricky….hi! Is that Lindy on the phone?"

"Oh God." Ricky groaned. "Do you believe it?" Ricky spoke into the phone.

Lindy recognized Carrie's voice on the other end of the line. "Oh no….can't we *ever* get away from her?"

"Is that Lindy?" Carrie asked again.

"Now who in the hell do you think it would be? Of course, it's Lindy."

"Just asking. Do you mind if I sit here?"

"Yes…I mind very much. In fact, if you sit down, I'm getting up and leaving."

"Why do you have to be like that? Why can't we at least be friends?"

"Baby, I'll call you a little later. Love you…" After he disconnected he stared at Carrie. "We cannot be friends because of what you did to Lindy. You just don't get it, do you? Lindy and I are always….*always*….going to be together. You don't stand a chance now, or before, or ever. You…will…never…be….my girlfriend. How much clearer can I make it? I don't like you, and I have never liked you. And that has nothing to do with Lindy. So get over it. Find a guy who can stomach you and leave me alone."

She stood at the table and stared at him—her look was one of confusion, like she really didn't understand.

Ricky threw his napkin on his plate and got up. "I lost my appetite. Thanks…you ruined my lunch." He picked up his tray and walked toward the exit, stopping only to deposit his lunch remains in a receptacle and stack his tray. Carrie stared after him, looking dazed.

He still had half an hour to go, so he wandered outside to the smoking area and bummed a cigarette off of one of the lab techs. He lit it and called Lindy back.

"Calm me down, Honey. That girl makes me want to smash bricks."

Lindy laughed. "What's she doing there? Certainly she doesn't have to work."

"From what she was wearing I'd say she's a candy-striper. Probably good for her father's image. He probably insisted that she do it. When I go back upstairs I'm going to tell Uncle Nick about it. He's going to have to do something to keep her away from me. Every time I see her I come so close to just smashing her face in."

"Well, don't do that….hey, Uncle Nick just called me back before you did. He said we're going out for steak dinners tonight. Cool, huh?"

"So you must have solved his problem. He said if you found the error that kept him from a break-through in the research, he was buying us steak dinners tonight. So I guess you really are a genius."

Lindy laughed her beautiful laugh. "Ricky? You're smoking right now, aren't you?"

"Yeah, I'm sorry, Babe…..I needed to calm down after seeing that bitch. God, you're psychic, too." He laughed. "See you after work. I'll brush my teeth so you don't smell it. Love you." He hung up and felt a whole lot calmer than he had when he walked outside. He wasn't sure if it was the cigarette or Lindy's lovely voice that had calmed him down, but he would put his money on Lindy if he had to choose.

Nick and Ricky walked through the door smiling. Nick, because the error Lindy had found clearly changed the research data favorably, and Ricky because he was so glad to see Lindy. Liz entered the condo right behind them, as Ricky strode to the den to greet Lindy. The four of them were going out for a steak dinner as Nick had promised.

"Rick, I'm starving….let's go." He walked in on Lindy and Ricky embraced in a kiss. "Oh, gees…..can't go in there….they're getting reacquainted. After all, they've been apart eight hours….a life time."

"Actually, it was nine hours and twenty-two and a half minutes…..it seems like a lifetime." Ricky's muffled voice came from the den.

Liz laughed. "Oh, Scrooge…where's your sense of romance?"

Nick shook his head. "In my ass, I guess." He and Liz laughed, both remembering that she had said that to him once.

\* \* \*

Another work week flew by. Lindy and Ricky paid the rent to Nick, and went grocery shopping the following Saturday. Independence Day was next week, and they wanted steak on the grill. Lindy was planning on making potato salad and Liz said she would bring another dish. During the day they were going to go to an air show, since neither Lindy nor Ricky had ever seen one. They would come home and cook on the grill on the patio. Angie planned on coming into town the following weekend after the fourth. She hadn't been back since the flare-up over Lindy's pregnancy. She hoped Lindy would forgive her, but most of all; she hoped she hadn't lost Ricky over it. She hadn't meant anything she said; she was just angry that Ricky's future was now in jeopardy. Lindy's, too, of course; but Ricky was her son—one she had high hopes for. She was impressed when Nick told her about Ricky working in the lab. She hoped he would find it interesting enough to want to pursue a career in medicine. Ricky found the lab work exhilarating, fascinating, and interesting; exactly what he would like to do in life. He was more interested in chemistry than he was in medicine; leading him to lean toward becoming a chemist.

Angie also was impressed when Nick told her of Lindy's findings and how she saved his research project. "That child she's carrying is going to have some real intelligence; don't you think?" Angie asked her brother during their phone conversation.

"Yeah….good gene pool. They are smart and each of them has a particular talent. Kid's going to luck out in that way….not to mention their good looks."

"Nick…..what can I do to make it up to her? The things I said….I didn't mean them…."

"Angie, that's why you should always put your mind in gear before you put your mouth in motion. You hurt her….and hurting her makes you an enemy with Ricky. I told you that when you first met her. Say anything bad about her and Ricky is gone. He loves her….why can't you understand that?"

"Oh, I do now. Hey, it's hard to imagine somebody so young actually being truly in love….you know that."

"Yeah, I had a hard time believing it myself…but I see them every day…and I can assure you…it's love. We older ones can learn a lesson from them. Oh, they have bank accounts now. Let me tell you the ingenious plan Lindy

328

came up with…." Nick explained Lindy's accounting plan to Angie, and she was again impressed.

"Very smart. Okay….I give up….I concede….they are in love. I have to do something to show how sorry I am for…you know…hurting Lindy like I did. I'll see you next weekend."

Angie replaced the telephone receiver in its cradle and sat in her chair a moment, thinking. She sighed, and quickly got up, went to her desk, and retrieved writing paper and a pen. She was much better at expressing herself in writing. She sat down with a fresh cup of coffee and composed a letter to Lindy.

\* \* \*

The Fourth of July holiday was a fun-filled day for all four of them. After the air show, they stopped at a petting zoo, where Lindy fell in love with a couple of baby goats. Nick's smile never left his face as he watched Ricky, Lindy, and Liz lavish affection on the animals. He was never an animal person, himself, although he wouldn't have minded having a dog. He wasn't home enough to devote time to a dog, so he never acquired one. Although he enjoyed watching his 'family' with these barnyard animals, he had no desire to go inside the fence and pet them himself.

Later on, after the steaks and trimmings were eaten, they all went to the park to watch the fireworks display. He kept his arm around Liz as he watched Lindy's and Ricky's faces with each explosion. 'They're beautiful,' he thought to himself. Rather than end the day abruptly, they went home and enjoyed toasted marshmallows over the grill. Ricky and Lindy took turns feeding each other the toasted marshmallows, and Nick openly teased and made fun of them; while secretly admiring their warmth and affection for each other. Ricky felt the time was right to give Lindy the framed charcoal sketch. He ran upstairs and carried the frame, still wrapped in newspaper, down to the living room. He handed it to Lindy.

"I was waiting for a special day to give this to you…. but every day is a special day for us….so go ahead…. unveil it."

Lindy tore off the newspaper and gasped. Liz came up behind her and stared.

"My God….it's so *good*, Ricky. It looks exactly like you two." Liz lifted the frame off the table and held it up for Nick to see.

"You did that?" He was obviously impressed.

"I love it. Ricky, it's so…..us." Lindy smiled at Ricky and slid her arm around his waist, tilting her head up for a quick kiss from him.

Nick picked up the frame and moved toward the dining area. He held the frame up against the wall behind the dining room table. "How about we put it here? I never liked the picture that's hanging here now." He removed the picture, replaced it with Ricky's work, and stood back to admire it.

"Excellent……excellent work. I like it there…what do you think?"

"You can have it there until we get a place of our own. Then you have to put your ugly picture back up," Ricky responded.

Work for everybody resumed the next day. Ricky hung back and kissed Lindy several times before Nick shouted to him. Ricky laughed, kissed Lindy again, only quickly this time, and trotted out the door. "Call you at lunch," he promised over his shoulder. Lindy began her work for the day, setting up for the line count, and downloading the dictation sound files.

Just before lunch she gathered the mail out of the box, and discovered the letter from Angie. She was reading it when Ricky called.

"Listen to this, Honey….." She read the letter to Ricky.

*Dear Lindy,*

*I owe you an apology. I never meant those things I said about you. I was just angry. I wanted a better future for Ricky, and of course, you too, if you are going to be in his future. It appears that you will be. Please understand that it is hard for me to believe that two people as young as you and Ricky can honestly be in love. So I'm wrong…you are in love…I can see that. Also, please understand that all of this came as a shock to me. Once I thought about it, I adjusted to it. I'm going to have a grandchild! My baby is going to be a father! Lindy, I mean this when I say it…I wouldn't want to see Ricky with anyone but you. I just would have liked to see you two wait a little longer before tying yourselves down with a baby and all the problems that come with it. But, Lindy, I want to help. I don't want to see you two lose out on life, so I want to help any way I can. Maybe you can find it in your heart to forgive me and maybe let me baby-sit once in awhile? Also, I'm offering you and Ricky a place in my home when I buy one. Lindy, let's make amends. I'm truly sorry. I love you like a daughter.*

*Love,*

*Mom DeCelli*

"So what do you think?" Lindy appealed to Ricky.

"Up to you, Babe. You can forgive her if you want…. but me? She better do something pretty spectacular to make me forgive her. But…on the other hand…we now have a baby-sitter…"

Lindy laughed at his remark. "You're terrible. Let's give her a shot, Ricky….okay? She's your mother and we don't want to start out on a bad note. All the holidays…. birthdays….the baby's birthdays….we want her there… don't we?"

"That's why I love you…you know that? You're so sweet and understanding…and forgiving. Okay. We'll call her tonight. Gotta go. I'm a working man, you know. Love you."

Nick came up behind him as he said his parting words.

"Aw….how sweet. Love you," Nick mimicked.

Ricky laughed, and then told Nick about Angie's letter.

"You know, Rick…she means well. If we could cut her tongue out, she'd be the perfect mother and mother-in-law." They both laughed walked back to the lab.

# Chapter 32

It was Friday, and Ricky was ready for another weekend with Lindy. He loved working and earning money, but he also loved being with her. He was washing some lab utensils before leaving for the day when Nick called to him.

"Hey, Rick….I have a meeting after work. Aunt Liz says she can drop you off."

"Okay…the meeting…you're not in trouble for anything, are you?"

"Oh hell, no….I applied for research funding and I find out if it was approved. There's always a meeting attached to finding out. I'll see you afterward."

Liz was standing at the doorway to the lab already waiting for Ricky. She dropped him off and left quickly. "I want to get home and get changed. I'll be back in about an hour. Nick and I are going out tonight and I planned on meeting him here."

Ricky nodded and thanked her for the ride, quickly jumping out to get to Lindy. Liz watched him sprint up the walk, smiled, and drove off.

Lindy had already finished for the day, and was upstairs dressing after a quick shower. Ricky knocked lightly and entered her room and discovered Lindy sitting on the bed wrapped in a towel.

"Now that's what I like to come home to." Ricky teased.

"But look how fat I'm getting."

She removed the towel and that was all it took for Ricky to shed his clothing and quickly wrap himself around her. As he kissed her, he whispered, "you're not fat….you're carrying my baby……and that makes you terribly sexy to me."

They made love, Ricky being ever so careful and gentle. They lay there in each other's arms for a few moments afterward.

"Aunt Liz will be back in a little while. We'd better get up and act like we didn't do anything…"

That caused them both to burst out laughing. Ricky stopped laughing and stared at Lindy's face. His hand dropped down and rubbed her belly. "I love the two of you," he said as he kissed her again.

Ricky thought he heard someone knocking at the door. "That can't be Aunt Liz already…." He quickly got dressed and ran down the stairs, Leaving Lindy in her room to get dressed, too.

Ray Riley was standing at the door when Ricky opened it. Ricky stared at him, not knowing that he was staring at Lindy's father.

"Can I help you?" Ricky politely asked.

"Where's my daughter?" Ray spoke in a low even tone.

"You're Mister Riley?"

"Yes…do you have more girls here besides my daughter? Where is she?"

"She…she's upstairs. She's the only one here with bruises from a belt on her back, so she *must* be *your* daughter."

"You're a smart-assed kid, aren't you?"

"Only when I stand face-to-face with a guy who beats a girl half to death."

Ray ignored Ricky's remark. "Get my daughter down here. I'm taking her home."

"I don't think so, sir…I don't think she wants to go."

"She doesn't have a choice. She's still under-age."

"Dad….what are you doing here?" Lindy came down the stairs on shaking knees.

"I'm here to get you. You're going home."

"No…I'm not. Not after what you did. It's been two months and I still have bruises on my back. I'm not going anywhere with you. I never want to see you again."

"You're a minor…you have to go."

"No….I don't. I'm pregnant…which makes me come under my own jurisdiction. Look it up. I can live where I want to live….and I'm living here."

"Look….Lindy, I'm sorry….I'm sorry for a lot of things. I wish I could explain but I can't…."

"Dad, I'm not going with you….I…"

"Look, Mister Riley…..she doesn't want to go. Maybe someday she'll heal emotionally and be able to see you again….but…not now."

"SHUT UP, PUNK!" Ray turned on Ricky. "You stay out of it! This is between me and my daughter! You don't have any claim on her just because you fucked her! You took advantage of her. She was innocent before she knew you!"

"How would you know, Dad? You hadn't spoken to me in three years. You ignored me, left me alone in the house for days at a time. How would you know if I was innocent or not? You don't know anything about me! Now....Dad...please leave."

"You heard her. So why don't you just go? Go have another beer. It smells like you've had a few already."

"Shut...the...fuck up, Punk! How about I blow your balls off for ruining my daughter?" Ray pulled a pistol out of his waistband and pointed it at Ricky.

"NO! Dad....please....okay.....I'll go with you.....just stop pointing that gun at Ricky!"

"Baby, you don't have to go. He'll hurt you again. He'll keep us from seeing each other....."

"You got that right! You ain't going to be fucking her again; that's for sure."

Ray pointed the gun at Ricky.

"No! Dad...you aren't going to keep us from seeing each other. I love Ricky...we love each other."

"Bullshit! You're too young to even know what love is!"

"Oh....and you do? You ignore her for three years... when she really needs you....then you finally acknowledge her by beating her? Beating her so badly she couldn't even walk. Is that love to you?"

"SHUT THE FUCK UP!" Ray once again turned the gun on Ricky, only this time he had his index finger on the trigger.

It happened so fast. Lindy screamed and shoved Ricky as the gun exploded in the room. Lindy gasped and fell to the floor.

"LINDY!!!!!!" Ricky shouted. "Oh my God….you shot her….you son of a bitch! Lindy? Baby, open your eyes. Lindy!"

Ricky felt for a pulse and found one, although it was weak. He jumped up, grabbed the phone and dialed nine-one-one. "I need an ambulance. Hurry! My girl friend's been shot!" He gave the dispatcher the address. She told him to stay on the line until the ambulance got there; assuring him that one was already on the way.

Ray stood there for a moment, frozen. He took a step toward Lindy and then stepped back. Dropping the gun, he ran out the door, jumped in his truck, and sped away, almost hitting Nick's car as he pulled into the driveway.

"Ricky! Who was….?"

"Uncle Nick….Help!"

Nick came around the side of the sofa and saw Lindy lying there, blood everywhere. "Oh my God. Did you call an ambulance?"

"Yeah….here…they're still on the line. So much blood….Uncle Nick…."

"Ricky, I'm a doctor….let me take over." Nick reached for the telephone. "This is Dr. Bazario….it looks like her spleen was hit. She's pregnant…"

Lindy opened her eyes and stared vacantly at Nick. "Uncle Nick….I'm ruining your carpet…."

"I don't give a damn about the carpet….just stay with me, Lindy….stay with me. Where the fuck is that ambulance?"

"Nick? What's going….? Oh dear God!" Liz dropped her purse and ran to Lindy. "What happened?"

Ricky was busily moving furniture so the paramedics would have room to maneuver, and then he went out and moved the cars to the side of the driveway. He had to do something to keep from losing his mind at the moment.

"Ricky? What happened?" Liz's voice sounded far away.

Ricky's voice was tight and raspy. "He shot her. Her father shot her."

Ricky heard the ambulance siren in the distance, getting louder as it got closer. He opened the front door, waited until it was in sight, and then went out to flag it down. He was shaking, and he felt as though his legs were going to go out from under him. 'Stay strong.... stay strong,' He reminded himself. 'Lindy needs you.' He heard Liz say Lindy needed blood. 'Oh, God!' He thought to himself. Behind the ambulance a police car pulled up, and two officers emerged from each side of it.

Inside, a flurry of activity was going on. "Lindy! Stay with us, Baby...stay with us!" He heard Liz yelling. Ricky felt like his head was swimming under water. He couldn't breathe and he felt as though his head were going to explode. He stood there as the gurney whizzed past him, one of the paramedics holding a bag of liquid up in the air. The gurney disappeared into the back of the ambulance, Liz jumping in, too. "I'm her doctor...I'll ride with you." Ricky heard the doors slam shut and the siren going off again.

"Hey, kid! I'm talking to you!" The police officer was standing in front of Ricky, his hands on his hips. "Are you deaf? Now....I'm going to ask you again...what happened here?"

Nick came to Ricky's rescue. "Hey, give him a break.....that's his girl friend. He's beside himself with worry and shock."

"Yeah, okay…but we need some answers." The other officer spoke up.

Ricky ran his hand across his forehead, stopping to stare at the blood on his hand and his arm. He looked down and saw blood—Lindy's blood—all over his shirt.

"He shot her." His voice also sounded far away to him.

"Who? Who shot her?"

"Her….father. Her own father….shot her. He was aiming at me. He wanted to shoot me… She pushed me out of the way…..oh, God…Lindy…why? Why did you jump in front of me?" He didn't realize that tears were streaming down his face.

"Kid….what is the name….her father's name?"

"Riley…..Ray, I think. Yeah, that's it…..Ray Riley. Lives….." Ricky made a gesture toward the area Lindy and her father lived, and then said the address. "I gotta go…to Lindy….I gotta get there…."

"Let's go, Rick." Nick appeared at his side holding a clean tee-shirt. "Guys, let us get to the hospital. The girl is critical. We'll be at University Hospital if you need us…. we're not going anywhere else."

Nick led Ricky to the car and jumped in behind the wheel. In minutes he was pulling into a doctor's spot in the emergency room parking lot. Liz was waiting for them inside the emergency room.

"Where is she?" Ricky seemed to be coming back to life.

"They took her right to surgery. Come on….we'll go up to the waiting room there." She shot a furtive glance at Ricky, and then used her eyes to communicate to Nick that it did not look good.

Ricky paced. He paced back and forth, and then around the perimeter of the waiting room. He paced out into the hall, and then back again, back and forth, not able to stand still; silently praying—begging—God to spare her life. He felt as though his entire body was put together with rubber bands that could snap at any moment.

\* \* \*

Angie pulled into the driveway, noticing that the only car there was Liz's. Where was Nick? The house looked dark. She got out of the car, walked to the front door, and knocked. No answer. She tried the door and found it unlocked. Oh, that was it. They ran out somewhere and left the door open for her. She went in and switched on a living room light and gasped. Blood. Whose? Where was everybody? What happened here? She started to back out of the room when a police officer entered, along with two men wearing suits. More police followed.

"What's happened? What's going on?" She appealed to a uniformed officer.

"Ma'am, you are…?"

"Angela DeCelli. My brother and my son live here. I came in from Chicago for the weekend. Officer, what has happened?"

"Shooting."

Angie gasped. "Who? Sir…who got shot? Please…I need to know."

"The young girl who lives here. Father shot her."

"Lindy? Oh my God! Lindy's been shot? Where is she? Where is everybody?"

"They're at University Hospital. I'm going there now…I can give you a ride." It was one of the suited men who spoke to her.

The other one interrupted their conversation. "Well, well…..look what I found." The nicer one, along with Angie and the uniformed officers turned around to see him holding a pistol up with his pen. "This must be the weapon."

The uniformed officer was already holding a plastic bag for the suited man to drop the gun into.

"Oh God." Angie murmured.

"Come on, Ma'am…I'll give you a ride up there. I have to interview the others who were here at the time."

Angie followed the detective out to the car, and as he held the door open for her, he offered his name. "I'm Detective Shultz. I'll be handling this case. Now how are you related?"

"Lindy is my son's girlfriend. Very sweet girl."

It was a short ride to the hospital. The detective helped Angie out of the car and they walked inside together. The detective flashed his badge and asked where the family for Lindy Riley would be waiting. The girl at the desk told him where and how to get there. He pushed the elevator button and waited.

"The girl must be in surgery. That's the surgery waiting area." Of course he was correct.

When the elevator doors opened, Angie immediately spotted Nick.

"Nick….my god…what happened?"

Nick stared at Angie, and then beyond her to the man standing just a step behind her.

Detective Shultz extended his hand to Nick. "I'm Detective Shultz. I'll be in charge of this case. Mrs. DeCelli got to the house a few seconds before our investigative team got there. She was totally unaware of what had happened so I offered to drive her here."

Nick nodded, indicating that he accepted the detective's explanation. Angie spotted Ricky standing by the window, his knee up on the sill, leaning against the frame. Her heart went out to him. She could see how he was suffering.

"Uh, you are…?" The detective stared at Nick.

"Oh, I'm sorry. I'm a little preoccupied. Dr. Nicholas Bazario. The condo you were in is mine."

"So what happened? Were you present at the time of the shooting? By the way…we found the weapon in your living room. He must have dropped it and ran."

Nick nodded again. "I wasn't there. He was." Nick pointed in the direction of Ricky's back. "My nephew, Ricky DeCelli"

Detective Shultz strode toward Ricky and offered his hand. "Hello Ricky. I'm Detective Ron Shultz. I'm sorry, but I need to ask you some questions."

Ricky turned and accepted the detective's handshake. He waited for him to begin.

"So just tell me what happened….from the beginning….when the shooter first got to the condo."

Ricky told the detective about the exchange of words, and how Ray Riley pointed the gun at him. "It all happened so fast. Lindy shoved me out of the way and….the next thing…I knew….she was lying on the floor….blood everywhere. Oh, Lindy….that bullet was meant for me. Why? Why did she jump in front of me?"

Ricky was openly weeping, making the detective feel uncomfortable.

"Things we do for love. She was protecting you, Ricky. It was instinct. Don't be too hard on yourself…or her. Anyway, we're going to make an arrest. He wasn't home an hour ago, so we planted someone outside the house. When he comes home, he'll be arrested."

The detective said his goodbyes with the promise to be in touch, and Ricky went back to staring out the window. Nick appeared at his side with a cup of coffee.

"Thanks." Ricky mumbled.

Nick put his hand on Ricky's shoulder and rubbed it for a moment. "Anything else I can get you?"

"No….thanks. It's been so long….shouldn't we know something by now? Shouldn't somebody be able to tell us something?"

"It's only been an hour and twenty minutes. That's not long for a damaged spleen, and we don't know what else got damaged. No news is good news right now. Just be patient. They are doing everything they can to save her. Aunt Liz demanded the best surgeons…..she has pull. Why don't you sit down for awhile? You can't really see anything out that window now that it's dark."

"I'm not looking at anything out the window. I'm praying."

Nick nodded. "Oh," he replied.

\* \* \*

Ricky wasn't the only one pacing. Ray was pacing up and down in Diane's driveway. Where was she? Ray needed her now. He was heartsick all over again. How could he? How could he have shot her? 'Lindy….oh God….Lindy.' These thoughts were going through his mind as he paced.

He hadn't meant to shoot anybody….just scare the punk kid a little. He had no idea the trigger was that sensitive. Now his Lindy may be dead or dying—he had no idea. He should be at the hospital, if that's where she was. He knew if he went there he'd be arrested. He needed Diane. Finally, he saw her car coming down the small street her house sat on. She pulled in and immediately got out of the car.

"Ray…..what's wrong?" By the look on his face, she knew she was going to hear something terrible….she just knew it. "Come on in. Tell me what's wrong."

"I shot Lindy."

Diane shook her head to clear her hearing. She didn't think she had heard him right. "What? What did you say?"

"I shot Lindy." Ray repeated.

Diane felt her knees begin to buckle. "What do you mean….you shot Lindy, Ray? What the hell are you talking about?" Diane could feel panic rising in her chest as she leaned on the car to steady herself.

"I didn't mean to. I pointed the gun at him….I didn't even plan on shooting him…just scaring him. The gun went off, and…..Lindy…fell to the floor. Oh God…Diane, I didn't mean to. It was an accident. The gun just went off…Lindy shoved him out of the way….and the bullet hit her…." Ray choked on a sob. "Diane….I'm scared."

"Ray….I….don't know what to say to you. I'm going to the hospital. You can stay here and hide if you want, but…I need to know if she's alive. Oh, God….that poor baby…..and what about the baby, Ray? You may have killed two people. Did you even think about that?" Diane's voice faded as she got behind the wheel.

344

"Diane, wait......I'll go, too. No...I didn't think about the baby. Lindy is my baby....she's the one I care about right now."

Diane drove carefully through the streets, not wanting to get stopped for anything. She was probably transporting a fugitive and didn't want to be involved in an arrest. Ray wasn't speaking, and for that she was grateful. Her mind was in turmoil. She thought she loved Ray, but how could she love a man who brutalized his daughter and then ended up shooting her? Diane thought about Lindy—her big blue eyes, her angelic face, her sweet disposition. How could anybody do anything to harm a girl like that? Yes, she got pregnant, but so do many girls. She fell in love. Ricky is a good-looking boy with a take-charge personality. Obviously he is devoted to her and very protective as well. How could a young girl not fall in love with him? Especially when that young girl has been ignored by her father and abandoned by her brother for three years? Diane glanced at Ray. He was sitting forward in the seat, holding his face in his hands. Diane pulled into a parking space and put the car in park.

"You know...if I go in there.....I'll probably be arrested." He spoke through his hands.

"You're going to be arrested anyway, Ray. What difference does it make where it takes place? At least, by being here it looks like you may be showing remorse for what you did, and that you actually do love your daughter."

"Diane, I do love Lindy! How could you think I don't?"

Diane sighed. "Well, let's see....ignoring her for three years, then brutally beating her, and then shooting her.

I can't find love in that picture anywhere....and neither will a judge. Now....I'm going in there. I know I'm going to face some flack, probably from Ricky, but I don't care. I care about how Lindy is, and I'm willing to take on the opposition to find out." She got out of the car and slammed the door.

"Diane...wait. You're right. I'll go up, too."

After inquiring at the front desk, they learned that Lindy was still in surgery. The girl gave them directions to get to the waiting area just off the operating room where they were working on Lindy. The elevator doors opened and Diane and Ray walked off the elevator, not exactly sure of where to go. Just inside a waiting room a nice-looking man in his early forties, and a pretty blonde lady stood together. They walked in and looked around. They spotted Ricky, leaning against the window frame, his back to them. The man approached them.

"Can I help you?" He asked.

"Is this where we are supposed to be when someone we love is in surgery?" Ray asked.

Nick nodded. "Who do you know that is in surgery? We're here for Lindy Riley."

"Yes...we are, too. I'm Diane...and this is her father, Ray Riley."

Nick couldn't hide his surprise at seeing Ray there. Ricky heard the exchange. Without warning, Ricky whipped around, strode across the room and sucker punched Ray in the mouth, knocking him down.

Nick went into action, grabbing Ricky and trying to pull him back. He was surprised at Ricky's strength. "Ricky, stop...this doesn't help matters."

Liz jumped up. "Ricky.....settle down. You're not helping Lindy this way."

"You're not so bad-assed when you don't have a belt or a gun in your hands; are you? You son-of-a-bitch.... you don't deserve to have Lindy for your daughter. I hope you rot in jail over what you did to her." Ricky's eyes were black and his nostrils were flaring. He could feel every part of his body revving up to go at this man again. He was straining against Nick's arms to break loose and hit him again.

Two orderlies showed up to assist Nick in holding Ricky back. He stopped resisting.

"Get him out of here. He doesn't belong here." Ricky turned from the orderlies back to Ray again. "Why couldn't you just...love her? Love her for who she is... unconditionally. That's how I love her. I love her for.... being her. Why couldn't you?"

Ray sat on the floor immobile, and stared at Ricky. He heard what Ricky was saying and he knew Ricky was right. He should have loved her unconditionally. Ray also saw that Ricky did love Lindy, more than he gave him credit for. He stood up and backed out into the hallway, tears streaming down his face.

"Diane, I'm going to wait outside."

"Fine. I'm going to find out how she is doing before I leave here."

Nick filled her in on what they knew about Lindy's condition. "The bullet passed through her spleen and tore off part of her stomach wall, and damaged her small intestine. We don't know where they are with the surgery, but we do know that they had to remove her spleen. That was the easy part. The rest...." Nick stopped and looked over at Ricky, who was once again staring out the window with his back to them. "The rest is…not so easy. That bullet fragmented a lot of her digestive tract. The repair is extensive. She…the odds are not in her favor."

Diane was trying to swallow the lump in her throat and she felt her tears running down her cheeks. "What about the….baby?"

"We haven't heard anything about the baby yet…. other than the heart is still beating."

Diane wiped her tears with the heels of her hands. "Look….I genuinely care about Lindy. She's so easy to love….I mean…the first time I saw her….I was…drawn toward her."

"We all were. Ricky loves her so much…you have no idea. I see them together all the time. He dotes on her. You know….when he introduced her to us….all of us…she immediately found a place in our hearts. I love her. I love them both…a lot."

Diane stared at the floor for a moment. "Well….the point is….Ray's screwed up. He loves her….but some…. circumstances….came about….when Lindy's mother was dying. I can't go into detail, but believe me….there is a reason for Ray turning his back on Lindy. I know how he hurt her, and he was wrong. Lindy didn't deserve the way he treated her. If….Ray had just….talked to somebody…. worked it out….we all may not be here right now." Diane pulled a pen and a used envelope out of her purse and wrote down her phone number. "Will you call me if there is any news?"

Nick took the envelope and nodded. "I'll keep you posted."

Diane thanked him and walked toward the elevators. Nick returned to the seat he had been sitting in and picked up the magazine he dropped when he jumped up to grab Ricky. Liz's pager went off, and she walked to the wall phone and dialed the number on the pager screen. When she hung up she called them all together.

"Nick…Ricky….Angie….they want me in there. They're going to take the baby. The baby is in distress now, and it's affecting Lindy's condition."

"What does that mean….they're going to take the baby?" Ricky asked. His voice held alarm in it.

"What it means, my young nephew….is that you are about to become a father."

Ricky sank down onto the window sill. "It's too soon. The baby is only six months along! The baby could die."

Liz was already out of the room and down the hall, on her way to scrub in for surgery.

"Ricky….the baby is in distress. They have to take the baby out of the uterus. Outside the womb at six months gives the baby maybe a thirty-seventy chance, not in the baby's favor….but being in distress inside the womb…. well, let's just say the odds become even less favorable….. for Lindy as well. Lindy is fighting for her life. She doesn't need two battles going on at the same time. Trust them…. they know what they're doing."

The room got quiet. Nobody spoke. Angie went and stood at Ricky's side and put her arm around his waist.

"Hey….." It was all she could say. She saw her son's pain and agony when she looked at him, and she broke down in tears.

Ricky put his arm around her shoulders as Angie rested her head on his chest. "You know…if all she needed was love to heal her right now….she'd be fine. The love for her in this room alone is so powerful. And Ricky…. I know….I know that you truly love her….and that she truly loves you. When she gets well….I'm going to be there to help you both out. Keep you together. I promise. I'm sorry for the hurt I caused…."

"You didn't do anything half as painful as her own father did, Mom. You know….if Uncle Nick hadn't have pulled me back I would have beat him to death. I hate him for what he did to her."

"I know. But Ricky….don't use your energy hating him….use it to pray for Lindy right now."

"I've been praying, Mom. She has to live….she just has to. She can't leave me…not now….not ever. Maybe I'm too young to be where I am…but I *know*….I *know* in my heart…that she is the *one*."

Ricky turned to the window again, and Angie returned to her seat and her rosary. Nick went to get more coffee for everybody.

When Nick handed Ricky a fresh cup of coffee, Ricky was tense. "It's been over four hours, Uncle Nick. Almost five. When will we know something?"

"I can't say….because I don't know. I know medicine, but I'm not a surgeon. I do know that this is a difficult surgery. They're doing the best they can."

"But what if their best isn't good enough? Uncle Nick? Lindy can't die…"

"Ricky…" Ricky's words were interrupted by Liz.

"Ricky….congratulations….you have a son." Liz appeared to be out of breath.

Ricky stared at Liz, disbelieving. When he realized what she had said, a smile came to his lips. "A son? The baby is born? Is he okay?"

"Well....he's very small.....and very weak....but he is alive. He's in natal intensive care. Want to see him?"

"Yeah." Ricky stopped and stared at Liz. "Lindy?"

"They're.....still working on her. Although now that the baby has been taken, her vital signs are a little better. They say it's going to be awhile, so let's go see your son."

Angie jumped up. "I have a grandson.....wow....who would have thought? Can I come, too?"

"Let's all go." Ricky offered, as he put his arm around Angie's shoulder.

They approached the window of the Natal Intensive Care Unit and waited for the nurse to position the baby so they could see him.

"Oh, Ricky....he looks like you." Angie offered.

"Wow...he's so little....I've seen bigger puppies." Ricky marveled.

"That's what a preemie looks like. They are small. See all those tubes and wires? They're doing his functioning for him. His organs were not ready for his departure from the womb, so medical science has found a way to compensate for that."

"What are his chances of survival?" Ricky looked straight into Liz's eyes as he asked his question.

Liz sighed. "It's hard to say....not good....but there's a chance. If he gets a little bigger and stronger maybe. Then you'll be able to hold him...just not yet, though."

Ricky nodded, and started back down toward the waiting area. He was becoming tense again, not knowing what was happening with Lindy. Nick had ordered a food delivery, and it was waiting for them when they got back to the waiting area. Ricky didn't realize how hungry he was until he smelled it. Although he took a couple of bites of the sandwich Nick had ordered for him, he didn't eat much more. When he looked up from the sandwich after the second bite, a surgeon was standing there looking uncomfortable.

"Are you all here for Belinda Riley?"

"Yes." Nick answered, and started to stand. Ricky, Angie and Liz began to get up, too.

"Just sit. I'm going to. I've just stood on my feet for over six hours. Okay…now…the surgery is over. We removed her spleen, repaired the hole in her stomach, and removed some fragmented intestine. The bullet was small, and of course so is Belinda, so when it emerged out the other side, it didn't leave a large hole like most bullets do. We repaired the hole it left."

"So how is she?" Ricky was showing his impatience.

"She's alive. They've taken her to the ICU."

Ricky expelled his breath and leaned back, not able to control the tears that just came without warning. He wiped his eyes with the back off his hand, but the tears continued to flow down his cheeks. Tears of relief.

"She's not out of the woods. The next forty-eight hours will decide her fate. We've done all we can. She's in the hands of a higher power now."

"Can I see her?" Ricky asked quietly.

"Well, give the nurses and aides a chance to get her settled, and get things hooked up…maybe you can see her for a few minutes. She won't know you're there, though."

"Yes, she will…" Ricky responded, knowing that Lindy would feel him there.

"Okay…well, keep in mind there will be a lot of equipment around her…she'll be hooked up to things…. so don't be alarmed."

Nick nonchalantly walked to another waiting area and called Diane's number. He gave her the details and promised to keep her posted. He asked if Ray was still with her, and she affirmed that he was. Nick suggested that she keep him away from the hospital, and she agreed that it would probably be best.

They gathered outside of Lindy's Intensive Care Unit, just waiting. Angie stood close to Nick and asked him if he thought that maybe after Ricky saw her they could persuade him to go home and get some rest.

"Not a chance, Angie. He won't leave here…you should know your son better than that."

Ricky's day and night vigil began. He did not leave the hospital, but sat by her bedside, holding her hand and talking to her.

"Don't leave me, Baby….please. I need you….our son needs you." He told her over and over again. He talked about their future; he talked about things they had done together; he talked about their son, hoping that she could hear him. "We have to name him, Baby. I'm not going to name him without knowing what you want."

When the hospital staff made him leave in order to change dressings, bathe her, or administer medical care, he went down to see the baby, always in hopes of seeing some improvement. There was none. He was still weak and nearly lifeless.

It was into the third day, and still no change in Lindy, either. The nurses shook their heads and clicked their tongues. 'So young, so pretty,' were their constant words. One of the nurses observed that Ricky had been there constantly, never leaving her side unless he was forced. 'Such devotion.' She had said.

Going into the fourth day, Lindy opened her eyes, and Ricky was there for her. Before he fell asleep with his head on her bed, he had placed her hand on his face and held onto her arm with his outstretched one. Lindy's eyes opened and she looked around her, not sure of where she was. She felt her hand touching…someone. Looking down at her hand she discovered Ricky asleep on the side of the bed, his head on top of the mattress. She ran her thumb across his cheek, awakening him instantly. He stared up at her.

"Hi." She croaked out.

It was the most beautiful word Ricky had ever heard. Again, he was fighting back tears. "Oh God….Lindy…. thank God…you're awake." He kissed her hand again and again, and then stood up to lightly kiss her lips.

"What….? Oh…..yeah….I remember." She ran her hand over her abdomen, and her face showed a mixture of alarm and confusion. "Ricky….the baby…?"

"We have a son." He smiled at her, causing her to smile back.

"We do? Is…he okay?"

"Well, he's real little and not very strong…..but he's fighting. He's like his dad…a fighter. My mom says he looks like me, too."

"Your mom's here?"

"Yeah….Uncle Nick, Aunt Liz, too….they've all been here."

"Will the baby….make it?"

"Honey, I don't lie to you…you know that. Aunt Liz says his chances aren't good, but he could. They want us to name him and have him baptized. We never thought about names…."

"I have. I've thought of only one name for him. Nicholas….I want to name him Nicholas Enrico DeCelli. What do you think?"

Ricky smiled down at her. "Yeah? That's your choice? Thank you, Baby….thank you so much for that."

"You're awake! Ricky, you should have told us." A nurse interrupted.

"Sorry…she just woke up."

"Now you have to leave for a few minutes. You can come back, but we have to do our jobs now." The nurse was accompanied by two more.

As Ricky was leaving the room he heard them telling Lindy, "Honest to God, he has been here day and night. Gotta be love, Sweetie."

He called Nick and Liz, and his mother. "She's awake," was all he said. They promised to be right there. Nick stopped to call Diane to tell her the news.

\* \* \*

Lindy's recovery quickened once she was fully awake. She convinced Ricky to go home and get a good night's sleep after she realized he had not left the hospital since the night she had been shot. He showered and changed clothes in the hospital daily, but had not slept in a bed in almost a week, nor had he had a decent meal. He agreed to go home when they told him that Lindy was going to be moved from intensive care to a regular room. He was back the next day with flowers, a card, and a big stuffed dog. Lindy laughed when she saw the dog, but then her face took on a serious note.

"Ricky, find out when I can go see our baby.... please?"

"I'm on it." He said over his shoulder as he walked out to the nurse's station. He returned with a wheel chair. "How about now?"

"They said it was okay?" She wanted to be sure.

"Yes...since you're not hooked up to things except that one I-V, and as long as you go in this chair. They don't want you standing up or walking for any length of time yet. So....your chariot awaits you....Juliet."

Lindy turned and looked into his eyes, and the electricity shot through both of them. Their eyes locked and they smiled into each other's face. Ricky Picked her up and sat her in the chair and wheeled her toward the Natal ICU.

"He's so little," Lindy commented as they stared through the glass at their son. "But he's beautiful....isn't he?" They watched as the resident pediatrician examined him, and they saw his frown deepen as he listened to his chest through the stethoscope. Lindy looked up at Ricky, a frown forming on her face. "What do you think he hears?"

"Don't know. Maybe he'll come out and talk to us." Ricky got the nurse's attention and pointed to the baby and then to them, gesturing that they were the parents. He saw the nurse say something to the doctor, and the doctor nodded. They waited.

Finally the doctor did come out to talk to them. "You are the parents of that baby?"

They nodded. "Please....talk to us....let us know where Nicholas stands." Lindy pleaded.

"You named him Nicholas, did you? It's my name. I'm Doctor Nicholas Kane, by the way. So tell me.... why was he born so soon? You don't look like druggies or anything....so what happened?"

"I was shot. I really don't know more than that. I was in surgery for hours....I do know that."

Ricky took over and filled the doctor in on what had happened and why the baby was taken from the womb. "But Doctor Kane....please be honest with us. We love our baby and we want to know what his chances of survival are. We saw you frowning, and..." Ricky stopped and waited for the doctor to speak, noting that his frown came back.

"Well, you both know that at six months a baby doesn't have as great of a chance of survival. I mean, it's possible, but....well, anyway, your baby's lungs are under-developed. They're not working, in other words. See, breathing is an...instinct, if you will...it's automatic. But little Nicholas...although the instinct may be there, the ability of the lungs to function on their own is not there. There's a chance that they might begin to function, but....it's a very slim one. But I also hear a murmur when I listen to his heart. That's what was causing my frown."

Lindy reached for Ricky's hand and gripped it tightly. "So you're saying our baby is going to die." Lindy's eyes filled with tears.

"Yes, there is a good possibility....to be brutally honest. I'm sorry."

The tears spilled down onto her cheeks. "Thank you for your honesty, Doctor."

Ricky wheeled Lindy back to her room, lifted her onto the bed, and held her while she cried.

# Chapter 33

$\mathcal{L}$ittle Nicholas lived another four days, when finally his heart just quit beating. Ray Riley was arrested and arraigned on murder charges an hour after Nicholas died. The police found him hiding at Diane's house. Lindy cried and cried while Ricky held her. Every time she thought she would stop, the tears came back. Angie stood by while Ricky held Lindy, and then she touched Ricky's arm.

"Can I say something to Lindy, Ricky...please? Let me hold her for a minute."

Ricky moved out of the way and made room for his mother.

"Lindy....honey, listen to me. I know how this hurts. Believe me, I do. But listen....just a moment. Little Nicholas had to be held. He wanted to be held, like all infants. He *needed* to be held. But we weren't able to hold him. He was too fragile." Angie put her hand under Lindy's chin and lifted her face up. "So....Lindy....he went to the only person who could hold him....his other grandmother. She was waiting for him, and he's probably in her arms right now."

Lindy stopped crying and stared at Angie through teary eyes. "Oh." She choked out before she wrapped her arms around Angie and cried on her shoulder. Ricky stood beside them and rubbed Lindy's back while Angie held her.

\* \* \*

Lindy was released from the hospital in time to attend little Nicholas' burial. Liz and Nick, and Angie and Ricky were there, of course, but she was surprised when Diane and then Lukas showed up. She cried when she saw other students coming in the door, too, all offering their condolences and support.

Ricky held on to Lindy throughout the service, crushing her to him even more when the final goodbyes to little Nicholas were said. He looked over at Nick in time to see him wiping his eyes. Lukas was openly crying with the rest of the students. It made Ricky realize that everybody not just loved them, but approved of them as a couple, and that they were lucky to have such wonderful friends and family.

After the service, almost everybody went back to Nick's place, where there was an assortment of luncheon foods and desserts dropped off by neighbors they had never met, and friends who cared. Ricky made Lindy sit on the sofa and he brought her something to drink. Normal food was not allowed yet, so Ricky would make her broth and serve her gelatin when everybody left. Lukas went over and sat down beside Lindy.

"Would you like to know how your dad found you?"

Lindy looked up at Lukas through hollow eyes. "Carrie?"

Lukas nodded.

Ricky was within earshot of their conversation. He felt his blood pressure begin to rise, and his heart start to

Carole McKee

palpitate. He was fighting hard to control the anger that was bubbling up inside of him. He had to remain calm for Lindy's sake, since she had been through so much already. He made up his mind that he was going to pay Carrie a visit and persuade her—no—order her—to leave them alone once and for all.

When all the visitors except Lukas had gone, Ricky put some chicken broth into a saucepan and started to heat it up for Lindy. He drew Lukas into the kitchen with him.

"Hey, how about doing me a favor? Tomorrow evening. I don't want to leave Lindy tonight, but I need to go somewhere tomorrow, if that's okay with you."

"Yeah, sure. When tomorrow? Well, I'm sure Lindy will be tired early, so after she falls asleep, maybe around eight-thirty or nine."

"Fine...are you going to tell me where you need to go?"

Ricky looked past Lukas to make sure Lindy wasn't listening, and was satisfied to see that she and Uncle Nick were talking quietly. "To Carrie's....I'm going to have it out with her. She killed my son, Luke, and she almost killed Lindy. Maybe she didn't pull the trigger, but she's the one responsible for Lindy's dad finding her."

Lukas glanced around to make sure Lindy was still occupied. "Rick, don't do anything stupid. I don't want to see you get into any trouble.....maybe even ruin your life."

"I'm just going to talk to her. What...you think I'm going to go kill her?" Ricky laughed at his own question. "It's not like it hasn't crossed my mind, I guess...but she's not worth it. I just want her to leave us alone. Leave Lindy

361

alone. You see how sad Lindy is? It breaks my heart to see her so sad, and Carrie's responsible for it. I want the torment stopped, Luke. I want it to end."

"Okay...fair enough. I'll pick you up tomorrow. Hey, I better get home. I actually got a job to go to."

"Yeah, I do, too, but I think I'll stay home one more day...for Lindy."

Luke hugged Lindy and told her to call if she needed anything, and then took off for home.

When Ricky brought the tray for Lindy into the living room, she immediately asked him about the carpet. "I know my blood was all over it. Was it cleaned or replaced?"

"Replaced….at least a section of it was. Why are you even worried about that?" Nick asked her.

She shrugged. "I was just curious. You know...I actually worried about that in the hospital. By the way, where is Aunt Liz?"

"Oh...she'll be right back. She and Angie went to the drug store. Aunt Liz is picking up a prescription for you to help you sleep."

"I guess I can use it. I'm really exhausted but I don't think I can sleep."

"You haven't touched your broth…."

"I'm really not very hungry."

"Well, you need to eat….to get your strength back. I can see you've lost a lot of weight." Nick told her.

"I think when she starts to eat regular foods again she'll gain some back." Ricky came to bat for Lindy. "But come on...eat that broth so you can have your delicious raspberry Jello." Lindy laughed at his humor, but declined the Jello; preferring to just go upstairs to bed.

"I'll be up to say goodnight in a few...okay?"

She nodded. He and Nick watched her slowly climb the stairs; both had worried looks on their faces.

Ricky took Lindy a capsule from the prescription Liz had obtained along with a glass of water. He sat down on the bed while she swallowed the pill with water, and then lay down beside her, cradling her in the crook of his arm. She fell asleep and eventually, he did, too. Nick looked in on them, lying there fully clothed, sleeping so peacefully and decided to let them be. He felt that they needed to be together right now, and he knew that they wouldn't be breaking his rules since Lindy still had staples in from her surgery, and they were both still grieving.

*     *     *

Ricky jumped in Lukas's car and they sped away. Ricky had been right about Lindy going to sleep early; she was sound asleep before eight-thirty. He sat on the bed and rubbed her back until she fell asleep and then left the room when he was sure she was sleeping soundly. He felt a little guilty that he hadn't told Lindy that he planned on going over to Carrie's, but he knew she would worry if she knew.

"You okay, Dude?" Lukas quizzed him.

"Yeah....I'm okay. I hurt...you know? I have this ache in my chest that won't go away. I see Lindy...all stapled up, and in pain....it hurts. She tries to act like she's not in pain, but I know her too well. I know when she's hurting. Then.....losing Nicholas...well, let's just say...I really wanted him....my kid....our kid. When they told me I had a son...well, I got visions of....things I would do with him....you know...teaching him how to ride a bike...taking him fishing...and just telling him all the things my dad told me. He was really beautiful…even if he was small. Besides the physical pain, Lindy has the heartache of Nicholas….not…making it….not to mention how it still hurts her that her own father caused all of her agony.…" Ricky fell silent until they reached Carrie's house.

"Uh, Dude….I'm not going to go in with you….is that okay? You'll be okay?"

"Yeah…..I'll be okay."

"I'll wait out here. Looks like she's in the game room downstairs. Just walk around the back of the house. There are sliding glass doors that open up into the game room. The rest of the house is dark, so maybe nobody else is home. I'll wait….parked over here."

Ricky nodded and got out of the car. He walked around to the back of the house and disappeared into the shadows. He found the sliding glass doors that Lukas had talked about, and peered inside. She was there, sitting on the couch with her feet up, reading a Glamour Magazine. Ricky pulled the door to the left a little and discovered it was unlocked. Very gently and quietly he slid the door open and slipped inside. The music on the stereo provided him an undetected entrance. Once he was inside he approached her from behind. When he was standing five feet from her, he said her name.

"Carrie…."

She jumped and gasped. "Ricky…..you scared me. What…..how are you?"

Ricky said nothing for a few moments; he just stood there staring at her.

Feeling uncomfortable and uneasy, Carrie stood up. "Ricky….are you okay?"

"My baby…my son…is dead. Are you happy now?" He answered.

"I….Ricky….*I didn't do anything*…I…."

"You killed him, and you almost killed Lindy."

"NO! I….*didn't*…..Ricky….I *didn't*."

"No…you didn't pull the trigger….but you told Lindy's father where to find her. Don't try to lie about it. We know you did." Ricky's voice was low and monotone. He stared at Carrie and held her attention.

"I….didn't…..I didn't mean for any of that to happen. I didn't expect him to go shoot her…." Carrie's hands were shaking and sweat was forming on her brow and upper lip. Ricky was frightening her.

"Oh…he didn't expect to shoot her either. The bullet was meant for me. Lindy…Lindy shoved me out of the way….and the bullet hit her. She almost died." He stared at Carrie, hoping to get some look of remorse from her, but he saw nothing in her face.

"I…I'm sorry. I didn't mean……"

Ricky cut her words off. "I wanted that baby…. you know? It hurts….It hurts so bad. The pain in my chest….." Ricky brought his hand up and tapped himself on the chest. "I can't cry! I want to….but I can't. If I could cry, this ache in my chest might go away. Lindy…Lindy cries. She cries a lot. I stay strong for her. Carrie….tell me why. Just tell me why. Why would you do something so…underhanded and cruel? You're an accessory….an accessory to murder. Lindy's dad….he's going to implicate you….."

"NO! I….I'm not responsible…."

"Oh, yes you are. You're guilty just as if you had pulled the trigger. Tell me....why? Why do you hate Lindy so much?"

"You should have been with me! Not Lindy! I saw you first. I should have been pregnant with your baby.... not her! Give me a chance, Ricky....please! Sleep with me! I can do things. Ricky....I can satisfy you.....like Lindy never could. Ricky....make love to me! You won't regret it!"

"You're a real sick bitch....you know that? You think because you want me I should be there? Like a new pair of shoes? What about the things that matter? Attraction.... *LOVE*? You see something....or someone...and you want it....so you should have it...have him? You're a spoiled brat....you know that? You're spoiled, selfish, and sick.... mentally sick."

"I love you, Ricky! Don't you know that?"

Ricky sniggered and then sneered at her. "*LOVE*? You *love* me? You have no idea what that even means. You don't love....you possess. You want to own me....like a trophy. And you want me even more knowing that you can't have me."

*"NO! That's not true! I liked you....wanted you....from the first time I saw you..."*

"But, Carrie....don't you get it? I never wanted *you*! YOU don't interest ME! Never *did*. You can't keep hurting Lindy because you're not getting what you want....or think you want. She has nothing to do with the fact that I don't want you. You....you're just not for me...and never will be."

"I...."

"I…what? You're guilty of murder. I'm going to the police and turning you in…as an accessory…" Ricky turned his back and started toward the glass doors. He had no idea if she could be considered an accessory, but it sounded good.

Carrie ran around him and faced him. "No….don't go…Ricky….stay." She reached for his arm and he brushed her off.

"Then just…..for right now….have sex with me." She lifted her arms and tried to put them around his neck. He pushed her arms away.

Carrie started to cry. "Please?"

"No…..Carrie, find someone who cares. Your tears mean nothing to me."

"You….bastard! Fuck you! Fuck you and fuck Lindy! I wish she had died!"

"I'm out of here, you demented bitch."

Once again, Ricky started to walk toward the doors. Carrie tried to stop him again. She grabbed the arm of his shirt and held on, causing it to tear when he pulled his arm away.

He reeled and turned toward her. She stopped abruptly when she saw the hate and murderous rage in his eyes. He took a step toward her and she took a step back. He glared at her.

"This ends now." His voice was raspy as he spoke through clenched teeth.

\* \* \*

It was late when Ricky unlocked the door of the condo and silently slipped inside. He quietly climbed the stairs and entered Lindy's room and saw that she was sleeping peacefully. He sat down in the chair near her bed and silently began to weep. The tears for Nicholas and then for Lindy silently slid down his face. He stared at her sleeping face through blurred vision, and somehow she felt his presence. She opened her sleepy eyes and peered at him; instantly knowing that he was weeping.

"Ricky?" She moved over in the bed. "Come on."

He swiftly got up from the chair and lay down beside her, laying his head on her shoulder as she had so often done with him. She ran her hand through his hair and kissed his forehead, and then wrapped her other arm around him. "We're going to be okay." She murmured in a sleepy voice, and then fell back to sleep.

He lay there feeling her warmth and felt the tension leaving his body. "I love you." He whispered before he dozed off to sleep.

# Chapter 34

$\mathcal{L}$indy awoke to find that she was alone in the bed. Had Ricky been there or had it been a dream? No. He had been there, and he was crying. Now she remembered. She remembered him sitting in the dark, and she instinctively knew that he had been crying—for Nicholas—and for her. She knew how it affected him when something happened to her. She tried to keep him from knowing how much pain she was in, but she realized he knew. He just knew. He had not cried when Nicholas died, and she knew he hadn't because he had to be there for her—be strong for her. Last night he had his cry, when he thought he was invisible in the dark, but she knew. She felt him there in the room, and he needed her. He needed her to hold him for a change.

She looked at her watch on the night stand. It was close to seven. She got out of bed and padded downstairs, where she found him in the kitchen making coffee. She put her arms around him as she stood behind him, and he turned to encircle her in his arms.

"Good morning." He smiled down at her and kissed the tip of her nose. "I thought I'd go to work today. You'll be okay?"

"Yeah, actually....I plan on working a little bit today, too. I also have a doctor's appointment at three. Hopefully the staples come out and I'll be able to eat food...instead of tasteless liquids."

Nick came out of the den when he heard her. "Lindy, I have a cab coming to pick you up at two-fifteen. The doctor's office is directly across the street from the front entrance of the hospital. Afterward, stop and see Liz. You should be ready to ride home with us. If not...you'll have to walk."

Both of their heads spun toward Nick.

"Ha! Gotcha!" Nick laughed.

"Uncle Nick, I'm going to work a little bit today, if that's all right."

"If you feel up to it....that's fine. I don't want you two getting behind on your rent." He winked at Lindy as he poured himself a cup of coffee. She smiled back at him. "I'd better get into the shower. Rick, you're going today?"

"Yeah, Uncle Nick....I've already showered...just waiting on you."

He watched Nick climb the stairs to go take his shower, and he sat down at the kitchen table with Lindy.

"I have to tell you something." He began. His tone got her undivided attention.

"Last night....after you fell asleep...I went to Carrie's house."

"You did? Why?"

"I wanted her to know that I blamed her for you getting shot and for Nicholas dying. I told her she was spoiled, selfish, and mentally sick. She...tried to talk me into going to bed with her....tried to put her arms around me. I pushed her away. Then she started screaming obscenities at me. I finally told her that I was going to get a restraining order against her.....and I think I'm actually going to. I'm going to talk to Uncle Nick about it. I want her bullshit to be over...over and done. I'm sick of it. Getting a restraining order may be the only way...let her deal with her dad's image over that one." Ricky smiled at Lindy. "You're not mad that I went over there?"

"No. If you went there it was for me. I trust you, and I truly believe you love me.....end of story."

"Good. Because you, my love, have nothing to worry about. I belong to you, heart, body and soul." He leaned over and kissed her gently.

"*AW, gees*! Do I have to see that this early in the morning?" Nick teased and then laughed.

Ricky and Lindy laughed, too.

\* \* \*

It was nearly five o'clock when Lindy and Liz walked into the lab. Ricky didn't see them come in but he caught the reaction of one of the lab technicians. He looked up and saw Lindy standing there with Liz, and smiled and waved. He made his way over to Lindy and immediately put his arm around her and kissed her.

"So what did the doctor say? Can you eat food yet?"

She smiled up at him. "Anything soft. Is filet mignon considered soft?"

Ricky laughed. "Let's ask the experts."

"Aunt Liz......Lindy wants to know if filet mignon is considered a soft food."

"No." Liz laughed. "I don't think so."

"Well, anyway...I can have mashed potatoes, pudding....anything soft. It doesn't have to be clear liquids like broth. So I guess that's an improvement. But it means I can have ice cream…..right?"

"You name the flavor, Baby, and it's yours. Of course… if we put filet mignon in the blender…it would be soft." He teased. "Did he take the staples out?"

"Oh….yeah….he did. God that hurt! And YUK to the blended filet mignon."

"So….is everything okay? I mean…..anything we have to worry about?"

"He says I'm going to be fine."

"That's a relief." Ricky hugged her and pulled her to him, just as Nick exited the culture room, as he called it.

"Hey….Lindy! Are you doing okay?" Nick joined them. "Hey, I'm ready to go home, if you all are."

The banter between the four of them was light, easy, and comfortable. It was accepted that Lindy and Ricky were an established couple just as Nick and Liz were. Nick Loved all three of them and regarded them as his family. At that moment they didn't have a care in the world and they were happy. Not one of them could foresee that in a few short hours fate would be serving up another plate of wreckage to their perfect world.

# Chapter 35

Before going home, they made a stop at the grocery store so Lindy could pick out ice cream. Armed with two half gallons, one chocolate peanut butter and the other chocolate caramel, they filed into the condo. As Ricky was putting the ice cream into the freezer, the telephone rang. He reached over and grabbed it.

"Ricky! This is Cindy."

"Hey! Cindy....how's it going? What's up?" He looked toward the living room to find Lindy. "Hey Lindy.... Cindy's on the phone."

Lindy quickly joined Ricky in the kitchen, smiling up at him and the phone.

"Ricky....have you heard the news? Turn on the TV."

"What news?"

"Carrie's dead. Murdered."

"What? When? Gees!" Ricky made a motion for Lindy to turn on the television, and she quickly complied.

"Last night. Her parents came home late and found her...in the game room....dead."

"Oh, wow.....Cindy....I went to see her last night. To tell her to leave us alone. She was fine when I left her.....

I mean…she was certainly alive. Do they have any idea how it happened? Who did it?"

There was dead silence on the other end of the phone.

"Cindy?"

"Ricky….they suspect….you."

"Huh? No way. I didn't….Cindy…..I didn't do that."

"I know, Ricky. You don't have to convince me….but you may have to do some convincing of others. I gotta go, Ricky. Good luck. Hey….I'll be there…for both of you…if you need me."

"Thanks, Cindy." Ricky hung up and joined Lindy in the living room. They had missed the bulk of the news, so Lindy still didn't know about Carrie. He immediately put his arm around Lindy.

"Baby….Carrie's…..dead."

"What? What did you say?" Lindy looked confused. "Carrie? She's dead? Carrie's dead? Ricky….when? How?"

"Somebody murdered her….last night."

"Who? Do they know?"

Ricky shook his head. "No….but Cindy says they suspect it was…*me*."

"That's ridiculous. You didn't do it. You *wouldn't*."

Ricky was relieved. Lindy's faith and trust in him knew no boundaries. The idea that it could have been him didn't even cross her mind. He pulled her close and kissed the top of her head. Nick and Liz had gone into the den when they first got home, and were just walking into the living room when the doorbell rang. Nick answered the door for Detective Shultz.

"Detective….hello. What brings you here?" Nick asked him.

"Is your nephew here?"

"Yeah…Ricky? Detective Shultz here to see you."

Ricky stood up and waited for the detective to start talking.

"Ricky….when did you last see Carrie Siverson?"

"Last night."

"And, uh….would you like to tell me about it?"

"Sure…no problem."

Nick's ears perked up. "Hey…wait a minute. What's going on?" Nick stared into the detective's face.

"Carrie Siverson was found murdered late last night. Ricky may have been the last one to see her alive."

"How do you know Ricky even saw her?"

"We found his prints on the glass door."

"So…what are you accusing him of?"

"Nothing. I just want to hear why his prints were there."

Nick stared directly into Ricky's eyes. "Got something to hide?"

"No." Ricky responded.

"Then talk to him."

Ricky sighed and sat down. "I went there to tell her to leave us—me and Lindy—alone. I told her I felt she was responsible for Lindy being shot and for our baby dying. I told her I wanted it stopped….I was not interested in her and never would be. She tried to….talk me into having sex with her. I refused. Told her she was sick. She started crying and begging. I told her that her tears meant nothing to me….so she started screaming obscenities at me….."

"What kind of obscenities?" The detective questioned.

"Oh……like fuck you….fuck Lindy….I wish she had died….I called her a demented bitch and started to leave. She grabbed me and tore my shirt…..begging me to stay. I told her it all ends now….that I was going to get a restraining order against her…to make her leave us alone. I told her to explain that to her dad when his image was tarnished….then I left. She was very much alive when I left."

"How did you get there? I know you don't have a license."

"Luke. My friend Luke drove me over there. He waited outside in the car. I was only there about twenty minutes, and then we went to the diner for coffee. We just hung out there for awhile."

"Okay, Ricky….how do I get in touch with this Luke?"

"He lives over on the other side of that little shopping area past Lindy's house."

"One-twelve Apple Drive. Lukas Byrom." Lindy interjected.

"Oh….that's Lawrence Byrom's son?"

"Yes." Lindy confirmed.

Detective Shultz focused on Lindy for a moment. "Lindy…isn't it?"

"Yes, sir."

"How are you feeling? I'm sorry about the baby. I was the one who arrested your father when…"

"Thank you for your condolences."

"Tell me what it was that Carrie Siverson did to you to make you go over there, Ricky."

"Well, for starters....she deliberately gave Lindy a black eye in gym class. But she called Lindy's dad and told him that Lindy was pregnant...which caused him to beat Lindy with a belt. She was hurt very badly. Then....she called him and told him where Lindy was staying. That's when he came up here with that gun and shot Lindy. She just wouldn't stop...."

"So you decided to stop her....."

"No....not like that....not what you're thinking. I really did plan on getting a restraining order on her."

"We talked about it this morning." Lindy interjected again.

"Why....what did she have against you two?"

"She wanted Ricky." Lindy stated simply.

"She was jealous of Lindy." Ricky added.

"Did you kill her, Ricky?"

"Oh hell, no! Why would I kill her? Do you really think I would do anything that could possibly take me away from Lindy?"

"Son....I hope not. I'll be in touch." Shultz got up to leave, taking a long hard look at Ricky before he walked toward the door.

"So...what was that about?" Nick asked as he walked up behind Ricky.

"I guess I'm a suspect. I mean....I never tried to hide how I couldn't stand the girl. But I'm not the only one. She isn't....wasn't...very well-liked. But since they found my prints on her sliding glass door....I'm a suspect."

"And what are your prints doing there?"

Ricky sighed. "I went there to...just convince her to leave us alone. Lindy's been through a lot....and a lot of it was caused by her. I....really did plan on looking into a restraining order against her. Enough is enough....she needed to stay away from us."

"Is that why you were asking me about that in the car this morning?"

Ricky nodded. "Uncle Nick, she was alive when I left there....I swear."

"I believe you, Rick. I just hope Shultz does."

* * *

Ricky kissed Lindy before he and Nick left for the lab.

"Make sure you eat lunch today. Remember.....to eat lunch. I'll call you at lunch time...and you better be eating." Ricky smiled and hugged her.

"I plan on eating Campbell's chicken noodle soup and ice cream. Is that acceptable?" She smiled up at him and slid her arm around his waist.

"Very acceptable. Gotta go." He kissed her quickly as he heard the BMW's horn. Nick was already in the car, and getting impatient.

Ricky ran out the door and jumped into the front seat with Nick. Lindy watched them drive away before she went into the den to start her daily work. She got a fresh cup of coffee while she waited for the computer to boot up, and began typing as soon as the computer was up and running. She became engrossed in her work, and stopped just before noon to heat up the can of soup that she told Ricky she would eat. She finished the soup and got out the ice cream when the phone rang at twelve-fifteen. It was Ricky.

"Did you eat?"

"Uh-huh....just finished the soup and am about to tackle the ice cream. Miss you."

"I miss you, too. I'm eating a greasy cheeseburger and fries. Should have had soup."

"I agree." Lindy chuckled. "But I can't wait to be able to eat a greasy cheeseburger and fries."

"As soon as you are able to, I'll buy. You can top that off with filet mignon if you want. Sound good?"

"Sounds wonderful." Lindy paused for a moment, and then spoke to him. "Ricky? Are my scars going to bother you? I mean...I have a lot of them. I know they'll fade but.....they'll still be there."

"Bother me? No, Baby....they aren't going to bother me. Hell, why do you think they would?'

"Well....because.....they're kind of ugly....and...."

"And what?"

"Well....maybe you won't find me attractive....."

"Baby," Ricky sighed. "If that bullet had hit me, I would be the one with scars. Are you saying that you would think they were ugly and I wouldn't be attractive to you any more?"

"No, of course not."

"Sweetheart, you took that bullet for me. You saved me. You couldn't be more beautiful to me. Every time I see those scars, I will see how much you love me...and that's beautiful. You're beautiful. And I love you....with all my heart. Now go eat your ice cream...but save me some. Gotta go earn the paycheck. We go to part-time pretty soon. I love you...bye."

Lindy hung up and sat for a few moments thinking about what Ricky had said. She believed him; he did love her enough to live with the scars on her torso. She considered herself lucky. She stood up and put her soup bowl into the sink and put the ice cream away. She would get it later. As she started toward the den to go back to typing, the doorbell rang. She answered the door to see Diane standing there. Lindy sighed, and moved aside to let Diane in.

"If you are here to try to convince me to go visit my father, don't waste your time or your breath."

"No, Lindy, that's not why I'm here. Can we sit down and talk for a few minutes? There are some things I need to tell you." She handed Lindy a wrapped package. "This is from me. Just something to say I'm glad you're okay."

"Diane." Lindy sighed as a look of sadness crossed her face. "I will never be okay. Something will always be missing from my life. I'm lucky I have Ricky; I know he loves me, but little Nicholas will always be in the shadows, for both of us."

"I know, Lindy....and I wish I could say something that would help, but I can't. There's nothing anybody can say that can take that kind of pain away. Anyway....why I'm here......I have several things to show you and tell you. Do you have any coffee? I could use a cup."

Lindy nodded. "I'll make a fresh pot. It will only take a few minutes."

Diane sat down and began spreading out the contents from the large envelope she carried in with her. Lindy got out cups and the cream for her own coffee, remembering that Diane drank it black. She also got a plate out of the cupboard, added some almond cookies to the plate, and set it on the table. As promised, in a few minutes, the coffee was done, and Lindy carried two cups to the table.

"Thank you, Lindy. Can you sit for awhile? I have a lot to go over with you."

"Okay, but I do work, you know. I work from here every day." Lindy proceeded to tell Diane about her job and Ricky's job.

Diane smiled and nodded her approval. "Dr. Bazario sounds like a wise man with a heart of gold."

"Yes….and that's why we named the baby Nicholas….. after Uncle Nick. He became the father-figure I missed the past few years. I love him as though he were my father."

Diane quickly hid the sadness and disappointment she felt in hearing those words. Ray deserved whatever he got, or didn't get from this girl. Obviously, her love and loyalty had been transferred from Ray to Dr. Bazario. Sad…..

"Okay, now……Lindy….the first thing I need to tell you is….the house is yours…."

"I don't want anything from my father….." Lindy interrupted.

"It's not from your father. Your parents never owned that house. Your grandfather did, and they lived in it…. raised you kids in it. That house….along with a lot of other things….was willed to you….by your grandfather. It was to go into your name when you became of age….which will be….next April. There will be a lot of paperwork, but other than that, everything else has been taken care of. The taxes are paid out of the estate and the insurance as well. The house is free and clear, no liens, no mortgages…..it's all taken care of and paid for. The house and all its contents belong to you. The estate attorney will contact you when you turn eighteen. You have to make arrangements for keeping the grass cut and maintenance…"

"What about Chris?"

"He is taken care of, too. There was more than one property and the wealth of the estate is extensive. Your grandfather set you both up very well. You were his only grandchildren. Now....did you ever get anything concerning a portfolio? In the mail?"

"Yes......but I didn't know what it was."

Diane laughed. "That's part of your wealth. Honey, you are worth quite a bit. There are other things that will just be presented to you when you turn eighteen. Your grandfather thought of everything. He set it up so that there would be money trickling into your possession all the time. I know, because I work for the attorneys who handled his estate. That's where I met your dad."

Lindy thought about the account with the debit card— the one she used for Christmas. She also remembered the large education fund for her. Was there more? Must be. She focused on what Diane was saying.

"If and when your dad gets out of prison, he will come live with me. He will never go back to that house. It belongs to you. All I ask is that you let me get all of his things out of it...." Diane hesitated, waiting for an answer.

Lindy nodded. "Of course. I don't really hate my father....I just really have no desire to ever see him again. But we can make arrangements for you to go there and get his things. Of course, he won't be out for a long time..... right?"

Lindy became alarmed when Diane hesitated.

"What? Tell me....he's going to be freed?"

"No....not right away....but he can get out in a couple of years. Since he pled guilty they reduced the charge to manslaughter, with a lighter sentence for saving the state the expense of a trial."

"So....that's what my baby was worth....great. I wonder if they would not have been so lenient had the baby's mother been older and married."

"I don't know, Lindy....but please try to understand.... that no matter when he gets out....he has to carry the burden of losing his only daughter....and killing his grandson. If you think that doesn't bother him....you're wrong. And if I tell you that he thought he was doing the right thing by avoiding you the past three years, you probably won't believe that either. His judgment was not good, Lindy...but he did what he thought he had to do to protect you."

"Diane, that makes no sense...no sense at all."

Diane stared at Lindy and then sighed. Should she tell her the truth? Would Lindy be able to understand? She couldn't let Lindy go on the rest of her life thinking that her father didn't love her, but how would she react to the truth? She sighed again, and thought to herself, 'here goes.'

"Lindy...do you know anything about....how sensitive a man's....penis...can be? How something will set it off and cause an erection for no reason?"

"Yes, I do. Ricky told me. He said sometimes something stupid will just cause it to get hard...for no reason."

"Yes....that's what I'm talking about...for no reason... it happens." Diane stared directly at Lindy and opened up. She told her what happened the day before her mother died, and how her father was afraid to go near her after that. "He doesn't know why it happened....God knows he never had any sexual feelings toward you….but he was afraid it would happen again. So you see….he thought he was protecting you…from himself. He….was so afraid. If only he would have talked to somebody….told somebody. It could have been explained to him that…it had nothing to do with sex….”

Lindy stared back at Diane; a sick feeling began to creep into her stomach. She wanted to get up and run to the bathroom but she didn't think her legs would carry her. They felt like rubber. Tears stung her eyes, blurring her vision.

“I'm sorry, Lindy….maybe I shouldn't have told you….”

Lindy put her hand up indicating that she wanted Diane to refrain from speaking. “No….you probably shouldn't have…..but I'm glad I know. I understand now. I…I thought he quit loving me….I always wondered what I had d-done to make him stop loving me….” Lindy was sobbing now; her sobs were coming out like hiccups. “I…I started t-to think he wished it was me who d-died…. in-instead of m-mom. I-I hated him…for not loving me….and then….af-after awhile….I j-just didn't c-care anymore….”

Sobs were racking Lindy's body now. Diane moved over to her and held her, stroking her hair and letting her cry; her own tears running down and falling on Lindy's silky blond hair. After she stopped crying, Lindy continued to let Diane hold her. It felt good to be held like her mother used to hold her. Diane reached for a box of tissues, handed Lindy one, and took one for herself.

“Oh, Lindy….you have cried way too many tears for a girl so young. You poor baby…you deserve so much more….so much more than you've gotten. I thank God for Ricky. I know he loves you. And Lindy?" Diane held Lindy at arm's length by her shoulders and stared into her eyes. "I love you. You would have been the daughter I never had….if things had been different. Please believe me when I tell you….I'll be there for you…any time. Not as your father's wife or girlfriend, but as a friend who cares for you….okay?"

Lindy nodded. "Diane….how do you explain…the beating….and then the shooting?" She dabbed at the new tears that threatened to erupt onto her cheeks.

Diane bit her lip and stared at her. Lindy had already had so much pain. She had to make her explanation good, even if she didn't totally understand the reasons herself.

"Well, Lindy….I think….the beating was partly because of guilt….shock, and frustration. He thought he was protecting you. He wasn't watching though. You got pregnant….behind his back. He blames himself for not being aware that you had a boyfriend, that you were actually having sexual encounters. He just snapped. You….didn't see him after he did that. He was a mess. He actually hoped the ground would open up and swallow him. We looked for you. I prayed you weren't hurt….he cried because he knew you were. He felt like….shit."

"And the shooting?" Lindy switched the focus from her father's feelings.

"Oh, Lindy….he never meant to pull the trigger on that gun. He only wanted to scare Ricky into letting you come back home. He knew…from what I told him…. that Ricky was protective of you. He knew that Ricky wouldn't let you go without a fight. He wanted you home again. He….wanted to try to make everything up to you. When Ricky gave him attitude….he got attitude in return. He was actually jealous of Ricky….still is. See…. you look up to Ricky; lean on him. Your dad wanted you to…be that way with him again. But Lindy…..I swear…. he didn't want to shoot anybody. That was an accident. He was sick over it. We went to the hospital when you were in surgery. We didn't stay. After Ricky punched your dad and knocked him down, we felt it was best to sit and wait at my house…."

"Ricky punched my father?"

"Knocked him flat on his butt. I still remember what he said to Ray."

"What? What did he say?"

"He asked him….why he couldn't just love you, like he did. Ricky told your dad that he loved you for just being you. Ray said to me later on that he wished it could have been different. He would have liked to have gotten to know Ricky….because obviously; Ricky is someone he can trust to look out for you."

"Well, that part is true. Ricky does watch out for me. He's very protective."

Diane smiled at her. "I know. Lindy, I only hope that some day you will be able to forgive your dad…. understand why he has done the things he's done. I know you can never feel the way you once did, but at least….be able to forgive him. I better go. There will be papers sent here…..concerning the estate. Congratulations….you're a very wealthy girl."

Diane got up and hugged Lindy. "Take care of yourself, Lindy…physically and emotionally. Don't let bitterness eat you up. You're too pretty for that." She smiled at Lindy once more and started toward the door.

Lindy stared after her, and then stopped her. "Diane....tell my dad......tell my dad that........I'm sorry....things ended the way they did."

Diane nodded, thinking that at least it was a start.

* * *

Lindy had thrown together some ground meat, onion, green pepper, and tomato sauce into a crock pot and the guys ate sloppy Joes for dinner. There were French fries for them and mashed potatoes for Lindy. The three of them were just finishing dinner when the doorbell rang. Nick let Detective Shultz pass when he opened the door. Shultz made a beeline for Ricky.

"Ricky, I have to arrest you....for the murder of Carrie Siverson."

Lindy screamed. Nick grabbed her before her knees buckled, but she slipped away and grabbed for Ricky. She clung to him, crying.

"This is wrong! He didn't do it! He didn't! He wouldn't!"

"Lindy, I'm going to have to ask you to step away from him." The detective warned.

"NO! Ricky didn't *kill* her. He's not a *killer*. You can't take him!" Lindy's words were replaced by sobs.

Detective had handcuffs in his hand as he read Ricky his rights. Lindy still clung to Ricky, sobbing.

"Can you give me a minute?" Ricky appealed to the detective.

Shultz nodded.

Ricky held Lindy tightly. "Baby, we know I didn't kill her. Look at me....please."

Lindy looked up at Ricky, vision blurred by the tears that gathered in her eyes before they rolled down her face, one after the other. Her body jerked with every sob.

"I'll be back.......damn it, I'll be back. I didn't do anything. You know that. I need you to be brave and strong right now. Hang tough. Please? For me? I love you and I know you love me. I'll be back home before you know it." His hand held her face as he spoke softly to her, kissed her tenderly, while Shultz stood by looking uncomfortable, as he shifted from foot to foot.

Ricky let go of Lindy and moved toward the detective. He turned around and put his hands behind his back so Shultz could put the cuffs on.

Lindy started to grab for Ricky again but was intercepted by Nick. "Where are you taking him?" Nick asked, holding onto Lindy. There was an edge in his voice.

The detective gave him the address of the police station he would be taking Ricky to, where he would stay until the arraignment. "Look....I don't like having to do this. Ricky seems like a good kid, but the evidence....all of it points to him. No other prints were found. Lukas isn't even a witness....he sat in the car. There is motive, opportunity, and the ability....."

"You'd have to arrest the entire school for motive.... nobody liked her." Lindy's voice was quivering. "I know Ricky didn't kill her. He wouldn't...."

Nick was on the phone talking to someone when Shultz began to lead Ricky away. Nick hung up, strode toward Ricky and hugged him. "I got you a good lawyer. I believe you when you say you didn't do it. Detective....

you see how he treats his girlfriend…..does that look like someone who would kill a girl?"

Shultz shrugged. "I've seen more unlikely killers." He led Ricky out to his car and placed him in the back seat, and then got in and drove away.

Lindy was visibly shaking and her teeth were chattering. Thinking she was about to collapse, Nick put his arm around her and led her to the sofa. He sat with her, holding onto her, while he called Liz.

\* \* \*

Liz didn't bother to knock, but came bursting through Nick's front door.

"Dear God, Nick! Why? Why would they think Ricky did it?" She stopped and stared at Lindy. "Oh, Honey," was all she said before she dropped down next to her, wrapping her arms tightly around her.

"Aunt Liz, h-he d-didn't. H-he w-wouldn't…." Lindy spoke as though she couldn't get air into her lungs; her voice was quivering.

"Lindy, you have to calm down. No, of course Ricky didn't do it. He's innocent. Uncle Nick's lawyer will prove him innocent….you'll see."

"Liz, can you stay here with her? I'm going to meet the lawyer and we're going over to the jail……oh, shit….. Angie. I have to call her."

"Nick…just go. I'll call her." Liz looked at Nick reassuringly, and nodded to reinforce it.

"Thank you." Nick turned toward the door and started to sprint, but stopped suddenly. "Liz….I love you."

She nodded. "I know." She watched him go out the door before she turned back to Lindy. "Come on, Lindy….

let's have some tea." She led the unresisting Lindy into the kitchen, sat her in a chair, and put the water on for tea.

Liz was pulling cups out of the cupboard when the doorbell sounded. Lindy jumped but didn't move toward the sound. Liz sighed and went to answer the door to two teenaged girls.

"Hi....is Lindy here? I'm Cindy and this is Shawna. We're Lindy and Ricky's friends."

Liz moved aside to let Shawna and Cindy pass, and then she led them to the kitchen and added more water to the kettle for the guests. Lindy's tears started again when she saw the two girls, and they both hugged her. Cindy was the first to speak.

"Ricky didn't do it....we know that. Lindy, we have to figure out who did. I hate my dad right now for arresting him. All the police care about is that they can pin it on someone....because of Dr. Siverson being who he is."

"Cindy, who is your dad?" Liz asked.

"Detective Shultz. I hate him right now. I told him he was making a mistake." Cindy's head quickly turned to Lindy. "You won't hold that against me, I hope."

Lindy shook her head, and then focused on Liz as she placed cups of tea in front of everybody. Shawna carried the sugar bowl and lemon to the table, along with a plate of almond cookies. When they were all seated, Shawna spoke out.

"We have to think of something. I'm going to lean on Sara. I'll bet she knows something we don't. Ricky didn't kill Carrie, but somebody did...and I'll bet it was someone both Carrie and Sara knew. You know....they both ran with older guys. Sara cheated on Luke all the time with older guys. Luke never knew it."

Liz listened to their conversation and approved of the interaction between Lindy and these two girls, who were obviously devoted friends to both Lindy and Ricky. She remembered seeing them at the services for little Nicholas. When she was sure that Lindy was calmed enough she got up and moved toward the den to call Angie.

"Oh dear God, Liz……did he do it?" Angie responded.

"Angie….how could you? NO…*of course* he didn't. You better change your way of thinking, Angie. That kind of thinking can put him away for life. We all believe he's innocent. Lindy's in the kitchen right now with friends from school. They all believe in his innocence…..and his own mother even questions it?"

Angie didn't speak for a moment. "I'll be there. I'll call off work and be there tomorrow."

"With a positive attitude and a belief in your son, I hope…." Liz retorted.

Liz hung up and glared at nothing in particular. She couldn't understand how Angie could even question whether her own son was guilty or innocent. She returned to the kitchen to find all three girls with their hands joined and their heads bowed. She broke the circle and added her hands to the group. Together, with Shawna's lead, they prayed aloud for Ricky. Liz fought back the tears that accumulated in the corners of her eyes.

\* \* \*

Ricky was led through the door by Detective Shultz and put into a room while the detective filed the paperwork. Another seasoned detective stood and stared at Ricky through the glass. Ricky couldn't see him but Detective O'Rourke watched him as he sat there waiting.

O'Rourke shook his head. "Kid didn't do it." He was overheard by a uniformed officer.

"Why do you say that? We found his prints."

"I've been a cop a long time. I know guilty when I see it, and I'm not looking at it right now. Besides.....why is it that the only prints you found were his? Nothing even from the victim or any family members were on that door. Only this kid's prints on the *outside* of the door, and he admits to being there. Do you really think that if he went to all the trouble to wipe away prints he would have forgotten to wipe the prints off from the way he came in? He seems like an intelligent kid. I say we got the wrong one."

The uniformed officer shrugged. "I don't know.....if not him....then who?"

Their conversation was interrupted by Nick and Attorney Harold Brewer, as they spoke with Shultz.

"Go ahead in. I'll be in shortly." Shultz told them.

Detective O'Rourke watched the interaction between the kid and his uncle, and then the attorney. "Innocent." He whispered under his breath.

\* \* \*

"Is Lindy okay?" Ricky asked Nick when he entered the room.

"Yeah...she's okay. Distraught, of course....but Aunt Liz is with her right now, so she'll be okay. You need to concentrate on yourself right now. It's your life you're fighting for."

"I know, Uncle Nick.....it's just that.....it breaks my heart when she cries."

Nick smiled slightly. "I know. She's something else."

"Her laugh is like music, but when she cries.... damn...it tears my heart apart."

"That's love, Rick. That's what love is. Now... concentrate on your defense with Attorney Brewer."

The attorney cleared his throat. "Let's start by you telling me what happened the night you went over to the Siverson's. From the time you got there....until you left. Actually...start with the reason you went there. Don't leave anything out. Remember, I'm your attorney....I have to know the total truth."

Ricky began. He told Brewer what happened to make him go to Carrie's house. The entire school year of torment was brought out in the open. Then he went into detail about the night he went to her house. He was careful to remember everything and not leave anything out.

"She was very much alive and screaming obscenities at me when I left. I swear it."

Brewer sighed. "I believe you. Really. I do. I think you are innocent, so let's see what we can do to convince a jury. Oh....and your concern for your girlfriend...how you care about her....isn't a liability. It shows that you are....compassionate....kind."

# Chapter 36

**Lindy** was awake when Nick returned from the jail. She had waited up for him so she could hear the details of what took place. She followed Nick into his den.

"Uncle Nick, is Ricky okay?"

"Funny….he asked me the same thing about you. He's okay. Would rather be here, of course."

"So what did the attorney say?"

"He believes Ricky's innocent….he just has to build a defense now. I….have to come up with a retainer. Not sure where it's going to come from. Most of my assets are tangible assets. I have very little cash."

"How much does he want?" Lindy asked.

"Fifty-five hundred as a retainer….then there are expenses and if Ricky goes to trial….the cost goes up. But just to keep the attorney it's fifty-five hundred. I'm not sure I can get that together within the next twelve hours. Ricky will be arraigned in the morning, and bail will probably be denied, so he'll have to be in there for awhile. Anyway, the arraignment is at eleven in the morning. I have to figure out where the money for Brewer is coming from."

"Uncle Nick……I have it."

"You? You do? That's five thousand-five hundred dollars, Honey. That's a lot of money."

"I have it. I'll go to my bank in the morning….if you'll give me a ride."

"Lindy, are you sure?"

She nodded. "I can't lose Ricky. No matter what my future is…Ricky's in it. And, Uncle Nick, I have money that goes into an account for me every month, but I never use it. It's mine to use for whatever I want….and right now I want Ricky home."

Nick stared at Lindy, a partial smile on his lips and at the corner of his eyes. He marveled at the unselfish love they both shared. No sacrifice was too big for either of them when it concerned the well-being of the other. To have a love like that was rare—rare and beautiful. He nodded at Lindy.

"Okay. We'll go to your bank at nine in the morning, after breakfast, and then to the attorney's office. I see why Ricky loves you. Now….go get some sleep. You really look exhausted."

Lindy hugged Nick before she went upstairs to bed, stopping to hug Liz who had just finished cleaning up the kitchen from the tea and cookies earlier. Lindy secretly wished that Liz would spend the night. She knew Nick needed her comfort and Lindy loved having her around, too. That wish came true for Lindy.

\* \* \*

Lindy, Nick, Liz, and Angie stood in the court room where arraignments were held. So far there was no sign of Ricky. Liz could feel Lindy's body trembling as she stood beside her. She was worried. Lindy had been through so much in the past few months, and Liz wondered how much more she could take. Ricky's arrest devastated her. Liz looked down at Lindy and gave her a weak smile, and was relieved when she got one back from her. She glanced over at Angie and saw the tightening around her mouth. Nick. Liz looked at Nick and saw the pain in his eyes. He loved Ricky, and this was hurting him very badly. Liz was pulled out of her thoughts by the sound of the large double doors opening. There was Ricky in handcuffs and shackles, flanked by two guards. Instinctively Liz put her arm around Lindy's shoulders and drew her closer.

Lindy's heart broke when she saw Ricky in those handcuffs and shackles. Their eyes met and held each other's briefly. When Ricky's back was to her, she put her head down to hide the tears that were already stinging her eyes. Ricky glanced over his shoulder and saw her with her head down. 'Baby, please don't cry,' he beseeched silently. Almost as if she heard his thoughts, she looked up into his eyes and bit her lip to keep the tears in check. Ricky flashed a very quick smile and quickly winked at her. She smiled back, her eyes sparkling with tears and love. She watched as Ricky's attorney took his place beside him. Of course Ricky pled 'not guilty', and although the attorney argued, Ricky was denied bail.

As the guards were leading Ricky back out through the double doors, he asked one of them if he could just see his girlfriend for a moment.

"It's against the rules, kid.....can't do it." The older of the two told him.

"Come on......look at her. Look how her heart is breaking."

The younger guard looked over at Lindy. "What can it hurt, Hutch? That little girl is crying her eyes out."

"Okay….motion for her to come out into the hall. But, kid, anything funny and I'll shoot the both of you…. got it?"

Ricky nodded. A bright smile came across his face as he saw Lindy coming out the door.

"Five minutes….that's all we can allow."

"Thanks….thanks a lot…..I mean it."

Lindy rushed toward Ricky and was stopped by the younger guard. "Whoa, little girl. You can't just do that. We have to make sure you have no weapons on you."

Lindy was trembling as she agreed to a search.

"Okay…..go hug your boyfriend."

She fell against Ricky and wrapped her arms around his waist, her tears dripping on him.

"I can't hug you back, Babe….but it feels so good having you touch me." He whispered as he looked down into her face and smiled. "I love you….you know that."

They were interrupted by the older guard. "Kiss her and we gotta go. We could get in big trouble for this."

"Okay. Thanks, man."

They kissed as Lindy hung onto him. "Wait for me…. I'll be home sooner than you think….and please….don't cry. It breaks my heart every time you cry. Okay?"

"Okay." She answered, her lower lip quivering as she tried to control her tears.

The guard touched her shoulder. "Just go back out those doors and don't say a thing to anybody. Remember…..we stuck our necks out."

"I won't say anything. Thank you….thank you so much, Sirs." She smiled weakly at the guards.

They watched her walk back through the doors and then turned to escort Ricky to the van that awaited him outside. "Nice girl." The younger one commented.

Ricky nodded, as he watched Lindy disappear through the doors.

\* \* \*

Lukas joined the others at the dining room table. Attorney Brewer had requested his presence at the condo and Lukas was glad to oblige. He reached for Lindy's hand and held onto it for a moment.

"Are you doing okay?" He asked.

"Yeah....I'm trying to stay strong...for Ricky."

"That's good. If you need....anything....just call me. Okay?"

Lindy nodded, before they turned their attention to Attorney Brewer.

Brewer looked around the table, scrutinizing all of their faces. He could read the emotional pain in their eyes. "Let's proceed." He began.

He asked Nick questions about Ricky's behavior and what their relationship was like. He only had a couple of questions for Liz and a couple more for Angie. Shawna and Cindy were only there for moral support, but Brewer had a couple of questions for them anyway. He wrote on a legal pad as they all answered his questions. Next, he focused on Lindy.

"So....Lindy...what kind of a boyfriend is Ricky?"

"He's....the best." Lindy brightened for a moment just before the tears gathered in the corners of her eyes. "We....never fight or argue...he always does....what he thinks will make me happy."

"He's so romantic..." Cindy interjected.

"How so?" The attorney focused on Cindy.

"Well...things he....says....things he does....for Lindy." Cindy proceeded to tell Brewer about the gorilla for Lindy's birthday and how Ricky told her that he and Lindy were married from the moment they met. "Everybody calls them Romeo and Juliet....because that's how much they love each other." Cindy concluded.

Brewer continued writing on his legal pad, nodding at the appropriate times. "Now....is it true that Ricky was willing to pay someone to beat up Carrie?"

Shawna started laughing. "Yeah....me....but I would have done it for free."

"Tell me about that." The attorney asked.

"Well....she was always doing things to Lindy. She deliberately smashed into Lindy causing her to have a black eye for weeks. She was so jealous because Lindy had Ricky...."

"She liked Ricky?" Brewer asked.

"Yeah....well....she said she did.....but we know her....knew her...too well. She was a spoiled brat. She only wanted Ricky because he was with someone else. Anyway...I offered to beat her up for a buck. Ricky laughed....but I was serious. It pissed me off that she hurt little Lindy. She was a lot bigger than Lindy. Then she was always making remarks about Lindy...saying things. Oh...and every time I saw her she was glaring at Lindy and Ricky together. She was so....jealous. She was always trying to humiliate Lindy in front of everybody....but what usually happened....no....what *always* happened... was Ricky would humiliate her. Like the time about the prom...." Shawna stopped and laughed.

"What about the prom?" Brewer coaxed.

"Well…Carrie made a crack that they wouldn't be going to the prom because they didn't make maternity prom gowns. Ricky went up to Sean and bought the tickets to go….he stopped at Carrie's desk and told her they would take pictures of Lindy in her maternity prom gown…since Carrie wouldn't get to see her that night. Carrie wasn't asked to go to the prom….and Ricky let the whole class know it. Made a fool of her in front of everybody…." Shawna stopped to laugh again, and was joined by both Cindy and Lukas.

Brewer turned to Lukas. "Lukas….tell me about the night you drove Ricky to Carrie's house. What did you talk about on the way over there?"

"Well…..I asked if he was okay. He said he wasn't…. that he was hurting because of the baby dying and Lindy in so much pain. He said he really wanted that baby…. that he had visions of teaching him things….telling him all the things his dad had told him. He wanted to be the kind of dad like he had. Then he said it hurt him so bad to see Lindy suffering like she was. He knew she was in pain, even though she never complained….but….he knew she had emotional pain, too. He said his heart hurt….that there was a hollow feeling in his chest…."

Lukas stopped when he realized there were sobs going around the table. Lindy, Cindy, Shawna, Angie, and Liz were visibly and openly crying; Nick sat with his head down with his eyes shielded by his hand as his elbows rested on the table. He watched as Liz reached for Lindy to hold her. He felt so helpless. Brewer cleared his throat.

"Lukas, what about after he got back in the car? What did he say? How did he act? Was he running? Walking?"

"Well, no….he was walking….walking and shaking his head. When he got in the car, the first thing he said was that Carrie was nuts…"

"Was nuts? Meaning past tense?"

"No….he said, and I quote 'that girl is nuts…really whacked out. She called me a faggot because I won't sleep with her. She just doesn't get it.'"

"So…he was talking in present tense the entire time?"

"Well yeah…we went to the diner and had coffee and talked about things when we left Carrie's. He never said anything that would make me think Carrie might not be alive…"

"What did you two talk about at the diner?"

"Things like…how he planned on being with Lindy forever….how he couldn't understand Lindy's dad….and we talked about me, too. I broke up with my girlfriend when I found out that she and Carrie called Lindy's dad and told him she was pregnant. We talked about that. We talked about my new girlfriend. He talked about Lindy some more. He loves her so much."

"Anything about Carrie? Did he say anything about Carrie at the diner?"

"Only that he couldn't figure out why she didn't get it that he wasn't interested in her and never would be."

Brewer continued his writing, and without looking up, asked Lukas, "Did you notice anyone…or anything…any type of activity around the house while you sat there?"

"N-no…..Only about two cars drove past me. One was a Mercedes and the other was an old, old Cadillac, I think. Light blue. I remember that one because the hood was a different color—yellow I think. It was a big car."

Nick's ears perked up. He listened attentively to the description of the car. Something about that description was tugging at his memory. What was it? He pictured that car in his mind. Where had he seen that car?

"Oh...and there was another car that went by. A dark sedan of some kind. I really don't know what the make or model was, but it was a black car, I think. That's about it, though. I didn't see anybody out walking or anything. It's a quiet neighborhood."

"So did you see where these cars went? Think about it..."

"Well, the Mercedes pulled into a driveway a couple of houses down from Carrie's...the black one went straight past the house and drove away. The big blue car, went up past the house, but then turned around. It went down to the next corner and made a right. I thought it turned into the service way behind the houses. In the city...that's an alley....but in Carrie's neighborhood, it's called a service way."

"What makes you think it may have turned into the service way?"

"I saw headlights, but then...." Lukas stopped and stared at the attorney. "...then...the headlights went out...."

Harold Brewer stared intently at Lukas. "They went out? Like someone turned the car off?"

"Yes. I wish I would have listened or paid closer attention. I didn't really think anything about it at the time, but that car didn't really fit into that neighborhood.... you know what I mean?"

Brewer nodded. "We have to see if we can find that car. I have a gut feeling."

Nick didn't say anything, but he also had a gut feeling. There was….something…

Something…what was it?

# Chapter 37

Ricky was led to a new cell in a new facility. He had no idea where he was, but he hoped that the attorney would know—and his family. Up until now, he had been brave and optimistic, but now he wasn't so sure. The judge already treated him like he was guilty. At least those two guards were okay. Letting him see Lindy showed him that they were at least human. Lindy. How it hurt to see her in tears like that. She tried to be brave, and tried to control them, but she was too distraught. What would she do if he were to be found guilty? 'Stop it….don't think like that, Rick. I'm not guilty. Certainly I can't be found guilty of a crime I didn't commit….can I?'

The guards stopped in front of his new cell and unlocked it. "You're going to have some company here." The younger guard told him.

Once he stepped inside, they removed the shackles and handcuffs. As he was turning around they closed the barred door in his face. He stood there watching them walk away, unmindful of the man lying on the bottom of the two cots in the cell. The man was watching him from under the pillow he had placed on his head.

"What the hell are you doing here?" He asked him.

Ricky whirled around and stared at him. Ray Riley sat up on the cot, ducking his head to keep it from hitting the cot above him.

"Ricky….isn't it?"

Ricky nodded, as he got his bearings and focused on Ray.

"What are you doing here?"

"They say I killed a girl."

"Who?"

"Carrie Siv….that girl who called you and told you about Lindy."

"She's dead?"

Again, Ricky nodded.

"And did you kill her?"

"No."

Ray snorted. "It was only a matter of time before somebody did. Snotty bitch. Why do they think you did it?"

"Because on the night she was killed I went to her house to have it out with her about all the shit she did to Lindy. She was alive when I left."

"She did other things to Lindy? Besides call me?"

Ricky nodded, and then told Ray of the taunting, the black eye, the snide remarks, the baby rattle, and everything else Carrie had done to torment Lindy.

"She was so jealous of Lindy…..it consumed her."

"You're their only suspect?"

"Seems that way. Should be the entire school, though. She wasn't very well liked."

"Hell, I didn't like her. I told her she was a very sick girl that last time she called me. She said she should have been with you; not Lindy."

"Yeah, that's what she said to me. Crazy bitch. She couldn't get it through her head that even if I hadn't met Lindy, she wouldn't have been the one. Didn't like her from the minute I saw her. She couldn't….understand that."

Ray was silent. He knew he had to say something to Ricky about the shooting, the things he said, and the baby, but he wasn't sure what he should say. He didn't want this kid beating the shit out of him right in this cell. Judging from his physique, the kid could easily whip his ass.

"How's Lindy?" He asked gingerly.

"Distraught….that would be the best way to say it. She totally lost it for a few minutes when I was arrested. I saw her today….she was trying so hard to keep from crying…."

Ricky stopped. Ray watched his eyes soften and the corners of his mouth tilt upward when he talked about Lindy.

"You really love her; don't you?"

"Yeah…..I do. How could anybody not? She's like……"

"An angel….I know. Everybody always said that about her….from the time she was little. They have little figurines out in shops….blond haired, blue eyed angels…. everybody always said that was Lindy. My wife started collecting them. Called it her Lindy doll collection…."

Ray got a far-away look in his eyes, as he remembered those happy days.

"I miss those days…..when Stacey was alive. We were all so happy then. When Stacey died…." Ray shook his head. "Can't dwell in the past, I guess. Doesn't do anybody any good."

"She sings like an angel, too." Ricky offered.

"Yeah....doesn't she?"

"That's how I met her. I opened the auditorium doors on the second day of school and I heard an angel singing. I couldn't go anywhere....I just went in and sat down and listened. I was hooked from that moment."

"That's a nice story." Ray commented.

Ricky moved toward the cots, and Ray flinched.

"I guess this top one is mine?"

"Yeah.....you can get up there all right, can't you?"

"Yeah....but what if I piss the bed? You're going to get wet."

"Is that a problem you have?"

"No." Ricky chuckled under his breath.

Both were silent for awhile. Ricky was looking around the small cell and visually taking everything in, even though there was not much to see. Two bunk-type cots, sink, toilet, small table with one chair and three bare walls and one barred one, and that was it. Ray lay on his back in the lower cot, ankles crossed, and his hands under his head. He tried to look relaxed even though he was aware that at any time the kid could grab him off of the cot and beat him severely. He knew he needed to apologize, but was afraid to approach the subject. How sensitive concerning the baby was this kid?

Ray sighed. "I'm sorry.....about everything. I never meant to kill anyone. Hell...I didn't even mean to pull the trigger. It just....went off."

"Want to explain why you beat her like you did?"

"Wish I could. I don't know…..I snapped. My God…. I was so sorry afterward. I…know….I'm a piece of shit. I know Lindy will never forgive me….because I will never forgive myself."

"The emotional scars will never go away. She'll remember it all for the rest of her life."

"I never…..never, ever laid a hand on her before that night. I don't know what….happened." Ray stopped talking, swung his legs over the edge of the cot, and stood up. He leaned against the wall of the cell across from the cots. "It was such…..a shock…when I heard that she was pregnant. I blamed myself for not watching….not being there. I couldn't….be there. I was afraid to be there…."

Ray stopped talking again and shook his head. Better not to go there with this kid. He stared at the cell floor. He had to ask about her, though.

"Is she going to be all right? I mean…."

"Well….physically, I guess. I mean…apparently you can live without a spleen. The scars bother her. Emotionally? I'm not so sure. Our baby died. That's hard for anyone…especially a loving mother…to take."

"Lindy was a loving mother?"

"Well yeah….she never even got to hold him while he was alive though. He was so….fragile. When he…. died…….we both held him for the first and last time. Lindy cried….she cried so hard….for days. My mother helped. She told Lindy that he needed to be held and cuddled, but we couldn't do that because he was so little and weak….so he went to be with the grandmother who could hold him. My mom told Lindy she bet that Stacey was holding him in her arms at that very moment. I don't know….somehow it helped."

Ray looked away from Ricky, but not before Ricky saw the tears glistening in the corners of Ray's eyes.

"And I'll bet your mother was right. Stacey was a loving mother, but as a grandmother....well, there would have been none better. I'm sure of that." Ray sighed.

Both Ray and Ricky were staring at the floor. This strange partnering was awkward but yet comfortable somehow. Ray had told Diane that he wished he could have gotten to know Ricky, and now, under these strange, unfortunate circumstances, he was going to get the chance. He knew Ricky wasn't guilty of killing that girl. The kid wasn't a killer. What his poor daughter must be going through right now. How much more could she take? She lost her mother, her baby, her father, and now Ricky. 'Lindy, I'm so sorry,' Ray spoke to her in his mind.

"Will she be coming to visit?"

"No. I don't want her in this ugly place...seeing me as a prisoner....no, I asked my uncle to make sure she doesn't come. God...I want to see her so bad...." Ricky sighed. "But not this way. She was at the arraignment.... crying....shaking. My aunt held her......at least she's in good hands."

"She's with your aunt?"

"And my uncle. They both love her...as much as they love me. They're both doctors....so they treated her when......for the welts. My aunt is an OB/GYN, so she was Lindy's doctor. She delivered Nicholas.....during the surgery for the bullet wound."

"Nicholas.....that was his name?"

Ricky nodded. "Nicholas Enrico DeCelli. For my Uncle Nick and my dad. It was Lindy's idea." Ricky smiled slightly and then stared at the floor. "He was so

pretty…you know? Even though he was born too soon….
he was too small….but still…pretty."

"You must have wanted him as much as Lindy did."

"Yeah….I did. See…I had a wonderful dad…and I
want to be the same kind of dad. Little Nicholas had two
parents that really loved him….even though the odds
were stacked against us. We would have made it though.
It would have been tough…but we would have provided
him with a home. I know that. As much as we love each
other and loved him….we would have made it."

Ray stared at Ricky. "Yeah, I believe you would have.
I'm….so sorry I took that away from you. I would have
been a good grandpa, you know….once I got over the
shock and realization that my daughter grew up and moved
on to adulthood behind my back. Me and Diane…..we
would have just spoiled him."

"You would have had to fight my mother for the
chance."

Both Ray and Ricky laughed at that remark. Ricky
glanced at Ray, thinking, 'he's not all that bad of a guy.
Somewhere something happened to make him do the
things he did.'

"Okay, let me give you the run-down on how things
work here. You'll be okay in here. Nobody fucks with me.
I'm going to get the word out that you are family….you'll
be fine. Do you smoke?"

"Occasionally. Lindy doesn't like it, so not very
often."

"Same here. Once in awhile a cigarette just…hits the
spot….I don't know. We get outside in about ten minutes.
Stick with me. We can have a smoke then. I have some,

and I'll share them with you. But you have to get the next pack. You have money in your bank here?"

"I had twenty-four dollars on me when I came in. My uncle was going to add more, so yeah…I have some."

"Okay. Cigarettes are five dollars a pack, but they'll last you almost two weeks, probably. You'll get a list of stuff you can order from the commissary. You check what you want for the week and they will bring it around. You have to pay for your own soap, deodorant, shaving stuff, shampoo….whatever you use. It's expensive. Hopefully, you won't be here that long, though."

"Yeah….hopefully."

"There are no other suspects? Really?"

"Apparently not."

The signal that the doors were going to open to let everyone outside for a thirty minute break sounded.

"Just stick with me…..okay?"

Ricky didn't have a problem following that advice.

# Chapter 38

**I**t was the first day of the new school year. Nick dropped Lindy off in front of the building and asked her if she would be all right. She shrugged and nodded. Nick watched her walk up the steps and enter the building, holding the schedule she had received in the mail. Ricky's schedule sat on his dresser, the envelope unopened.

She was greeted by Lukas and Shawna when she entered the building. They walked with her to her homeroom, not talking. A couple students waved at her, but many just gawked at her, wondering what it was like to be the girlfriend of a murderer. Sarah passed the three of them and whispered something under her breath, but they couldn't actually hear what she said. Lindy was glad that the classes would be on an uneven schedule for the week. She really wasn't ready for class regimen yet. In one short summer, she had lived a lifetime of drama, and all she wanted to do was crawl into bed and just stay there. Cindy dropped down into the seat next to her.

"Hey, hangin' in there?"

"Yeah, Cin….trying to, anyway. I hate the way some kids are staring at me."

"I know. You're quite an attraction. How's Ricky doing?"

"He-he's okay. I haven't been to see him because he doesn't want me to see him in jail. He...tells Uncle Nick to tell me he loves me and he'll see me soon, but....." Lindy stopped, not trusting herself to speak any more. She didn't want to cry.

"Well...here's a little bit of good news. I heard my dad talking to another cop yesterday. He says their case against Ricky is weak."

"That's...good, right?"

"Right."

\* \* \*

Lindy was waiting impatiently for Nick to get home. He had gone to see Ricky and promised to tell her everything when he got home. Ricky had made Nick promise not to let Lindy go to the jail, so consequently, Nick made Lindy promise him she wouldn't go, but with the stipulation that he would tell her everything. She had done her homework, and was trying to concentrate on a television program, but she was too restless. The clocks seemed to have stopped. Finally, she chose to turn on the computer and type some reports. She just finished the fifth report when she heard Nick pull into the driveway. Closing out, like she had been taught, she shut down the computer, and went to greet Nick.

"Well? How is he, Uncle Nick?"

"He's okay, Honey. Asked about you. I told him you were being strong for him. I didn't mention that you cry yourself to sleep every night"

Surprised, Lindy stared at Nick.

"You didn't think I knew that, did you?"

"No." Lindy shook her head.

"Anyway, He said to tell you that he's okay....that he loves you.....and that he misses you. I gave him an update on the progress of the investigation. The police don't really have a lot to go on. If this goes to trial....the jury isn't going to see a lot of hard evidence....."

"I hope they can see that Ricky is innocent. He's so...."

"Sweet....yeah, I know. How about some dinner? I'm hungry, and I know you haven't eaten. Steak? You can eat now."

"No." Lindy shook her head. "Ricky promised me he would buy me filet mignon when I could eat real food again.....so.....I'll wait for that. Italian would be good, though."

"Good deal. Let's go to Luigi's for spaghetti. Outside of Ricky's, it's the best I've ever had."

# Chapter 39

It was already the third week of school, and Ricky was still incarcerated. The trial date had been set for November fifteenth, right before Thanksgiving. Thinking optimistically, Lindy believed they would have something wonderful to be thankful for—Ricky coming home. Her life, as well and Nick's and Liz's life, was on hold until then. Nick and Liz had planned on getting married at the end of September, but postponed it because they wanted Ricky there. Angie sold the house and was in the midst of house-hunting in the area. She was looking for a two or three bedroom home, in hopes of having Ricky and Lindy there. Lately, she had become resigned to the fact that if there was no Lindy, there would be no Ricky either. They came as a package deal, so to speak.

Nick came home to find Lindy crying, holding Ricky's picture in her arms. He went to her and put his arm around her shoulder.

"I know this is rough for you, Honey. We have to believe that they will find him not guilty. Why don't you call one of your friends? Go to the mall, maybe. You need to get out."

Lindy just shook her head. "He's going to call tonight. I have to be here."

Nick had forgotten about that. Ricky would be calling in about an hour. Nick told Lindy to accept the charges when he called—it was okay.

"Okay. I'm going to order us some Chinese. Is that okay?"

Lindy nodded. "Is Aunt Liz coming over?"

"No, not tonight. She was tired so she went right home to bed."

The Chinese delivery arrived and both Nick and Lindy devoured it. Lindy hadn't eaten all day and Nick had a very light lunch, trying to avoid Tom Siverson. He hadn't seen Siverson since the funeral, and he was glad. Siverson gave him an accusing look when he and Liz showed up at the funeral. Ricky and Lindy made an appearance that day as well, but left after a brief visit. It was a very sad event, as it always is when a young person dies. Very few students from school attended the funeral, but then it was well-known that she wasn't very popular.

Shortly after they finished eating, the phone rang. Nick answered it and accepted the charges, and then turned the phone over to Lindy, as she tried to control her breathing.

"Hi." There were butterflies in her stomach and it hurt to breathe. She was biting her lip to keep from crying.

"Hi, Baby….I miss you."

"I-I miss you, too. Are you okay?"

"Yeah….I'm okay. I just want to be home with you; but you already know that. Is school okay?"

"It's not the same without you. I've been keeping a record of all assignments for you. Oh…Shawna and Cindy said hi….and get back to school. Lukas asked about you, too. Mr. Wise…well, he's upset. Says to tell you hello, and get back there to take care of his star pupil. And I....I just....I just want you to hold me again." She bit down on her lip hard, trying to keep from crying.

"Write me a letter...okay? Send me some pictures. The ones I have of you are in my wallet, and I'm not allowed to have that. Will you do that? I'll write you back..."

"Yeah....of course. I'll write tonight."

"I only have a minute left, Baby. Can I talk to Uncle Nick? I love you, and I miss you."

"I love you and I miss you, too." She said, as she turned the phone over to Nick.

"Hi, Uncle Nick. Just wanted to say thanks for all you've done. You're looking out for her, aren't you? She's eating?"

"Yeah, we had Chinese tonight. She....has her moments, but she's doing okay. She'll be better when you're out of there. So will I."

The operator announced that there was only fifteen seconds left, so they said their good-byes and hung up. Nick looked at Lindy as she broke down crying. He felt like crying himself. He still had his mind on that car. If only he could remember the significance of it. He was racking his brain as he mechanically made tea for himself and Lindy. Together, they sat on the sofa, drinking tea and watching a television sitcom. Neither of them laughed during the entire show. Nick got up and stretched and walked to the bar. He poured himself a good sized portion of bourbon, and sat down on a bar stool to drink it. Something.....something....what was it? He knew he had the answer somewhere in his brain. It was important, too. Why couldn't he think of it? Lindy went up to bed at ten o'clock, kissing his cheek before she went. He watched her climb the stairs, and then poured himself another glass of bourbon. An hour later, he climbed the stairs up to bed himself.

\* \* \*

Nick jerked awake. He glanced at the clock. Two-thirty. He sighed and stretched out on his back, staring at the ceiling with his arms behind his head. His mind was roaming. Suddenly he sat up. He had it. That car. Now he remembered. He looked at the clock again. He had to call Liz. He lifted the receiver and then stopped. It was two-thirty. No....he had to call her now. She wouldn't get mad—not at something this important. He dialed her number. She answered on the fourth ring, sounding very sleepy.

"Liz.....sorry to wake you...."

"Nick? Is everything okay? What's wrong?"

"Listen....try to remember, okay? When we were sitting in the diner that morning. Remember the couple arguing outside?"

"Y-yeah....I do."

"Remember the car? The one they drove away in?"

"Yes. An old Cadillac......oh my God, Nick. It was light blue with a yellow hood. The girl....was Carrie Siverson. Now I remember. Oh, Nick...."

"I'm calling the attorney. No....I can't. It's the middle of the night. Liz, what do I do?"

"First thing in the morning, right after Lindy leaves for school. I'll be there. We'll go see the attorney, and then the police. Nick....this could be the break we've been looking for...."

"I'm not going to say anything to Lindy. I don't want to build up her hopes, and then....well, you know."

"Yeah….I know. Is she okay?"

"She talked to him tonight. He called. She cried after they hung up, but not while he was on the phone. She can be a trooper."

"Hey, listen….I'm going back to sleep. I'll see you bright and early…g'night."

Nick hung up, and stood up. He doubted that he would get back to sleep. He went downstairs, made a pot of coffee, and waited for daylight.

\* \* \*

Liz rushed through the door two minutes after Lindy left for school.

"Ready?" She asked Nick.

"Yeah……I hope the attorney is in this morning. If not….I'm going to the police station and finding Shultz."

The attorney was in, but with a client. They agreed to wait, after he agreed to see them on such short notice. They told his secretary that it was urgent. Nick was showing his impatience, so Liz was glad when the secretary told them they could go in. Nick and Liz told Brewer about the car.

"It was a light blue Cadillac with a yellow hood. Carrie Siverson was with the guy who drove it. They were arguing, and I remember he grabbed her arm, and then grabbed her face and held onto it so she couldn't move her head." Nick related this to the attorney.

"Are you sure about the car?"

"Positive."

"Oh, and Shawna told us that Carrie and her friend Sarah ran with much older guys. This guy looked to be about twenty-six—twenty-eight, maybe."

"Okay....we need to get this information to Detective Shultz. Did it look like he was hurting her when he grabbed her?"

"Yeah, I thought so. I tensed up when he did it."

"Okay, let's go over to the station and see if Shultz is there. This is new evidence. He'll want to interview all the kids again, and then this Sarah. Who is she?"

"She used to be Luke's girlfriend. He would know her last name." Liz added.

Shultz was on the phone when they got there, so they sat down to wait. "Let me do the talking. Don't talk unless he speaks directly to you. Remember, I have something to lose here...my fee. So he'll listen to me. The District Attorney will probably be called, too."

When Detective Shultz was free, they all sat down around his desk. Brewer explained about the car, and the other circumstances in which this car could be identified. Shultz listened attentively, and then got out a binder full of pictures of cars.

"See if you can find the car in there. I'll give Lukas the book to see if he can identify it, too."

Nick reached for the book and opened it. He began searching the pages, and then stopped. "Here it is....right here."

"You're sure?"

"Yeah....it's even the right color....except for the yellow hood."

Shultz began working on his computer, and then turned to them. "There are only three of those in the county. One is in the junk yard, so that leaves two. Now the guy...could you identify him? How about a description of him?"

Nick shrugged. "Brown hair, about six foot, average build."

"Prominent jaw line. Sort of jutted out a little beyond his face….if that makes sense. He had a scowl on his face….seemed angry." Liz added.

"What about her? What was her demeanor like?" Brewer inquired.

"Her back was bristling until he grabbed face. I don't know what he said to her, but it sure did subdue her. She appeared…..compliant….docile."

"They kissed and made up in the car, before he sped away. He appeared to have complete control over her, though."

Detective Shultz made a couple of phone calls while they sat there. "I'm sending a uniformed officer to the school to pull Lukas and that Sarah out of class. This is too important to wait."

A man in uniform appeared at his desk, and Shultz handed him the book. He gave him instructions and the uniformed man hurried away. The District Attorney appeared and sat down. He listened while the detective briefed him on the latest information.

"So what are you saying? We may have another suspect?"

"It looks that way."

"All right. We'll wait for Officer Tanner to get back here. See what he says." The DA excused himself, and told Shultz to call him when Tanner got back.

Shultz looked at his watch. "It's almost noon. You folks have anywhere to be right now?"

"Nowhere we want to be until we hear back from the officer."

"Look." Shultz sighed and shifted in his chair. "I don't want Ricky to be the one. I want you to know that. I like him. And that girlfriend…..she could melt the heart of a granite statue. If we can find another suspect.:..we can at least get Ricky released from jail….for the time being, anyway. A confession from the other person would be…well, let's not assume anything."

"I only hope that Luke can identify the same car…. or at least one close to it."

"I have to tell you….my daughter hates me for arresting Ricky."

"Oh….Cindy…..I know. She was at the house the night you arrested him. They're all good friends." Liz answered.

"I've made plenty of arrests in my day….but never have I made an arrest where nobody….absolutely nobody believed I had the right one. I hope everybody is right."

He punched some more buttons on his computer and came up with two names from the DMV, both names of men around the same age. He wrote them down, along with the addresses listed for them. He looked up at the group around his desk.

"Why don't you all go get lunch? Be back here in about an hour….hopefully the police officer will be back here by then. I want to run background checks on these two guys while you're gone."

\* \* \*

Nick and Liz sat at a small table in the small restaurant across from the police station. Attorney Brewer went back to his office to see another client, but promised to be back at the police station as soon as possible. Although Liz and Nick ordered food, they didn't eat. Instead, they pushed it around on the plate, pretending to eat. Each of them had a glass of wine, which helped calm them.

"Remember….we say nothing to Lindy. I don't want her getting her hopes up."

"Got it." Liz answered. "I just…..pray something comes of this. I never did fall back asleep last night."

"That makes two of us." Nick countered.

When the hour was over they paid the check and went back to the police station. Detective Shultz was engrossed in a conversation with Officer Tanner when they got there. He waved them over.

"Okay. Lukas said it could be the car, but it was dark, and the car was too old for him to instantly recognize. The color was definitely right. He also told Tanner that Carrie was screwing a twenty-eight year old guy. Sarah had told him that. Now Sarah…according to Tanner is kind of a snot. She was hostile from the beginning. But she did say that the guy Carrie was seeing was someone named Ken something. He had video-taped them having sex and controlled Carrie by threatening to put it on the Internet, and sending a copy to her father at the hospital. I wrote down Kenneth Trent off of the DMV list. He's the first one I'm targeting. No real rap sheet….just a DUI four years ago. Here's his picture….can you make a positive ID from it?"

He laid the picture in front of them.

"That's him." Liz responded. "I'm positive."

"Well…let's just see what he has to say for himself. I'll get back to you as soon as I can. It may take a couple of hours or a couple of days. Hopefully this guy hasn't decided to leave town. As soon as I know something, I'll get back to you. Be patient."

Shultz got up to leave, giving them the hint that their time was up. Neither of them wanted to go to the hospital, but they also didn't want to go home and anticipate the outcome of their information.

"How about a trip to the mall? I'll buy you whatever you want. I want to get Lindy something, too. She put up the retainer money for Brewer. You can help me pick it out."

# Chapter 40

Ricky sat on his cot sketching Lindy, while Ray Riley was out in the visitors' area. Since it was early afternoon, he was fairly sure he would have no visitors. He didn't mind not having visitors since Lindy was the one he wanted to see. He liked having Uncle Nick and Aunt Liz and his mother visit him, but he wanted Lindy. She would be there in a heart beat if he asked her, but he just didn't want her to see him in prison clothes behind a heavy glass. He didn't want to have to talk to her on a telephone that only God knew who had touched it before she would. Seeing her would make it extra tough on him, because he would want to hold her so badly. He heard the bars sliding open and looked up to see Ray return. He was usually very talkative after his visit with Diane, and today was no exception.

"Diane is going to send us some books. I see you like to read."

"Yeah, I read."

"Good. Diane asked how you were. I already told her you were my cellmate. She was worried you would….you know….fuck me up. I told her we were past that."

Ricky nodded.

"Rick, I'm so sorry for everything. You know that; don't you?"

"Yeah, I guess. But Ray....I'm not going to apologize for punching you. You deserved it...you know you did. I'd do it again if you ever did anything to hurt Lindy again."

"I know. I did deserve it...I know. Have you talked to her?"

Ricky handed Ray the pictures Lindy had sent. "I got a letter from her today. You can see the pictures."

Ray took the pictures and studied all four of them. There was one of her in her prom gown, another of her in her Christmas Ball gown, her school picture, and a snapshot that Nick had taken. That was Ricky's favorite. She was wearing a running suit and a smile; her eyes sparkling. Ricky remembered when Nick took the picture. They had been down at their place and had gone back to the condo, and Nick was there when they walked in. He called her name, she turned around, and he snapped the picture. She looked so gorgeous in that picture. Ricky watched Ray's face as he studied the pictures. He knew Ray was hurting, and he knew that if Lindy saw his face right now, she would forgive her father. Maybe he should work on that with her, just like she did with him and his mother. He hadn't told her that her dad was his cellmate, but he planned on it, hopefully when he got out of this place.

"She's beautiful; isn't she?" Ray's voice was thick like he was trying to swallow a ball of cotton.

"Yeah, she is. Pretty on the outside, beautiful on the inside. The combination makes her gorgeous."

Ray nodded in agreement, still staring at the pictures.

"She makes me laugh….you know?" Ricky continued. "She's witty, but also….kind of…childlike. Her menagerie of stuffed animals….they all have names…did you know that?"

"No. I didn't know that. There's a lot I don't know, I guess."

"I love how her face lights up when I suggest we go somewhere she likes, or do something she likes. You should have seen her when my uncle suggested we go look for a Christmas tree last year. My uncle could have saved on electricity the way she lit up the whole room. Then her enthusiasm when we picked it out and bought ornaments for it…wow. It was great."

Ray looked up at Ricky and saw the wistful look on his face as he talked about Lindy, and he was suddenly very glad that Lindy had him. As long as he was there, Lindy would always be okay.

* * *

Nick and Liz presented Lindy with the new outfits they had selected for her when they went to the mall on Monday after seeing Detective Shultz. Liz had taken the clothes home with her with the idea that they would both be there with her on Friday night. They realized that she had not even gone shopping for new school clothes, so they thought it was a good idea to shop for her. Liz laughed at Nick's reaction when she asked the saleslady for something in Lindy's size.

"A size two? That's for infants, isn't it?"

And when the saleslady brought out a pair of jeans, Nick asked if they were for a Barbie Doll. Liz relayed the story to Lindy as she looked at the purchases they made, without much enthusiasm. She was grateful to them, but nothing could fill the emptiness in her. She missed Ricky so badly.

"Thank you, Uncle Nick....Aunt Liz. I appreciate it....really. I just can't seem to get excited about anything any more. The only time I seem to be happy is when I'm sleeping....because I dream about Ricky. He's with me.... in my dreams. When I close my eyes....I can pretend he's....right there.....with me. I....I *do* like everything you bought for me...even if I...don't show it. I'm sorry."

"We understand, Sweetie. It's okay. We also brought dinner. You have to be hungry...."

She nodded and then joined them in the kitchen. Shortly after she ate she went up to bed, even though it was only seven o'clock on a Friday night. Nick watched her go up the stairs and he sighed.

"It's like the lights went out....ever since Ricky was arrested. All the light that girl brought into a room with her is gone. I look at her eyes and the sparkle is gone.... damn it....why haven't we heard from Shultz? It's been four days."

"He said it might take awhile, Honey. I'm sure he's working on it. And who knows? Maybe that guy skipped town. Just be patient."

Nick nodded. He knew he had to be patient, but it was so hard to see Lindy so sad and lifeless, not to mention imagining Ricky in a jail cell. Sighing deeply, he reached for Liz's hand and offered her a weak smile. Angie had gone back to Chicago to take care of some things—she said. During the week, she had found a couple of small houses that she liked and were within her price range, and she made an offer on one of them. She had to make arrangements for movers, although many pieces of the old furniture would be replaced with new ones after she settled into a new house. Before she left yesterday morning, she received a call from the realtor telling her that she could have the house. She might have been truly excited had Ricky not been locked away in some dirty, nasty jail.

Nick sat in front of a cup of coffee at the kitchen table, just dwelling on these thoughts as he clung to Liz's hand. The doorbell startled him. He knew it was Angie, since she had called him earlier to say she would be there before eight o'clock. She followed him back to the kitchen where Liz was sitting, and helped herself to a cup of coffee. Nick told her Lindy was in bed when she asked about her. Clicking her tongue, she shook her head and sighed.

"It's like….she's in mourning."

"She is. Ricky's her life right now. Angie, imagine what it would be like to lose your mother, then your brother, your child, your father, and the man you love in a short period of time. She isn't even fully over her mother's death yet. She was only fourteen when she lost her. Lindy's been through a lot. If there is anything I can do to ease her sadness, I will do it." Nick sighed as he sat back down in front of his coffee cup.

"Me, too, Angie. Nick and I both care about her….. very much."

"Well….I care, too. I don't like it that she's sleeping so much. That can't be good. It's an escape from reality."

Nick explained to Angie that Lindy had dreams about Ricky so she enjoyed sleeping. Angie just shook her head. They sat at the table in near silence, only talking when necessary. 'We're all in mourning,' Liz thought to herself.

Once again the doorbell sounded. Nick got up from his chair and went to open the door. Standing in front of him was Ricky and Detective Shultz. Nick's mouth dropped open. Shultz spoke up.

"When I realized he was innocent, I went and got him myself. It was the least I could do."

Nick grabbed Ricky in a big bear hug. "God, I'm glad you're back."

"Me, too, Uncle Nick."

Angie and Liz jumped up and ran into the living room when they heard Ricky's voice, both of them in tears. They hugged Ricky at the same time. He was holding a bouquet of flowers, but he hugged them both.

"Where's Lindy?"

"Upstairs sleeping." Nick responded. "I guess those are for her?"

"He asked me to stop so he could get them." Shultz offered.

Ricky smiled and started toward the steps.

"Oh no, you don't." Liz intercepted. "I'm not going to miss this reunion for anything. I'm going up with you to watch."

"Count me in." Angie added.

Ricky took the stairs two at a time and quietly entered Lindy's room. In the darkened room he could just see the outline of her face. Liz and Angie stood just inside the door and waited. Ricky bent over her and kissed her gently on the lips. She stirred, and then her eyes fluttered.

"Sleeping Beauty is awakened by a kiss from Prince Charming….once again." He spoke softly and quietly in his 'for Lindy only' voice.

Lindy's eyes opened and she stared at him for only a moment. Suddenly she gasped loudly, and in one fluid movement she flew into his arms, crying and laughing at the same time. They hugged each other as they planted kisses on each other's face and neck. Lindy was breathless.

"Oh…..oh…..Ricky……I thought I was dreaming…." she cooed as she held his face and looked into his eyes. "Is it over? Are you home for good?"

"Yeah….and I am never leaving you again….if that's all right with you…."

"Yes….that's….perfect." She laughed as she was wiping tears away.

"Oh, I brought you these." Ricky remembered the flowers that he had cast on the bed.

Lindy let out a small laugh. "Thank you. Oh God, Ricky….I've missed you so much. I….."

"I know, Baby….I know. I've missed you, too. But hey, everybody is downstairs. The detective is down there and he wants to see you."

"Okay, but I'm not letting go of you."

"And that's just fine with me….'cause I'm holding onto you, too."

Liz and Angie had gone back downstairs after Ricky woke Lindy up. Both of them had fresh tears in their eyes.

"That was worth watching. It was just…beautiful…. Oh, Nick….you should have seen her…"

Nick touched Liz's shoulder to silence her. "They're coming down."

Nick watched them as they walked down the steps together, arms around each other. He marveled at the change in Lindy. 'The lights have come back on,' he thought to himself. Lindy's eyes had the old sparkle back in them.

"So tell us how it came about that Ricky was freed." Nick asked Shultz.

"Well, thanks to the information you provided me, I followed up on the lead, and I found this guy. He's a two-bit creep who dabbles along the border of legal and illegal, but he's not real bright. At first he acted like he didn't know what I was talking about. Said he didn't know anybody named Carrie. Well, I told him he was seen with Carrie....so he says that he knew her....finally. I asked him where he was the night she was murdered...he said he was home. No witnesses, though. I told him his car was seen at Carrie's house, and he opened up like a faucet."

"So he went there and killed her? Why?" Nick asked.

"Well, apparently....do you mind if I sit, by the way? I've had a long day. I'm off duty now, and I'm exhausted."

"Oh, of course." Nick gestured to the arm chair. "Since you're off-duty, can I get you a drink?"

"No....but a cup of black coffee would hit the spot."

Angie went to the kitchen and returned with a cup of steaming coffee. She set it down on the table next to the chair.

"Thanks." Shultz nodded to her. "Well, anyway.…..
apparently he had his own key to the house. He knew
her parents weren't home and he came in through the side
door off the kitchen. He said he heard voices so he stayed
real quiet. He heard Carrie begging Ricky to sleep with
her…telling him she could do things to him….saying she
loved him. He heard Ricky reject her….and heard her beg
him some more. It…pissed him off. He heard Ricky tell
her to leave him and Lindy alone, and that he was going
to get a restraining order. Then he heard Ricky go out and
slam the sliding glass door. That's when he confronted
Carrie. She denied everything, and he called her a liar.
He slapped her around, and when she refused to have sex
with him, he killed her. Strangled her."

Ricky felt Lindy's arm tighten around him as her
body tensed up a little.

"He killed her because she wouldn't have sex with
him?" Lindy asked.

"Well…it's a little more complicated than that. He
heard her begging Ricky for sex, and then she refused to
have sex with him. Apparently they had been having an
affair for two years, and suddenly she was turning him
down. It was an ego thing, I guess."

Lindy looked up at Ricky and smiled crookedly. He
smiled back at her and shrugged.

"Anyway, he was going to let Ricky take the rap for
the whole thing. He said he laughed when Ricky got
arrested. Then he said he felt bad when he heard about
the baby. Said he remembered reading the story about
the shooting, but he didn't connect it to Carrie until that
night. He told me that Carrie was a real evil bitch…."

"We'll go along with that…" Ricky interjected.

Detective Shultz stood up. "Guess I have to go over to the Siverson house and tell them everything."

"Do you have to be blunt about it all? I mean...can you give them a break? They just lost their daughter...can you spare them a lot of the details?" Nick appealed to Shultz.

"Oh....yeah....I can leave some stuff out. Don't worry...I'm not totally heartless." He laughed.

"Anyway, after I finish up over there, can I talk you people into meeting me for a drink and a little celebration?"

Nick noticed that the detective glanced at Angie just a little longer than was necessary. 'Hmmmm,' Nick thought to himself. 'I think the detective may just have a crush on Angie...'

"Yeah, I'm up for that. It's not late. What do you say, girls?"

"What about Ricky? He just got home....."

"Angie...I don't think Ricky will mind."

Angie followed Nick's line of vision and watched Ricky gently kiss Lindy's forehead and then smile into her eyes.

"Oh....I guess not."

"Come on, Shultz....I'll walk you out...then we can discuss where we want to meet up."

"It's Ron. Call me Ron."

"Okay...Ron. I'll be out in a sec."

When he was sure Angie couldn't hear him he whispered his belief into Liz's ear.

"I think he likes my sister."

Liz grinned and showed her approval with her eyes.

After agreeing on a local spot to meet, Nick came back inside and joined Ricky and Lindy in the kitchen. He hugged them both, and smiled at Lindy approvingly. "It's good to see the lights on again." He smiled at her. "We're all going out with the detective to celebrate your freedom. You don't mind, do you?" Nick lowered his voice, and added. "I think the detective likes your mother."

Ricky grinned. "No. I don't mind…because I like this girl right here. She's who I want to be with tonight. He likes my mother?"

Nick nodded. "Okay with that?"

"Yeah….I guess so. Maybe that will mellow her out a little." Ricky's grin got wider.

Nick punched Ricky's arm. "You two be good."

He rounded up the women and led them toward the door, glancing back at Ricky and winking.

\* \* \*

When the door closed, Ricky led Lindy to the sofa. After they sat down he pulled her close and began planting gentle kisses all over her face, ending with her lips. They kissed tender meaningful kisses, while gently touching each other's face.

"I missed you…so much…." Lindy whispered.

"Yeah….I missed you, too." He answered as he kissed her again.

"Ricky……can you be…..gentle?" Lindy smiled at him.

"I can be very gentle." He spoke into her mouth, still kissing her.

"I mean….very, very gentle."

"Very, very gentle….like a lamb…"

"Like a lamb?"

"Um-hmm."

"Want to go upstairs?" She whispered.

Ricky continued to kiss her. "You realize you just asked me for sex?" He whispered back.

"Do you realize you haven't responded yet?"

"That's what you think. Parts of me have." Ricky chuckled.

"Well? Let's go then."

"I thought you'd never ask." Ricky smiled at her as he studied her face. "I love you….so much. You know that; don't you? But I don't have any…."

Lindy nodded as she stood up to go up the stairs. "I'm on birth control. We're safe."

In the darkness of her room they made love, gently and tenderly, murmuring words of love to each other. Holding each other, they lay there in silence, Ricky's lips pressed against Lindy's forehead. Ricky broke the silence.

"I wonder how long we have before the guards get back."

Lindy laughed and repeated, "Guards."

"In a few minutes let's get up and go down to the kitchen and have tea. I have things to tell you." Ricky kissed her forehead again.

"Yeah….okay…..as a matter of fact….I have things to tell you. Things I was going to tell you the day you got….. you know."

"Yeah….I know. That's something I'd like to forget."

"Were you scared?'

"Oh, hell yeah."

"You didn't act scared."

"Because of *you*. I couldn't let you see how scared I was. You were freaking out. I had to act brave for you. I knew how it panicked you to see Shultz take me out of here. You were terrified for me....I could see it in your eyes. So I had to make you believe that I wasn't scared. Anyway....it's over....I'm back....and we're together. That's what matters now."

Lindy smiled at him in the darkness and kissed his chest. "Ricky, something else may matter."

"What's that?"

"Well, what if your mother and the detective start going out, and then get married? You and Cindy will be siblings.....sort of."

"Cindy? Shultz is her dad?"

"Yep. I have lots to tell you."

"Let's get up, then."

Wearing sweatpants and tee-shirts, they met in the kitchen, where Ricky already had the water heating in the teakettle. Lindy automatically got out the cups and the sugar, choosing lemon instead of her usual night-time choice of milk. Ricky dropped the teabags into the teapot and added the boiling water when it was ready, while Lindy carried the cups to the table. Ricky poured the tea into the cups and they sat down at an angle so they could face each other the way they had sat there so many times in the past. Lindy began by telling Ricky about Shawna and Cindy coming over the night he was arrested, and what they talked about.

"Well, how did they end up finding that other guy?" Ricky asked.

"I don't know....we'll have to find out from Uncle Nick....or maybe even Cindy. I don't know about any of that."

"Somebody was playing a good detective….I just want to know who I owe thanks to. So what else you got for me? You said you were going to tell me something that day…"

"Oh….yeah…."

Ricky listened attentively as Lindy told him about the wealth she would acquire when she turned eighteen.

"I never knew any of this. I knew about the education fund and the expense account, but I had no idea about the rest. Apparently my grandfather owned a lot. I remember him…..but I never remember him as being wealthy. He was Grampa to me…and I loved him dearly."

"He was your mother's dad?"

"Yeah….and he would come over every Sunday. Sometimes he showed up during the week, too….just to bring me and Chris something. I don't remember it being anything expensive, though. Usually candy or fruit. It never mattered….it came from him and that made it special."

"He sounds like someone I would have liked. I mean…anybody who treats you special like you deserve to be….."

"Yeah…you would have liked him. Anyway, the house is mine. My parents never owned it…Grampa did. He left it to me." She smiled and winked at Ricky. "So stick with me and you'll have your own pool table."

They both laughed and hugged each other. Ricky became serious for a moment.

"So….we could get married….and live in the house…. right?"

"Yeah....right. Ricky, are you still thinking about getting married? I mean...even though we...I'm not.... there's no baby..."

"Stop." Ricky spoke abruptly. "Baby, I *want* to marry you. Get it? *I want to marry you.* You're the only one I could ever want to be with. And I still believe that even though we're young, we can make it. We have strength. Here, let me show you."

Ricky got up from the chair and grabbed a dish towel. "Okay, now look. See how these threads are interwoven?" He pulled on the towel and gave her a demonstration of how pulling the towel tightened the threads. "See how they pull together? Well, that's how we are. When faced with adversity, we pull together and tighten up. We can get through anything. We're too young, we're too inexperienced, we're too immature, we're too uneducated....but we're also too much in love to be apart. Baby, without you I could probably succeed and become something great, but *with* you....*with you*...I could be something so much greater....and it would have so much more meaning."

Lindy knew that what he was saying was true. She felt that way, too. She knew she was talented and bright, but it became so much more important to her since she met Ricky. She knew she was pretty, but it was important that she be most beautiful girl in the world to Ricky. She looked into his face and his eyes met hers. They each felt the familiar bolt of electricity surge through their bodies as they reached for each other's hand.

"So...yes....I still want to marry you. I'm hoping you still want to marry me."

"Oh God....of course I do."

"Even though I'm an ex-con?" He teased her playfully.

"You are *not* an ex-con. And yes...I want to marry you because we are a dish towel." She started laughing her musical laugh and he joined in, pulling her to him and hugging her tightly.

Lindy moved from her chair onto his lap. "Oh Ricky...." Was all she could muster before placing her lips on his.

She pulled away after the kiss ended. "Oh....I'm sorry....you said you had things to tell me.....so....now it's your turn."

"Oh....yeah. Well, I wanted to tell you about how I bought a sketch pad and a pencil from the prison commissary. I kept from having enemies by sketching pictures from the other guys' pictures of their families and loved ones. I had a sketch of you and somebody saw it hanging in my cell. He asked if I could do one for him, and he gave me a picture of this little girl. So...I did it and he loved it. Everybody began asking me. It's a good thing I'm fast, or I might have had some enemies...."

"That's so cool, Ricky! What did you do with the one you did of me?"

"I think it's upstairs with my stuff I brought home."

"So....what about your cellmate? What was he like?"

Ricky was quiet for a moment. He sighed and looked into her beautiful trusting face. "He was your dad."

"What?"

"My cellmate was your dad."

"No way!"

"Yes…. It's a good thing he doesn't hold a grudge, too. He kind of looked out for me."

"Well, I'm glad of that….but…how did you handle that?"

"I told him I would hurt him again if he ever did anything to hurt you again. And he said he understood…. and was glad you had someone who cared about you and wanted to protect you."

"Did he tell you why he treated me like he did the past few years?"

"No…but that he's so sorry he did."

"Yeah….well, Diane told me why."

Lindy always told Ricky everything, and this time was no exception. She told him exactly what Diane had told her. Ricky sighed and looked into her eyes.

"Oh man…..that is so *stupid*. And that's why he avoided you…stayed away from you?"

Lindy nodded.

"*That is so stupid*! Do you know how many times that happens…for no reason? Anything can set it off. Just the way your clothes touch it can make it do that. I mean….I can understand how it must have shocked him when it happened….but he certainly couldn't think that it would happen all the time, or again, even. That's so *stupid*! All that time…you two could have had a nice father-daughter relationship…and he fucked it up by something that stupid."

"Yeah….that's what Diane said, too. She said he was afraid he was some kind of latent pervert…and that he would….do something…to me…eventually. That's why he stayed away from me….was afraid to even talk to me. He thought he was protecting me. When I got pregnant he realized instead of protecting me from himself, he should have been watching me more closely. Been there. Diane said he snapped. She also said he never meant to pull the trigger on that gun…"

"Yeah, he told me that. He said he was shocked when it went off."

"She also told me that they came to the hospital….and you punched my dad…"

"Yeah….I did. I'm sorry. I would have told you, but I didn't think about it….I was so worried about you…."

"I know. So…did he ask you to talk to me about forgiving him?"

"No…not at all. He said he knows you'll never forgive him….because he'll never forgive himself. When I was finished packing up my things to

leave….he….hugged me…and told me to take care of you. He also said he wished things could have been different…."

"Yeah…me too." Lindy got a wistful far-away look in her eyes for a moment, but then focused on Ricky's face again.

"Do you think I should….forgive him…I mean?"

"That's up to you, Babe."

"I might be able to forgive him for the past three years….but for the beating….and the shooting….never."

"Again, Baby….that's up to you."

Lindy thought for a moment and was about to speak when the front door opened.

Ricky groaned. "The guards have returned."

They both sniggered as they listened to the activity in the entry way and living room. Ricky whispered to Lindy. "I smell food."

# Chapter 41

Ricky returned to school with Lindy on Monday. Many students greeted him, telling him they were glad he was back. Nick drove them to school since it was required that he be accompanied by a parent or guardian, and with proof that he was exonerated from all charges. Detective Shultz appeared at Nick's side, ready to vouch for Ricky. Cindy loved her father again. Lindy and Ricky, hands joined, walked down toward their homerooms after Ricky was cleared to return to school. He was caught up on his classes, since he and Lindy worked all weekend getting him there. Lukas met them in the hallway and clapped Ricky on the back, truly glad to see him. Life was good once again, and Lindy and Ricky were happy. They returned to their normal routine of sitting together in all the classes they shared and in the lunchroom. There was no Carrie to glare at them, but they did get an occasional nasty stare from Sarah. Lukas and his newest girlfriend, Bethany joined them for lunch a couple of times a week. Bethany felt intimidated by them and was uncomfortable around them, and Lukas asked her why.

"I don't know," she answered. "It's like they know a secret that no one else knows. They communicate without ever saying a word. It's spooky."

Lukas laughed. Bethany obviously didn't understand about true love and being soul mates. Lukas did, and he envied Ricky and Lindy.

Life at the hospital returned to normal, except that now Angie was a staff member. Tom Siverson appeared in the lab Monday morning, after Ricky and been released, the tell Nick he was sorry that he doubted his nephew's innocence. They talked for a few minutes, catching up on each other's news. Nick told him Angie had just purchased a house in the area and was looking for a job at the hospital. Tom agreed to endorse her as an employee, so when Angie applied, she immediately got a job in medical records at the new Women's Health Center. Liz was impressed by her professionalism and accuracy on the job.

Before Thanksgiving, Angie moved into the new home, which was only a block and a half away from Lindy's house. Lindy had hired a maintenance man who was well-known and trusted, to handle any maintenance and upkeep on her house, and extended his contract to include Angie's house. Ricky hadn't moved into the new house with Angie yet, since he was waiting to see where Lindy was going to go. Lindy wanted to go back to her house, but had not been inside it since that night her father beat her. Up until she found out that the house was actually hers, she had no desire to go there, but now she wanted to see it as her own. She knew she couldn't live there alone, even though she was practically alone when she lived there with her father, but she wanted to get the place ready for when she and Ricky moved in. She knew there had to be dust everywhere, and that the air in the house would be stale and musty, so she and Ricky planned on going to the house over Thanksgiving weekend to dust, vacuum and air the house out. Thanksgiving was held at Angie's, and two more guests had been added to the family. Detective Ron Shultz and his daughter, Cindy joined the family for Thanksgiving dinner. Shultz, a divorced man of three years, had been wining and dining Angie since Ricky's release, and even helped her hang curtains in the new house. There were several toasts proposed around the table at the Thanksgiving meal. Nick's toast was for the family. Angie toasted Nick and Liz, hoping there was a happy ending this time. Shultz toasted Angie and congratulated her on the superb meal, and Angie reminded him that Ricky was also responsible for it. Liz proposed a toast to the most beautiful couple in the state, Ricky and Lindy. The entire gathering stood up for this one, while Lindy and Ricky exchanged that secret smile they had adopted for only each other.

Everyone was happy and contented, but with only one concern—where was Lindy going to live? Ricky would not stand for them to be separated, but Angie didn't feel it was right that she live with them. 'It's like inviting the hungry, raging hormones to a feast,' she had told Nick. Nick just shook his head.

"Angie, do you really believe you can stop them from having sex by not having them under the same roof?"

"No, but I don't feel I should be encouraging it by letting them sleep under the same roof either."

"Well, first of all, wherever Lindy is going to be is where Ricky is going to be. You'll never see him. Second of all, they didn't exactly sleep together when they both stayed with me."

"And you know that for sure?"

"Yes....I do. Never mind....Lindy is welcome to stay with me. In five months she'll be eighteen....she can legally live wherever she wants. And just remember, Ricky will be eighteen, too.....so keep that in mind."

Nick and Liz, once again, made wedding plans. They chose the second Saturday of January as their wedding day. Ricky and Lindy, as well as Angie and Ron would be in their wedding party. The wedding would be small, but elegant.

After the Thanksgiving dinner ended, Lindy and Ricky, accompanied by Cindy, went to the kitchen to clean up. Working with the precision they generally used, Ricky and Lindy had the job done in no time while Cindy watched in awe. By the time she had the table cleared and wiped off, Lindy and Ricky had the dishes rinsed and stacked in the dishwasher, the counters cleaned, and the leftovers put away. Instead of joining the adults in the living room, they remained in the kitchen, sitting around the table, talking about the events of the past year. The talk turned to the future.

"Are you two considering college?" Cindy asked.

"Of course. We're thinking about going to the local university. That way we will have a place to live and be together, and still get educated." Ricky told her.

"And...the school has an excellent chemistry program. Ricky wants to be a chemist." Lindy added.

"And how about you, Lindy? What do you want to do?" Cindy asked.

"Music. I want to study music. The school has a good music program as well. But I'm also considering elementary school education."

Cindy started laughing. "You two always have your classes together....I can't see how you can combine classes in those two subjects."

"Oh, we'll just have to tough it out, I guess. We're not used to being separated for that long...under normal circumstances, that is." Ricky smiled at both Lindy and Cindy.

After a dessert of traditional pumpkin pie and a blueberry cheesecake, Lindy's contribution, Liz and Nick got up to leave. As they were saying goodnight Ricky appeared with his and Lindy's jackets.

"Ricky, why don't you and Lindy stay here tonight?" Angie asked. "Lindy can sleep in the guest room."

Ricky looked at Lindy. "Want to, Babe?"

Lindy shrugged. "If you want."

"Okay, mom, but Lindy and I have things to do this weekend. We're going to go up to Lindy's house and clean it and air it out for awhile."

"You can do that. Where you sleep shouldn't affect that."

"Well, we have to go to the condo tomorrow morning to get the key. Is that okay?"

"That's fine, Rick. Liz and I both have to go to work, so make sure you have your key to get in."

"Thanks, Uncle Nick."

Lindy hugged both Nick and Liz and kissed their cheeks before they closed the door. Shultz and Cindy were sitting on the couch and made no attempt to get up, so Angie put on another pot of coffee. Lindy and Ricky went to find something for Lindy to wear to bed.

Rummaging through Ricky's drawers to the dresser Angie had the movers bring from Chicago, Ricky found an old pair of sweat pants and a tee-shirt that was much too small for him and too big for Lindy. The sweat pants were too big, too, but would be fine for a night. They turned the light out and fell into each other's arms in the darkened room.

"Only five more months, Baby. We can legally get married without anybody's permission. We'll still go to school and college, but nobody can keep us apart after that."

"It's going to be hard to wait that long." Lindy sighed as she put her arms around his waist. "I feel so homeless… like I'm a burden on everyone."

"No, Honey, you're not. We all love you. There are just certain….protocols that have to be followed." Angie spoke to them from the doorway of the darkened room. "Come on out and have coffee with us. Lindy, Uncle Nick is going to petition for you to live with him until you're eighteen….but Ricky will have to live here."

Lindy and Ricky gave each other an unhappy look and went with Angie to join the Shultz's in the living room for fresh coffee; just long enough to lure Cindy back out into the kitchen in order to leave Angie and Shultz alone in the living room. They listened while Ron and Angie made plans for Friday night.

"Do you think I should tell them no hanky-panky?" Lindy and Ricky laughed, and then shared the joke with Cindy, telling her about Nick telling them that last Christmas.

* * *

Lindy and Ricky entered the condo a little after nine in the morning. Nick, Liz, and Angie had all gone to work, so they walked to the condo from Angie's new house. Lindy ran upstairs to change, but was quickly joined by Ricky. Their clothes came off and they made love slowly, savoring the feel of each other's body.

"I'm so lucky to have you." Ricky whispered into her ear.

"We're lucky to have each other." Lindy whispered back. "I can't imagine ever being with anybody else."

"No….me neither. I love you so much." He spoke breathlessly as he entered her at the height of their arousal.

Lindy gasped as her spasms started, causing Ricky to plunge in deeper. They clung to each other tightly as both their bodies were racked with spasms. They lay together still entwined, while their breathing returned to normal. Lindy smiled at Ricky as he kissed the tip of her nose.

"Will it always be this exciting?" She asked him.

"I hope so. There are so many things we haven't done yet. You'll see…."

"Like what?"

"You'll see. We better get up; don't you think? We have a lot to do. Not that I want to….I could do this with you all day." He grinned and started tickling her.

"Stop…stop." She laughed, as she turned her back to him and curled up so he couldn't get to her belly.

"Not fair." He laughed as he slid his arm around her.

She slid out of bed and ran toward the shower, and he followed her.

\* \* \*

Lindy found the key to her house in her suitcase. They were dressed and ready to work as they sat at Nick's kitchen table having the last of the coffee from the pot.

449

As Lindy got up to rinse out the coffee pot and the cups, the doorbell rang. Ricky got it. Two strange women were standing there with plastic smiles on their faces when he answered the door. Both of them had their chunky bodies stuffed into dark blue blazers. The older of the two had short cropped gray hair, and the younger one had a long frizzy brown ponytail. She wore a gray skirt while the other one wore gray pants.

"Can I help you?" He asked.

"We're here for Belinda Riley. Is she here?" The older of the two asked.

"Lindy!" He called, but turned back to the women. "Who are you and what's this about?" He asked them.

"We're from Social Services. We've been informed that Belinda Riley, a minor female is living here with men other than her family."

"We're her family." Ricky countered.

"Biological family?" The younger one asked.

"No...well, no, but...."

Lindy appeared beside Ricky.

"Are you Belinda?" The older one asked.

When Lindy nodded, the older one said, "Belinda, you are to come with us."

"For what?" Lindy's voice held a note of alarm.

"Well, we have found you a nice foster home to live in until you are of legal age to decide for yourself where you want to live."

"NO! I'm not going anywhere with you! Who do you think you *are* to make this choice for me? You don't even *know* me!"

"Well, nevertheless, we have a court order to take you out of this home and place you in a home with two

450

foster parents.....a male and female couple. It's a lovely home..."

"NO! This is a lovely home. Uncle Nick loves me.... Ricky loves me." She slowly slithered toward Ricky and locked her arms around his waist. "You're not taking me anywhere."

"Oh yes, we are. We can have the police here in a moment if you don't cooperate. We have a court order...." The older one stepped toward Lindy and she tightened her grip on Ricky's waist.

"A court order? Is it signed by God? I haven't done anything wrong....I'm not going."

"Belinda, you have no *choice*...."

"Oh...everybody has *choices*. There are *always* choices. I choose not to go."

Ricky reached for his cell phone and called Nick at the lab. "Uncle Nick....there are two women here trying to take Lindy away."

"What? Who are they? Why?"

"They say they're from social services....I haven't seen any ID yet. What should I do?"

"I'm on my way. Keep them at bay."

Lindy was becoming terrified. Their perfect world was being rocked again. The tears were running down her face as she held onto Ricky and confronted these women.

"Why now? When I'm happy? Is that the idea? Keeping people from being happy?"

"Belinda, you're a minor. You are living in an unwholesome environment for a girl your age."

"That's bullshit!" Ricky interjected.

The older woman stared briefly at Ricky and saw his eyes turn black as coal and his nostrils flare. She reached out to take Lindy's arm, and Lindy shrieked.

*"Don't touch her!"* It came out as half a hiss and half a growl.

The woman shrank back momentarily. A car pulled into the driveway as she was about to reach for Lindy again. It was Detective Shultz.

"What's going on here?" He asked as he flashed his badge at the women.

"Oh....we haven't even called you yet. How did you know?" The younger one commented.

"I don't know what you're talking about. I'm not here for you; I'm here for these two. What are you trying to do here?"

The frizzy headed girl handed Shultz the paperwork. He took it from her and sat at the dining room table to read it. Nick rushed in as he was reading the paperwork.

"Lindy....are you all right?" Seeing her in tears angered him. "What the hell is going on here?"

The older one appealed to Nick telling him that Lindy was a minor and that they had a court order to place her in a foster home until she became of age.

"Why can't this be her foster home?"

"Well....you're a male figure....no wife.....and he's.... from what we hear....her boyfriend." She gestured at Ricky. "It's just not acceptable."

Nick was becoming angrier by the second. "And who decides what is *acceptable*? Where were you when she was practically living alone, or when her father beat her so badly she couldn't walk? I was there....so was he." Nick gestured at Ricky. "I helped her up off the floor and got her medical attention, gave her a safe place to live, looked out for her....how is that *unacceptable*? *Huh*?"

"I am sure you have done your best for her....but she is still a minor living under the roof of an unapproved guardian."

"Why can't this be her home? Tell me....we love and care for her....all of us. My fiancée, Ricky's mother, me, Ricky.....we all love her."

"And then why didn't you petition the court to become her legal guardian?"

"I didn't think this would happen.....it's not like she's being abused or mistreated."

"I know, sir....but there are laws governing the state of affairs of minors. She's legally not allowed to live here."

Liz came running in a flourish. "Nick, what's happening?"

"They're trying to take Lindy."

"NO! Oh, no. Please.....please don't take her."

"You are?" The older one faced Liz looking like she was ready to do battle.

"She's my fiancée." Nick answered for her.

"What's going on? Nick?"

"They say it's not *acceptable* for Lindy to live here."

"Well, she can come live with me. I have three bedrooms....can we do that?"

"We have a court order....if you want to challenge it, or petition the court for custody of Belinda, you may do so. We have our orders...." The older woman stood up straight and looked Liz directly in the eye. "Have you even thought about petitioning for guardianship?"

"Yes....of course we have. I was going to get the ball rolling this week...."

"…and she's been living here how long?"

"Well, she was pregnant when she came here….I was told she was under her own jurisdiction…."

"True."

"Then she was so badly injured that we….we just didn't think about it again. We just…worried about her recovery."

"Yes, her recovery. And then the boyfriend went to jail….it's all in the report."

"He was released when it was discovered he was innocent…" Nick's voice was taking on a hard edge.

Lindy was clinging to Ricky. "Please, Ricky….don't let them take me. *Please*." She whispered.

Ricky's arm tightened around her. "Not without a fight."

Shultz handed the papers to Nick. "They're in order, and they are legal documents. There's no way to fight this. It's court ordered," he whispered.

Nick felt his heart sink; he felt like all the air had left his lungs. He turned to Lindy and spoke in a hoarse voice. "Lindy….we can't do anything about it. You have to go with them."

"NO-OO!" Lindy screamed. "Uncle Nick….*please*. Don't let them take me. *Please*!"

"Lindy….I can't break the law."

"Uncle Nick, isn't there anything…anything at all you can do?" Ricky appealed to him.

"Ricky, if there was, I'd be doing it." He turned away from Lindy and Ricky, but not before Ricky saw the tear slide down onto his cheek.

Ricky wanted to cry, but he couldn't let Lindy see him cry.

"Where is she going? Will she be going to the same school?" Liz asked.

"Oh…no…we have to get her enrolled in another school."

"But she graduates this year! She went to school with these kids around here all her life! Certainly you can see how important it is that she graduates with them…"

"Ma'am….with all due respect….the issue is that we put her in an acceptable, healthy environment. The couple who is taking her in has a very nice home…never had any children. They're both professional people….."

"Oh….and I'm a sloth…...I'm just a research doctor…." Nick flung the words at her.

"Sir, we do not question your integrity….not in any way. We have to abide by the court order."

"And how did this court order come about? You would have no idea Lindy even existed unless somebody brought it to your attention. So who did?"

"We can't disclose names…...it was a concerned citizen who lives over in the Estates….Old Mill Estates."

Lindy was shaking as she looked up at Ricky. "Sarah…...Sarah lives there."

The wind left Ricky's lungs. "Christ." He murmured.

"Now…Belinda, I'm going to ask you to get your things together. You have a half hour to pack and be ready."

Lindy couldn't even see; her eyes were so blurred with tears.

Liz asked the older woman. "What would it take to get her back with me?"

"A court order." The woman answered.

"Of course….a court order." Liz murmured.

"Lindy…..I'm going to do my damnedest….to get you back. I swear I will." Liz couldn't hide her tears any more. She reached over and held onto Lindy's hand.

Lindy was hysterical. Ricky was holding onto her tightly as she sobbed.

"This isn't fair." He said directly into the older woman's face.

"Well, take it up with the court. Now, Belinda….get your things together. You are leaving with us."

A police car pulled up behind the other cars and two officers came in through the partially opened door.

"Is everything all right?" One of them asked.

"Yes, officer…everything will be fine." The older woman turned to Ricky and challenged him. "Nobody needs to be arrested here. Belinda will come willingly."

Lindy stiffened. Was she talking about arresting Ricky? She looked up at Ricky through teary eyes. "I have to, don't I?"

"It's only five months, Babe. You'll be eighteen then. You can come back here and finish school here then. I'll figure out a way to see you….just let me know where you are."

"Can you come help me pack?"

"Yeah. Wait a minute." He turned to the two blazered women and said, "I'm going to help her get her things together. She'll go….but not willingly. She's being forced. I thought this was America."

He held Lindy as they went upstairs to gather her clothes. She gave Ricky the key to her house, and the portfolio information she had gotten in the mail a lifetime ago.

"Protect these. Maybe Uncle Nick will let you put them in his safe."

"Okay. Baby....Oh, Baby....I can't stand it." He held her so tightly, trying to fight the tears that were threatening to come.

Lindy was shaking in his arms, terrified. "I can't.... Ricky, I can't. I can't leave you."

Liz, openly crying, followed them up the stairs and into Lindy's room. "Oh, Lindy....we have to let you go. You have to go with them. I promise....I promise...when I leave here I'm going straight to a lawyer's office. Okay?"

Lindy nodded, her upper torso was quaking.

"Now let's get your things together...as painlessly as possible."

Liz began opening drawers and taking Lindy's clothes out of them, and Ricky lifted the suitcase onto the bed and opened it. Lindy began putting things into the suitcase, sobbing as she worked. When it was full, Ricky shut it for her, keeping his eyes averted from her.

"I can't look at you, Baby. I just can't....it's too painful." His voice had become raspy. "I can't believe I'm losing you."

"No....Ricky....no. D-don't s-say that. You'll n-never l-lose m-me." She was stuttering partly because of her sobs and partly because of her tremors.

She sat down on the bed and stared at the side of Ricky's face. "Ricky, please...p-please l-look at me. I-I c-can't st-stand it."

He turned and looked at her and then grabbed her up into his arms. He held her so she couldn't see the tears sliding down his face. Liz saw, and she knew she had to do something to give Ricky a chance to compose himself. She turned to a practical side.

"Lindy, do you need money?"

"No. Thanks."

"Do you need anything? Anything at all?"

"No."

Liz dug a business card out of her purse and tucked it into the side pocket of the suitcase. She got another one and put down the phone numbers for Nick and her own cell phone. "Ricky, let me write your number down on this, too. What is it?"

Ricky repeated his cell phone number to Liz and she wrote it down. Nick appeared at the bedroom door.

"They're chomping at the bit down there. Do you have everything together?"

Lindy nodded.

Nick grabbed the suitcase to carry it downstairs for her. "Rick….five minutes. Okay?"

Ricky nodded, and Liz went out with Nick.

They were alone. Five minutes to say their good-byes. Ricky felt sick. He knew after she went he would vomit. He felt it. Lindy felt numb; her world was being torn away from her. She couldn't speak or stand up straight; she was shaking so badly. Ricky held her.

"I love you….I love you so much. I'll wait for you to come back. You're the only one for me…you know that; don't you?"

"Yes. Oh, Ricky…..there will never…..ever be anybody but you. Promise you'll be here when I get back? Promise?"

"Oh, God….yes….yes….I promise." He lifted her face by her chin and looked into her eyes. The electricity was still there; they both felt it. He leaned down and kissed her sweetly. "I promise."

One of the officers cleared his throat as he stood outside the bedroom door. They turned toward the sound.

"I'm sorry, miss….but they're waiting and you have to go."

Lindy nodded, as she placed one leaden foot in front of the other. She couldn't breathe. Slowly she tried to move her lungs in and out.

"I'm sorry I have to be a part of this." The officer said to Ricky. "I can see what this is doing to her….and you. Doesn't seem right…."

The officer put his hand under Lindy's elbow in order to escort her down the stairs. Ricky put his arm around her waist on the other side of her. Together they managed to get her down the stairs without her falling. She was grateful for it because she didn't think her legs would hold her.

"Let's get going, Belinda." The older one ordered. "I told the couple you would be there before two. They are waiting for you. Young man, let go of her. She can walk."

Ricky removed his hand from Lindy's waist and she stumbled; her legs felt like rubber. The officer grabbed her and kept her from falling.

"Officer, will you escort the young lady out to the car, please?"

He shrugged, and held onto Lindy's arm. "Just lean on me," he whispered.

Lindy nodded, and glanced at Ricky as he stared at the floor. He looked like he was going to fall to the floor, too. New tears blurred her vision before they fell onto her cheeks. She looked over at Liz and saw that she was crying so hard that her chest heaved up and down. Nick was holding her and holding a tissue to his own eyes. Uncle Nick was crying! She glanced once more at Ricky as he raised his head and stared into her eyes. Briefly their eyes locked as they conveyed their love for each other. The officer helped Lindy out the door and into the back seat of the plain dark brown nondescript sedan. The two social workers followed them out. When Lindy was secured into the back seat with the door closed, the women climbed into the front seat, the younger one behind the wheel. As they pulled out of the driveway Lindy looked back once more just in time to see Ricky come outside and stare at the car before it pulled away. He saw her looking back and raised his fingers to his lips slowly. He kissed his fingers and lightly blew the kiss towards her. He saw her reach up and grab the kiss and press it to her lips. Slowly he walked back inside, shut the door, and slid down onto the floor in front of the sofa, staring at the floor. Nick joined him. Liz grabbed her purse and car keys and started out toward the door.

"Where are you going?" Nick asked her.

"To find a custody lawyer."

"Let me know what you find out. Hey.....and thanks."

"Nick, I'm not doing this for you or for Ricky. I....I love her, too."

Nick nodded and got up to kiss her. "I'm so glad you do."

Liz pulled out of the driveway and Nick returned to the floor beside Ricky. Neither of them spoke. Nick heard a tiny sob come from Ricky and his heart broke.

He put his arm around Ricky's shoulders and pulled him in close.

"Let it out, Rick….just let it out."

Biting his lip, Ricky looked over at Nick. "It hurts…so bad, Uncle Nick. I…I can't imagine life without her."

Nick nodded. "I know." He looked at Ricky and saw the drops falling from his cheeks onto his chin, and began biting his own lip. It didn't work, and he finally gave in to the tears he had been trying to hold back. "She really gets to your heart, doesn't she? Did I tell you what Shultz said about her? Shultz said….she could melt the heart of a granite statue." Nick let out a small laugh. "And I think he's right…"

Ricky also let out a small laugh. "I think he's right, too. She's so…..so precious, you know? Everything about her is….special. And she makes everything around her special…..you know what I mean?"

"Yeah, kid…..I do. She's a delight to have around." Nick smiled into the air as he thought about some of the things she did. "You know what?"

"What?"

"I'm paying for a wedding when she comes back….if you both still….."

"We do."

"Then….it's settled. So we have something to look forward to…okay? I approve. I know you're young, but hell….I've never seen two people more in love and more in tune with each other than the two of you. And I'm still willing to help you both until you graduate from college. After all…you are my only nephew. I want the best for you." Nick punched Ricky's arm lightly before he stood up.

"Uncle Nick…..thanks."

"Sure."

\* \* \*

The brown sedan pulled into a driveway in front of a gray stone ranch-style home. Lindy made no attempt to get out as she stared at the house. She had cried all the way there, having to put up with the two battle-axes trying to make small talk with her. She watched as the front door opened and two people came out toward the car. The man went around to the trunk to retrieve the suitcase, and the woman stopped just in front of the rear car door. Old battle-axe jumped out and opened the rear door, giving Lindy a meaningful stare.

"Loraine, this is Belinda. Please get out of the car, Belinda."

Slowly, Lindy got out of the car giving (Loraine, was it?) a wary look. She was an attractive woman, sort of on the tall side; but what drew Lindy's attention was the stylish haircut and perfectly manicured nails. The woman extended her hand in order to shake hands with Lindy. Out of politeness, Lindy accepted the hand and shook it. The man came around from the back of the car, and set the suitcase down on the lawn. He also extended his hand to Lindy.

"I'm Nelson. Nelson Sutter. You are Belinda?"

Lindy nodded and accepted his handshake as well. Nelson was close to the same height as the woman, and appeared to be in excellent shape, salon tanned, and well-groomed.

"Well, come on in. We have fresh coffee….do you drink coffee?"

"Yes."

"Well, good…..we also have cookies. My wife made 'em."

"There are some papers to sign…." The younger battle-axe spoke up. "We'll have to go over a few things…."

"Fine…fine. Come on, Belinda. Is that what people call you?"

"Most people call me Lindy."

"Well, then….Lindy it is. Come on, and I'll show you your room before we get to the coffee and cookies."

Lindy followed Nelson inside and down a hallway to a closed door on the right. Nelson opened the door and gestured for Lindy to pass through the doorway. In spite of everything, Lindy thought the room was lovely. It was large and airy and the colors were of turquoise and purple hues, very close to the colors of her own room. Sitting on the bed was a large stuffed shaggy dog.

"Couldn't resist that. I know girls like that kind of stuff." He smiled as he pointed out the dog.

Lindy noticed that there was a computer on a computer table near the window. She hoped there was Internet access so she could email Ricky. Nelson set the suitcase on the bed.

"You can unpack later. You have your own bathroom and there is plenty of closet space and drawers here for you. Is this all you have? I think we need to go shopping."

"I have clothes in two different places….and only one suitcase."

"Oh. I can see where that might be a problem. Let's go get some coffee."

He placed his hand under her elbow, just as the officer had done, but somehow when he did it, she was uncomfortable with it. She shrank back a little.

"Come on….nobody is going to hurt you."

She relaxed a little and followed him out to the bright oversized kitchen. The two social workers were going over paperwork with Loraine as they walked in. Lindy overheard part of the conversation.

"….and under no circumstances is she here as a maid or servant or a slave. She can have chores like in any household, but you did not just receive a domestic. She is to be treated like your daughter….is that acceptable to you?"

"Yes…of course."

"Good. Oh, here she is. Do you like your room, Belinda?"

"Lindy likes it's just fine." Nelson answered for her as he pulled a chair out for her to sit down.

Loraine got up from the table, poured a cup of coffee, and then set it in front of Lindy.

"Thank you." Lindy said quietly and politely.

Loraine smiled her approval at Lindy's politeness. "You prefer to be called Lindy?" She asked her.

"Either one. Everybody calls me Lindy, though."

"Well, then…we will, too. Try one of my cookies. I baked them especially for today….for your arrival."

"Thank you, Ma'am."

"Oh please….call me Loraine. Ma'am makes me sound old."

"Okay….Loraine."

"And you know to call me Nelson…right?" Nelson interjected.

"Yes."

"Good."

The two social workers stood up. "We have to get going." The older one announced. "Belinda, you are to behave. There will be no contact with anybody from the place we just brought you from. Contacting them could mean jail for one or both of them, and a detention home for you."

"Oh…now…there's no need to threaten her like that…." Nelson came to her defense, for which Lindy was grateful. "I'm sure Lindy will do what is expected of her."

"Well, I hope so. Give us a call if there are any problems."

Loraine saw them out and returned to the kitchen.

"Those two have got to be the homeliest women I have ever seen." Nelson spoke to Loraine, but for Lindy's benefit. Lindy chuckled quietly—a reaction he was hoping for.

"Nelson…..that's not nice. True….but not nice."

Loraine got the same reaction from Lindy, and was pleased. She could feel Lindy relaxing a little. She sat down with a fresh cup of coffee and turned her attention to Lindy.

"So…tell us about yourself."

"Before that….tell us where you were living and what makes it so bad for you to contact anybody from there?"

"It's bad because those women have dirty minds. I was living in my boyfriend's uncle's house. Ricky lives there, too. They looked out for me…really cared for me. It…it wasn't the unwholesome living arrangement those two made it out to be. I had my own room and rules to follow….and so did Ricky. We both love and respect

Uncle Nick. We would never do anything….that was against his rules."

"So tell us the whole story. Tell us how you ended up living there…..from the beginning. We care, too….and we want to know. We can't be sensitive to your feelings if we don't know anything."

"It's a long story…."

"We have the time. We set aside this whole weekend just for you."

Lindy opened up and told them everything…. about her mother….her dad…meeting Ricky….Carrie's jealousy….little Nicholas. Just everything. She stopped several times to keep her tears under control. Nelson handed her a box of tissues when he realized that it was impossible for her to keep them under control. Loraine refilled Lindy's cup as well as her own and then Nelson's. She made a fresh pot when that one was empty. Loraine had tears in her eyes when Lindy got to the part about Nicholas. Both she and Nelson listened patiently and attentively, stopping her to ask a question here and there. By the time Lindy was finished with her story, Loraine needed a couple of tissues.

"You poor kid…..you've been through hell, haven't you?"

"Being taken away from Ricky hurts…so bad. He… he…." Lindy couldn't say anything more; the tears were coming again, and the lump in her throat was beginning to choke her.

Loraine patted her hand. "It's okay….you don't have to say anything more. I understand."

Nelson tilted back his chair and stared at Lindy. 'She's so pretty....and sweet. How did she manage to stay so sweet through all of this?' he wondered silently.

# Chapter 42

Ricky returned to school alone on Monday after Thanksgiving. Cindy met him just inside the door.

"I heard what happened. It sucks. How are you going to handle this? God, Ricky...."

Ricky kept silent. He wasn't sure he could trust his voice or his tear ducts at this point. He had cried. He cried as he lay in bed the night after she was taken away. He reached for Sherlock—the stuffed dog she had given him—and the tears came. He held onto the dog until they subsided. He couldn't sleep that night. He sat up and turned on the lamp on the nightstand, seeing a frame with her picture in it. He picked it up and traced her face with his finger, feeling the hollow spot in his chest grow even bigger. He had decided he needed a walk. He quickly and quietly got dressed and left the house. He walked until he found an all-night convenience store where he purchased a pack of cigarettes. It was warm for November, so he decided to walk a little further and smoke a cigarette. He walked until he found a bench to sit on. The bench was just located off the sidewalk facing over the hill. He looked down over the hill and discovered a river. He wondered what river it was as he watched the lights on a lone tugboat pushing a barge. He imagined that in the daylight this was a pretty place. He would have to bring Lindy—'no, don't go there,' he scolded himself silently. He quickly stood up and began walking back toward the condo, lighting another cigarette as he walked. Walking and smoking—he had survived the weekend.

"Ricky! Are you there?" Cindy was still standing in front of him.

"Sorry. My mind drifted. I...don't know what I'm going to do. Five months...it's like forever...you know what I mean, Cin?"

"Yeah...it sucks. Hey, I gotta run. See ya later."

Ricky rounded the corner and ran into Lukas, and they headed toward their homeroom together.

"Where's Lindy?" Lukas asked.

"You don't know?"

"Know what?"

"They took her....just took her away."

"Who?"

"Two old hags from social services. They had a court order....to put her in a foster home. Said living with us was unacceptable...unwholesome."

"Why? That doesn't sound right. I mean....your uncle didn't let you two sleep together or anything....what the hell was the problem?"

"The problem is that some concerned citizen..." Ricky made imaginary quotation marks in the air with his first two fingers on each hand when he said 'concerned citizen.' "Some concerned citizen who lives in the Old Mill Estates reported her living conditions to social services. Told about her being shot, me being in jail....some concerned citizen told all that."

"Sarah…." Lukas said it like a statement, not a question.

"I believe so….yeah."

"Wait until I see that fucking bitch."

"You and me both."

\* \* \*

Loraine drove Lindy to her new school and went in to register her. She was asked to produce the necessary paperwork that proved she was legally staying with the Sutters, and of course, she had it. Lindy was given a schedule after she filled out a questionnaire. She would have the same courses that she started with at the beginning of the year, since her transcript was immediately faxed over from the old school. The schools were similar, but this one didn't have Ricky. She was handed a lock and a locker number, and books. The principal met with her and Loraine and asked if Lindy had any questions.

"You're a straight A student. That's impressive. Also, according to your transcript, you also sing. We have an excellent choir program here, along with private voice lessons, if you're interested. Have you ever sung professionally?"

"No, but I won the talent contest at the fund raiser for the Women's Center at University Hospital."

"Well, that doesn't count as professional, so you would still qualify for voice lessons. I think I remember seeing that on the news. That may be why you look a little familiar to me. Okay, well…run along. Your first class is already in session, but you can probably be in the second class this morning."

Loraine walked with her to find her locker. "I didn't know you could sing, Lindy. And…you get all A's in

school? I had no idea we were housing a talented genius."
Loraine smiled at her. "By the way, now that he mentioned
it, I saw you on the news, too. I think I may have seen you
one other time. Prom Queen....right?"

"Yes." Lindy answered her and instantly got that far
away look in her eyes.

She felt like she was only half there. Something was
missing. No. Someone was missing. 'Oh, Ricky....Ricky....
I miss you....so much.' She silently communicated to
him.

"Well, I'll pick you up today. Nelson will pick you
up on the nights that I work late. You'll like those nights.
He usually orders take-out....pizza, junk food. I eat at
the office on the nights I work late, since I don't get
home until around ten. So I'll see you at three o'clock
then....okay?" Loraine quickly kissed Lindy's forehead
and walked toward the exit.

Lindy watched her walk away and then checked her
schedule to see where her second period class was located.
Judging from the way the numbers on the doors ran, it was
just three classrooms away. She looked around to get her
bearings so she wouldn't have any trouble finding her way
back to the locker later on in the day, and then she went to
see where the lunchroom was located. Loraine handed her
money for lunch and she started to decline it until Loraine
explained that money was given to her by social services
for things like school lunches. There was also a clothing
allowance, in case Lindy was interested. She located the
lunchroom and walked back to the classroom she would
be entering when the bell rang. When the doors opened
at the end of the period, students began rushing out into
the hall. All the strange faces stared at her as they passed.

She suddenly felt lonely and vulnerable as she entered the strange classroom that was filling up with strange kids, many of which were staring at her. The teacher walked in and spotted her right away.

"Do you have an entry slip? I'm Mr. Peters, your teacher."

"Yes, Sir….here it is." She handed him one of the slips of paper she was to hand to every teacher in every class. He smiled at her, tentatively. You started the year in World History? What century were you on before you transferred?"

Lindy told him where they ended the class the day before Thanksgiving and he grinned approvingly. "Good. That's right where we are. Have a seat. Your name is…."

"Lindy." She interjected. "Lindy Riley."

"Okay…so you prefer Lindy to Belinda….am I right?"

"Well, it's just what everybody has always called me."

"Fair enough. You'll be Lindy here, too."

He turned his back to her and began writing on the board. She found a seat that appeared not to belong to anybody and sat down. Students were still staring at her, making her feel uncomfortable. Finally a boy sitting in the seat next to her leaned over and simply said, "Hi."

Lindy returned the 'hi' with a slight smile. Thus began Lindy's life in a new school, without Ricky.

\* \* \*

Lukas and Ricky were walking out of the lunch room when they spied Sarah sitting with a new boyfriend. They made it a point to walk past her table behind her.

"Rick....look who's getting lucky with Sarah now. She sure does pass it around, doesn't she? I wonder if this new guy knows about the twenty-five year old she screws."

"Shut up, Luke." Sarah hissed at him.

"Why? I should think you'd appreciate someone opening up and speaking the truth....being the concerned citizen you are...." The words hung in the air.

"Tell me, Sarah....how concerned would your parents be if...say...they were to see those pictures I have of you? The ones you insisted I take of you?"

"You wouldn't...."

"Oh, but I would....because of what you did. Why couldn't you let the torment die with Carrie? Why? Tell me....tell me right now what Lindy ever did to you."

Sarah was visibly shaking, causing the boyfriend to begin to stand. Ricky put his hand on his shoulder and pushed him back down in his chair as easily as if he were a small child.

"I think you need to hear this....Ryan....isn't it? You see...this is what you're in for if you ever do anything she doesn't like. She's a vindictive bitch....and this is your warning." Ricky stared into his eyes and spoke deliberately and softly.

The boy remained tense, but did not attempt to get up out of the chair again.

"So....Sarah.....I'm waiting. What did Lindy do to you?"

"Nothing." She answered, barely above a whisper.

"Nothing? So that means what you did was pure meanness and vindictiveness...right? You just had to hurt her in some way. Am I right?"

Sarah shrugged.

"Answer the question, Sarah…."

"Yes….okay? You're right. *Miss pretty, pretty, oh so sweet Lindy.* Everybody loves her….everybody looks out for her….everybody *protects* her…no matter *what*…..I am sick of it! Luke, why don't you tell Ricky how you're in love with Lindy?"

"Because I'm not in love with Lindy. Think the world of her? Yes. Care about her? Yes."

"And no matter how you see that, Sarah….I know Luke would never do anything to hurt her." Ricky spoke up.

"Leave me alone….both of you."

"Oh, we're going to leave you alone….but will anybody else after those pictures appear in public?" Lukas grinned at her.

"Luke, you….wouldn't. I mean…we meant something to each other…once."

"Yeah….once. That was when you had me fooled."

"Luke….would you really do that? I mean….put those pictures out somewhere?"

Lukas made an effort to smile at her and then turned toward the door. Ricky followed him, glancing back to see Sarah defending herself against the words he and Lukas had said. The new boyfriend looked skeptical and uncomfortable. Ricky smiled.

"Hey, I'm going outside and grab a cigarette before my class starts. Want to walk out with me?"

"Yeah, sure. I didn't know you were smoking again."

"I started up that night after they took Lindy. I'm not….sleeping very well….you know? When I do sleep, I have bad dreams….of Lindy. I can hear her crying."

"It's probably not a dream, Pal. I'm sure she's crying herself to sleep every night. I know she must miss you. You're probably picking it up telepathically…I mean…you two were kind of like that with each other….reading each other's thoughts."

"I wish she would make contact with me….just so I know she's okay."

"She will. If she can…she will. You know that. Can I bum a smoke?"

*   *   *

Nelson was waiting in the car for Lindy to get out of school for the day. Loraine would be at the office late, have dinner there, and be home around ten, as was usually the scenario on Thursday nights. Loraine's late days were usually Mondays and Thursdays, but she chose not to work late on Lindy's first day of school. Loraine would have been a good mother if she had ever had children; Nelson could tell. Already she was dedicated to making Lindy's life perfect, and Nelson could tell that Loraine already had a maternal love for Lindy. But then again, the girl was so easy to love. Nelson watched as the students began filing out of the school. He spotted Lindy immediately and watched her as she was speaking to another student. 'She is making friends—Good,' Nelson thought inwardly. He was glad she was talking to a girl in lieu of a boy. He really didn't want boyfriends in her life, but then, she probably wasn't over the boyfriend she left behind yet, so he didn't really think there was much to worry about. He leaned over and opened the car door for her as she approached the car. She slid into the front seat, dropped her book bag into the back seat, and fastened her seat belt without saying anything.

"How was school today?"

"Okay. Same as always."

"What kind of food do you want to junk out on tonight? Pizza? Chinese?"

Lindy shrugged. "Doesn't matter. Whatever you like."

"Oh well…I think I like *you*….letting me make the choices like that. I think it will be pizza…..deep crust…. with all the stuff it will hold on top of it. What do you like on yours?"

"Onion, green pepper, black olives."

"Okay….then you can pick off what you don't like and give it to me. Fair?"

"Okay."

Lindy stared out of the front window. She knew he was watching her and it made her uncomfortable. He patted her knee and she jerked it away from him.

"Hey….relax. I was just going to tell you that we are going to be junk food junkies together twice a week. When Loraine is home we have to eat sensibly….but when the cat's away…..we eat junk food! Gees….don't be so jumpy."

"Sorry." She mumbled.

"It's okay. So….do you have homework?"

"Always."

"So get your homework done, and then we can watch a movie while we're eating pizza."

"What kind of work do you do?"

"Me? I sell electronics to major corporations. Why?"

"Because I have to do a paper on an occupation that has to do with modern technology. I guess that would fit."

"Yeah, it sure does. I'll give you some literature on it, and also my job criteria. Will that help?"

"Yes, it will."

"When is this due? Not tomorrow, I hope."

"No….next Friday."

"Fine….I'll bring home what you need tomorrow." Nelson smiled at her as he pulled into the driveway.

"Oh….I was wondering…..that computer in my…the bedroom. I notice there is no Internet access on it."

"Yeah, well…Social Services recommended that we don't have it."

"Then how do I do any research?"

"Good point. I'll see about it. So let's get inside so you can do your homework and then we pig out….sound good?"

Lindy nodded, and she opened the car door and grabbed her book bag out of the back seat of the car. Noting that Nelson had gone directly to his home office, she hurried into her room and immediately started her homework. Since she didn't have much, she finished it quickly and put her books away. As was her long-time habit, she got out her clothes for school the next day. She chose the designer jeans and top that Liz had bought her for Christmas last year and hung it on the inside hook on the door. She stood staring at it for a few minutes, feeling the tug on her heart as she remembered last Christmas and how happy she was. She absent-mindedly played with the ring on her left hand with her little finger, wondering if Ricky still wore his. 'Of course he did!' She chided herself. The hollow spot in her chest was aching as she closed the closet door. Wiping the tears from her cheeks, she wandered out into the hallway and then down toward the kitchen. She stopped to stare out of the sliding glass doors that opened up onto a large stone patio. She imagined it would be a wonderful place for cookouts in the summer.

"All done?" Nelson asked as he approached and stood behind her.

She flinched. "Yes. For another day, anyway."

"Good. Let's order pizza…oh….and you can select a movie out of the cabinet over there."

Lindy nodded; as she remembered how many times she and Ricky had exchanged the very same words. Pizza and a movie….their favorite cold night activity. Of course, she remembered a few times when the movie was forgotten and the pizza had gotten cold….'No….don't think about that,' she reminded herself. But she did think about it, and she wished longingly for Ricky's arms around her. It hadn't been a week and yet it seemed like it was a long time ago. Five months would seem endless. She hoped he would wait for her…

"Hey! Did you go deaf on me?" Nelson's voice brought her out of her reverie.

"What? I'm sorry….did you say something?"

"Yeah, I asked what you wanted to drink."

"Oh…a diet soft drink will be fine."

"You don't need the diet stuff…."

"I know….but I don't like the sugared stuff."

"Okay. Diet coke, then. So what were you thinking about? That had you in another world, I mean."

"Just….last year…how happy I was at Christmas….. being with Ricky and his family. There was so much love there….I'll miss it."

"There's love here, too…just not as many people."

His remark made Lindy laugh a little. There weren't all that many people there either, but Ricky's mom usually made it seem like it. The pizza arrived and they ate it in silence except for the parts of the comedy movie where they laughed. Lindy relaxed a little. When the movie was over Nelson got up and stretched.

"I have a couple more contracts to look over so I'll leave you to your own resources."

"Okay....I think I'll just go in and get ready for bed"

Nelson watched her hurry away down the hall before he went into his office. Lindy went into her room, changed into a simple nightshirt, washed her face and brushed her teeth. She was sitting on the bed brushing her hair when Nelson tapped on the door and then opened it and entered without waiting for a response.

"Hi....I....just...." He stopped and stared at her for a moment, and then he strode the distance between the door and her bed, grabbed her and forced her down on her back.

"What are you doing? NELSON! STOP!"

"Shh......" He yanked down her panties as he held her down.

*"NO! STOP! PLEASE! DON'T DO THIS!"*

Lindy felt him groping between her legs as she struggled. She heard his zipper come down while he fumbled with his pants, all the while pinning her to the bed. She was gasping for air as she strained against his arm that held her down. He pushed her legs apart with his knees and then he penetrated her. She screamed and he covered her mouth, cutting off her air supply. She turned her face into the pillow and bit down hard on it, sobbing as she endured his painful thrusts. Then it was over. She felt him stiffen as he released into her, and then his body flopped down onto her, holding her in place for a few moments. Her chest was heaving as she sobbed and tried to catch her breath. He sat up and pulled her up with him.

"We'll let this be our little secret. Nobody has to know. I mean….the last girl who blabbed about it…. well, they never found her body. And we wouldn't want anything to happen to you…now…would we? Stop crying. It wasn't that bad."

Lindy stared at him through tear filled eyes. "How could you? Oh God….why did you do this?" She choked out the words, still not able to breathe normally.

"Hey, it's not like I just deflowered a virgin, Honey. I'll bet you and that boyfriend of yours humped like bunnies every chance you got."

Lindy gave him a murderous look and he laughed.

"Now….mum's the word. Like I said….we wouldn't want anything to happen to you. You do want to see your boyfriend again, don't you?"

Lindy stared at the coverlet on the bed, trying to get control of herself. He squeezed her knee and laughed again. "If you're good to me….well…we'll see about you seeing…..what's his name? Ricky."

Lindy felt her stomach jump when Nelson said Ricky's name. 'Oh Ricky, Ricky….help me,' she silently conjured him up in her mind.

\* \* \*

Ricky had just finished his homework and was lying on his bed staring at the ceiling. He looked over at the clock. It was just past eight-thirty. One more lonely day of school for the week and then another lonely weekend. Tomorrow would make a whole week without Lindy. As he lay on the bed thinking about her, he suddenly got an uneasy feeling that he couldn't describe. He felt that something was wrong and that it involved Lindy. 'Oh, God, Baby....where are you? Are you okay?' He silently spoke to her. Ricky became restless and got up from the bed. He began to pace in his room, not quite knowing what the feeling meant. He stopped at the dresser and picked up a picture of Lindy. He stared at it hard, and then spoke out loud. "Baby, if you're in danger....just tell me somehow." In his head he heard her scream.

He left the house and began walking mindlessly; not knowing where he was going. Where is she? He knew she was in danger; he just knew it. He stopped at a crosswalk and stood there wondering which way to go. He had no idea. Leaning against the trunk of a tree, he ran his hand through his hair before he pulled out a pack of cigarettes and lit one up. Drawing the smoke into his lungs, he tried to think rationally. Was Lindy in trouble, or was that some kind of panic attack? No. It's real. Lindy needs him. But how does he find her? He had to talk to Uncle Nick. Walking as fast as he could, he headed toward the condo, and was relieved to see lights on. He knocked before using the key that Nick insisted he keep even though he had officially moved in with his mother. Nick seemed glad to see him as he offered him a soft drink. They sat down and Ricky explained the feeling he had gotten.

"You don't think maybe it's because you miss her?"

"No. Uncle Nick....this is real. You know Lindy and I are always....on the same page...you once put it. Something is wrong. I feel it. Lindy needs me....us."

Nick let out a short sigh. "All right. Let me see what I can find out tomorrow. I may have to call those two ugly broads from social services. Okay?"

Ricky was a little relieved as he walked back to Angie's house. He had to walk past Lindy's house first, and he said a silent prayer that she was okay. "We'll be together again, Baby.....just stay strong." He said the words aloud, thus giving himself a comforting feeling that Lindy was near.

# Chapter 43

Lindy and Loraine entered the house through the front door after Loraine picked Lindy up from school. It was Friday afternoon and Loraine was just happy that the weekend finally arrived. She had certainly had a rough week and was looking forward to just doing nothing. Maybe she would talk Lindy into going to the mall with her, but that was the only game plan she had for the weekend. Just as Loraine kicked off her shoes, the doorbell rang. Loraine groaned.

"Lindy, can you get that?"

Lindy opened the door to the two beasts from social services, as she had secretly referred to them.

"Hello, Belinda. How are you doing?" The older one attempted a smile that looked more like a grimace. "Is Loraine here?"

Lindy stepped out of the way and let them pass through the door.

"Hi, Loraine. We just stopped by to see how everything is going. Any problems? Anything we need to know about?"

"No...I don't think so. What do you think, Lindy? Is everything okay?" Loraine appealed to her.

"Y-yes….everything is okay. Do you ladies want some coffee? I could make it…."

"Oh, no….we really can't stay. We were in the area and thought we would stop to see if everything is going okay. Belinda looks fine."

"Well, I'm enjoying her company immensely." Loraine assured them.

'And your husband plans on enjoying my body immensely,' Lindy retorted silently.

Oh, how she wanted to scream that out loud, but she was afraid of how Nelson would retaliate if she did; not to mention how it would hurt Loraine. Lindy realized that she liked Loraine. 'Too bad her husband is a pig,' Lindy thought in silence.

\* \* \*

Nick picked up the laboratory telephone on the second ring. After his greeting he listened intently to the social worker's account of the visit to Lindy.

"She seems….fine." It was the older woman who had placed the call.

"What do you mean 'she seems fine'? You don't think so?"

"Oh, no….she's fine…it's just that she seems very nervous. Maybe we intimidate her….I don't know. Look….Dr. Bazario….I know you think what we did was wrong…but Lindy has to have growing space. She needs to find a circle of friends….other than the boyfriend. She's too young to settle down with one boy. You should know that. Now I know you are worried about her…because I believe you do care about her…but trust me….we put her into a good home where she will be able to expand her horizons. If she is meant to be with your nephew, she will be….but later on in life. The separation is good for her…. and for him. If what they feel is real…well, it won't go away….it will be there when they are older."

"Thank you for checking for me….and thank you for the counseling session."

Nick hung up abruptly. He had an uneasy feeling that something really wasn't right. Ricky's feeling was too real, and the old bitch on the phone wasn't all that convincing. He decided he wouldn't tell Ricky about his feeling. Ricky was going out of his mind about the whole thing as it was, and living with Angie was turning into a replay of Chicago. Ricky showed up at his place more than once during the week just to escape Angie. How could he tell his sister that she was making a very huge mistake?

\* \* \*

Lindy came out of the school and spotted Nelson's car. Her heart sank, and then she remembered that it was Monday—Loraine's day to work late. She squared her shoulders and made up her mind that she would go directly to her room and lock the door. Inside the car, she huddled as close to the door as she could, even though she realized that he could still touch her in his small Mercedes.

"So….what's for dinner?"

"I-I'm not hungry."

"Well, you might be in a little while." He reached over and pinched her knee and she jumped.

"Don't! Don't touch me!"

"And what are you going to do about it? Tell my wife? She'll wonder why you waited so long….especially when I tell her you came on to me….."

"You're a pig."

Nelson laughed. "And you're my little lamb chop." He said as he rubbed her thigh.

She stared out the passenger side window, feeling the sting of tears in her eyes.

"Please? Please don't do it again. Please?"

Thinking this approach may help her, she pleaded and cried. He laughed.

"I didn't hurt you. You weren't exactly pure as snow."

"But you did hurt me. It hurt! It hurt a lot!"

He laughed again. "Can't help it if I'm well endowed, Babe."

"It's not that. I'm still recovering from…the surgery."

"Not likely…but nice try, though."

Lindy turned away from him again. 'He's ruthless,' she thought.

Nelson swung the car into the driveway and hurriedly got out and came around the car to take Lindy by the arm. "Come on, little girl….we'll have our fun first and dinner later."

Lindy's heart was pounding and she began to tremble. She focused her mind on Ricky, and silently begged him to help her. Nelson guided her into the house, helped her with her coat, and then put his arm around her waist and led her to her room. He shut the door and took her chin in his hand.

"Stop crying….just stop." He tapped her cheek hard with his fingers. It stung and she gasped. He pressed his lips against hers and kissed her hard, shoving his tongue into her mouth. She twisted her face away from him, struggling to breathe. He fumbled with the zipper on her jeans and succeeded in pulling it down. Forcing her onto the bed, he pulled her jeans down and then off. While holding her down, he worked at his own pants and got them off. Her panties tore as he yanked at them. She sobbed as he forced her legs apart and forcibly slammed into her. His thrusts were more brutal than the first time, and she prayed it would be over soon. She was relieved when she felt him stiffen, because that meant that it was ending. Once again he flopped on top of her until his breathing was normal, and then he got up and smacked her on the thigh.

"Come on....let's eat. I'm starving....I'm going to order Chinese tonight, so what do you want? Or is that my choice, too?"

Sobbing, Lindy lay on her side facing away from him. "D-does it m-matter?"

"I'll order you sweet and sour chicken. Pull yourself together....we're eating in the dining room." He talked over his shoulder as he left the room, acting like nothing had happened.

Lindy lay on her side, praying to God, and then switched to praying to Ricky.

"Oh Ricky....help me....please help me." She went back to praying to God, begging for a sign to a solution. Her prayers were interrupted.

"Lindy! Come on, Sweetheart. Food is here......and I expect to see you out here for dinner."

She sighed, and went to wash her face, picking up the torn panties on the way. The answer was right there in front of her, in her hand. She looked down at the torn panties and whispered, "Thank you, God. At least I can prove what he is doing to me." She got the other pair out of the hamper, used both pairs to blot away his semen, and put them both into a plastic bag.

* * *

Fate was on her side again. Loraine picked her up from school on Tuesday afternoon and they went out to eat. Nelson was working on a deal in the next county and wouldn't be home until after eight o'clock. That was a relief in itself to Lindy, but even more of a relief was when Loraine told her they had a Christmas party to go to on Thursday night, and that she wouldn't be working late that night.

"Do you mind, Lindy? That's usually when they pass out the Christmas bonuses, and I'd like to get mine that night."

"No, Loraine….I don't mind at all. I have that paper due on Friday, so I will be busy typing it that night. Besides, why should your life stop because of me? That wouldn't be fair. Remember, I practically lived alone when I was living with my dad. He would go away for days and leave me there alone. I think I can handle one evening."

"Well….it usually lasts until midnight….are you sure you'll be okay?"

"Yes, I'll be fine. Besides, I'm asleep before ten-thirty… I won't even notice that you're not home. And….now that I know about it, I would feel very bad if you didn't go…. because I would know it was because of me."

"You're a very sweet child…do you know that?"

"So I've been told." She smiled at Loraine, as she thought to herself 'your husband thinks I'm a sweet woman.'

Lindy was relieved. No Nelson attack on Thursday night. It was going to be like a holiday in her mind. They would be gone until….after midnight. Ricky…she could see Ricky. Lindy told Loraine she had to type her paper, but it had already been typed. She had another one to type. And she had to pack. She was leaving….running away. She couldn't stay there and be raped twice a week for the next 4 or 5 months. She had to go. Nobody would believe her if she told anyone…he appeared to be a decent citizen. She would look like a kid vying for attention. And besides, he promised to hurt her if she told. He would, too. No, her only option was to disappear. She had to see Ricky first.

\* \* \*

Ricky answered his cell phone and was surprised to hear Lindy's voice.

"Ricky….."

"Lindy! Where are you?"

"Ricky….meet me at our place. Can you?"

"On my way." He snapped the phone closed, grabbed a coat, and took off in a sprint toward the steps down to the creek.

Lindy hung up the phone at the phone booth on the corner and headed toward the steps. She left just after six o'clock and hailed a cab to the restaurant she and Ricky used to frequent after their visit to their special place. She remembered there was a payphone she could use. She stood in the shadows under the trees waiting for Ricky.

Ricky ran down the steps, almost falling on the ice that had formed on them.

"Lindy? Are you here?"

"Ricky!" She flung herself into his arms. "Oh, Ricky." Tears began to flow, and then borderline hysteria.

"Baby….Baby….oh God, I've missed you." Ricky held her tightly.

"Ricky….I'm running away."

"Baby….no. They'll find you and put you in some detention home. We can wait the five months….four and a half now…."

"He's….he's raping me."

Ricky held her at arm's length. "What? What did you say?"

"He's raping me."

"Who?"

"The man who lives in the house they took me to. Nelson is his name."

Ricky dropped her arms and walked away from her, and balled up his fists.

"Son of a bitch! I'll kill him!" He reached for her and wrapped his arms around her, holding her tightly. "Okay…. we're out of here. Tomorrow. Can you be ready?"

"Yes. But Ricky….you can't go and ruin your life…."

"Baby, you *are* my life. Without you…nothing even makes any sense. And besides….do you really think I'm going to let you go off by yourself? You need me to protect you. The world can be an evil place for a pretty young girl like you. So…you go; I go."

"Okay…At least we can be together again."

"Yep. Okay…let's plan this. You go home and pack. Go to school like you normally would, then leave after first period. Go home and get what you packed….we need help. I'll call Luke. We can trust him. He can take us to the bus station. We'll go somewhere by bus, because every way else you need to show I-D."

"I'll give you directions to the house. Can Luke pick me up there?"

"What time do you have to get back tonight?"

"They went to a Christmas party. They said they would be home around midnight, but I need time to pack."

"Let's call Luke."

They walked up the steps and called Lukas. He was there within ten minutes. He got out and hugged Lindy, which brought on tears again.

"Luke….we have a situation here. Lindy and I have to go. We need your help."

"Hey…sure…anything…"

Ricky laid out his plan for their getaway, and then they both drove Lindy home. Lindy handed Lukas a twenty dollar bill. "Get some gas in the car." She told him. Ricky kissed Lindy when she got out of the car.

"See you tomorrow. I love you."

"I love you, too. Ricky…I…are you sure you want to do this?"

"Does a bear shit in the woods? See you tomorrow. Remember…go to first period and then leave the school, walk to the corner. Luke knows where the school is. He'll meet you on the corner."

"And take me to the bank? We need money, and I have it."

"Yeah….okay. Luke? Before you pick me up can you stop at Lindy's bank so she can get some money?"

"No problem."

"Okay….just follow the plan we agreed on. See you tomorrow. And Baby? We'll be okay….as long as we're together…we'll always be okay."

Ricky got back into the car, and Lindy went inside, straight to her room to pack and prepare for her departure tomorrow. 'Nelson, you have a big surprise coming....I hope.'

* * *

Lukas approached the ticket window at the bus station and purchased two tickets for South Carolina.

"That's at least an eight hour separation from here, Luke. So that's a good head start for us."

So it was agreed upon that they would head to South Carolina. After dropping Lindy off the night before, Ricky told Lukas what was happening to Lindy. Lukas became almost as angry as Ricky, and had the urge to go back and wait for Nelson.

"No....let's just get Lindy out of there. He threatened her if she told anybody...and she's right....nobody would believe her. It's best we just get her the hell out of here."

The bus was boarding and Lindy hugged Lukas. "I'm so glad you and Ricky became friends. Take care, and as soon as we can, we'll get in touch with you."

Lukas shook Ricky's hand and told him to take care of Lindy.

"Always, Luke.....always." Then Ricky hugged him, too.

"Remember....you know nothing. You were home with a virus."

"Got it, Pal....don't worry."

Lindy and Ricky boarded the bus and found a seat near the rear. Ricky reached for Lindy's hand and held onto it as the bus pulled away from the station.

"This is it, Baby. This starts our life together." He pulled her hand to his lips and kissed it.

She smiled up at him. "Why do I always feel so safe when I'm with you?"

"Because that's how you're supposed to feel. I'll never let anything happen to you again. You don't know how bad Luke and I wanted to wait for that guy last night…. and just beat the shit out of him. We didn't because we knew you'd still be there after we ended up in jail…..and you'd be at his mercy. So we decided it was best to get you out of there."

The ride was long and tiring. They reached a town in South Carolina after dark and somewhere close to ten o'clock, and were told that was the end of the line. They got off in the middle of the town and looked around, with sinking hearts.

"Looks like a ghost town, doesn't it?" Ricky spoke as he looked around. "Well, let's walk that way." He pointed in the direction that seemed to have more structures.

They started walking. "I'm glad these suitcases have wheels. We'd be exhausted if they didn't. Let me carry the book bag." Ricky suggested, as he reached for it.

Lindy had decided to bring along the book bag, filled with drinks and a couple of sandwiches. Ricky thought that was smart thinking on her part, since he didn't even think about food on the trip. He had brought all the money he had, which was about five-hundred and thirty dollars. Lindy said she had money, so he paid for the tickets out of his money, and had a couple hundred left.

"I didn't think it would be so cold here…but it feels colder than when we left."

"Yeah…it does. I have gloves if you need them, Babe." He reached into his pocket and produced a pair of gloves for her.

"I think we're in a summer resort town, Ricky. Everything is closed for the season…didn't you see that sign back there?"

"Yeah, I saw it. I was hoping you didn't. Don't worry…. we'll find something open. We just have to….look…up there…I see a light in that big window…."

They picked up the pace and headed toward the lighted window of a motel. A man was standing behind the counter, and they quickly entered.

"Closed." The large man behind the counter said as they entered.

"Oh. We saw the light on and hoped….Well, do you mind if we get warm a little? We're freezing."

"No….you can stay a bit."

"We need a place to stay. How far before we find a place that is open?"

The man laughed. "Miles. Miles and miles. This is all summer resort business along here. We close up and enjoy spending the money you tourists from the North bring us all year long." He laughed at his own remark. "But you two aren't tourists….am I right?"

Lindy and Ricky looked at each other.

"No. We're not tourists." Ricky answered.

"On the run?"

"Something like that."

"Nothing can be bad enough to make you two run away…."

Without warning, Lindy started crying and Ricky immediately put his arm around her.

"That's what you think, sir. Thanks for letting us get warm. Appreciate it."

Ricky held the door for Lindy and they went out into the cold and started walking. Lindy looked up at Ricky with a frown on her face.

"I'm cold, tired, dirty, and hungry. I'm a homeless person." She laughed at her joke. "But at least we're together, and in spite of everything….I am so happy about that."

"Me, too."

As they walked out into the cold, the man's wife joined him behind the counter in the motel office.

"They remind you of anybody, Sam?"

"Yeah. They do. Go call them back in here."

Lindy and Ricky stood on the corner not knowing which way to go. They heard a woman's voice behind them telling them to stop. They turned to see a middle aged woman running toward them.

"Stop….kids….stop. We can let you have a room for the night. That's what you want, isn't it?"

"Yes, Ma'am." Ricky answered.

"Okay…come on back."

Lindy and Ricky looked at each other for a moment, but it didn't take much coaxing to get them back into the warmth of the motel office. They followed the woman.

"Okay….I'm going to let you two have a room for the night…on one condition. I want the truth as to why you're running away. Are you in any trouble?"

"No, Sir…we're not in any trouble. We just had to go….I mean….Lindy had to go….and I wouldn't let her go alone."

"So you're name is Lindy…and your name is…?"

"Ricky. Ricky DeCelli. This is Lindy Riley." Ricky gestured toward Lindy.

"So…tell me…Ricky….why are you two running?"

"Well, it's a very long story up until this point…but…. well, due to circumstances, Lindy was put into a foster home with this couple. The guy was raping Lindy."

Lindy started crying again. The man's wife was carrying out a tray of hot tea when she heard Ricky say it.

"Oh…..you poor thing!" She exclaimed.

Ricky's arm went around Lindy, protectively.

"Why didn't you go to the police?"

"Because," Lindy swallowed hard in order to talk. "He threatened to do something to me if I told….then he said a week later that nobody would believe me since I waited so long. He-he said….they never found the body of the last girl who tried to tell. I didn't know what to do…so I decided to run away."

"And let him get away with it." The big man spoke flatly.

"No…maybe not. I-I did something."

"What?" Both Ricky and the big man asked her at the same time.

"Well…I saved the…underwear with his….semen… on it…and put it in a plastic bag. It's in my locker at school. One pair is torn…he tore them. Anyway, then…. I had a paper to turn in today…but I turned in two. One was the real one and the other was the entire story of how he raped me….what he said….everything. I also put in the paper where they could find the….underwear with the semen on it. There was also a brochure he gave me with his fingerprint and DNA on it…..and I said to tell his wife, Loraine that I was sorry for hurting her, but her husband is a pig. Anyway, hopefully someone will take it seriously and investigate."

She looked up to find Ricky staring at her. No, he was smiling at her.

"Baby, you're a genius. I didn't know you were going to do that….but it's brilliant."

"Yeah, Lindy…it is. Good thinking. Maybe he won't get away with it. Anyway, we haven't introduced ourselves. I'm Sam and this is my wife Renee. You two can have the second room from the stairs on the top floor for the night. Tomorrow, we'll see what we can do for you. Are you hungry? We don't have anything to eat since we plan on leaving for a well-deserved vacation, but I was going to go out and pick something up. Ricky…you're welcome to ride along."

Ricky looked at Lindy for a sign that she would be okay if he went.

"Let's get your stuff into that room, and then decide if you want to go."

"How much do you want for the night?" Ricky asked.

"One hundred dollars."

"Sam!" Renee scolded.

"Just kidding. Twenty for the night, since there are no accommodations except the room. No snack bar, beach rental items. But there is electricity, water and heat."

"Right now that sounds like paradise." Lindy spoke up.

Ricky and Sam carried the suitcases up the stairs and deposited them on the floor inside the room. Lindy looked around, approvingly. There was a small kitchenette, a bed and a small loveseat. A television stood on a stand near the loveseat. In front of the window was a small round table, perfect for two. A blue tablecloth covered it. The room was decorated in blues and greens, reminding Lindy of the sea. She went past the bed to check out the bathroom, also done in blues and greens, but with a splash of orange and olive here and there. Lindy loved it.

"Baby, I'm going to go get us something to eat. I'm locking the door on the way out. Don't open it for anybody....okay?"

"Okay....I'm going to take a shower while you're gone."

"Be back soon. Do you care what I bring back?"

"As long as it's edible....no."

Ricky got into Sam's car and Sam pulled out of the parking lot. They talked while Sam drove. Sam wanted to know why Lindy was put into a foster home, and Ricky obliged by telling him of the beating, the shooting, the baby dying, and then the part where he was accused of murder. When he was finished with the abbreviated version of the story, Sam remained quiet as he had throughout Ricky's tale. Finally, he cleared his throat and spoke.

"She's been through hell...hasn't she?"

"Yeah...she has. She's so sweet, Sam...you have no idea. It hurts me to see her hurt. When she cries.... damn....I can't even begin to tell you what it does to me."

"I guess you love her, then?"

"With all my heart....since the day I met her." Ricky absently smiled as he remembered the day he met her.

Sam was quiet again. When he began speaking, Ricky was almost startled.

"You two remind me and my wife of us....when we were young. We ran away...but not for the same reason. We ran away to another state to get married. Her parents didn't approve of me...still don't. They wanted better for their little girl. Figured a college educated guy would have been better for her....but....we've been married thirty-seven years, raised two kids, never had one unhappy day in all that time...I say she did all right. I know I did, too. We're still in love....you know what I mean? That's important. We love each other, but we are still in love with each other. If you can stay that way...you can stay married for fifty years."

"We're going to get married. We're not going back until we are married. Nobody is going to break us apart again." Sam heard the bitterness in Ricky's voice.

"I bet you would like to kill that guy, huh?"

"You got it."

"Well, put the thought out of your head. Let the law handle it. Here we go....hope fast food is okay. That's about as good as you're going to get tonight."

* * *

Ricky unlocked the door to the motel and set the bags of food on the table. Lindy came out of the bathroom in a gray fleece football jersey nightshirt that went all the way to the floor. She had just finished drying her hair. Ricky thought she looked adorable.

"Dinner is served, m'lady." He smiled at her.

"Ricky....this is our first home together."

"Yep...it is. Even if it is for only one night."

"There are dishes and pot and pans in the cupboards."

"So...you've already checked the place out, huh? Hope you're hungry....I bought enough to feed more than two."

They sat at the small round table and ate; feeling more relaxed than they felt since they left Pennsylvania. After they finished eating, and put away the leftovers, Ricky went in to take a shower. Lindy turned on the television just in time to catch a late news broadcast. She wanted to make sure that the news of their disappearance didn't trickle down this far, if at all. Ricky came out of the shower, wrapped in a towel, and stared down at Lindy, who was fast asleep on the bed. He watched her for a moment, smiling; and then he turned off the television and the light, pulled on a pair of sweatpants he had taken out of the suitcase, and crawled in beside her. The last thing he remembered of the night was wrapping his arm around her and pulling her close to him.

# Chapter 44

*M*iss White, the first period teacher sat down to grade papers on Friday evening. She sighed as she pulled the stack in front of her and began reading. The third paper was Lindy Riley's. Miss White smiled because she knew this one would be a good one. She read through it, smiling, and then placed an A on the top of it. She picked up the next one. It said Lindy Riley again. She began reading, and then sat up straight. She set the paper on her knee and then picked it up and began reading again. She rose from the sofa, went to the phone, and dialed the principal's number.

"Jim, I think you need to see this paper. I don't think it's a hoax. Can I bring this over?"

"Yeah, sure, Amy. We just finished dinner"

Amy White drove the short distance to Jim Thompson's house and rang the bell. She handed him the paper and watched his expression as he read.

"Oh my God....is this possible? I mean...credible?"

"I think it is. Lindy Riley is a sweet girl....I can't imagine her making this up."

"We need to take this to the police....we are legally obligated to do so." Jim Thompson grabbed his coat and the two of them left for the police station.

\* \* \*

Angie called Nick around nine o'clock on Friday night.

"Nick, is Ricky there?"

"No, Angie...I haven't seen him all evening. Maybe he's with Luke."

"Yeah, maybe. Well...if you see him can you tell him to give me a call?"

"Everything all right?"

"Oh...yeah....I just want to know where he is."

"Okay...will do."

Nick hung up and turned the television volume up again. "She needs to stop hounding him." Nick said to nobody in particular.

\* \* \*

Loraine hurried home to see if Lindy was there already. She wasn't. 'Maybe Nelson picked her up,' Loraine thought to herself. Nelson walked in an hour later with no Lindy.

"Nelson, do you know where Lindy is?"

"No...weren't you supposed to pick her up from school?"

"She wasn't there. I waited until there were no more kids coming out of school. She just wasn't there."

"Maybe she went somewhere with a friend."

"Without letting us know?"

"She's a kid. Sometimes kids aren't the most considerate people."

"Yeah....but Lindy seems very considerate. What if something's happened to her?"

"Did you check her room?" Nelson was already halfway down the hall to Lindy's room.

"Loraine? Her clothes are gone."

"What? Oh my God...why? Why would she go? We treat her like a daughter."

"Want to bet the boyfriend is gone, too? Or that she's there with him?"

"We have to call social services. Let me find that card those women left here."

\* \* \*

Jim Thompson and Amy White stood in front of Lindy's locker while the police officer used a bolt cutter to open it. Using a large flashlight, the officer looked into the locker, sorting through books and papers.

"Here we go." He pulled out a plastic bag holding two pairs of panties and a brochure of some electronics company. "Let me submit this to the lab. If we find what she said we would find in that paper she wrote, we may have a good strong rape case."

They left the school and went back to the police station.

"Should those foster parents be notified?" Jim Thompson asked the officer.

"No. They should be reporting her missing. I don't want to....alert him that we're investigating him. In that paper she says the lady is really nice and she is sorry if this is going to hurt her. She feels sorry for her...what's her name? Loraine. I feel sorry for her, too."

"So we shouldn't say anything?"

"No...not to anybody. You say this was foster custody? They should be notifying social services. In the meantime...this has to be kept quiet. Remember, Miss Riley is a minor. If this gets out there can be law suits. I'll keep you posted." The officer stood up signaling to them that the interview was over.

In the car on the way back to Thompson's house, Amy was exceptionally quiet.

"What are you thinking? You're awfully quiet."

"Do you know Lindy?"

"I met her the day she registered here. Sweet girl. Bright and talented, too."

"I'm just thinking…..how could someone do this to her? Any child, really."

"Well, we haven't proven anything yet. We don't know if it's true."

"Oh, it's true. I can feel it. Lindy Riley is not the kind of kid who goes around making false accusations….I can tell you that."

* * *

Nick's telephone and doorbell were ringing at the same time. He grabbed the phone and carried it with him to answer the door. Angie was on the phone, sounding frantic. Ricky had not come home all night. Nick opened the door to the two social workers, and he instinctively knew why they were there.

"Angie….come up here. Right now." He hung up the phone and stared at the two at the door.

"Ladies….come in. What can I do for you?"

"We would like to speak to your nephew."

"He's not here. He moved back in with his mother more than a week ago. Is there something I can help you with?"

The two of them exchanged glances and then stared at Nick.

"Belinda has run off."

"You don't say."

"Where is your nephew?"

"Don't know. His mother is on her way here. You can ask her."

"We will."

"Can I offer you some coffee?"

"No."

Angie came in with a major attitude. "Nick? Who are these women?"

"They're from social services."

"Social what?"

"Services. Apparently Lindy has run off."

"And…they think Ricky is with her? Ricky has had no contact with her."

"Why would Lindy run away?" Nick asked the two women.

They exchanged glances again. Although the Sutter's were not to be alerted to anything, Social Services had to be told, lest they try to replace Lindy with another child. They were sworn to silence, and told that there was an investigation going on, not to mention that they were responsible for putting Belinda there.

"Have you checked your son's room, Mrs…..?"

"DeCelli. No, I haven't. I didn't think I needed to."

"I'm going to look upstairs, Angie…to see if I can see anything that would indicate….whatever it is we need to know. Call Liz for me. Tell her to come over. She'll be concerned about Lindy….and Ricky."

Nick came out of Ricky's room and walked down the stairs slowly, reading the note that Ricky had left for him. He read it once before he left the room, but he was reading it again for clarification.

"Find anything, Nick?"

"Sure did. Listen to this….." He stopped and stared at the two social workers and then began to read. "Uncle Nick, I'm sorry, but I had to go. That guy where Lindy was living was raping her and she had to get away. I couldn't let her go by herself, so I went along to protect her. Tell my mom I'm sorry, but Lindy's safety is too important to me. When we know it's safe, we will come back. Love, Ricky….."

Angie started crying. "Oh God, Nick….now what?"

Nick stared at the social workers. "Did you know about this?"

"The police told us about a paper Lindy turned in to her teacher. There was possible evidence in her locker. The police told us about it this morning."

"The fine upstanding male half of the fine professional couple you took her to live with was raping her. Great…. just great. Now…let me get this straight. You took her from here….a place where she was loved and cared for…. because this home was unsuitable…*unacceptable*. And then you placed her in a place you considered suitable, *acceptable*, and she gets raped. Do I have it right?"

"Doctor Bazario…we had no idea…."

"Oh, but you were so sure this place was…all wrong."

Liz was standing in the doorway listening to Nick. 'Lindy raped? Oh my God.' She thought.

"So now….Lindy is gone…and apparently Ricky went with her…to protect her….which is what you two said that you were doing!"

"Dr. Bazario….we did what we thought was best…for her. I know she feels she's in love. I remember when we

506

drove her out to the foster home….she cried and cried. I told her there would be other boys…."

"And I wonder if that sounded as stupid to her as it just sounded to me. They had a child together! That would be like telling the survivors of the Titanic that there would be other boats!" Nick could feel his blood pressure rising as he spoke through clenched teeth. He could have choked these two women at the moment.

Liz broke the silence. "So both Ricky and Lindy are gone? Gone where?"

"We don't know, Liz. I thought Ricky may have stayed up here last night, so I called Nick this morning."

"As soon as I saw those two standing at the front door, I knew. The part where she was raped was a real shock. Our sweet Lindy….God, how awful for her." Nick shook his head and stared at the floor.

The younger of the two social workers spoke up. "Well, I don't understand….if she was being raped why didn't she go to the authorities?"

Nick's head whipped around and he stared at her in disbelief. "Lady, is your brain stuck on stupid? *You* are the authorities….to Lindy. You're the authorities….and you put her there….against her own free will. You placed her in harm's way! Now…why…would…she…go…to the authorities?"

The older woman stood up. "Well, this is getting us nowhere. So it's established that they are together then? We will have to inform the police of that. They were only looking for a small blonde girl."

"Why are they bothering to look? Lindy is safe now. Ricky will take care of her…believe me…I know my nephew. I trust him more than I trust you two."

The women got up and left without another word. Nick helped himself to a glass of scotch and sat at his bar.

Angie watched him and then spoke up. "It's not even noon yet."

"Shut up." He responded to her.

"Have you tried calling his cell phone?" Liz asked Nick.

"Wouldn't do any good. It's upstairs. He knew I would try to call. He doesn't want to be found. And I don't blame him. You know how he feels about Lindy. It probably about killed him when she told him. Damn it.... it's killing me."

Without warning, Nick's eyes filled up with tears. "Poor baby.....that son of a bitch....how could he?"

"You know, Nick....I was thinking...that if Ricky didn't go with her....he would have gone out and found that house...and confronted....no, attacked...the guy. It's probably good that he went with her...not to mention he will protect her...keep her safe."

"I know he will. She would have been safe here, too. But...oh no! Cagney and Lacey knew what was best for her....RIGHT!"

\* \* \*

Lindy and Ricky awoke at the same time and rolled over to stare into each other's eyes. Ricky kissed her nose.

"Ready to get up and check this place out in the daylight?"

"Sure....but I'm hungry again. Can't we heat up the leftovers from last night?"

"If that's what you want...then absolutely."

He pulled her close and held her for a moment. A knock on the door sent him flying out of bed, and sent Lindy under the blankets.

"Who's there?"

"Sam and Renee. We brought you breakfast and a proposition."

Ricky opened the door to see Sam holding a large tray; Renee stood behind him with a coffee pot. A yellow streak whizzed past Ricky's legs and appeared to fly onto the bed. The streak was a yellow Labrador retriever. A very surprised Lindy came out from under the covers and immediately reached for the dog.

"Well, hi!" She ruffled the dog's fur around his neck and he plopped down beside her on the bed.

"He's great! What's his name?"

"Baxter."

"Cool name. Well, Baxter….I smell food….so let me up."

Baxter jumped off the bed and followed Lindy to the table.

"He likes you." Renee offered.

"Yeah…most dogs do. I like dogs."

"Well…then you may like our proposition."

"Okay….what kind of proposition?"

"Well, we are leaving on vacation….and we were going to put Baxter in a boarding kennel for three weeks. We're going up north to visit family, and a couple of the kids are allergic to dogs…otherwise we would take him. Anyway, here it is….we need a dog sitter….and you two need a place to live. So…how about if we leave Baxter with you for three weeks and that way….you can stay here for that time and take care of him?"

Lindy sucked in her breath. "Ricky? Can we?"

"Of course. I always wanted a dog, but my dad was allergic to them. I know Lindy will love taking care of him, Sam. So yes, we can do it. Only one problem...I don't know if they are going to look for us or not...but if they find us...and you're not here...what would happen to Baxter?"

"Yeah...that could be a problem. But here's the deal.... if that happens....we will leave you a number to call us. I'll call one of the local policemen to come get Baxter. They will take him until I get back. But let's hope that doesn't happen."

"Yeah...let's hope.....so it's settled then. Lindy and I are dog sitters for three weeks. And I don't even have to turn around to see the big grin on her face....it's warming the back of my neck."

Renee and Sam laughed. "So let's eat this wonderful breakfast my wife prepared. And Lindy...Renee wants to take you food shopping before we leave. So be ready by noon today....okay?"

Lindy nodded, her hand resting on top of Baxter's head.

\* \* \*

Lindy and Ricky waved good-bye to Sam and Renee as they left for their vacation. Baxter stood beside Lindy, apparently already having adopted her as a surrogate owner. Renee had taken Lindy shopping for food so they had plenty of it. They had gone to the dollar store where Lindy bought a couple of candles and a coffee pot so they could have coffee. Renee told her of the convenience store that was a mile in the other direction in case they needed milk or bread. Sam told Ricky that he alerted the local police that his wife's young nephew and his young bride were going to stay and watch the place on a sort-of-honeymoon, so the police wouldn't be nosing around too much, as Sam put it. He also told him about the hardware store near the convenience store. The hardware store held more than just hardware, Sam told him, as he reminded him that Christmas was two weeks away. Ricky knew that he would be surprising Lindy with a Christmas tree.

"We'll be passing through the Western Pennsylvania area, so we'll listen to the news to hear if there is anything you should know. We'll ring your phone in your room if we hear anything." Sam patted Ricky's shoulder. "Take care of your little girlfriend. She's a cutie." He said it as he watched Lindy throwing a ball for Baxter to fetch.

"Yeah, she is. She's very special." Ricky watched Lindy absently for a moment, and then called her over so she could say good-bye to them.

They stood with arms around each other, and watched the car drive away before they ran onto the beach to play with Baxter.

Sam watched them in the rearview mirror. "Those two are going to make it, I think. They have what you and I have." He winked at Renee and then accelerated toward the freeway.

# Chapter 45

$\mathcal{L}$indy couldn't sleep. She slipped out of bed and sat on the loveseat with her feet curled under her. They had been in the motel for more than a week, and in that time Ricky had not even tried to make love to her. Was it because Nelson had touched her? Maybe Ricky didn't find her appealing any more. It would devastate her if that were the case. She looked over at his sleeping face, and her heart swelled with the love she felt for him. She had to make him want her again. Sighing, she got up and removed her nightshirt and stood beside the bed.

"Ricky…..Ricky….wake up."

He opened his eyes and focused on her. "What are you doing, Babe?"

"Ricky….I need you to make love to me."

He stared at her nude silhouette in the darkness, not knowing how he was supposed to react.

"I don't want what we had to be over….because of what happened with Nelson. I….I want you to want me again." Lindy's voice was husky with emotion, and even though she didn't want to cry, her tear ducts were betraying her.

Ricky lifted up the blanket and moved over so Lindy could crawl in, and then he reached for her and pulled her close.

"I want you, Baby…..I want you just as much as I always did. But I had to know that you were ready. I know…that what that son of a bitch did to you was traumatic…and I was afraid that you….you know…. wouldn't want to. I just wanted you to be able to make love without thinking of him…..and…I had to know that when we….did…it…that you felt me making love to you…not him attacking you. Oh, God, I want you. I want to make love to you." He whispered as he held her, stroking her hair and kissing her face.

Ricky began kissing her tenderly, and slowly and gradually progressed to making love to her; being gentle and tender as he always had been. He softly spoke words of love and endearment to her, cajoling her until she climaxed. He kissed her while he erupted inside of her, enhancing the pleasure even more.

They lay in each other's arms, as Ricky caressed her shoulder.

"I love you, Lindy. That will never change. Now I need sleep. I'm a working man, you know." He kissed her once more and then cradled her in his arms, and quickly fell back asleep.

\* \* \*

Ricky unlocked the door and entered quickly. It had gotten very cold outside and he didn't want to let any cold air in. He hid his package outside so Lindy wouldn't see it until he had a chance to set it up. It was a Christmas tree, fully decorated with lights included. It was small, but their little motel room was not big enough for anything bigger. Ricky had started working at the hardware store a couple of days before purchasing the tree. Earlier in the week, he had gone off to the hardware store to see what kind of things besides hardware were sold there, when he saw the 'help wanted' sign in the window. He told the proprietor, Mr. Carter that he was interested in the job and filled out an application. Mr. Carter looked over his application and called him into the office.

"You have no work history."

"No, Sir....I don't. I've never had to work before."

"And why do you have to work now?"

"I want to support my girlfriend...or at least cover part of the expenses."

"This only pays minimum wage, kid."

"I know....but it's also the only place that's hiring."

Mr. Carter laughed. "I like your honesty. Anyway.... it's minimum wage plus a commission of five percent on your sales. It will probably only last through Christmas.... is that okay? Won't buy a lot of groceries...."

"That's fine. Actually, I have money to buy groceries..... I need money to buy her a Christmas gift...and a tree. She would be so excited if I brought home a tree."

"Well, we have 'em here....and you get an employee discount."

"Really? Does this mean I have the job?"

"Yeah....I'm the only one hiring and you're the only one who applied....so we both win by default. Start tomorrow?"

"Great!"

Ricky began working at the hardware store the next day. Lindy was saddened that they wouldn't be spending every day together, but she had Baxter to fill her days, and

she took pleasure in cooking dinner and having it ready
for Ricky when he came home in the evening. Tonight
was no exception. Ricky smelled the cooking as soon as
he closed the door.

"Smells good….whatever it is."

"Beef stew. Hope you like it."

"Perfect for the weather outside. Gees, it's cold! Why
does it feel so much colder down here than up in P-A?"

"I don't know…but it does. Dinner is ready when
you are. I'm going to run in and take a quick shower,
if that's okay. I cleaned and then cooked, so I feel like I
need one."

"Go ahead…..I'll set the table"

As soon as she disappeared into the bathroom, he ran
out and got the tree. He quickly set it up and plugged in
the lights before she came out of the shower. They would
be eating on the loveseat until after Christmas, because
the only place to put the tree was on the table. He knew
she wouldn't mind, though. He heard her coming and
turned out the lamp by the loveseat. She gasped when
she saw the tree.

"Oh, Ricky…..we can have a Christmas." She wrapped
her arms around his waist and smiled up at him.

"Baby, I can't promise you a lot just yet, but I can
promise you that we will always have a Christmas."

He placed a kiss on her lips, tenderly and slowly.
Baxter sat beside them, whined and let out a small 'woof'.
Ricky patted his hip.

"Come on up, Baxter…..group hug…"

Lindy laughed her lovely musical laugh as Baxter
stood on his back legs with his front paws around each

of them. Ricky sobered for a moment and looked into her eyes.

"We're happy....aren't we?"

"Yes.....we're very happy."

"You and me....and Baxter makes three." He kissed the tip of her nose as he said, "Feed me, woman. I'm starved."

\* \* \*

Liz came up behind Nick and put her arms around him.

"Christmas is a week away. I know it's not the same as last year, but are you planning on doing anything for the holiday?" She nibbled his ear while she asked.

"I don't know. I'm worried about Lindy and Ricky, but I also miss them. Christmas last year was really great.... wasn't it?"

"Yeah....it was."

"Do you think they're okay?"

"I'm betting they're okay. Ricky is very resourceful.... and they're both pretty smart. I say we just wait. They said they would come back when it was safe...so we wait for them."

"How will they know it's safe?" Nick asked her.

"Think about it. When they're eighteen. But...at any rate....I did buy them gifts for Christmas. We may have to have Christmas at a later date."

"Yeah, I bought them things, too....hoping that maybe...."

Nick's words were interrupted by the doorbell. Liz opened the door, knowing in advance that it was Angie and Ron Shultz.

"Nick, any word?"

"No. How about you, Ron? Anything?"

"No. I don't think they're looking too hard for either of the kids. The boys in the next township are focusing on Lindy's accusation and the trail of evidence she left. Believe me, if they can prove anything from what she left for them...that is what they will work on...not two runaway kids who aren't in any trouble."

\* \* \*

Loraine answered her front door and was taken by surprise to see two uniformed police officers filling up the entrance. A smaller gentleman wearing a suit stood in front of them. He was the spokesperson.

"Ma'am....is Nelson Sutter home?"

"Yes, he is." She looked to her left and called to him. "Nelson?"

Nelson sauntered out to the entrance foyer and was taken back by the sight of the police. "Can I help you gentlemen? Donation time?"

Not one of them smiled at Nelson's little joke.

"Nelson Sutter? I'm Detective Robert Bruno. You're under arrest for rape."

Loraine gasped. "Rape? Who? Nelson...what are they talking about?"

"I don't know, Loraine. They have the wrong guy."

One of the uniformed officers had Nelson's hands behind his back putting handcuffs on him while he read him his rights. Loraine felt helpless as she stood and watched.

"Should I call a lawyer?"

"Yeah....Loraine! Call a lawyer."

"I'll see you.....where?" She appealed to the spokesman.

Detective Bruno told her where they were going and she went to the telephone to call their lawyer. He agreed to meet her at the station where Nelson would be. She grabbed her coat and immediately drove there and parked. They had Nelson in an interrogation room when she got there, and she was escorted in. The detective was sitting across from him.

"Detective…what is this about?" She asked, obviously confused.

"Do you know a Belinda Riley?"

"Yes…of course….she was a foster child….living in our house. She ran away."

"Yes….she ran away. She left a long letter and evidence in her school locker…all incriminating your husband."

"I-I don't understand."

"Loraine, did you call our lawyer?" Nelson interrupted.

"Yes…I did. Now…what does Lindy have to do with any of this?"

"The girl left a letter with one of her teachers. Said she was running away because your husband was raping her….on the nights you worked late. In the note she said we could find some underwear with….your husband's semen on it. We did. One pair was torn…she said he tore them off of her."

"Loraine…it's a lie. You can't believe that…." Nelson interjected.

"And was my husband's semen on them?" She stared at the detective.

"Yes, Ma'am. I'm sorry."

"What else did Lindy say…in her letter?"

"That your husband threatened to do something to her if she told. And...also...she said to tell you she was sorry if this hurts you....she likes you...but your husband is a pig. We can let you read it...if you like."

"Yes. I would like to read it."

"Loraine...you don't want to read the lies of some teenaged girl. She probably wants money.....or something...."

"Shut up, Nelson." Loraine ordered. She couldn't look at him.

The detective opened a folder and took out the paper Lindy had turned in before she took off, and handed it to Loraine.

"Loraine...." Nelson attempted to distract her. She ignored him and continued to read. When she finished she handed it back to the detective without speaking. She sat for several minutes mentally digesting what she had read, and she knew.....Lindy was not a liar. Her husband violated that sweet girl. She stood up and reached for her coat that she had placed over the empty chair next to her.

"Loraine....where are you going?" Nelson's voice held alarm in it.

Without any warning, she turned and slapped him across the face—hard.

"You did it...didn't you? You raped that sweet child!"

"*No*....she's lying!"

"No...she's not a liar. You *raped* her! *Raped her!* She's right...you are a pig. I'll be getting my own lawyer...you *bastard*!" Loraine turned to the detective. "You might as well just keep him here…he no longer has a home. Good-bye, Nelson."

Loraine walked out of the room and closed the door behind her. She felt the sting of tears in her eyes, but they weren't for Nelson. They were for Lindy and for what she must have endured. She only wished Lindy would have come to her, but she understood why she didn't. She wished Lindy would come back, but she knew she wouldn't. She wished her well.

\* \* \*

Angie called Nick after eleven o'clock. He was just getting ready to go upstairs to bed when the phone rang. He ran to it, thinking it may be news about Ricky and Lindy.

"Nick…did you hear the news?"

"What news, Angie?"

"They arrested that Nelson guy…and charged him with rape."

"No shit? So the evidence checked out then?"

"I guess it did. Poor Lindy. It must have been awful for her."

"Yeah….I hope she's okay now. Both of them. Hey, thanks for letting me know. Good night Ange."

Nick debated calling Liz, but his thoughts were interrupted by the ringing phone. It was Liz. She had watched the eleven o'clock news, too.

\* \* \*

It was two days before Christmas. Nick's heart was not into it, but he decorated the windows just as Ricky had done last year. Liz was bringing a tree, convincing him that he should have it up just in case the kids showed up. He agreed to it, thinking that maybe they just might.

He doubted it. He had just plugged in the window lights when he heard the doorbell. He opened the door to a stranger—a young man in uniform.

"Uh, hi....I'm looking for my sister.....Lindy Riley...."

"You must be Chris."

"Yes....is she here?"

"Come on in. I've got a story to tell you."

He sat Chris down at the kitchen table, poured him a cup of coffee, and briefed him on the past year of Lindy's life. Chris was shocked, since Lindy had never said anything.

"Well, she didn't want you to be worried about anything here. She figured you had enough to worry about taking care of yourself. She told me that."

"So where is she now?"

"We don't know. She and Ricky took off."

"This guy was raping her?"

"Yes....he was arrested for it just yesterday."

"Lindy....my God....she was an innocent kid when I left. Now you tell me she's been beaten, shot, raped, and somewhere in between all of this, she became a mother?"

"Yeah, that's pretty much it in a nutshell. Poor kid. She is still so sweet. Chris, I love her like she were my own daughter. She's....very special."

"So what about this Ricky...your nephew. She did write to me about a boyfriend...Ricky...that was his name. What's he like?"

"Devoted. Devoted to her. They're devoted to each other. I never saw two young people more in love...."

"My little sister….in love. Hard for me to picture. So my dad is…in jail? For shooting Lindy?"

"Yep. He didn't mean to. It was supposed to be Ricky….but Lindy jumped in front of Ricky. Actually, I don't think your dad meant to shoot anybody. The gun went off. But it caused the death of Lindy and Ricky's son….so they arrested your dad and charged him with…murder…that changed to involuntary manslaughter."

Chris sat in silence, obviously not knowing what to say.

"So…Chris…are you home for good? If you are, Lindy wouldn't have to be in foster care, if we could find her, that is."

"No…I have to go back….but I will be out at the end of April. Then I plan on going to school."

"Good for you. I wish you had come home to better news…."

"It's okay….I probably shouldn't have left when I did. I saw how hard it was on everybody when my mother died. I should have been there….for Lindy especially."

"Well, you know what they say about hindsight…you did what you thought you had to do. Hey…listen….you're welcome to spend Christmas with us. We're having a hell of a feast for just four of us. Join us…please. I'm sure everyone would love to meet a relative of Lindy's. You would be the first."

"Thanks….maybe I will."

\* \* \*

It was Christmas Eve. Lindy and Ricky were curled up on the loveseat in front of the television, watching a Christmas special. Outside of the television, the only light in the room came from the tree lights. Baxter lay stretched out in front of the loveseat. Ricky was absently stroking Lindy's shoulder with his thumb. The ringing telephone shook the tranquility of the scene. Ricky and Lindy stared at each other for a moment.

"It has to be Sam, Honey." Ricky reached over and picked up the receiver.

"Merry Christmas, Rick! It's Sam and Renee."

"Hey! Merry Christmas to you. Enjoying your vacation?"

"Yep. How's my dog?"

"I think you mean Lindy's dog. He adopted her." Ricky laughed.

"Yeah, he's fickle like that. Everything okay?"

"Yeah. Everything is fine. You know....if I want to take Baxter out, he looks at Lindy first. I don't know if it's to see if she's going to go, too, or if he's asking her permission."

Sam laughed. "Hey, I got some news for you. That guy....was his last name Sutter?"

"Yeah...I think....why?"

"He was arrested on rape charges a couple of days ago. That story was on the news in Ohio. Said he raped a teenaged foster child that was living in his house. That would be Lindy?"

"Yeah.....it would. I'm glad to hear that."

"So let me say Merry Christmas to Lindy. I won't mention anything....that's your responsibility..."

"Okay." Ricky handed the phone to Lindy.

Lindy smiled and told Sam she hoped he was enjoying his vacation, and Merry Christmas. Yes, she loved his dog, and no, she wouldn't steal him away from them. She handed the phone to Ricky to hang it up, and caught the serious look on his face.

"What?"

"What do you mean 'what'?"

"I know that look, Ricky….so…what? What is it you're afraid to tell me?"

"I'm not afraid….I just don't want to spoil our evening."

"Oh…now I know you're going to tell me….what is it?"

"They arrested Nelson Sutter for rape a couple of days ago. Charged him with raping a foster child living in his home."

"That's me they're talking about! They got him! Merry Christmas, Ricky! That's good news. Why do you think I wouldn't want to hear that?"

"It's not that I didn't think you'd want to hear it…. it's just that…you just stopped crying and writhing in your sleep a couple of nights ago. I just don't want that to start again."

"I didn't know I did that. Why didn't you wake me up?"

"I just……held you….and told you I loved you…..it seemed to calm you down."

Lindy looked at Ricky appreciatively. "I've put you through some real emotional stuff over the past year…. haven't I?"

"Nothing that I regret. I'd do it all again for you. We kind of put each other through stuff….but…you know what? We stayed strong and became stronger….agreed?"

"Yeah….agreed. We've come a long way in a year…. haven't we?"

"I'd say it's more like…we've been a long way in a year. A lot has happened."

"I hope we're over the bad parts. Maybe we can focus on good things happening to us from now on. Ya think?" She twisted around and smiled at him. Their eyes connected and they felt the electricity again. "Do you think Baxter would mind if we were to go over to the…bed?" She whispered.

"Yeah…he would….but let's do it anyway."

\* \* \*

Nick and Liz tried to create a festive mood for everyone on Christmas day. Lindy's brother had agreed to join them for dinner, and Liz was looking forward to meeting him. Angie and Ron Shultz would be showing up for dinner at any moment, along with Ron's daughter Cindy. It wouldn't be the same for any of them without Lindy and Ricky, but they were all going to make an effort. Angie and Ron were now considered a couple, and she had managed to get him to go to midnight mass with her on Christmas Eve. Nick laughed and sang 'The things we do for love' when he heard that.

The doorbell brought Chris, holding a bottle of wine and a tin of cookies. Nick greeted him warmly, silently wishing Lindy could be there to see him. When dinner was ready, they all sat around the dining room table and said grace. Cindy added to the prayer by asking God to keep Lindy and Ricky safe. Angie dabbed her eyes with her napkin. The conversation turned to where they might be.

"I've done some checking. Lindy didn't take any of her money that may have been easy to trace. She has a debit card with quite a bit of backing behind it, but she didn't take any of the real money."

"Lindy has money?" Liz asked.

"Lindy has lots of money….and there will be much more when she turns eighteen. Our grandfather took care of us….particularly Lindy. She was his favorite."

"I had no idea. Now I know why she didn't bat an eye when she saw the cost of the ball gown for the Christmas party last year. She just paid for it before I got a chance to offer."

"Our grandfather owned everything around here at one time. The land that the hospital sits on was his. He sold it to them for an enormous amount. That's why there is a plaque with his name on it in the front lobby….. William Stockwell….I'm sure you've seen it."

"Yeah….but I never made the connection." Nick spoke up.

"Because our name is Riley….My mother was a Stockwell. The only child of William and Belinda Stockwell…..thus Lindy's name, Belinda."

"So does Lindy have access to any of this money?"

"No…only the money for her expenses, which is probably a sizeable amount….and some emergency fund my grandfather set up for her. Only she knew how to get to it. She was to use it if it was a life and death emergency…. and I don't know where the money is….or how she would get to it."

"Running from a rapist would definitely be considered a life and death emergency. I'll just bet that's what they left with. I'm kind of relieved. At least I can believe that they aren't sleeping under some bridge out in the cold." Nick expelled air from his lungs, definitely feeling a weight being lifted off of his shoulders.

"Yeah, grampa left us very well off. He hated my father, but he loved our mother and he loved us. The house....where we lived....is Lindy's. My parents never owned it. It becomes Lindy's when she turns eighteen. There is another one that was left to me. It's rented out for now. There is other real estate that is handled by an executor in my grandfather's attorney's office. Grampa was a brilliant man....he made sure that we would never want for anything. Money will always trickle to us, and what doesn't trickle will always be working to make more. Brilliant."

"I should say." Nick laughed. "I'm totally impress-ed."

"Uh, I went to see my father yesterday. He's really sick over what he did. You have no idea how much he always loved Lindy. He loved us both....but Lindy....well, I'm sure you already know that special quality she has. She's so endearing...goes right to your heart. Everybody has always seen that about her."

"Yeah....I know exactly what you are talking about. We all feel that way about her." Liz told him.

"I just can't figure out what happened. Why he turned his back on her...when he loved her so much." Chris sat at the table pondering his own questions. "Anyway, the cookies are from Diane, my dad's girlfriend. When I left the jail I went to see her. She said to say Merry Christmas to all of you...and....I guess she didn't know about Lindy running away, did she?"

"No....I didn't call her. I guess I should have."

"Anyway, she cried.....hysterically. I told my dad and he looked like he was going to cry. He blames himself for all of it."

"Sorry to say this, Chris....but so do I." Nick looked Chris square in the eye. "So do I."

# Chapter 46

$\mathcal{S}$am turned into the driveway in time to see a yellow streak flying after an orange round object—a Frisbee. He and Renee got out and watched for a few minutes. Lindy and Ricky were throwing the Frisbee and Baxter was trying to retrieve it from them. He was barking and they were laughing. It looked like such a normal scene that Sam almost hated to disturb them. He quietly walked toward the activity. Lindy spotted him coming.

"Baxter, look who's here."

Baxter looked to his right and then his left, and then looked at Lindy quizzically.

"You forgot to look behind you, Dummy!"

Baxter ran toward Sam when he heard his voice, then stopped and looked back toward Lindy. Sam laughed.

"Now he's really confused…torn between us."

"Hi, Sam." Lindy ran alongside Baxter to greet him. "Baxter is a great dog. We had so much fun. How was your trip?"

"Long. And I'm glad you and Baxter bonded. I knew he was in good hands. How did you kids make out?"

Ricky joined them in time to hear the question. "Good, actually. I got a job at the hardware store and worked through Christmas. We had a nice holiday...just the three of us."

"Yeah, Santa Claus brought Baxter things." Lindy chimed in.

"Is that so? Well, he must have been a good dog." Baxter heard the term and barked, causing the three of them to laugh.

"Need any help carrying things in?" Ricky fell into step with Sam as Lindy went around to the other side of the car to help Renee.

"Oh, and happy new year, by the way. What did you kids do for New Year's Eve?"

"Watched the ball drop. Oh, and wait 'til you hear Baxter sing!"

"I can't wait for that." Renee laughed.

"The two of them had me laughing so hard my side hurt. They sing a duet together." Ricky informed them.

They quickly got the car unloaded so Lindy and Baxter could perform. Lindy sang and Baxter threw his head back and howled in time to her singing. Sam, Renee, and Ricky laughed until they cried. After wiping his eyes, Sam had an announcement.

"Kids, you don't have to leave. Ricky, I have lots of work to do around here so if you two want to stay on, I could use your help with repairs and maintenance. What do you say? Our season opens in May, so maybe if you could help out, you can stay until then."

"Lindy?" Ricky asked.

"I'm for it, if you are, Ricky. We won't be eighteen until April."

"Your birthdays are close to each other?" Renee asked.

"Ricky's is the fourth and mine is the fourteenth of April. It's up to you, Ricky."

"Well, then….it's settled. We stay until we are eighteen…..and married. Nobody is going to separate us again."

"Ricky….did you just propose to me?" Lindy asked.

"Uh, yeah….I guess I did. Lindy? Will you marry me? After the fourteenth of April?"

"Why I'd be delighted." She answered in her best southern accent.

\* \* \*

The holidays ended and Chris left to go to his next and final assignment in North Carolina. He would be separating from the service at the end of April, and going home for good. He was extremely disappointed that he didn't see Lindy, and he only hoped that she would be back when he was discharged. Ricky's family seemed like good people, and he was glad they all seemed to care for Lindy. He prayed that she was all right and that Ricky, the boyfriend was watching out for her. He was still a little surprised that his baby sister had actually had a child, and saddened that the little boy didn't live. Lindy must have been through hell in the past year. He should have been there, he guessed. What was their father thinking? Why did he abandon Lindy emotionally? Chris might never know the answer, but the question would always be there.

Life for everybody in the family returned to normal— minus Lindy and Ricky. Without them, Nick doubted that life could ever be normal. He had hoped that they would contact him over the holidays, but he supposed that Liz was right—they wouldn't return until they were of age to manage their own affairs. 'Lindy and Ricky will make sure nobody can ever separate them again,' Nick thought to himself as he drove to the lab the day after New Year's Day. He wondered what they were doing at that moment.

\* \* \*

Ricky and Lindy were eating a breakfast, cooked by Ricky. He still loved spoiling Lindy with all sorts of delicious dishes. His dad would have been proud of him; he knew. Not only was he treating his woman like a queen, but he was working hard as well. He started helping Sam do repairs on a couple of units, and they planned on replacing a hot water heater in another room today.

"So what are you going to do today?" He asked her.

"Renee and I are going food shopping. Want anything special?"

"Yeah….how much money do we have?"

"Lots. What do you want?"

"Stuff to make spaghetti sauce…let me write down what I need, okay?"

Lindy got up and got a pen and writing paper, and set it down in front of him.

"Ricky, I was thinking…..we should learn to drive."

"Well….I know how to drive…but I can't until I'm eighteen. That's when my probation ends. Besides, what do we drive?"

"First of all…I don't know how to drive….and I want to learn. Second of all…we have lots of money. We could buy a car."

"You keep saying that. Exactly how much money do we have?"

Lindy got up again and went to her side of the dresser they shared, where she pulled out a manila envelope. She reached into the envelope and pulled out a couple of stacks of bills.

"I think this is enough to buy a car."

"Baby, there's fifteen thousand dollars here. Where did you get it?"

"I told you I had lots of money. Remember when I had Lukas take me to the bank before we left? Well, I went to my grampa's and my safe deposit box. He left this there for me in case of an emergency. Running from that pig would be considered an emergency...don't you think? Anyway...I only took half of it. We have this much left in there. I already had six hundred dollars in my suitcase."

"Wow....why didn't you tell me?"

"Because I didn't want you to go all macho on me. Whatever I have is yours, too, but I didn't want you to get mad that I had so much. I was kind of embarrassed that I had that much....considering you have been paying for almost everything. But, anyway....we could buy a car with this...right? Then we could drive back home instead of taking a bus. We would have our very own first car. What do you think?"

Ricky laughed. "I think you're incredible. And, yeah...let's see about getting you a license. I can get mine right after my birthday. Ask Renee if she'll teach you to drive."

He got up and kissed her. "Gotta go. Love you."

\* \* \*

Lindy and Renee went grocery shopping late in the morning. The weather was turning very cold and wintry, and there was sleet expected before late afternoon. Renee agreed to teach Lindy to drive but not while there was the chance of ice or sleet on the roads. Renee explained that they had no winter road maintenance like the northern states allotted for during the winter. They got very little snow or ice on the roads, so when it happened, they just stayed off of the roads until it cleared up.

"You have to get a permit, Dear. We'll go get you one. Oh, wait….you need proof of age…."

"I have my birth certificate with me. My mom always said to keep it handy…so I have it with me."

"Well, good…then we'll go when the sleet has passed. Maybe tomorrow."

Lindy smiled at her. "Thanks. I want to buy a car so we can drive home instead of taking a bus. We've acquired more things, so taking a bus would be…a pain."

Renee smiled back at Lindy. She was so glad she and Sam agreed to let them stay on. Sam was sure enjoying Ricky's company as well as his help. They had been a big help by agreeing to take care of Baxter while she and Sam were gone. The kennel wanted seven hundred fifty dollars to keep him, so letting the kids stay during that time gave them much more spending power on their trip.

"Oh…don't be surprised if you're invited to dinner some night this week. Ricky gave me his list of things to buy for his spaghetti sauce, so he'll be making it. I need a can of beer….for the sauce. His sauce is terrific."

"Ricky certainly is mature for his age, isn't he?"

"Yes…..he is. He saw a lot of….things…when he lived in Chicago. It made him the way he is….plus, his dad did a lot of things with him. Talked to him all the time…telling him what is right and what isn't. His dad was to him like my mother was to me. And....he misses his dad as much as I miss my mother."

"You two are perfect together...but you know that; don't you?"

"Yeah....we knew from the moment we met."

# Chapter 47

$\mathcal{L}$indy ran up the stairs and burst into their motel room.

"I passed my test! Ricky, I passed my driver's test!"

Ricky was lying under the covers, with a blanket wrapped around him. He was shivering. "That's good, Baby. I'm glad."

Lindy heard the quivering in his weak voice. "Hey…. what's that matter?"

She approached the bed and put her hand on his forehead. He was burning up. She quickly left the room and ran down to the office. Sam was inside.

"Sam, Ricky is really sick."

"I know. I told him to go to bed."

"Do you have anything for fever? I notice he has a cough, too."

"No….but you and Renee should go get something, because whatever he has, I'm getting it, too. I'm not feeling so well."

Renee came out into the office, already wearing her coat. "Lindy, let's go to the drugstore and get some supplies for the sick."

Lindy was frantic. For as long as they had been together, Ricky had never been sick. She bought everything she could find that might work to make him better. They stopped at the store and bought some tea and lemon, some chicken soup, and a bottle of rum. Renee promised to give Lindy some for Ricky's tea. When they returned home, Lindy ran back upstairs to Ricky. He was sleeping, so she left him alone, but stayed nearby.

Ricky awoke after dark, still burning with fever. Lindy heated up the soup and made him some tea, added the lemon, and then the rum that Renee had shared with her. She spoon-fed him a little of the soup, but he didn't have much appetite. He drank the tea, and she gave him some cough medicine. He fell back asleep, after she covered him with yet another blanket. Lindy picked up the remote to the television, but set it back down. The noise may awaken him. She looked out of the window and saw Renee walking Baxter, so she went out to walk with them.

"How's Ricky?"

"Sick. How's Sam?"

"Sick."

"Do you think we'll get it next?"

"I hope not, but if we do....we already have the supplies."

"I guess that's true. Did Sam eat?"

"Not very much."

"No...Ricky didn't either. Ricky has never been sick for as long as I've known him. This....scares me."

"He'll be okay, Honey. This is just a flu bug. Just keep him covered and keep the tea concoction coming....he'll be fine."

When Lindy got back upstairs, she immediately went to the bed to check on Ricky. His forehead was still very hot. He stirred and opened his glassy-looking eyes.

"Can I have something to drink?"

"Whatever you want. Juice? Water? More tea?"

"All of it. I'm just so hot…."

Lindy went to the kitchenette and opened the refrigerator. She returned with a glass of water and a glass of orange juice, with a straw in each glass.

"I have water on for tea. Are you hungry at all? Want more soup? Toast?"

"Toast would be nice." His voice was raspy and his cough seemed to be getting worse.

"Okay…..toast then." She quickly got up and put two slices of bread into the toaster and got out the butter. "Do you want jelly or cinnamon on it?"

"Cinnamon….please."

"You got it."

She sat beside him while he forced a couple of halves of toast down past his sore throat. He couldn't eat any more, but he drank the rest of the juice and some water, and then sipped the spiked tea.

"Is there booze in here?"

"Yes…..Renee gave me some for you."

He managed a weak smile. "Thank you, Baby."

"For what?"

"For taking care of me like this."

"Don't mention it. You've done this for me a couple of times, as I recall." She smiled back at him. "And…. who knows? In three days Renee and I may end up sick like this, too."

"I hope not."

\* \* \*

Ricky and Sam recovered and were almost back to normal within a week. Lindy stayed at Ricky's side and nursed him back to health during that time. One night during his illness, Ricky awakened to find Lindy sponging him with warm water that smelled like alcohol. It felt good to him, but he wasn't sure why she was doing it. His fever broke that night. Neither Renee nor Lindy caught it from them, which was a relief to all four of them. Sam and Ricky went back to doing repairs on the motel, and Renee and Lindy resumed their daily routines. Lindy had begun working on embroidery to frame and hang on the wall. She envisioned it hanging in her room in her house back in Pennsylvania. Lately she had been thinking of the house a lot. In just a little more than two months she would be eighteen and the house would legally be hers. She planned on moving back into it with Ricky right beside her. They had already discussed it, and decided it was the right decision, since they could both go to school and not have to worry about rent. Utilities—yes, but not rent. Between the two of them, they had enough income to cover expenses, and utilities, so they weren't concerned about them. She was working on her embroidery when Ricky came in the door.

"What's that you're doing?" He looked over her shoulder. "Hey….that's pretty."

"Thanks. Are you done for the day?"

"Yeah. Sam wants to know if you want to go car hunting. He's willing to take us."

"Okay….now?"

"Yeah….let's go."

\* \* \*

Lindy drove back to the motel in the almost new silver Toyota. It was five years old, but had low mileage. Sam checked it out for her, and told her it was in good shape, and the engine was clean. The dealership registered it for her and collected the money for the car and the registration and taxes. She purchased a six month insurance plan, and she was all set to go. She drove and Ricky rode in the passenger seat, just a little nervous since he had never ridden with Lindy as the driver before. He had to admit that she was a good driver, though. He noticed that she hadn't taken the smile off of her face yet.

"You look happy."

"Ricky...it's our first car....our first purchase together....yeah...I'm happy...and excited."

He grinned back at her. "Good. You're a pretty good driver....you know that?"

"Thanks. That's what the trooper who rode with me when I took my test said."

"Did you see that salesman's face when you pulled out all that cash? I'm glad Sam told him you cleaned out your savings account, or he would have called the police, I think. He was pretty surprised to see all that money."

"Yeah....I noticed. You don't think he will...call anyway....do you?"

"And have to give it back? No....I don't think so. He just made a good day's wages off of you....he's happy. He'll probably write it up so it looks like he sold it for less, and then keep a little extra for himself.....but that's not our concern."

Lindy pulled into the motel parking lot and eased into a space just under the location of their room. They waved to Sam and thanked him for taking them, and went upstairs to celebrate in their own way—by making love.

\* \* \*

The temperatures were warming a little. It was February, just one day before Valentine's Day. Sam suggested that he and Ricky take a little trip to purchase Valentine's gifts.

"I just usually do the flowers and candy thing. Renee appreciates it and says that's what the day is meant to bring....flowers and candy. So....want to?"

"Yeah....sure. I was just thinking about last year. I got Lindy red roses, and a gold locket, shaped like a heart. She still wears it. Our pictures are in it. I cooked her dinner....and...then we took a walk in the snow. It was really coming down, as I recall. She gave me a framed picture of us....in a heart....and some art supplies that she knew I wanted. You know.....I love her more than I did last year....and I didn't think that was possible. My love is growing....not diminishing...like people said it would. She's my most favorite person in the whole world....and I never get tired of being with her. She's all I need...you know? I don't need guys to hang out with...or other girls....just her."

"Yeah....you got it like I always had it for Renee. My one and only....all I ever needed. That's what drew me to you....and that's why I was so willing to help you out. You're for real....and what you feel is genuine. I wish you both the best....always. So....roses, huh? Well...this place has roses...so let's get some."

* * *

Nick answered the door and recognized the detective who was working on the rape case. He invited him in.

"Dr. Bazario, have you heard from either of the two kids?"

"No....I wish."

"Without her….Belinda, I mean….we're going to have to let Sutter go. No victim to testify…"

"I would have thought her letter would have been enough. I mean….she's a minor…don't they usually make concessions for minors not to testify?"

"Yeah…in the courtroom….but the minor still has to talk to a district attorney in most cases."

Nick sighed. "I wish I knew how to get a hold of them. I honestly do not know where they are. I pray every night that they're okay…"

"I'm sure you do. Well, if you hear anything….call me."

"Yeah, I sure will."

Nick sat down after the detective left. He only hoped that he would hear from the kids before the police had to let that son of a bitch go.

\* \* \*

Ray Riley sat in the prison yard smoking a cigarette as he stared at the man leaning against the fence on the other side of the yard. It was him; Ray was sure. The bastard that raped Lindy was only a quarter of a football field away. It was all he could do to keep from running over there and beating the crap out of him. A voice pulled him out of his thoughts.

"Hey, Riley….why you look so pissed?"

"See that guy over there? Leaning against the fence?"

"Yeah….that's Nelson somebody-or-other."

"That's what I thought."

"Why? You know him? Want him to come over here?"

"NO! I mean…..no…I don't want him to come over here."

"Who is he to you, then?"

"He…he's the guy…..that raped my daughter…."

"Oooh…..well, I tell you what…..I get the word out. He be dealt with."

"I don't want him dead. I want my daughter to have her day in court….when she comes back. That bastard made her run away….but she'll come back….I know she will."

"Well, we just fuck him up a little….okay?"

"Yeah….okay." Ray produced a hard thin-lipped smile. "That'll work."

\* \* \*

Nelson couldn't open his eyes. Every part of him hurt. He had to think for a moment, and then he remembered. The beating. And the rape. He remembered walking back from the showers and hearing a noise. He stopped to listen and then WHAM! He was hit from behind and dragged. There were four of them. They slammed his face into a wall, almost knocking him unconscious. He fought back, he remembered. One of them hit him in the face—hard, and then in the gut. He doubled over, and then took a couple of punches to the kidneys. He almost lost consciousness again, when he felt them taking down his pants. He began to fight again, but was rendered helpless by another blow to the side of his head. That was when the four of them raped him. He only remembered the first, since he actually did lose consciousness, but he remembered that first guy asking him how *he* liked it. That was when he knew—this happened to him because of Lindy.

He could only see a sliver of light through one of his eyes. He listened for sounds and realized that he must be in the hospital. He tried to raise his arm and realized he was handcuffed to the bed. He felt someone near him.

"Who's there?" He asked.

"Mister Sutter….I'm your nurse. My name is Annie. You're awake. Let me call the doctor."

"Where am I?"

"You're in University Hospital. You had a pretty bad accident."

"So that's what they're calling it, huh?"

"Yes, Sir. That's what the chart says. I'm going to go get the doctor now."

Nelson lay there unable to move. He was in more pain than he had ever been in his life. 'They're calling this an accident.' He thought to himself. 'What…I slipped and fell and landed on some guy's willie? That's what they want this hospital to believe?'

His thoughts were interrupted by a hand around his wrist. They were taking his pulse, and a thermometer was popped into his mouth. It hurt. He felt a cold stethoscope being pressed to his chest, and then a cuff put around his arm. He just lay there in too much pain to resist. A male voice spoke to him.

"Mister Sutter, how do you feel?"

"Like….I washit by….a…train."

"No doubt….You suffered some pretty severe injuries. You'll be fine, but you're going to hurt for quite awhile. We're going to keep you in here for about five to seven days. You should be feeling better by then."

The doctor wrote on the chart and then left the room. Nelson felt a needle going into his arm and welcomed the blanket of fog that followed.

* * *

In South Carolina, the winter was evolving into spring. The days were mild, and the winds were warm, and some of the trees had begun to bud. March, and its gusty winds, had passed. Ricky was about to celebrate his eighteenth birthday; and with the turning of eighteen, he would be off probation and able to get a driver's license. Lindy was busy in their little kitchenette, baking him a birthday cake while he was off with Sam picking up some things from the hardware store. She had just put the finishing touches of the decorations on the cake when Renee appeared at the door.

"Want to go shopping for Ricky? I know where there's a men's store."

"I'll get my jacket." Lindy answered.

Renee drove to a small strip mall several miles from the motel. There were ten stores linked together with a small parking lot in front. One of the stores was indeed, a men's clothing store, offering clothes for all occasions. Lindy looked for some shorts and tees for Ricky, and found a couple of nice ones. Then she spied the light grey three-piece suit. Ricky would look wonderful in it. She looked for Renee.

"Renee, look at this suit over here. Ricky would look so good in it….and if he's serious about getting married…. then he would need a suit to wear….right? I mean…..I would like to have….not a wedding….but at least some pictures……and I would want Ricky to wear a suit." Lindy pulled Renee by the arm to show her the suit.

"That's a good-looking suit. Do you know his size?"

"Yep." Lindy was already checking the size on the pants. "These are right, and the jacket looks right, too."

Renee reached up and took the jacket off of the hanger to see what size it was. Lindy tried it on.

"I think this is right. At least this is how his clothes fit me when I put them on."

A store salesman approached them. "Can I help you?"

Lindy smiled at him. "I want to get this suit for my......fiancé...but I'm not sure if it's the right size. I mean...it's close....and it might be....but...."

"But it has to be perfect....right?" He finished for her.

"Yes."

"Well....we do offer free alterations....so if something needed to be altered....he could bring it back and it would be done for free."

"Cool! Renee, I'm going to get it."

Renee smiled as she watched Lindy's face light up and become animated.

"Can you wrap it? I want it to be a surprise......for his birthday."

"Certainly.....I'll get my wife to do it right now. We have boxes big enough....."

He disappeared through the doorway in back of the store, while Lindy and Renee waited.

"I have no idea what I'll be wearing.....but at least Ricky will look good."

"Let me think about it, Lindy. I may have an idea for you."

"I have a dress with me. It's a nice dress, so I may wear that. It's blue and white….that's appropriate….isn't it?"

* * *

Angie awoke crying around two in the morning. Ron rolled over and raised his head to see her face.

"What's wrong?"

"I just had a bad dream about….Ricky."

"What was it?"

"I don't remember, exactly." Angie's throat felt swollen as she tried to speak. "It….it was dark….and…he….he was lying there…..so….cold. He had…..Lindy's hair…. her hair was in his hands…..but she….she wasn't there." Angie began to shiver.

"Come here…..it was just a dream." Ron pulled her close to him and tightened his arms around her. "They're fine, Angie….both of them. I'll just bet we're going to see them real soon."

"Ricky turned eighteen today. Eighteen. I may never see him again." She cried.

"Of course you will, Honey. Of course you will."

"I said some…..really mean things….about Lindy. Ricky may never forgive me for them. Sometimes….I feel like he left….just to punish me….for saying those things. I mean…" Angie sat up. "Ron, who would imagine that two people that young could really be in love? They're still children! But….Ron….they *are* really in love….I know it now. I….I just hope….they are okay." She fell against him, crying.

"Me, too, Angie. We have to believe they're okay. And Ricky didn't leave to punish you….he left to protect Lindy. That's very noble and honorable of him. You should be proud." Ron stroked her hair and held her until she calmed down.

* * *

It was Lindy's eighteenth birthday. Ricky surprised her with breakfast in bed before he left to go help Sam. After they finished the work they had planned for the day, Sam had promised Ricky that he would take him for his driver's exam and then they would go shopping for a birthday present for Lindy. Ricky planned on surprising her with his driver's license, and then surprising her with the engagement ring he purchased when he and Sam were out buying supplies earlier in the week. Since they planned on returning to Pennsylvania shortly after the day of their wedding ceremony, Ricky took a chance and withdrew some of his money from his investment account that his father had set up. Not long before he and Lindy left, he had arranged for those monthly checks he received to be directly deposited into his account. He still had a debit card for that account, but was not sure he could safely use it without being traced. Tomorrow he and Lindy would go to apply for their marriage license, and get married on Saturday. Sam and Renee told them they could use the room that was adjacent to the office for the ceremony. They used that room for continental breakfasts during their season, and it was empty at the moment. Sam called his pastor to see if he would do the honors of performing the ceremony, and he said he would be delighted.

Renee was very fond of both Lindy and Ricky. She had a few surprises of her own. During the evenings she had spent her time decorating the room with flowers and put a wedding tablecloth on the table in there. She also had a very special surprise for Lindy. She had taken apart her white wedding dress and created a dress for Lindy. It was simple, but elegant, and very up to the minute in style. She felt sure Lindy would look lovely in it. She took a lace curtain, and by adding a couple of stitches, had turned it into a beautifully designed veil. The night before the wedding, she would make a two-tiered wedding cake, perfect for the small wedding. She and Sam would stand up as witnesses for them, and the hardware store owner, Mr. Carter would be there with his wife, who agreed to take pictures. Renee sighed. She even invited the mailman and his wife, just so there would be enough people to make a small reception. It would be beautiful even if it was small. The love those two had for each other would make it beautiful. She came out of her thoughts and put her jacket on to take Baxter for a walk. She planned on getting Lindy to walk with her and then come in to see the dress. She hoped she liked it.

* * *

Speechless, Lindy stared at the dress. Her eyes were shining with tears.

"Oh, Renee…..it's…..beautiful! Are you sure? That you want me to have it? I mean…..it must mean so much to you….."

"Lindy….if I didn't want you to have it, I wouldn't have remodeled it and altered it to fit you. Come on….. try it on."

Lindy quickly removed her sweatshirt and sweatpants and her sneakers and reached for the dress. Renee helped her slip it on over her head and zipped it up for her. She turned Lindy to face the mirror and Lindy gasped.

"So…..what do ya think?"

"I-I don't know what to say….Renee, it's beautiful…. and it's a perfect fit. How did you do this?"

Renee laughed and then smiled at her. "I've never been a bad seamstress….I've sewn all my life. Honey, it looks perfect on you…..but….that's not all. Wait here."

Renee disappeared through a doorway and returned quickly, holding the lacey veil. She positioned it on Lindy's head and turned her toward the mirror once again. Lindy's gasp said it all.

"Good? Huh? What do you think, Lin?"

"Oh….it's so….perfect."

"Okay….now we'll do your hair up…..with some wisps hanging down framing your face. You'll get dressed down here on Saturday….this will be a surprise for Ricky. Don't tell him about the dress…..we'll surprise him. I mean….. he may love you….but seeing what a pretty package he's getting never hurts."

Renee helped Lindy take the dress off over her head and then she hung it up. Lindy quickly got dressed, but not before Renee saw the scars on her torso. They weren't terrible, since they had faded somewhat, but it was sad to see such a beautiful girl scarred like that.

"Now…..we have to think of other things. Your dress is taken care of….but now….let's see. We have the mailman and his wife, Mister and Missus Carter, me and Sam, you and Ricky, the pastor and his wife…..we have to think of a luncheon of some sort. What do you and Ricky want for food? Never mind…..I'll take care of it. I know. You're going to have a nice wedding….small, but nice."

Lindy smiled at Renee. "I don't know how I can ever thank you enough. You and Sam have been…. wonderful….like family to us."

"Honey, that first night you two showed up….well, I looked at Sam and asked him if you two reminded him of anybody. You two are us…..thirty-some-odd years ago. The love, the passion, the adoration…….we had it all…. and still do. You and Ricky just brought our youth to the surface again…..so this wedding is our pleasure."

Lindy couldn't have asked for a better birthday. Ricky's special birthday breakfast, and then the wedding dress from Renee made her day wonderful. Ricky found a little restaurant where he planned on taking her when he was done working for the day. He had a special speech planned for her before he gave her the ring. He knew she was not expecting a ring, and he also knew that to her an expensive ring was not important; and that was one of the reasons he loved her so much.

Ricky bolted up the steps and into the room as soon as he and Sam got back from their shopping trip. Lindy was working on her embroidery when he rushed through the door.

"Baby, I'm taking you to dinner. I found a nice little place that is open until ten tonight, so let's get ready and go. You'll love the place. It reminds me of that place Uncle Nick took us for your seventeenth birthday."

"Okay….sounds great. Casual?"

"Yeah…..and….by the way…." He slipped behind her and held his license in front of her. "I'm driving."

Lindy squealed. "You passed your test! Cool! Ricky…. think about it. We have accomplished so much on our own. We got licenses, we got a car, and we have maintained a decent life for the past five months….well, with the help of Sam and Renee, anyway. Uncle Nick, Aunt Liz, and your mom should be proud of us…"

"We should be able to tell them everything in about a week, I guess." He kissed her cheek. "Gotta shower.... I smell like caulking compound. Be out in a couple of minutes."

\* \* \*

The restaurant was small and dimly lit, with very little noise since there were only a few people dining at the time. Ricky imagined that in the peak of the tourist season every booth and table was filled from open to close. He and Lindy were eating the seafood they had ordered and exclaiming how delicious everything tasted. The waitress removed their empty plates and brought them coffee and dessert menus to ponder over.

"Go ahead, Babe....order some dessert. I'm looking at that caramel and nuts thing myself."

"I'm eying the cheesecake with cherries.....so let's go for it. That way, I can taste yours." She laughed.

After the ordered desserts were placed in front of them, Ricky stared at Lindy, looking very sober.

"Lindy....you know....before I met you....when I still lived in Chicago....I was a bad-assed punk. I was rude, crude, and I had no respect for any of the girls I knew. Then I moved in with Uncle Nick.....and I met you. You...." Ricky smiled at her. "You were so....decent and sweet.....and so much like an angel......anyway....I guess I was yours from the moment we met."

"I felt that way, too." Lindy smiled back at him.

"Well....remember that weekend when Uncle Nick went toNew York?"

"You mean the weekend I got pregnant with Nicholas?"

"Yeah…..that weekend. Well, that first night when we went to sleep…..I put my arm around you and fell asleep…..when I woke up in the morning my arm was still around you."

"I remember…." Lindy smiled at him.

"Well, Honey……I decided that weekend…..that no matter where I went in life…or what I did….or what I became……I knew….that I wanted to fall asleep every night….and wake up every morning….with my arm around you."

"And that's okay by me. I love you so much." Lindy's voice was husky with emotion.

"Anyway, Babe….I know we talked about getting married, and we are…on Saturday. But I never really made it official…never really asked you formally." Ricky grinned at her. "Now….here's where it gets good." He laughed and slid out of his chair, and down on one knee.

"Ricky…."

"Will you marry me, Lindy?" He had the opened ring box ready in his hand, as he held it out to her.

Lindy gasped in surprise, tears already forming in the corners of her eyes. "Oh, Ricky…..Ricky…..yes……YES! Yes, I will marry you!"

They didn't realize that they held the attention of the entire patronage and wait-staff of the restaurant until they heard the applause from everybody as Ricky slid the ring onto Lindy's finger. Surprised, Lindy looked around and saw the smiles on everybody's faces. At that moment, the whole world seemed to approve of their love. Ricky held her face in his hands as he wiped away the tears with his thumbs. He kissed her lightly.

"I love you.....with all my heart and soul......I love you......and I always will."

"I feel that way, too, Ricky......I always will. Oh God... this ring....is so...beautiful. I......I didn't expect it."

"I know.....that's why you deserve it."

The waitress brought their check to the table, and a man stopped and picked it up.

"If I don't pay this check, my wife will never forgive me. She thought that was the most romantic display of love she has ever seen. I don't let her get out very much." He winked at them when he said it. "Anyway..... congratulations. You make a fine-looking couple....and your dinner is on me. Don't even try to argue about it...... because I won't take no for an answer." He added when Ricky began to protest.

# Chapter 48

$\mathcal{L}$indy sat still as Renee piled her hair on top of her head, and curled the wisps that fell down with a curling iron.

"You're gorgeous. Now….just a little bit of lipstick…." Renee spoke as she applied a little pink lipstick to Lindy's lips. "Perfect. Now let's get the dress on. I can hear Ricky and Sam out in the lobby right now."

Lindy slipped the dress over her head and slipped her feet into the white shoes she and Renee found the day before when they were out shopping for wedding napkins and paper plates. They hadn't thought about shoes until they passed a shoe store. It was then that Lindy remembered that she had no shoes to wear with the wedding dress. Inside the shoe store, they found the perfect pair of white shoes in Lindy's size and purchased them. Lindy only hoped that they wouldn't hurt her feet.

She sat back down while Renee fastened the veil onto the crown of her head and then stared at herself in the mirror. For the first time in her life she thought she really looked beautiful. She smiled up at Renee. It was just about three o'clock and time for the ceremony.

"I have butterflies."

"I'll bet. Excited?"

"Uh-huh. He's so…..Ricky is wonderful. I couldn't do better."

"Yeah…..he's so mature for his age, too. He even looks older than he is. I think that constant five o'clock shadow is sexy."

"Me, too." Lindy laughed up at Renee. "I think he's sexy….every part of him."

"Well……I'm glad of that. Ready? Let me go see if everything is in place and ready for you. Wait right here."

Renee ran out into the lobby area and Lindy stood up and looked at herself in the dress from all angles. She approved of what she saw. She was glowing. This was right; this was how it was supposed to be. The two of them belonged together forever.

Renee slipped back into the room. "All set. Now…I walk out first….and when you hear the music for you…. just start out. Lindy….look at me."

Lindy stared at Renee for a moment.

"Lindy….love each other. Love each other forever…. no matter what. Nothing will ever be as important as the love you share. And…." Tears welled up in Renee's eyes. "Don't forget me and Sam. We are very fond of both of you."

"How could we ever forget you?" Lindy smiled at Renee and kissed her cheek.

The musical sounds from the old upright piano started. Renee turned and began to walk into the room designated for the ceremony. The reverend himself was playing the piano as Renee walked across the small room. Then the reverend went into the traditional wedding march, and

Lindy came through the door. Renee watched Ricky's face turn from expectation to adoration as Lindy walked up and took her place beside him.

The ceremony was short and simple. Ricky and Lindy repeated their vows and then the reverend gave Ricky permission to kiss his bride. Those who were present applauded them and threw rice. Ricky and Lindy were husband and wife. Lindy was both surprised and thrilled by the small double-tiered white wedding cake that sat in the middle of the decorated table where Renee had placed trays of food. Everyone took pictures with the promise of getting them developed before Ricky and Lindy left to go back up north. Reverend Taylor's wife took some pictures and promised to have them printed by the next day. Ricky and Lindy posed for pictures and then some candid shots were taken. Many of them would show the love and adoration they had for each other. The traditional pictures were taken, including one where they cut the cake and fed it to each other. The day was a happy one that they would always remember. There were wedding gifts to them from the small party of guests, which was something they hadn't expected or even thought about. Lindy made a mental note to get all of their addresses to send thank you notes when they returned to Pennsylvania. At dusk, the guests were getting ready to go home. Lindy and Ricky profusely thanked them for making their day so special. When the last guest was gone, Lindy and Ricky hung around to help Renee clean up.

Sam cleared his throat as they finished putting everything away. "I'm taking my wife out for awhile. She looks really pretty, so I thought I'd show her off somewhere. Do you two want to go with us?"

Ricky put his arms around each of their shoulders. "Naw....you kids go have fun. The wife and I are going to go up and watch some television and then get to bed." He looked over at Lindy. "Unless you want to go?"

"No....you two go ahead. Ricky and I want to.... talk.....about the immediate future...."

"Okay. Well....then...Renee, are you ready?"

Arms around each other, Ricky and Lindy stood on the first step and watched Sam's car drive away.

"I hope we're like them thirty-five years from now." Lindy smiled at Ricky.

"Oh....I think we will be. How about we take our shoes off and walk on the beach for a few minutes? See the moon and the stars? The whole universe is smiling down on us right now."

Lindy already had her shoes off as she stood waiting for Ricky to get his off.

\* \* \*

They had just finished breakfast and were enjoying the quiet of the Sunday morning after the wedding. Lindy had showered while Ricky made breakfast and she was ready to begin packing up. They decided they wouldn't leave until Wednesday morning since the wedding guests promised to have the pictures back to them before they left. They were a little melancholy about leaving Sam and Renee, but they realized that not only did they have to go home and face the music, but Sam and Renee had to get ready for tourists. They couldn't stay in the room at the prices Sam charged and it wouldn't be fair to expect to pay less. No—it was time to go home. Lindy imagined that Ricky's mother must be sick with worry and grief, and they would have to deal with it eventually. Ricky came up behind Lindy's chair, bent down and put his arm around her.

"What are you thinking about, Babe?"

"Oh…..I was just thinking that maybe we should go to Uncle Nick's first….when we get home. Your mother is going to be…..well, you know how she got when she found out I was pregnant."

Ricky snorted out a small laugh. "Yeah….I sure do. We'll go to Uncle Nick's first. Besides….I think I want to stay there….instead of at my mom's."

"We'll be going to our own place….remember?"

"Yeah, but won't it have to aired out and cleaned? We never did that….remember?"

"Oh yeah….you're right."

"Not to mention….the pipes may be broken from the cold weather. I'm sure the heat wasn't on."

"Yeah….true. I'm thinking….no, I'm hoping…. that Diane took care of things. I'm sure she knows what happened and that I'm not there."

"How would she know?"

"Uncle Nick tells her stuff…..so she can tell my dad. He doesn't think I know that….but I do. I don't get mad about it because….Uncle Nick thinks it's the right thing to do. As long as I don't have to see my dad people can tell him anything they want."

"Well….hopefully he told Diane enough so that she is taking care of the house for you. Gees, I hate to leave here….how about you?"

"Yeah….me too. We have to, though….but we can come back on vacations….right?"

"Right….I'm going to take a shower."

"And I'm going to go take Baxter for a walk after I throw in this load of laundry. I'm going to miss that dog." Lindy put her jacket on and picked up a laundry basket full of clothes.

"Maybe as soon as we're settled….we can get one of our own. What do ya think?" Ricky asked her, already knowing the answer.

"Really? Oh wow! I'd love it….you know that."

"Yeah….I do. Hey, take this thing back to Sam for me, will ya?"

"What is it?"

"It's a knife….we used it to tear out old caulking on tubs. Be careful….it's really sharp."

"Okay…..I'll be back. Enjoy your shower." She dropped the knife into her jacket pocket.

"Want to stay and join me?"

"Next time." Lindy laughed and blew him a kiss. She opened the door to the bright sunlight and stood marveling over the sparkling ocean before she started down the steps. Sea gulls flew over her head and she watched them circle the beach and finally land at the water's edge. She sighed and started down the steps.

As she stepped down onto the last step and hand shot out from the side of the steps and grabbed her around the throat. She was pulled off the step; the laundry basket fell to the ground. She managed a short scream before another hand clamped down on her mouth.

"You didn't think I was going to let you ruin my life and then just let you disappear…now did you? Did you miss me, Baby-doll?"

'Nelson…..oh God!' Her mind screamed and she choked on a sob.

"Didn't think I'd find you….did you? I told you…..
it's a shame, too….because I really didn't want to hurt
you. Why couldn't you just disappear? You had to leave
evidence behind." He hissed into her ear. "My wife threw
me out…I lost my job…I have no home….and…I spent
three months in jail…all…because….of you. If you go
back….I'll be hunted like an animal….they'll want to
have a trial….I'll go to prison. I can't have that."

Lindy's body trembled. He was going to kill her; she
knew it.

"Now….where's the boyfriend? Upstairs? I have to
deal with him first. And….by the way….Lindy-Baby….
your dear daddy had me worked over when I was in jail.
You'll have to pay for that, too."

He pressed Lindy's back up against his chest as he
kept his arm wrapped around her neck. He reached into
his pocket and pulled out a small revolver and dragged her
back onto the first step. He started up the steps backwards,
dragging her with him, the gun jammed into her side.
Annie Taylor, the reverend's wife pulled into the motel as
Nelson was dragging Lindy up the steps. She saw what
was happening, and she plainly saw the gun pointed at
Lindy's side. She ran into the office hysterically screeching
at Sam to call the police.

When they reached the top of the steps, Nelson turned
around to face the door to their room, putting Lindy in
front of him.

"Open it." His breath felt hot as he hissed into her
ear.

"No," she retorted.

"Yes….open the door…..or I'll kill you right here and
then go in and kill him anyway. You won't even get to

say goodbye to…the love of your life. Open…the…door."
Nelson ordered her through his clenched teeth.

Lindy turned the knob on the door and it opened. She
didn't see Ricky at first and assumed he was still in the
shower, until she heard his alarmed voice.

"What the…..? Who the hell are you? Let go of my
wife!"

"Wife, is it? I presume you're Ricky?"

Ricky nodded. "Who are you? No…never mind…..I
know. Nelson Sutter….the rapist."

"Now is that what she told you? She loved every
minute of it….didn't you, Lindy-baby?"

Lindy didn't answer. She quietly sobbed and tried to
think of something she could do to get away from him.

"I doubt it." Ricky responded. "Let her go."

"No….you see….she has a debt to pay. I have to kill
her." Nelson quickly ran down the list of losses for which
he blamed Lindy.

"She didn't do anything to you that you didn't bring
on yourself. Big man….aren't you? Forcing yourself on a
small defenseless girl like Lindy. So you can't get lucky
with someone who is willing? You have to attack the
unwilling?"

"Shut up!" Nelson became agitated and pointed the
gun at Ricky. "Say good-bye to your sweet Lindy."

"No—oo!" Lindy wailed.

Sam stood outside and waited for the police to get
there. Two squad cars pulled into the driveway, and
Sam quickly told the driver of the first car what had
happened.

"Do you have any idea who this guy is?" The police
officer asked.

"No….not really….but I have my suspicions."

"Well? Who?"

Sam filled the officer in on what had happened to Lindy and why she and Ricky ran away. "Anyway….I have a strong feeling that it might be the guy that raped her. She left a letter and some proof before she ran away. This guy had been arrested, but he could be out of jail…. on bond…maybe."

"Do you remember his name? And from what part of the country?"

"Sutter….I think that was the last name….somewhere in Western Pennsylvania."

The officer nodded and talked into his radio. "We should know shortly."

Sam, joined by Renee, waited impatiently. Both he and Renee loved Lindy and Ricky, and would be devastated if anything happened to them. The officer got out of his car, and signaled for the man in the other car to get out, too.

"It could very well be him. He was released a couple of weeks ago….nobody to testify against him. We have to get up there….somehow."

\* \* \*

Nelson held the gun steady on Ricky while he tightened his grip on Lindy. She looked up at Ricky and he saw something in her eyes that he couldn't quite understand. He knew she was trying to communicate something to him—but what? Keeping his eyes locked on hers, he didn't see her reach into her jacket pocket.

"I'm going to kill you first….then me and little Lindy here are going to get it on for a while….right, Sweet-cheeks?"

"Oh, HELL NO....you son of a bitch!" Her words came out like gravel.

Like lightning, in one fluid motion Lindy's hand came out of her pocket and she sliced Nelson's arm with the knife Ricky had handed to her earlier. It was obvious that the knife that tore into his flesh severed a muscle or a tendon because he could no longer hold the gun upright as it dangled on two of his fingers. He made a noise that sounded like a wounded animal and tried to turn the gun toward Lindy. She twisted her body and brought her knee up into his crotch, causing him to scream and double over. Blood was streaming down from his arm as he dropped to the floor still trying to use the gun. It fell from his fingers and exploded when it hit the floor. Nelson and Lindy screamed, but Lindy was still standing. She reached down and grabbed the gun up into her hand and pointed it at Nelson, just as the police burst through the door.

When the gun went off, Ricky flew across the room, thinking that Lindy had been shot again. He stopped when the police broke through the door. He slowly made his way toward Lindy as she held the gun pointed at Nelson. One officer had his gun drawn.

Ricky stared at him for a moment and then said, "I'll get it."

He closed the gap between him and Lindy and softly spoke to her. "Baby.....give me the gun. It's over. You're safe now." He placed his arm lightly around her shoulders, quietly took the gun out of her hands, and held it out for the police officer to take it. Lindy fell against him, crying, and he tightened his arms around her, rocking her gently. He looked at Nelson writhing in pain and almost laughed when he saw that the bullet had hit him in his buttocks.

The room suddenly filled up with police and paramedics, and of course, Sam and Renee.

"What is your name, sir?" One of the paramedics asked him.

Lindy answered for him. "Nelson Sutter. His name is Nelson Sutter and he's a rapist." She turned her face away from Nelson and clung to Ricky.

He held her trembling body tightly as he watched the paramedics trying to stop the bleeding from Nelson's forearm. An officer holding a notepad approached Lindy and Ricky. Sam and Renee were right behind him.

"I'm going to need a statement.....I know she's upset....but....."

"Can't you get it later? When she calms down, I mean."

"Yeah...I can do that. I'll be back a little later this evening."

One of the paramedics approached Lindy. "Are you all right, Miss?" He then looked at Ricky. "I can give her something to calm her down.....is she hurt anywhere? Where is the blood coming from?"

Ricky looked down and saw the blood on his shirt and held Lindy at arm's length for a moment. He noted that his shirt had blood on it because Lindy had blood all over her hands and wrists.

"I don't think it's hers. She grabbed the gun. His blood was all over it. Something to calm her down would be good..."

Ricky still held her tightly while Renee wiped her hands with a wet soapy washcloth. The paramedic gave Ricky a small cup with a capsule in it.

"Give this to her…..I'm a medical physician just along for the ride….so it's okay if I give it to her."

"I didn't know doctors rode in ambulances…." Ricky commented.

"It's something new that we're trying. I'm a resident at the hospital. Is she going to be all right?"

"Yeah…..I hope so. Thanks."

As the paramedics were going out the door with Nelson on the gurney, Renee handed Ricky a glass of water for Lindy. Ricky eased her down onto the side of the bed and handed her the capsule and the glass of water.

"Here….take this, Babe. You'll stop shaking."

Lindy obediently took the capsule and the glass of water. She shuddered after she drank from the glass.

"Anything we can do, Ricky?"

"No….thanks….I'll be here for her….she just needs to sleep right now."

Renee and Sam walked out with the last of the police officers and closed the door behind them. Lindy was already groggy when Ricky covered her with a blanket. He sat down to watch her sleep, but then decided he needed to be busy. He began making dinner, although it was only just going into the middle of the afternoon.

* * *

Lindy awoke to the smell of Ricky's cooking. He saw her eyes open and sat down next to her on the bed.

"Hi…..hungry? I cooked."

"Yeah….a little."

"You know……you really fucked him up…."

Lindy smiled and turned her face toward Ricky. "I did….didn't I?"

"Yeah…..now I know never to piss you off."

Lindy laughed lightly and raised her hand to touch Ricky's face. "I'd go easy on you..." She smiled as she gently rubbed his cheek.

"Are you okay? I mean....sorta?"

"Yeah....I think so."

"You know....you keep saving my life. I'm beginning to think you like me."

Lindy laughed a little harder. "We have had way too many guns pointed at us.....don't you think?"

Ricky laughed, too. "Yeah, I agree."

They stared into each other's eyes for a moment before Lindy spoke again. "Ricky....can we just maybe take a day...or two....on the way home to....sorta have a honeymoon? Just stop somewhere a little romantic.....or at least somewhere quiet and pretty...and be alone in the world together before we....get back?"

"Sure. If that's what you want....you got it."

Lindy smiled and sat up. She draped her arms around Ricky's shoulders and lightly kissed his lips. He kissed her back and slowly kissed her again. The kisses were becoming ardent when they were interrupted by a knock on the door. Ricky groaned and got up to see who was there. It was the officer who promised to be back.

"Sorry to bother you folks.....but I have to have a statement from you."

"Sure. No problem.....come on in.....Lindy?" Ricky turned toward Lindy and saw that she was already getting up from the bed.

"Hi, Miss....are you feeling okay?"

"Yes......thank you for asking."

"I don't want to take up too much of your time. The other witness told us that Mister Sutter accosted you.....

so whatever you did was in self-defense. We know that. We just have to have some details."

Lindy told him her story, and he listened sympathetically, taking notes on his notepad. Ricky stayed in the kitchenette area putting dinner on plates, including one for the police officer. He carried the plates to the table and set them in front of both Lindy and officer who was Theodore Greer, according to his name tag, and then went back to retrieve his own plate.

"This smells good. How did you know I haven't eaten all day?"

"I didn't....but we have plenty and I like to show off my cooking when I can."

Officer Greer took a forkful and then asked, "Are you two married?"

"Yes," They answered in unison.

"Lucky for you, Miss, because I was going to propose... to him. I'd marry anybody who can cook like this."

Lindy and Ricky laughed.

"Anyway.....the cop who was handling this rape case wants you to call him. He needs you there. Sutter is going to be transported back to the jail he came out of in Western Pennsylvania." Officer Greer handed Lindy his cell phone.

Lindy hesitated and then picked up the phone. She glanced up at Ricky.

"I'll be with you every step of the way, Baby. Go ahead....call him."

She dialed the number that Officer Greer read aloud from the notepad in front of him. She held the phone and waited as it rang. A man answered and identified himself as Detective Bruno. Lindy hesitated a moment and then spoke into the phone.

"This is Lindy Riley….." She spoke nervously and tentatively.

"Well…..I'm certainly glad to hear from you. Are you…..how are you?"

"I…I'm doing good. I'm coming back…..to Pennsylvania…."

"We need you here……you shouldn't have run away like you did…"

"I….I was scared. He said nobody would believe me…..and he said he would….do something to me if I told anybody. I….believed that.. and after today, I believe it even more."

"When will you be back?"

"Friday or Saturday at the laest. Sir? Can you *not* say anything to Ricky's family? We want to surprise them."

"No….there's no need to say anything to them, but I want you to call me when you get home……promise?"

"Yes, Sir….I promise."

"Where did you two pla on going when you get back? Dr. Bazario's house?"

"Yes….that's what we planed."

"Okay……I'm counting on hearing from you. We can put this guy away for a ng time if you come back here."

"I'll be there…..I promise…..and I don't break promises."

"Good, Belinda. I look fward to meeting you. Your letter to your teacher…..the idence you left…..brilliant. Good work."

"Uh….detective? How Loraine Sutter?"

"She's….okay. She kinda flipped out on her husband when we arrested him. He tried to say it was all a lie. She must really like you….because she didn't buy it. Slapped him across the face. I'll see you soon, Belinda."

Lindy snapped the cell phone closed and reached for Ricky's hand as she handed the phone back to Greer. She smiled nervously at Ricky.

"You'll be fine, Baby….I'll be there for you all the way." He gently squeezed her hand. "Nelson Sutter has to pay for what he did to you."

# Chapter 49

It was a tearful good-bye. Renee and Lindy clung to each other, promising to keep in touch. Sam and Ricky embraced in a bear hug, both more emotional than they wanted to admit.

"Take care of her, Rick.....she's...."

"Like an angel.....I know."

Sam and Renee walked to the car with them, neither wanting to let go just yet.

"Be good to each other....stay in love." Renee offered.

Ricky smiled. "We will. We had a couple of good role models...so we'll be okay."

"You two be careful. Do you have everything you need?"

"Yeah.....we're good. Thanks for everything. After all you did for us....thank you doesn't seem....enough."

"We loved it. Please come back." Sam's voice was huskier than usual.

"We will....we promise."

Baxter barked and ran up to the car. Lindy stooped down and took his head between her hands. "Baxter..... you take care of Sam and Renee....okay? I.....I'll miss you, boy."

Wiping a tear from her eye, Lindy stood up. "I guess we're ready. I…we…love you guys."

Renee and Lindy hugged once more before Lindy climbed into the passenger side of the Toyota. Ricky put the car into gear and eased out of the parking lot and headed north. Sam and Renee stood together and waved until they couldn't see them any more. All four pairs of eyes were shining with tears.

"We really lucked out when we found those people…. didn't we?"

"Yeah….I hope they like their gift." Ricky smiled at Lindy. "Ready to go face the dragon lady?"

Sam and Renee went up to the motel room that Lindy and Ricky occupied for the past four months. They opened the door and gasped.

"Well, I'll be….damned." Sam said in awe.

Leaning against the back of a dinette chair was a framed portrait of Sam and Renee, signed by Ricky. A small potted plant and a thank you card stood to one side.

"It's beautiful, isn't it?" Renee whispered. "This is worth so much more than we ever did for them…don't you agree?"

"Yeah….but I guess when you lend a hand to someone in need it comes back in triplicate. We are lucky to know those two."

\* \* \*

"Uncle Nick should be pulling into his driveway about now. We should be pulling in behind him in about forty minutes." Ricky glanced at Lindy and smiled.

It was Friday evening, just about six o'clock. They had entered the state of Pennsylvania only a few minutes ago and were now getting very close to Nick's condo. After they left Sam and Renee, they traveled north on the interstate for about six hours. Ricky had been watching the billboards for advertised attractions and thought he saw one that would appeal to Lindy. He had gotten off the interstate at the exit advertised and found a lovely hotel with a vacancy. The tourist season had not yet begun, so vacancies were common everywhere, he'd guessed. After a good night of love-making and then sleep, they visited the farm that was advertised on the billboard. Ricky enjoyed watching Lindy's face when she spotted the new-born foals. In addition to horses, the farm had goats, cows, cats, and ducks, along with a couple of huge black dogs. To Lindy, this was heaven. She loved animals and enjoyed being around them. The owners of the farm opened it up to the public and found that they could make more money using it as an attraction than by farming it. They were courteous and friendly, and after the tour, brought out delicious foods for a nice lunch. There were souvenirs for purchasing, and Ricky bought Lindy a stuffed horse and a set of crystal barnyard animal figurines. He also purchased a set for his mother and one for Aunt Liz. He found a decorative pen knife with hand-painted barnyard animals on it for Uncle Nick 'At least we come bearing gifts,' he had said to Lindy. They spent Thursday night in another motel a little further north. There, he and Lindy toured a couple of caverns before they headed even further north toward their destination. They were now very close to the condo.

"Ready? I can see Uncle Nick's car....he's home."

\* \* \*

Nick was surprised by the doorbell, since he and Liz rarely got visitors. He was even more surprised when he opened the door. He gasped and grabbed for both of them, dragging them inside.

"Liz! Liz!" He held onto them tightly like he was afraid if he didn't, they would disappear again. Liz started down the stairs and when she saw them, ran the rest of the way. Crying, she joined in the hug.

"Oh…..you two! We have been so worried! I'm so glad you're back!"

"Better call Angie…..right away. She's had nightmares over you being gone."

Nick went for the phone as Liz took over the hugging, crying with relief.

Angie answered her phone.

"They're back, Angie."

"What? Who?" Then it hit her. "Ricky? Ricky's back? Ricky and Lindy?"

"Uh-huh…."

Nick heard a noise like Angie dropped the phone, and then heard Ron's voice on the line.

"What's up? Angie just fainted."

"The kids are back."

"Be there in a few." Ron said as he hung up.

"I have a feeling it's going to be a long night. Want me to make coffee, Uncle Nick?"

"Ricky…..I haven't had coffee like yours since you left. Please do."

Angie and Ron arrived in a flourish. Angie cried and hugged Ricky, while Ron hugged Lindy. Angie chastised them both for running off, but thanked God that they were both okay. When the coffee was ready, they sat around the dining room table listening to Lindy and Ricky talk about their adventures, saving the best news for last. They told them about Sam and Renee, and about getting their driver's licenses, and then purchasing the car. Lindy talked about Baxter and Ricky's job at the hardware store, and Ricky told of how he worked with Sam on maintenance and repairs. Then they both told the story of how Nelson found them, and of Lindy's heroic act.

During the course of the conversation, Liz had served pizza that Nick had ordered from the local pizza shop.

"It's getting very late. I'll bet you two could use a good night's sleep." Angie suggested.

"Where did you plan on staying tonight?" Nick asked.

"Well, Uncle Nick.....let me just say this. Lindy is no longer my girlfriend.....she's my wife. So no matter where we sleep, it will be together."

Everyone suddenly got very quiet; all eyes turned to them. Ricky lifted Lindy's hand and showed off the rings she wore; surprised that nobody had noticed them before. Then he raised his hand to show off his.

"And we have a marriage license to prove it." He and Lindy smiled at each other.

"Wow....I didn't see that coming. I never even thought about it. I mean....I kind of figured you would wait until you were both eighteen to come home....but I didn't think that you would come home married." Nick couldn't hide the emotion in his voice.

Angie began to cry. "Oh, God.....now what? Are you pregnant again, Lindy?"

"No.....I'm not. We got married because we wanted to....not because we had to."

"Oh God….how could you? What about your future? Ricky, how could you throw your life away?"

Ricky stiffened. "Throw my life away by marrying Lindy? The girl I love? Don't start, Mom….just don't start. Say anything bad, and you'll regret it. You'll never see me again."

"That's no way to talk to your mother, Rick." Ron spoke for the first time since they sat down.

"That's no way for my mother to talk about my wife."

Nick turned to Angie. "Angie, I think you better think back….to when you and Enrico got engaged. His family wasn't very happy about it….they had their hearts set on him marrying that girl from Italy. Remember how you felt? Don't do that to your son's wife. Ricky, you and your wife can stay here tonight."

"Lindy…..I don't want you to take it personally when I say stuff like that to Ricky. I love you. I don't mean that I think he ruined his life by marrying you…..I just think he's too young to be married. You, too. You're both only eighteen…what will you do to support yourselves?"

Ricky interrupted her. "Mom…we have it all worked out. Maybe you don't realize this, but Lindy and I have money. Lindy has lots of it. I have a nice little nest egg myself….thanks to dad. We plan on finishing school, going to college, and pursuing careers. We just want to do it together. We can…..and we will. Just watch. And thanks for the offer to stay here, Uncle Nick. It won't be for long. After we get the house aired out and cleaned, we'll be moving into Lindy's place."

"Oh, Lindy.....I almost forgot. Your brother was home. He's gone again, but he said he's getting out of the service sometime soon."

"Oh....wow. Is he okay? I'm so sorry I missed him."

"Yeah, he's fine. He had Christmas dinner here with us. Nice guy."

Lindy smiled. "Thanks. I can't wait to see him. I take it you filled him in on everything?"

"Yeah....we did. He went to see your father, and then Diane. It was a lot for someone to come home to....but he took it all well."

Lindy sighed. "I can't wait for *you* to meet him, Ricky."

"Me neither, Babe. And by the way, Uncle Nick.... Aunt Liz....are you two married now?"

Nick and Liz looked at each other and then started laughing.

"No.....I'm living here, but....well, we wanted to wait for you two to get home to tie the knot again. So.... now that you're back...we can plan our wedding. Right, Nick?"

"Yeah....as soon as you want."

Ricky looked back and forth between Liz and Nick, and then turned to Lindy.

"Lindy....I think there's some hanky-panky going on here."

Both Lindy and Ricky burst out laughing.

# Chapter 50

**After** a good night's sleep, Lindy and Ricky made breakfast for the four of them. Lindy called the detective to tell him she was home, and Ricky called Lukas. Nick called Diane. Lukas told Ricky he would meet them at Lindy's house to help them clean, and that he would call Shawna to come help. Diane came right over to the condo. When she saw Lindy, she burst into tears.

"I was so worried! I didn't know what happened to you until Chris came to my house. What about the guy? Is he in jail?"

Lindy sighed as she set a cup of coffee in front of Diane. She quickly told her the story of Nelson's confrontation with them in South Carolina. "He's being returned back here to stand trial. I will testify."

"That can be rough, Honey…." Diane sniffed.

"I know…..but I'm ready for it. Ricky will be there with me, so I'm not afraid. Oh, Diane….in case nobody told you….." Lindy showed Diane her left hand.

Diane sucked in her breath. "Well……I guess congratulations are in order."

"Yes….they are. We are….so happy." Lindy smiled at Diane for the first time since she walked in.

"Well.....I'm happy for you. Do you mind if I tell your father?"

"No....tell him anything you want. I understand, from Nelson, that my dad had him beat up in the jail. Is that supposed to prove that Daddy loves Lindy?"

Ricky came up behind Lindy and put his arms around her. "Shhh.....don't be so bitter. Luke and Shawna are going to meet us at the house. We have help cleaning, so we'll be able to move in sooner."

"Oh.....I took everything out of the refrigerator and cleaned it for you. Everything would have gone bad in there." Diane told her.

"Thanks, Diane. Are the utilities on?"

"Yes....I handled it just like your dad told me to do. The utilities are paid and so they are still on. None of the pipes burst this winter.....I had my handyman go over and wrap them."

"So.....what do we owe you?"

"Oh Lindy......don't worry about it."

"Well.....you had to have paid the handyman.....let us give you the money for that."

"It wasn't very much. I paid him fifty dollars."

Ricky reached into his pocket, pulled out some bills, and leafed through them until he found a fifty dollar bill. He handed it to Diane. "Are you sure that's all we owe?" He asked.

"Yeah.....I'm sure. The estate took care of everything else."

"Diane....when we get settled in....would you like to come for dinner some night?"

Lindy's question took her by surprise. "Why, yes.... yes, Lindy.....I'd love to come."

"Good. I'll call you. We have to get going, though. We have friends meeting us at the house. Thank you for all you did while I was away. You know, Diane.....if my dad hadn't have done what he did....you and I would have been good friends by now."

Diane smiled at her. "Thank you, Lindy....maybe there is still a chance."

\* \* \*

It was a tearful reunion with Lukas, Shawna, and Cindy. After Lukas hung up with Ricky, he called Shawna, who in turn called Cindy. Her father had already told her that Ricky and Lindy were home, but she didn't know they would be at the house until Shawna called her. After the initial hugging and the tears, and the gushing over the wedding rings, they each started on a room, first opening the windows, and then sweeping, dusting and scrubbing. Lindy called for a delivery of deli foods for everybody. When it was delivered, they all took a break and ate at the kitchen table.

"I'm so glad you're back." Cindy smiled at them. "....and married! That's so cool!"

"So what are you two going to do about school? Or are you just going to live on love from now on?" Lukas laughed as he asked his question.

"We're going to finish, and then go on to college. We'll just be together when we do it....that's all. Nobody is ever going to separate us again."

"Oh....that's so...romantic!" Cindy gushed.

"Yeah....like a real modern day Romeo and Juliet. You two have been through some shit...haven't you?" Shawna grinned at them. "But I always knew you two would make it. I can't tell you how happy I am for you. And....

I'm damn glad to see you! Ricky...when you didn't show up at school...I didn't know what to think. Taking off like that...not telling anybody. We didn't know anything about Lindy...about what happened to her...."

"Luke knew...." Lindy responded.

The two girls turned to Lukas, two pairs of eyes staring him down.

"You knew? And you just let us worry? Bastard!" Shawna snapped at him.

Lukas laughed nervously. "I couldn't take a chance by telling anybody. I was the only one who knew.....and I couldn't let it get out. I wanted to tell you both...but...I made a promise...."

"Luke's a true friend. I knew I could trust him. Besides....it was best that nobody knew. It kept the cops away from your doors. Except Cindy, of course....she lives with one."

"Yeah, and from what I hear and see....your mother may be living with one soon, too." Cindy grinned at Ricky.

"I just wish he could mellow her out. Man....that woman doesn't shut up!"

All five of them burst out laughing.

* * *

Lindy and Ricky slept at Nick's one last night before moving into their own place. The house had been spotlessly cleaned and had an aroma of freshly cut lilacs. All they had to do was make up the bed, but they were entirely too exhausted to do it. They planned on moving their clothes and personal things in after breakfast on Sunday. Nick and Liz agreed to help, as well as Luke, Shawna, and Cindy. They were having a leisurely breakfast with

Nick and Liz when the doorbell rang. Nick went to the door while the others continued eating and chatting. Lindy saw Liz's face change and her eyebrows go up just before someone covered her eyes with his hands. Lindy recognized those hands.

"Chris!!" Lindy turned and flew into his arms, wrapping hers around him. Crying, she hugged him. "Oh, Chris.....I'm so happy....to see you!"

"Me, too, Pumpkin. My God....you've grown up! You did that behind my back!"

"You have to meet Ricky....my husband."

"Your WHAT?"

"My husband. We got married in South Carolina.... and....we're so happy! Ricky?"

Ricky stood up and offered his hand, but Chris still had his arms wrapped around Lindy. Realizing the awkwardness, Chris put Lindy down and extended his hand to Ricky.

"I guess we're brothers-in-law...right?"

"Yeah...I guess we are. It's nice to finally meet you. I've heard so much about you."

"Yeah...well.....I'm sorry I let her down. I should have stayed around after..."

"Hey....it's in the past. You did what you had to do. When I met her I tried to look out for her the best I could....when people weren't interfering, that is."

"Yeah....I heard." He looked down at Lindy. "Are you okay?"

"Yeah.....I'm great now! I have to go see the police tomorrow....about Nelson. Ricky's going with me."

Chris looked back at Ricky. "Do you mind if I go, too?"

"No….not at all. Lindy?"

"No…..I don't mind. Having two men who care about me going there with me makes me feel even more confident."

\* \* \*

Ricky quickly made breakfast for Chris and invited him to sit and join the rest of them.

"We're moving our personal things into the house, Chris. Ricky and I will be living there…..and you are welcome to stay there as well….you know that."

"Well….thanks. Actually, I was going to let the tenants in my house know that they were going to have to move. I'll be moving into that house. I planned on giving them a three month's notice."

"Well, that's okay. You can stay with us…..get to know Ricky…..get reacquainted with me….is that okay with you?"

"Well, I guess…….but don't you two want privacy? You're newlyweds….."

"And you're her brother….." Ricky interjected. "We wouldn't have it any other way. You're family."

"And…..you can sleep in your old room." Lindy laughed. "I'll bet you still have those toy soldiers you used to play with. You can get them out again," Lindy teased.

It was Chris' turn to laugh. "I think I've had enough army play. I think I'll just donate them to some organization. But thanks, you two. I appreciate you offering me my old room. I'll try to stay out of your hair."

The game plan was for Ricky, Nick, and Lukas to move their things while Liz and Lindy went to the grocery store. There was no food in the house, so Lindy would be buying a lot of groceries. By the time she and Liz got to the house, the guys would be done moving everything in, and would be able to help unload the groceries out of the car. All went as planned and soon Ricky and Lindy were sitting together drinking coffee at the kitchen table in their home.

"I think we should go shopping for new bedroom furniture and move into the master bedroom. What do you think?" Lindy waited for Ricky's answer.

"Whatever you want. We have the money for new bedroom furniture?"

"Uh-huh…..so…we do it then?"

"Sure." Ricky smiled at Lindy. "I can't refuse you anything when you look at me with those big blue eyes."

"Diamonds and furs?"

"If you want them."

"Mercedes Benz?"

"Yep."

"Anything?"

"Anything."

"How about a roll in between the sheets with my husband? Make love to me?"

"Oh, hell yeah. I love it when you talk dirty!" Ricky quickly stood up and reached for Lindy. He swooped down and picked her up off of the chair and carried her into the bedroom, where they spent the rest of the afternoon and into the early evening.

\* \* \*

Lindy sat at the kitchen table working on finances while Ricky stood at the stove making pancakes, one of Lindy's favorite evening meals. Both were wearing robes, so they were momentarily taken by surprise when the front door opened, but relaxed when they saw it was Chris.

"Hi….is it okay to come in? I mean…."

"Of course it is……come on in and sit down. I'm making pancakes for my bride. I can make you a couple while I'm at it."

"Pancakes, huh? I remember that was one of your favorite meals, Lindy."

"Still is. Ricky makes them so good, too."

"I take it Ricky is the cook in this duo."

"Yeah….kinda…" Lindy laughed.

"She cooks, too, but I usually do it when I'm home. I love to cook, so she indulges me by letting me."

"Not to mention, Chris….that my stuff is edible…. but Ricky's cooking is….*magnificent*!!" Lindy laughed as she kissed her fingertips and tossed the kiss across the room and a sweeping gesture.

Chris laughed, and then stared at Lindy. "You certainly have grown up. I'm so sorry, Pumpkin…….I didn't know what was going on here. I mean….I can't believe dad just ignored you all those years. He loved you so much…..I remember."

Lindy sighed. "Yeah….he did. Then after mom died….at first I thought it was because he was grieving so bad….and then maybe because I looked so much like mom…but that wasn't it."

"What was it, then?"

Lindy looked up at Ricky and then back at Chris. "You have to promise you won't let anybody know that you know this….okay? Promise?"

"Yeah….sure…."

Lindy told Chris what Diane had told her. Chris' face went ashen at first, and then turned red.

"That's the reason? He got a boner? Gees....that's.... f...messed up."

"But Chris....you know that happens for no reason sometimes." Ricky interjected. "It doesn't necessarily mean anything."

"Yeah....I know. I just can't believe that my dad would totally shun Lindy, his pride and joy, because of something so stupid."

"And you have no idea how bad it hurt, Chris. For three years....it hurt....and it hurt worse when I found out that while he ignored me on every holiday, he was spending them with Diane."

"I feel real bad, Honey. That must have been awful for you."

"Oh....speaking of Diane....I have to call her. Ricky.... we can afford a new bedroom suite and a new comforter and sheets as well. How does a black and white bedroom sound? Black and white with a couple of touches of red and maybe some gray?"

"It sounds nice....so why do you have to call Diane?"

Lindy was already dialing her number, and put her finger up signaling to Ricky to wait a minute.

"Hi....Diane? Lindy....hey, when are you going to get my dad's things?"

"Any time you want me to, Lindy. Tomorrow if you like."

"That's fine. Do you want the bedroom furniture, too? Ricky and I want to get new bedroom furniture."

"Sure.....I have a spare room it can go into. I'll see about a truck tomorrow."

"Great.....talk to you then."

Lindy hung up and turned to Ricky. "So when do you want to go shopping for a new bed?"

"How about after we leave the police station tomorrow? I think you may want a shopping trip for something nice.....okay?"

"Great. I'm excited. Chris....it's the second purchase we will make as a couple."

\* \* \*

Lindy, Ricky, and Chris showed up at the police station to see Detective Bruno on Monday morning. Lindy told her story, crying in some parts, and answered all of the detective's questions. He told her she did a good job and that he would be in touch with her, noting her new address and phone number. He told her that Nelson was somewhere halfway between from South Carolina and the county jail, and they expected him sometime during the night. Ricky's arm stayed around Lindy as they left the station, and found the car. As promised, they went shopping for bedroom furniture and bedding. Lindy was delighted that they found exactly what she wanted—black lacquered furniture, and a black, white, and gray bold abstract blocked comforter, and of course, red satin sheets. Lamps with red bases and black and white shades set everything off perfectly. The room had hardwood floors, so Lindy purchased black oval rugs and a red oval rug to be set strategically around the bed. The delivery was set for Wednesday, and they promised to be there.

"So.....now that we have that taken care of....what now?" Ricky asked.

"School. We have to see about getting back in school and graduating."

"Uncle Nick said he would check into that for us. We should call him when we get home. He said he was going to talk to the head of the school board, the principal, and whoever else it takes to get some satisfaction. He said be prepared to return to school."

The three of them returned to the house, and found Diane waiting for them. She had contracted two movers who were busily moving the bedroom furniture onto a truck. There were boxes of Ray Riley's personal things already loaded onto the truck. Lindy invited Diane in for a cup of coffee while the movers finished their job.

"The place looks great....smells good, too."

"Thanks, Diane. How about coming over for dinner next Sunday?"

"Sunday? Sure....that will be great. I look forward to it."

When Diane, the movers, and the moving truck left, Chris suggested that they let him treat them to lunch. They didn't argue, but instead headed out the front door to the car.

\* \* \*

Ricky and Lindy planned on calling Uncle Nick around six o'clock when he usually got home from the hospital. They didn't get the chance to call him, since he pulled into their driveway at five-thirty.

"Be ready tomorrow morning. I'm taking you both up to talk to the principal. A member of the school board will be there as well. You shouldn't have too much hassle.... considering the circumstances under which you left here. Actually...the county is embarrassed over what happened. They pride themselves on choosing good homes for foster kids....and they really blew it this time. There won't be much of a problem."

"Great. We really do want to graduate....and then go on to college." Ricky assured him. "Uncle Nick....you've been great. Thanks. Oh....and by the way...any chance of us getting our jobs back?"

"I think so....glad you asked. Let's see where we are with the school thing and then decide on a schedule for both of you. See you in the morning."

He hugged them both, hopped in his car, and drove toward his place. Lindy and Ricky, their arms around each other, watched him drive away and then walked into the house to start dinner. They were excited and filled with anticipation about returning to school.

*     *     *

Everything went better than they expected. Since they had almost finished the first semester of their senior year, all they had to do was pass the end of semester tests with a C or above. They both knew they could do that. Then they could go on to summer classes, and if they passed everything, they could be ready to start college in the fall. 'Piece of cake,' they both agreed. The next step was getting into a college by the fall. They both agreed that they wanted to go to a local college, preferably the same one. Knowing that the larger colleges would already have their classes closed for the fall semester when they finished summer school, they both accepted the fact that the first semester would have to be at the local community college. At the community college, they could get in all their pre-requisites for their majors. Lindy was sure she either wanted to teach first grade, or possibly be an elementary school music teacher. She made her choice as she changed clothes in the bedroom. Ricky came up behind her and wrapped his arms around her as she stood in her underwear.

"Ricky.....I think I've made up my mind. I'm going to become an elementary school teacher. I'll just keep the music fun. You know....sing lullabies to our children...sing just because I'm happy. Sing for charity. What do you think?"

"It's your choice, Babe."

"What about you? Have you made a choice?"

"Besides being your love slave; you mean? Yeah.... I have. I'm going to go further with the chemistry and keep the artwork as a hobby. Maybe once in awhile enter something into a show....so we both choose to use our great talents for fun, and our great minds for our careers. I think we are going to be fine."

Lindy took on a serious look as she stared up at Ricky.

"What's up, Babe? I know that look."

Lindy sighed. "Ricky.....I want us to love each other....forever."

"We will, Sweetheart. I'm sure of it." He smiled down at her and kissed her forehead. "We have so much to do. Work....school...household chores. It will be a lot of work."

Lindy took a step back and held him at arm's length. She smiled up at him, the love shining in her eyes. "We can do this." She spoke quietly, but with conviction.

Ricky smiled back at her; the same love light shining in his eyes. "We can....and we will. You and me.....together.....forever."

*The Beginning*

# About the Author

Carole McKee bases most of her writing around the Western Pennsylvania area, where she grew up and where she resided for much of her adult life. Now living in Florida, Carole attends Argosy University in Tampa as a non-traditional student, and is working on a Master's Degree. As demonstrated in the writing of her novel, "Perfect" Carole's writing style conveys passion and emotion, inducing the reader to laugh and to cry with the characters in the story. "Choices" is the first of three in the series. Readers will fall in love with Lindy and Ricky as they evolve from youth to adulthood.

Carole McKee began writing in 1996, when she wrote a heart rending tribute to her black Laborador Retriever after he passed away. Her story brought tears and laughter to readers. 'Carole writes from the heart,' a fan stated. 'Her writing always cleanses the tear ducts.'

Printed in the United States
114293LV00001B/158/P